RAILROAD TRAIN

is dedicated to

Dolly Leo
Anney Thomas
Kathleen Maher
rhoda penmarq

Second Edition: 2018

ISBN: 9781717851444

The Olney Press
2102 S. 12th Street
Philadelphia PA 19148

danleo@mindspring.com

RAILROAD TRAIN TO HEAVEN

The Memoirs of Arnold Schnabel
Volume One

transcribed by
Dan Leo

RAILROAD TRAIN TO HEAVEN

The Memoirs of Arnold Schnabel
Volume One

Editor's Foreword

Once upon a time there was a man called Arnold Schnabel. Born in 1921 of humble German immigrant parents in the Swampoodle section of North Philadelphia, he was raised in the strange neighborhood known as Olney. Arnold's father died when the lad was only thirteen, and young Arnold quit school to go to work and help support his mother and three younger siblings. At the age of seventeen, with the help of an uncle, Arnold obtained employment with the Reading Railroad, for which he worked as a brakeman for many years, interrupted only by three years' service with the army engineers in World War II.

Starting in 1938, Arnold began creating the poems for which he has become justly if posthumously famous, publishing one of these small masterpieces each week and every week for over thirty years in his local newspaper, the estimable *Olney Times*.

In January of 1963, Arnold (who had never married and had always lived with his loving mother in their row home near the corner of B Street and Nedro Avenue, across the street from the Heintz metalworks) suffered a severe mental breakdown, resulting in his hospitalization for almost three months at the Byberry state mental hospital in Northeast Philadelphia. As grave as Arnold's collapse was, he nevertheless continued to keep to his schedule of one finely-chiseled poem a week, and indeed many scholars consider the poems he wrote from this point on to be his "golden period".

After his release from the hospital he attempted to go back to work on the railroad, but was soon put on an indefinite leave of absence at half-pay.

That summer his mother took him to stay with her three maiden sisters at their boarding house in the quaint Victorian resort and fishing town of Cape May, New Jersey.

Sometime in June of that summer Arnold began to compose the present sprawling memoir, in small copybooks which he bought at the local Kresge's 5&10. The volume you hold now is only the first in a planned series of a dozen or more, comprising a massive opus which is surely destined to become recognized as one of the great classics of world literature.

— Dan Leo, Professor of Classics and Phys. Ed., Olney Community College, Philadelphia, PA.

Railroad Train to Heaven

Chapter 1

I hate the beach, and truth be told I'm not all that crazy about sunshine.

But I have come here, to my aunts' guest house in Cape May, because my mother thinks it would be good for me, and because she likes to see her sisters now and then.

My mother also has no interest in the beach. She spends her days mostly working in the garden, or trimming the hedges.

I have my own room, a very small room, in the attic.

I read, walk around, try to stay sane.

I go to mass every morning without fail, and I think that helps. (Or so I pray. I pray that the daily mass helps. I pray that my prayers help.)

Occasionally I stop in a bar and nurse a beer. I look at baseball games on the television.

Sometimes I get into conversations with people. My fellow Americans seem to be a friendly sort by and large. People like to talk, and with little or no prodding they will and do tell you everything about themselves.

I listen, or sort of listen, I like to think I have always been very much a nice guy, but I do not reciprocate their autobiographical effusiveness.

What can I tell them?

That I am a Catholic bachelor, forty-two years old, that I live with my mother and except for the few years of my decidedly unheroic military career have always lived with my mother, that, again excepting for my time in the modest service of Uncle Sam, I have worked my entire life as a brakeman for the Reading Railroad, that last winter I went completely out of my mind and spent twelve weeks in the Byberry mental hospital?

That after a while I returned to work but, following a few embarrassing episodes (some of which I was aware of at the time, others to which I was oblivious), it was strongly suggested that I take an extended leave of absence on half-pay?

That I was on prescribed pills but stopped taking them?

That after ceasing to take these pills I would occasionally suffer the most frightening hallucinations, hallucinations which while they were happening were as real as anything I have experienced in my life?

And that — knock on wood — it has now been a few weeks since my last "episode"?

No, I choose not to share all this with my new temporary friends.

I won't say no one wants to hear this sort of thing because actually people love to hear horror stories, as of course do I.

No, I simply don't want to be the one telling them, with me as the subject; except for here, in this copybook, where it's all between me, myself and that other lunatic: I.

Chapter 2

Also staying here is my cousin Bert and his wife and three children, all of them squeezed into one small apartment of my aunts' shambling big old house. How odd that they leave their nice three-bedroom semi-detached home in Lawncrest to cram into these two cramped and stuffy un-airconditioned rooms with a tiny kitchenette and call it their vacation. But I suppose my aunts give them a good deal on the rent, as they do for me and Mom. The one boy, Kevin, sits and reads comic books for much of the day. Nearly every morning he goes to Wally's cigar store and pool room on Washington Street and trades in his already-used comics (the titles on the covers snipped off) for a fewer number of new used comics. There is some complicated financial formula involved, but the upshot is that for about a quarter a batch he seems always to have at least a half-dozen new used comics to read and obsessively re-read until he wearies of them and trades them in.

He's an unprepossessing lad, pale, un-athletic, taciturn. I have attempted to engage him in conversation, just to be a good avuncular sort, and I have failed miserably. However, I have taken a liking if not to the boy then to his comic books, and now each day I sit with him on the porch and read them. I wait patiently till he finishes the first one — he won't let me look at any until he's "finished" with it. But when he does finish one he passes it magisterially over to me. After we have read all that day's comics we read them all again, but this time more slowly and luxuriously, savoring each word and image.

And so I have been introduced to this new heroic and fantastic world. {*See Arnold's poem, "The Hawkman and I" in the Appendix. — Editor*} I find this very soothing. My own world these past months has grown far too fantastic in itself. It's a serene pleasure to read the adventures of this Dr. Strange, whose universe makes even mine look fairly mundane. Or another fellow named Strange, Adam Strange, who periodically gets transported by something called a Zeta-Beam to some entire other planet where he is a rather dashing gallant in a skintight suit with a jet pack on his back and a ray gun on his belt. And, of course, he has an attractive girlfriend.

I would like to be this Adam Strange fellow. If only I could find this Zeta-Beam to transport me to some other world. Oh, but that's right, I *have* been transported to other worlds. The only thing is I didn't like much what I found on those worlds, and I had neither jet pack nor ray gun, nor, needless to add, an attractive girlfriend awaiting me there.

Chapter 3

I did something I should not have done yesterday. Against not only several doctors' orders but my own personal experience and supposed good sense, I had one too many last night, all right, perhaps two, what am I saying, three, all right, say four, four too many considering two is my limit and I had six, but no, wait, I think I had seven.

It was at the Ugly Mug on Washington Street. Normally I prefer the slightly more refined Pilot House, but since I had been to the Pilot House two nights running and still felt like going out for a cocktail I chose "the Mug".

All went well, considering, until that sixth Manhattan. I had a sort of conversation with a couple of coast guardsmen, primarily on the efficacy of Pancho Herrera as opposed to Johnny Callison {*Callison and Herrera were players on the 1963 Philadelphia Phillies baseball team. — Editor}*, and I managed not to disgrace myself. Then a sort of chat with a charming middle-aged couple from Allentown. Well, boring middle-aged couple, but then I was no Steve Allen or Victor Borge in the sparkling repartée department either. Then a blank hour or so staring at the TV and a Yankees-Red Sox game. An hour I shall never retrieve. Then a jumbled sort of exchange of grunts and whinnyings with a couple of young college guys, about God knows what and who cares anyway. Then a period of void vague silent drunkenness, surrounding by chatter and madness, and then it happened.

It happened again, this leaving of the body, this departure from within myself to without, myself cooly observing the wreckage of myself leaning upon the bar, surrounded by laughing yelling people shouting words that meant nothing even though the beings shouting them thought they meant something, but none of it meant anything, not their words, nor their thoughts, nor them, nor that drunken wreckage leaning upon the bar there, that thing called me.

I considered leaving it all for good. Just floating away, and this time no punking out and coming back, in no matter how comatose or psychotic a state. Just leaving it all for good.

Well, obviously I didn't.

Somehow I found myself reeling home through the cool salt ocean air. Arriving at my aunts' house I heaved myself into my accustomed wicker rocker on the porch. By the dim porch-light I saw on the blue wooden floor a pile of my young cousin's comics, all of which I had read and reread earlier that day. I shoved my hand down and scrabbled them all up, laid them in my lap.

Which super-hero shall I be tonight? I thought, riffling through the comic books. What about Iron Man, after all I wear a layer of iron around me twenty-four hours a day. Or The Thing, because the way the Thing looks is exactly how I look inside, the Human Torch because I am aflame, Mr. Fantastic because I can stretch myself endlessly, the Invisible Girl because no-one, not even I, sees the real me. Or the Incredible Hulk, because I am scarcely credible and fully a hulk, or Spider-Man because a spider is my soul, but no, here we are: the Ant-Man. Yes, that's it. I am the Ant-Man. Digging my little hole, crawling about looking for my grains of sugar, crawling back into my hole with my precious sweet cargo, I am Dr. Henry Pym, at your service, sir, yes: The Ant-Man.

Perhaps I should write a poem based on the above tale.

But then again, no.

Chapter 4

Two days of tedious sobriety following which I found myself in the Pilot House with a Manhattan before me. The call of the wild. Outside brilliant sunshine and shimmering heat, people in their bathing suits and sandals herding by to and from the beach. But inside the Pilot House all is cool and dim, the dulcet vocalizations of Pat Boone and Perry Como exuding from the jukebox. I prepare myself for oblivion. All is well. Home (my aunts') is a mere few blocks' staggering distance.

Or, who knows, perhaps I shall do the sensible thing, have one or two, okay three at most, four at the absolute outside and then go home.

While pondering these alternatives and still on my first drink, wondering "Why?" for the thousandth time, and answering myself, "Why? Why anything?", and reflecting what little good attending mass that morning had done me — *mirabile dictu*: a woman spoke to me. She was sitting one stool away at the bar. If she had been there when I came in I had failed to notice her.

"Pardon me," she said, holding her cigarette in that up-tilted way that women do, "Do you have a light?"

"Of course," I said.

Like the perfect gentleman I always am unless I am in a state of insanity or extreme drunkenness, I quickly scrabbled up my Zippo from the bar, reached across and lighted her cigarette.

She began to chat with me. She was not bad-looking I suppose, although who could be sure, what with the layers of multi-colored clown-makeup on her face. Mid-thirties, possibly early or late thirties, what did I know? With the hard forbidding blonde hair that is in style these days. She was not very interesting at all in conversation, downright boring in fact, but I listened with I hope an interested and affable expression on my face, or at least what could pass for one. After a while she suggested I sit on the stool next to her, and who was I to say no, so I did.

In due course she revealed that she was single, divorced. When she asked me if I were married I told her the truth, that I wasn't, nor had ever been.

"You're not one of *those*, are you?" she asked, pointing her cigarette towards a table of elegant men with extravagant voices, a group of fellows who reminded me disconcertingly of some of our priests and parish ushers in the latter stages of one of our Communion breakfasts at the Schwarzwald Inn after a few rounds of Old Fashioneds had been served.

"No," I said. "I suppose I've just never found the right girl."

As if it were up to me.

She looked in my eyes, for once not saying anything. In a little while she went to the ladies' room. I gestured to the bartender to fix us two more drinks. When he laid them down he said:

"Looks like you made a conquest, buddy."

I smiled, or at least stretched the corners of my mouth outward a bit in an imitation of a smile.

She came back. We each had several more drinks. She became very merry indeed, and after a while Freddy Ayres the singer and accordionist came on with his supposed wife Ursula the saxophonist, and they played their songs. The woman of whom I write, her name was Rhonda, insisted that I dance with her. I did, in my clumsy fashion. She smelled of perfume, she was warm and moist with sweat, her Aquanetted hair abraded my nose. Her breath smelled of whiskey and cigarettes, as no doubt did mine. On about the fourth dance she said into my ear:

"Let's get out of here."

Soon we were walking along Decatur Street, in the direction of the beach. Swirly whirling night had fallen.

"Take me home," she said.

"Of course," I said.

We came to one of the rooming houses on Hughes Street.

"Let's go around the back way," she said.

"Okay," I said.

Once around the back, surrounded closely by ivy-covered house-wall and enormous fragrant azaleas and rhododendrons she put her arms around my waist.

"Kiss me," she said.

"Oh, I don't think we should do that," I said.

"Why not?" she said. "Don't you like me?'

"Of course, I do" I said, which was not quite true, but it was a white lie.

"Then why don't you want to kiss me?"

"Well, it would be a near occasion of sin," I said.

"You're joking, right?"

"No," I said, "I mean, if we kissed, which in itself may not be sinful, we could very well be making it more likely for us to go a bit further, which would be a sin."

I took out my cigarettes, offered her one, she shook her head no.

"You're not serious," she said.

"But I'm a good Catholic," I said, lighting my Pall Mall.

"But — how old are you?"

I let out that first fine lungful of smoke, then told her my age, shaving off only a few years out of vanity.

"And — you won't let yourself kiss a woman?"

"Well, I suppose if I were engaged to her — or of course if I were married —"

"But, how are you gonna know you want to marry a woman if you won't even let yourself kiss her?"

"Well, I like to think Jesus would tell me."

"Jesus."

"Yes. I like to think he would somehow let me know."

"Okay."

She paused a bit, then said goodnight and went into the back entrance of the house, the screen door flopping shut loudly behind her.

I started to walk home, but when I was almost there I changed my mind. I turned and headed back to the Pilot House. There seemed little point in stopping now.

And hey presto, I was there again, and ordering another Manhattan.

"So, buddy," the bartender said. "You sure work quick."

"Um," I said. "Uh."

"Always leave 'em wantin' more. That way they come back."

"Yeah, you're right," I said. I always agree with bartenders, no matter what.

I took a sip of my drink, and I lit up another excellent Pall Mall. I turned on my stool and listened to Freddy Ayres sing. *"Tiny bubbles,"* he was singing, *"in the wine, make me happy, make me feel fine. Tiny bubbles make me warm all over with a feeling that I'm gonna love you till the end of time. So here's to the golden moon, and here's to the silver sea, and mostly here's a toast to you and me..."*

I might commit the nasty but venial sin of inebriation tonight but at least I would not double the offense by committing the far more vile and mortal sin of fornication.

I sipped again, took another drag of my cigarette, and let the music and the drunkenness suffuse my being. Life was, if not good, then at the very least not damnable. Or so I hoped.

Chapter 5

What have I done.

The day after my previously recounted escapade at the Pilot House was no worse than what might have been expected, *viz.*, killing hangover, suicidal depression, pathetic and meaningless remorse and guilt, and unremitting boredom relieved only by an infinite self-loathing, in other words nothing to get excited about, just another day at Villa Schnabel. But the following afternoon, having vowed for the 13,769th time never to touch alcohol again I was sitting over coffee at a small formica table at the Cape Coffee Shoppe, enjoying the first day of the rest of my life and feeling quite pleased with myself for having written — and quite successfully I thought, at least by my standards — a sonnet on the subject of having neither talent nor inspiration {*See Arnold's poem "Inspiration" in the Appendix. – Editor*}, when who should burst through the door but she.

She being this woman from my disgraceful evening at the Pilot House, this "Rhonda" or whomever.

"*You!*" she shrieked. "*You!*"

At first I didn't recognize her but then she shrieked again.

"*You!*" she shrieked.

"Oh," I said.

"How *are* you?"

"I'm, uh —" I stood up, trembling I'm sure visibly, but if I was it fazed her not one bit.

"What are you writing?" she shrieked, and to avoid repetition I'll just stipulate here that she shrieked on the average every other phrase.

"It's uh —" I gestured dismissively at the damning dime-store notebook lying on the table, "it's nothing."

"It can't be nothing!" I should note that although she shrieked approximately half her phrases, she didn't necessarily alternate shrieking with speaking in a normal voice, normal for her anyway, phrase for phrase. "I mean it's gotta be something!" No, there was no pattern. "Is it your diary? What is it?"

I learned a long time ago that it's a mistake to talk to people about my bad poetry. But still I do it anyway, God knows why. But now, bored already to the point of screaming, all I wanted to do was to escape. I grabbed the notebook and shoved it into my Bermuda shorts pocket.

"Well, it was nice seeing you," I said, "but I'm afraid I have to —"

"Oh! Don't go! You know you don't have to go! You're just shy. I think that's so endearing! And you're such a gentleman! Won't you ask a lady to have a cup of coffee with you?"

Don't ask me how or why — cowardice, weakness, perhaps-more-than-half insanity — but before I knew it I was sitting back down with a refilled coffee cup and she was sitting across from me with a cup of her own, not that she needed it.

What happened next was like a Gestapo interrogation; without the extracted fingernails, it's true, but after a few minutes I was ready to pull out my own fingernails. Oh, sure, she was asking me all about me, but I did not want to talk about me, I am sick of me, I am stuck with me every second of my life, and besides, it's all so pathetic it's embarrassing, unless I lie, and then if I lie it's more embarrassing still.

In the end she got it all out of me anyway, or at least a *Reader's Digest* version: the lifelong celibacy (well, all right, lifelong except for one drunken and depressing episode in the army, which I changed for Rhonda's benefit to a one-night affair with a German girl, leaving out the fact that she had been a prostitute), the living with one's mother, the poem a week in the *Olney Times*. I even told her of my mental breakdown and hospitalization, of my returning to work after a few months and then being sent away from work indefinitely on half-pay — thinking maybe all this would scare her off. Ha.

"Arnold," she said, "I'm going to make you my project."

Oh no.

"Well, I really must be going," I said, and started to get up.

She put her hand on mine.

"Sit down," she said. "I know you don't really have to go. Let's talk a while."

I sat down. And she talked. But now she went on to a subject even more boring than me: her.

I won't go into it all, and besides I wasn't listening to half of it, and half of what I was listening to I've already forgotten and it was only yesterday, but just for the record, she's from Upper Merion, she works as a dental hygienist, she was married but is no longer, she has a child, a girl of some age I forget, whose name I forget. The child was with the former husband while the mother our heroine was enjoying this, her first ever vacation all by herself. It was all too dull, too much, too real, too little.

"Arnold," she said, seeming to indicate a shift away from her autobiography. "Such a cute name. Say, you do remember my name, don't you?"

"Of course I do," I said.

"Then what is it?"

"It's Rhonda," I said.

"What?"

"Rhonda?"

"My name's not Rhonda."

"Oh," I said. "I'm terribly sorry."

"You don't remember my name?"

"Um, Veronica?"

"No."

"Um —"

"I can't believe you can't remember my name." I hadn't realized it but the shriek in her voice had gradually diminished in frequency and volume while she had been talking about herself, replaced by a non-hypnotic drone, but now the shrieking returned. "You *jerk*!" she shrieked.

"Uh, I was drunk, I'm afraid."

"I was *plastered*, but I remembered your name."

"Sorry."

"You really don't remember my name."

Okay, this went on for way too long, but at long last she broke down and told me her correct name:

"Mona. My name is *Mona*."

"Oh," I said. Rhonda, Mona, they were pretty similar really.

"*Rhonda*," she said. "I should never talk to you again."

"*You're right*," I thought. "*You shouldn't. Please don't.*"

But she did. And now I must leave off. I must change for dinner. Because I am taking this Mona person to dinner at the Merion Inn.

I am doomed.

Chapter 6

It's occurred to me that I started writing this nonsense with the idea of a memoir and yet so far I've only written about my present state.

No matter.

It's all the same, past, present, the future, if there is a future.

When I was a child I knew just barely more than nothing, teetering my tiny steps forward into this massive incomprehensible universe.

Now my poor brain is a universe itself, filled with absurd memories, and still I teeter willy nilly forward through time, the universe no less incomprehensible than when I was three years old.

No matter.

Even sitting still I teeter forward through time, through this universe. These scribblings are my tiny evanescent footprints…

I went to meet her at the Pilot House. I was dressed in my only summer suit, from Krass Brothers, a shimmering dark grey conservative suit, suitable for a Catholic usher.

Supposedly I've sworn off drinking again, but I ordered a beer as I waited for her. A beer seems hardly to count as drinking.

She arrived, stepping in from the still-bright but dying summer daylight. I suppose she felt she looked radiant. Her hair was like some modernistic light fixture with a hundred-watt bulb turned on inside it. She wore a flowery dress of what looked and eventually felt like wallpaper, and she reeled towards me on high heels. I arose from my barstool, the gentleman as always. She kissed my cheek, suffusing me in a miasma of warm perfume, and I only wanted to go home, or to my aunts' home, to get out of this suit and sit on the porch with a paperback thriller or a nice stack of my young cousin Kevin's comic books. I felt a great boredom descending upon me already and for the ten thousandth time I thanked God (silently) for the blessing of alcohol.

After a couple of Mai-Tais (her suggestion) we walked over to the Merion Inn. I'd never been there before. I've never seen the point of these allegedly fancy restaurants, but it was her idea. A burger at the Pilot House or the Ugly Mug would have been fine with me, or as fine as things could be expected to be since I didn't want to have dinner with her in the first place, but I have always been a good boy and done what was asked of me.

It could have been worse. Maybe it was the dim lighting and the desperate-looking waiters in their iridescent black vests and choking bowties, but there was very little of the shrieking of the previous day. Apparently she could turn that off and on.

I ordered a steak, she ordered Surf 'n' Turf. When the food came she suggested we drink wine, and I said okay. (We'd each had another Mai-Tai while waiting for the food). The waiter handed me a wine list. All I knew was you were supposed to drink red wine with meat and white with fish. But she had ordered lobster and meat, making the choice impossible. I settled on a bottle of Mateus rosé. She did shriek at this, declaring Mateus to be her favorite wine.

It's all too tedious to recount so I'll hurry to the climax and *dénouement*. We were sitting on a bench on the promenade, near Frank's Playland, the pale beach and the dark living enormity of the ocean spread out before us. She snuggled against me. She told me she really liked me. I realized it was now or never. Either come up with something quick or I was going to marry this boring woman, I would become stepfather to her nameless child, she would hurry and become pregnant again with a child of mine, which would prove incontrovertibly that she was almost as mentally unstable as I.

No.

I was a poet, albeit a mediocre one. I had written a poem a week for almost twenty-five years, somehow wresting a grouping of rhymed and at least semi-coherent words from my brain when often I had no idea for a poem at all when I sat down to write one. I could do this.

"Mona," I said, for that was her name, and this time I remembered it. "I must tell you something. I'm in love with another woman."

She drew her hard bristly head from my shoulder.

"You are? Why didn't you tell me?"

"Because — because I thought that perhaps I could make myself forget her. You see, we — she and I — had a quarrel — that's why I came to Cape May, to, to, to try to —"

"To forget her."

Good, now she was helping me.

"Yes, to forget her. But I can't. I just —"

"You can't."

"Yes. I tried. But I can't. I think I'm going to have to resign myself, to the fact that that I'm just hopelessly —"

"In love with her."

"Yes."

"I thought it might be something like that. Why you were so distant. What's her name?"

Name.

"Uh, Rhonda," I said.

"Oh," she smiled, "that makes sense. That's what you thought my name was."

"Yeah. Sorry," I said.

"So she lives back in Philadelphia?"

"Yes," I said, in a comfortable improvisational mode now. "In my neighborhood. We — we grew up together."

"That's so sweet. But how come you never married."

"She —" That was a good question. "She became a nun," I said.

"She's a nun?"

"Yes."

"You're in love with a nun?"

"Yes."

"Arnold, that's insane."

"But she quit the convent."

"Oh, that's different."

"Yes. She moved back to the neighborhood, back in with her parents. We met again, and — well —"

"Sparks ignited."

"Yes."

"What did you quarrel about?"

"Quarrel?"

"Yes, you said you had a quarrel."

"Right. It was about —"

I had no ideas, nothing.

"You wanted to marry her," said Mona.

"Yes," I said, almost as a question.

"But she wasn't ready yet," she said.

"Right," I said, "she didn't want to rush it."

"But you did, because you'd waited so long."

"Yeah," I said. To tell the truth I was getting a little bored with it all.

"Go back to her," she said. "Go back to her, Arnold, and tell her, you've waited this long for her, you can wait a little longer. But not forever."

"Right," I said.

So I walked her home. She gave me a chaste kiss on the cheek. She told me she was leaving Cape May the next day, which was good. That meant I wouldn't have to hide from her.

"Y'know," she said, "I probably shouldn't tell you this, but I was probably going to sleep with you tonight, Arnold."

I let that go by without comment. She went inside and the screen door made a gentle flopping sound behind her.

I headed toward the Pilot House for a nightcap.

I decided just to have a beer this time, and the bartender brought me a chilled mug of Schaefer.

"So, pal, how'd it go tonight?"

He grinned lewdly.

"Good," I said. I exhaled Pall Mall smoke, lifted the mug and drank.

"Get your end wet?"

"A gentleman never tells," I said.

"Ah, you bastard, ya."

I turned on my stool. Freddy Ayres and his alleged wife Ursula were performing on the tiny stage.

"Oh, there's a lull in my life," sang Freddy. *"It's just a void and empty space when you are not in my embrace."*

I have to say, life in that moment was good, very good.

Chapter 7

Since the previously-related incident I have had an interesting thought, i.e., what if I never go back to work? After all, I've been working full-time since I was fourteen, and except for my three years in the army I've been on the railroad since I was seventeen. What if I simply continue this indefinite leave-of-absence? I was a mere cog in the mighty machine that is the Reading Railroad, they won't miss a pittance like the half-salary they're giving me, and besides, I could take an early retirement anyway and get nearly as much for my pension. Is it wrong of me to think this way? Is it my duty as a Catholic to work, even if Mother and I can easily get by on my half-pay and my savings?

Does writing this memoir count as work?

To be honest the thought of working at any sort of job fills me with a sort of dread, whereas the thought of continuing my present idle existence fills me if not with joy then at least an almost complete absence of dread, if an absence of something can be said to be capable of filling something. And I think this can be said. I have filled most of my life with absences. The absence of friendship. The absence of romantic love. The absence of sex. The absence of marriage and children. The absence of meaning. I could go on all day adding to my litany of nothingnesses.

But now I feel this something entering my life which before was not there. After the events of the past year I know well that this something could simply be another stage of insanity, perhaps one from which there is no return. But for some reason I am not afraid. Perhaps I am not afraid because I am already insane, or I should say insane again, although certainly nowhere nearly as far gone as when I had to be taken to Byberry.

So, that's settled, for now. Back to my memoir.

I was born in a section of Philadelphia called Swampoodle, in the shade of Shibe Park. My parents were German immigrants, with little education. My earliest years were poor but bearable, but then came the Depression. My father lost his factory job. I had two brothers and a sister, all younger than me. For two years we were always hungry. Then at last my father got work at the Heintz metalworks in the Olney neighborhood. We moved into one of the plain new rowhomes right across the street from the factory. The area seemed positively bucolic after the grimy old streets of Swampoodle. This was a good move for my father because now he could simply walk across the street to work. My father was a stoker. All he did was shovel coal into an enormous hellish furnace, hour after hour, all day long. He was a bull, a beast of burden, and he knew it, and he accepted it. He found solace for this purgatory of a life in food, cigarettes, and beer, most importantly beer. He would inhale two quarts of Ortlieb's beer on his lunch hour, and after work he would drink beer until he fell into his deep snoring sleep, only to wake up and do it all over again. One day in 1935 he didn't wake up.

I quit school and went to work. I helped the milkman deliver milk in the mornings in his horse-drawn wagon, then I sold newspapers on the street for the rest of the day. When I was seventeen my Uncle Hans got me onto the railroad, and there I stayed. In 1942 I volunteered for the army, even though my job on the railroad and my status as primary breadwinner for my siblings and mother exempted me from the draft. Because of my trade I was put into the engineers, and I never saw combat, although I served all through the long campaign from Normandy to Berlin. After the war I returned to my job as a brakeman for the Reading.

My siblings got married and left home but I did not. I worked, I ushered at St. Helena's church, I volunteered for parish and diocesan activities. I had taken up boxing in the army and for many years I coached a CYO boxing team.

Oh, I forgot to mention the poems. In 1938, when I was eighteen or so I wrote a poem and sent it in to the *Olney Times*. It was a bad poem, but the *Olney Times* published it anyway, I suppose because it was very sentimental and simple, or maybe they just had space to fill. The next week I wrote another poem and sent it in, and they published it as well. And so on. I have published a poem a week in the *Olney Times* every week of my life since. That's twenty-five years. That's roughly 1,300 poems, nearly every one of them utter nonsense, but it's a habit now, like my cigarettes and my Manhattans and beer, and I can't quit.

They call me the Rhyming Brakeman. There was an article about me a few years ago in the *Philadelphia Bulletin*. The article, like my poems, was nonsense, full of my dull platitudes, presenting myself as some sort of noble workingman artist, when the truth was that I was an odd fellow, living with his mother, fearful of life, living half a life or less while others all around him lived full lives.

However, even into the dullest life a little luridness may fall, and so it has been with mine. I have had my shameful moments, just about all of them under the influence of alcohol, but I would be lying if I said these moments were solely due to the alcohol. Perhaps I will cover some of this swampy ground later. Perhaps not.

Then I went insane, which was actually the most interesting thing I've ever done. Not that there was anything willful about it, so perhaps I should say it was the most interesting thing that ever "happened" to me. Leaving me having never done anything very interesting at all, unless you call the thirteen hundred poems interesting, and I suppose the fact that I wrote and published that many poems is slightly interesting even if the poems themselves were not, are not, will never be.

So much for my memoir. I've now succeeded in boring even myself with my own story. But there must be something of interest I can relate from this lifetime of nothingness.

There must be something.

But nothing comes to mind right now.

Chapter 8

Somehow I have let two weeks or so slip by since my last entry in these my memoirs, but I've not been completely idle.

Just this morning I added the finishing touches to, and mailed off to the *Olney Times*, my weekly poem, on the subject of my new daily occupation of swimming. *{See Arnold's poem "Swimming", in the Appendix. — Editor}*

Occasionally I do little odd-jobs about the house, but there isn't much for me to do, what with my three aunts and Mom all looking to keep busy. But they know I'm willing and able to leap up from my comic books or paperback thrillers at a moment's notice should some task present itself that calls for a man's strong back or long reach.

But my aunts actually have a handyman who has worked for them for years, an ancient and somewhat incomprehensible Negro named Charlie Coleman, and I hate to take any of Charlie's work away from him. So when this week a rain of shingles fell from the roof in a storm and my Aunt Elizabetta asked me if I would like to replace them, I declined and said it was probably a job more suited to Charlie's talents. To be honest I think she was perhaps hoping I would do the job for free, but, too bad. Charlie needs to earn a living, and my aunts can well afford what little they pay him. They all worked the switchboards for Bell for forty or fifty years and they've got nice little pensions as well as what they make from their rents and various canny investments over the years.

(Not to mention that they, like my mother, never spend money on anything but the bare necessities. To my knowledge none of these good women has ever had a meal in a restaurant, nor has any of them ever had a single drop of any alcoholic beverage, nor smoked a cigarette. I don't think any of them has ever read a book, or even a magazine or newspaper, except to look for supermarket coupons or to read obituaries.)

When Charlie and his son or grandson arrived to fix the roof I did bestir myself long enough to spot the ladder for them while they climbed up to the roof. Charlie spoke to me before I did this, but I couldn't tell you what he said, beyond (I think) thanking me for the spot. His son or grandson said not a word.

I returned to my place on the porch where I was sitting in "my" wicker rocker reading comic books alongside my young cousin, who had not remarked, nor even glanced up, at either my departure or my return.

But the noise of Charlie and his offspring's work distracted me, so I got up to take a walk...

These are the days of our lives.

Oh, the swimming.

I had gone swimming in the ocean now and then since coming down here, but I didn't much enjoy it. Too many people, too much sun.

Then one day, maybe it was the day after my so-called date with Rhonda or Mona or whatever her name was, it occurred to me to take an early-evening swim along that long curving cove that sweeps from the so-called fishing jetty way on down past the abandoned World War II bunker to Cape May Point, with its white lighthouse sticking up like an accusing finger into the sky. There was no one about at all. I guess you're not even supposed to swim there. There are no lifeguards posted there even during the day, and the currents are alleged to be treacherous. I walked down almost half way to the Point, then took off my flip-flops and worked my way down the pebbly shingle into the water. I dove in, and swam out, and it's true, the waves and currents did feel strong, but after I got out to a depth where I could no longer touch the slimy bottom with my feet the water was calmer, and I swam around for a bit until I got tired, then headed in, exhausted and heaving for breath.

I lay on my back on the towel I'd brought with me, staring up at the greying sky. Then I had a cigarette from the pack I'd left on the towel. This was good.

The next morning my muscles were so stiff I could barely get out of bed, but that evening I went down to "my" beach again, and swam for an even longer time, and went out farther.

Now, after a couple of weeks of daily swimming, already I am so strong I can swim as far out as about a mile, and I like to stop after a while, and turn, keeping myself afloat with a steady movement of my arms and legs, looking back to the rocking shore.

That's what I wrote the poem about.

I'd be lying if I said I didn't sometimes have a slight urge just to keep going, to swim out endlessly toward the horizon, but so far I've always come on back in. (Obviously, or I wouldn't be writing this.)

Suicide is a mortal sin, after all.

But I don't think this urge is necessarily a wish for death, no, it's just an urge to go, to go outward, away from the world I know, to escape that world and my absurd place in it.

What's the rush, after all, that day will come, who knows when, but it will, I'll escape the world as we all do.

I swim back, gloriously exhausted, and each day it's later in the evening when I stagger back up the shingle to my towel and my cigarettes and lighter, my old wallet and my t-shirt. This evening I lay there on my back for some time, staring up at the sky which had turned deep blue during my hour-long swim, the stars twinkling by the thousands, I didn't know their names, had no desire to know their names.

I thought I saw Jesus in the stars, but now I'm pretty sure it was just some wispy clouds, that and wishful thinking. I lit up a smoke, and headed back in to town. I stopped at Sid's Tavern for a beer.

Chapter 9

Now that I have each day absolutely and completely free from indentured servitude to that great iron beast The Railroad I wonder at how awful my life was, with five days a week dominated by work and going to and from work and recovering from work.

Now I wake each morning in my tiny attic room, I stretch and yawn, another glorious day of idleness awaits me.

Each day teems with adventures great and small.

Cousin Bert and his wife and two of their children have completed their dubious vacation and gone back to their red brick life in Lawncrest, but for some reason or reasons unknown to me they have left the eldest son Kevin here. Yesterday he surprised me by actually inviting me to come with him to Wally's, the shop on Washington Street where he buys his comic books. So off we went. It's a cigar store among other things, and there's a cigar store Indian in front. I'd never been in there before. It was dark and cool, and there was a pool table in the back part. I stood with my hands in my pockets as Kevin went intently through the rack of used comics.

A round old man with a bald head and a cigar in his mouth and thick spectacles on his nose stood behind the counter. I suppose this was Wally.

"Is that your boy, pal?"

"Well, no," I said. "He's my cousin's son."

"Nice kid. Quiet."

"Yeah, he's quiet," I said.

"Not like some of these snotnoses around here. They got no respect. They don't care about nothin' or nobody."

"Yeah," I said.

"Animals."

"Yeah," I said.

"Scum. An atom bomb falls on 'em it'll serve 'em right."

"Right," I said.

"It ain't like the old days."

"Yeah," I said.

"Punks," he said.

I stared out the open door at the bright street. For just the slightest moment I felt on the verge of one of those attacks I sometimes have, where I feel as if I'm merely a ghost in the world, separate from physical reality; but I used one of my familiar methods to gain control of myself, i.e., I concentrated my attention on something in this physical world, in this case a copy of *Look* magazine. There were people in the magazine, or pictures of people, and words, and by forcing my attention on them I somehow felt my being settling back within my corporeal host.

Kevin came up with a bunch of comic books. He had already laid a stack of comics he was returning on the glass cigar counter. The old man performed some abstruse formula with pencil and notepad and told Kevin it would be twenty-seven cents.

"Hey, Cousin Arnold," the lad said, "can ya help me out? I'm a little short today."

I realized then that Kevin's invitation was merely a ploy to get me to buy these comic books for him. But I didn't mind his duplicity. After all, if Kevin doesn't buy the comic books then I don't get to read them either, and as I have said somewhere else in these pages (unless I dreamt it) I have myself become addicted to these lurid fantasies.

I bought his comics and also picked up a carton of Pall Malls at a good price.

And this was only the beginning of my day. What other heroic adventures lay in store?

Kevin led the way out onto the sidewalk with our treasure.

He examined the comics' covers all over again as we strolled back to Perry Street.

"You can read one first if you like, Cousin Arnold," he said.

This was something. Normally of course I had to wait till he was finished with one before he would let me read it.

"Which one do you want?"

"What do you have?"

"Here –" he held up a *Kid Colt,* "here's a good one for you to start with."

I knew he wasn't crazy about Kid Colt, and to tell the truth neither am I. He was holding out on the good stuff, *The Fantastic Four, Spider-Man, Tales to Astonish* with the Ant-Man.

"Okay," I said. "Thanks, Kevin."

"You're welcome," he said.

He quickened his steps. Now that "business" was over he was anxious to get back to the porch, to our adjoining wicker rockers, to escape into his little dream world.

And to tell the truth so was I.

Chapter 10

A curious incident later in the day.

As usual of late, after digesting my supper over a novel (*The Outfit*, by Richard Stark) on the porch, I took my towel and my cigarettes and walked down to that bereft long stretch of pebbles and sand and desolation where I take my daily swim.

When I got to the beach there was no one there, as usual. The sun was dipping down beside Cape May Point lighthouse, as usual. I took off my pocketed t-shirt and rolled it up in my towel along with my wallet, cigarettes and lighter, then tossed the towel into a tuft of scraggly grass under that long high wave of sand that edges the beach, with a fence of wire and sticks running drunkenly along its crest.

I strode into the water, and when I got about thigh-deep I dove in, and swam out.

Each day I'm getting stronger, each day I swim farther out, and I swim for a longer time.

Sometimes I wonder about sharks. Or cramp. Or even a heart attack. Would my body be found? And in what awful condition?

A mile or more from the shore I treaded water, the sun had now sunk beyond the bay, and on the upsurge of the swells I could clearly see the lights of Delaware, as if beckoning. Well, I may be a strong swimmer now, but not that strong, and, besides, what would I do in Delaware?

I headed back in, and as I swam I noticed a small living light against the grey dimness of the beach.

Sloshing in with the surf I saw a group of four people gathered around a little fire. I would have ignored them except they were sitting right near where I'd left my rolled-up towel. I walked towards them. They were all sitting cross-legged, smoking, they had a large wicker wine jug and they were drinking out of Dixie cups. There were two young men and two young women. The men had short beards and the girls had long hair, one blond, the other dark. The girls wore long loose dresses, the men wore khaki shorts and t-shirts.

"Hi, there," I said. "I'm just getting my towel and stuff. I left it over there."

"Cool, man," said the one fellow. He had luxuriant curly dark hair.

I stepped past them and got my towel out of the weeds. I unrolled it. Everything was still there.

"That was some long swim you took, buddy," said the other guy. He had slightly sun-bleached hair, a bit overgrown, and his beard was trimmed like Shakespeare's. "We were digging you out there."

"Yeah, I like to swim," I said.

"It's so cool you go out here at night all alone," said the blond girl.

"Yeah, I like it that way," I said. I was rubbing myself with the towel with one hand, holding my t-shirt, wallet, cigarettes and lighter awkwardly all in the other hand.

"You look in great shape," said the dark-haired girl.

I didn't know what to say, so I said, "Um."

"These guys never get any exercise," said the dark girl.

"I'm exercising right now," said the curly-haired fellow, and he took a long pull on his hand-rolled cigarette.

He held in the smoke for a very long time and then exhaled.

He blinked, smiled, and said, "Hey, buddy, you want a toke?"

"A toke?"

"Some of this."

He held out the handrolled cigarette.

"Oh, I've got my own," I said.

"Try this, man. It's Mary Jane."

"Really?"

"Yeah, go on. It'll open your mind."

"I'm not sure with me that's a good idea," I said.

"Come on, live dangerously."

Don't ask me why, but I sat down with them and smoked some marijuana. This was my first ever social encounter with beatniks, and the first time I had ever tried "reefer". Let's face it, I've been a goody two-shoes for most of my life, and where did it land me but the loony bin?

Before long I was telling them my whole life story. Well, I gave them the short version. They listened politely, and even, oddly, seemed to be interested.

"You seem fairly sane now," said the curly-haired guy, whose name was Gypsy Dave.

"Yeah, I guess so," I said.

As sane as I'll ever be, I thought, which might not be saying much.

"I think you had a mystical experience," said the blond girl, who went by the name of Fairchild, or Fair Child, I didn't know how she spelled it.

"That's one way of looking at it," I said.

"Like Paul on the way to Damascus," said the Shakespeare guy, whose name was Rocket Man.

"Or, like Wile E. Coyote when the Road Runner tricks him into going off the edge of a cliff," said the dark-haired girl, whose name was Elektra.

"Yeah, it was more like that," I said.

"I want to read your poems, man," said Elektra.

"I assure you they're not good," I said.

"I don't care, man. I think they must be really, like, deep."

We sat smoking and talking for another hour or two, and then all of a sudden we realized we were all very hungry.

Chapter 11

My new friends invited me to their so-called "pad" for dinner. Of course I had already had dinner at our usual time (6:00 PM) but I was now ravenously hungry, I could have gnawed on one of the logs in the fire, I could have bounded back into the surf and swum under water with my mouth open, devouring seaweed and small fishes; in short I said, "Sure. Thanks."

We walked townward. How merry it was to walk along the sand in this new exuberant (if slightly reminiscent of my previous psychotic fugues) state. I felt like some silly large dog, prancing ahead of and around some new-found human friends. They seemed so much more interesting than the dull people I had met and invariably not befriended (or not been befriended by) all my life.

They lived above a jewelry shop on Jackson Street. An apartment hung with tapestries and beads, with candles in Chianti bottles and bamboo rugs and lots of oriental cushions and pillows on the floor.

Elektra and and the girl called Fairchild or Fair Child set to work making spaghetti in the kitchen that was open to the small living room. Rocket Man put a record album on. It was a very strange sort of saxophone jazz, strange to me, anyway, who normally never listened to anything stranger than Lawrence Welk or Larry Ferrari, although I suppose they're pretty strange too in their own ways.

"You dig coal train, man?" said Gypsy Dave.

"Coal train?" I asked.

"Yeah. Train, man."

"Train?"

"Yeah, John, coal train."

Now I was totally confused. Why was he calling me John?

I said nothing.

The strange saxophone wailed.

"I think he digs the train," said Rocket Man, coming over to where we were sitting on the floor around one of those great wooden spools that you normally wrap cable around. He sat down, smiling. "Doncha, Arnold. You dig the train, man."

"Well, of course I do," I said, doing one of my little imitations of a sane person. "The train, after all, has really been my, my whole life —"

"Your whole life?" said Gypsy Dave. He was rolling another "joint" on a record album cover. It was *The Freewheelin' Bob Dylan*, whoever he is. "That is really heavy," he said. "I mean, I dig the train, and the bird too, and you know, a lot of cats, but I wouldn't say that they're my *life*. But the train means that much to you."

"Well, it wasn't really, um, uh, voluntary –" I said.

"No, man," said Gypsy Dave. "It wouldn't be *voluntary*. But that's the beauty of it. It just, like, takes over you. And that's beautiful man. Wait, listen, now miles is coming in."

"Miles?"

Gypsy Dave held a finger in the air. I could understand now. Me leaning out from the cab of a hurtling locomotive, staring ahead, watching the myriad storming miles coming in, always coming and speeding by underneath the train's wheels. All those miles coming in for all those years, how many thousands, perhaps millions of miles, coming in, and going...

"Miles," I said.

"Miles," said Rocket Man. "He digs miles, too."

"Coming in," I said.

Gypsy Dave handed me the now-rolled "reefer", and I lit it with my lighter. A muted trumpet wailed sadly but wisely, and we stopped speaking and just listened.

Chapter 12

After a while the girls brought out plates and cutlery and a big bowl of spaghetti that Fairchild or Fair Child nestled neatly into the hole in the middle of the big spool we were sitting around.

"There's no meat, I'm afraid," said Elektra.

"That's okay," I said. I was so hungry at this point I could have eaten the spaghetti raw and uncooked.

They filled my plate and I confess I immediately dug in. It was the most delicious food I had ever tasted, and when I came up for air I told the girls so.

"It's just vegetables from our garden," said Fairchild or Fair Child, "and garlic and olive oil."

What did I know about garlic and olive oil? All I knew was that the food was sublime.

"You want some more wine, Arnold?" asked Gypsy Dave, and I said yes, thank you. We were drinking red wine from another one of those big bottles wrapped in wicker. We drank out of Flintstones jelly glasses.

For a time we simply ate and did not talk much. A record was playing. I had asked them to put on *The Freewheelin' Bob Dylan* because I liked the cover picture, a young chap walking arm-in-arm down a winter street with his girlfriend, something I myself had never done. After my second plate I sat back and lighted a cigarette. The others were still eating.

"Is he a hobo?" I asked.

"Who?" said Rocket Man. "Bobby Dillon?"

I picked the record sleeve up off the floor. "Bob Dyelan," I said.

"It's Dillon," said Rocket Man. "He pronounces it Dillon, like Dillon Thomas."

"Oh, I don't know who that is," I said.

"He was cool, he was a poet like you, man," said Rocket Man.

"Oh," I said.

"Bob Dylan's a poet," said Fairchild, Fair Child, the blonde girl.

"A hobo poet," I said.

"Well, he's not really a hobo," said Rocket Man.

"Arnold's right, though, he does sound kinda like a hobo," said Gypsy Dave.

"When I first started on the railroad there were always lots of hobos around the train yards," I said. "I was just a kid. Sometimes when we stopped I could hear them out there by their fires, singing. They sounded like Bob Dyelan, I mean Dillon."

"That's really heavy, Arnold," said Elektra. "How old were you, man?"

"I was seventeen."

"And you've been on the railroad ever since?"

"Yeah, except for a few years in the army, and in the army they had me working on railroads too."

Elektra looked at me. She had very dark eyes. It's always made me shy to have someone look at me, man or woman, but I suppose because of the marijuana and the wine and the food I just didn't care any more, and I even looked back at her.

"So do you miss it?" she said.

"The railroad?" I said. "No. No. I feel like I've wasted my whole life actually."

"How old are you?"

"I'm forty-two."

"You still have a whole life to live," she said.

"I feel like I've lived a thousand lives," I said. "And yet I feel like I haven't lived even one life."

She pushed her plate away and reached over and picked up my pack of Pall Malls.

"Can I have one of these?"

"Sure," I said.

Gypsy Dave was to my right, and Elektra was to the right of Gypsy Dave. I reached across and gave her a light.

She inhaled, blew out the smoke and looked at me again.

"Let's go out and have a smoke, Arnold."

"Where," I said.

"Out on our back porch."

"Okay," I said.

I heaved myself up, I was stiff from sitting crosslegged; Gypsy Dave grabbed my forearm and gave me a boost. Elektra for her part seemed to float up as if she were a weightless spirit. She led the way to the rear of the apartment, through the kitchen, and I followed.

We came out onto a second-floor wooden porch, looking down on a dark garden. Trees billowed and waved and whispered in the starlight. There were a few mismatched chairs on the porch, a small wicker table. Elektra went to the rail and leaned on it. I went over next to her, but I didn't lean on the rail, I'm a little afraid of heights – even though I've walked along the roofs of fifty thousand hurtling train cars in my career, I'm still afraid.

After a minute she turned and looked at me, her cigarette smoke trailing up into the night.

"You're a very strange man," she said.

"I know," I said.

She looked out at the moving trees. The air was clean, so much cleaner than the metallic harsh air I'd breathed all my life living right next door to the Heintz factory, and then on the trains, all those thick engine fumes, breathing them in all my life. And of course here I was smoking.

"What are you thinking about?" she said.

"The air," I said.

She paused, staring at me.

"The air," she said.

"Yeah. It's nice."

She turned sideways to the rail. Her dark hair swirled into her face, but she didn't seem to mind. I could hear the ocean gently crashing beyond the sounds of the rustling trees. It occurred to me that oddly I actually liked being where I was at the present moment or series of moments, although I did rather strongly have that feeling I'd done my best to keep submerged these past months, that feeling, or knowledge, that without too much effort, or rather by surrendering all effort, I could float upward and away, saying fare-thee-well to this world I'd never understood or felt at home in.

"Give me your cigarette," she said.

I did as I was told, and she went over to the wicker table and stubbed out both our cigarettes in a tin ashtray. Then she came over and stood near me.

"Come here," she said.

Chapter 13

I was only about a foot away from her. I didn't have very far to go, to go to her. I took a step forward. She put her hands around my waist.

"You're a real man," she said.

"Technically, yes," I said.

"Those other boys in there, they're boys, not men."

"They seem like nice guys," I said.

"Boys," she said. "Not men."

Now she was pressing against me.

"I want you to kiss me, Arnold."

What the hell, I've always aimed to please people. I kissed her. It didn't kill me to do so. And for once I surrendered, and I fell, and it was as if a great part of me at last opened up to life. Previously I had felt that nothing could be quite as pleasant as lying in bed on a cool afternoon with nothing to do, staring at the ceiling and dreaming of a world beyond this world, but now I was not so sure.

We disengaged, she laid her head on my chest. I had an erection. Perhaps I was not completely out of the norm after all.

And I had a thought.

"Wait," I said. "Elektra, aren't you Rocket Man or Gypsy Dave's girlfriend?"

"No," she said. "But I don't dig these labels. What does that even mean, 'girlfriend'?"

"I don't know," I said, honestly enough.

"Do you want to go to bed?" she said.

"Oh," I said. "Yeah, it is getting a little late, I suppose, but I don't usually go to bed quite this early —"

"No," she said. "I mean go to bed with me. Here. Now," she said.

"Oh," I said.

"I can tell you want to," she said, pressing her hip against my erection.

"I — this is embarrassing," I said, "but I'm a practicing Catholic. I don't believe in extra-marital sex."

"Oh, give me a break, Arnold. You can't really believe all that crap. What good does it do you? You just had a complete mental breakdown you said.

Give *yourself* a break. Sex is natural, man. You think the priests don't have sex?"

She had touched on a delicate subject. In my work as a parish usher and as a CYO boxing coach I had heard rumors. Many rumors.

"Arnold," she said, hugging her body close to mine. "I can feel you."

And indeed I could feel myself. I knew of course that it was the marijuana, the wine, my own barely controlled insanity, but I felt all of myself now suddenly within my erection. It almost felt as if it were pushing me away from her. She had my back against the rail now as she pressed herself against me and it almost felt as if this damnable erection I was suffering was, as I say, pushing me back, trying to push me up over the railing and off the porch, perhaps even up and out above the trees and house-tops behind me.

I took a breath.

"I think we should go inside now," I said.

Chapter 14

Her eyes, which seemed suddenly to have grown enormously, looked into mine. I felt as if I could fall into them. So here I was, precariously suspended between being thrust backward out into the stars or falling into this interior universe which seemed to me just as unknowable.

"You're a very, very strange man," she said.

This was the second time she had said this, now with an extra "very" attached.

I think I sighed slightly.

"Those other guys try to be strange," she said, "but you don't have much choice, do you?"

"No," I said.

Now she was touching me, immodestly. What the heck, I thought. I masturbated on a daily basis: that was a mortal sin. Every week I went to confession and like clockwork I would confess to seven or more acts of willful self-abuse; the priest would usually not even bother to give me a lecture, and after all, I knew deep down inside that the priest masturbated too, if not worse, so who was he to be judgmental. But the point was, if I was going to go to hell for masturbating, why not go to hell for doing what I was imagining doing when I masturbated? But then it occurred to me that performing sexual intercourse with another person was involving that other person in a mortal sin as well. Unless...

"Are you Catholic?" I asked.

"Oh, God, no," she said. "My parents are Jewish, but I'm not anything."

"Oh," I said.

"I think all religions are nonsense. Or not so much nonsense as superstitions, myths."

"Oh."

"Think about it, Arnold. There's a thousand or more religions in the world, and every one of them thinks they know the score. Why should one religion be any better than another one? And why does there have to be a God? And why should we worship a God even if there is one? Is he that insecure that he needs all these little humans to worship him all the time?"

"But —"

But nothing.

It's true that I had imagined Jesus speaking to me once, and it had seemed real to me at the time, but then look where it had happened: in a mental hospital. *{See Arnold's poem "A Guy Named Jesus" in the Appendix. — Editor}*

"Religions only came about so that people could make some sense out of the randomness of life," she said. "This is it, Arnold. Here. Now."

With that last phrase she pressed her hand particularly forcefully against that organ which had been such a bother to me my entire adult and adolescent life.

"So — extramarital sex would not be a mortal sin for you," I said.

"Not necessarily," she said.

She took my left hand and placed it on her right breast. I caressed it. It was pleasant to do so.

"Wait," she said.

"Yes?" I said.

"You're not a virgin, are you?"

Well, there was that one night in late May of '45 in Frankfurt when I got drunk with a couple of the guys in my outfit and they dragged me to a whorehouse, so:

"No," I said.

I hadn't wanted to go to that whorehouse, but my buddies talked me into it. Despite my inebriated state I huffed and puffed and managed to reach climax, albeit into a rubber. I felt guilty, and sorry for the German girl. It was not an experience I have ever looked back fondly on, but at least (at the age of twenty-three) it had taken care of the virginity business, so:

"No," I said, again, hoping she wouldn't ask for details.

Chapter 15

"I think we should go inside now," she said, still touching that organ which never seemed to give Jesus or any of the saints any trouble.

"Oh, wait, I can't go in just yet," I said.

"Why, Arnold?"

Again she pressed herself hard against me; but a curious thing, when a girl presses hard she feels soft.

But unfortunately I was not.

"Why can't you go in?" she asked again.

"Because, well, I have an, uh, you know —"

"A hard-on?"

"Well, yes," I admitted.

"So what? Can't you walk with it?"

"Well, yeah, I suppose, so, but, well, the others, Gypsy Dave and Rocket Man, and — Fair Child?"

"Yeah, Fairchild."

"Is that one word or two?"

"She spells it as one word. Her real name's Mary Margaret."

"Ah, okay. But, anyway, maybe we should wait —"

"Arnold, we'll just go right past them and straight into my bedroom."

"Oh. Right into the, uh —"

"You don't want to?"

Those universe-sized dark eyes stared up at me again. Who was I to disappoint her?

"Um, is Elektra your real name?" I asked.

"It's Betsy," she said.

"Ah."

"But I changed it to Elektra."

"Good," I said. "Much more — striking."

"Great," she said. "Now let's go in."

"Go ahead, Arnold."

It was a man's voice. Behind me. I turned and saw Jesus, just sort of hovering there, right beyond the railing.

I hadn't seen him since him since that one night in Byberry.

"Really, Arnold," he said. *"It's all right. It's perfectly natural. Go ahead."*

"What is it, Arnold?" said Elektra. She brought her body around so that she was between me, and the railing, and Jesus, who was now drawing a pack of Pall Malls (my brand!) from within his robes.

I couldn't bring myself to tell her what I was actually seeing, so instead I kissed her again.

"Oh, Arnold," she said, in a very quiet voice.

"Yes?" I said. She tasted of wine and cigarettes and spaghetti (as no doubt did I) but this was not a bad taste.

"Arnold," she breathed.

"Yes?"

"She's just saying that, old boy," said Jesus, smiling, exhaling a cloud of smoke that swirled and danced and flew up to the sky to lose itself in the Milky Way. *"It's an exclamation,"* he continued, *"and it requires no verbal response. Go ahead, put your hand under her dress."*

This took me aback I have to say, and I stared at him. Wait a minute, I thought. What if he were not Jesus, but the Devil, or at any rate *a* devil. (I doubted that the Devil himself would deign to appear to the likes of me; more likely he would send one of his lesser minions).

"No, Arnold," he said, reading my thoughts. *"It's really me. Jesus. Now stop staring off into space and kiss that girl again."*

I obeyed his injunction.

I began to wonder if I would ever get off that damned porch, but I had to admit this was a pleasant sensation, more pleasant than clocking out at the end of a workday, more pleasant than lying in bed and wishing I were dead, more pleasant than drinking beer and watching Sgt. Bilko, more pleasant by far than receiving Holy Communion had ever been.

After a minute or two, or maybe three, Elektra drew her face away from mine.

"Wow," she said.

I went to kiss her again but she stopped me with a hand on my chest.

"I just realized," she said. "You are incredibly stoned on that grass, man, and that's why you're acting so weird."

"Oh," I said. "You know, you're absolutely right."

And suddenly I realized that this could be the explanation for Jesus standing there in mid-air, smoking a Pall Mall: I was, as Elektra said, stoned.

"Hey, now wait a minute, Arnold," said Jesus, *"I'm really here!"*

I closed my eyes. If he is a figment of the marijuana, I said to myself, he will be gone when I open my eyes.

"Wait, Arnold, don't —" he said.

I opened my eyes.

He was gone.

Okay.

"Right," I said, to Elektra. "So, do you want to go inside now?"

Chapter 16

We went back in, through the kitchen, into the living room where the other three were still sitting around their wooden spool-table, listening to music, an old Negro man singing with a guitar.

I suddenly became aware again of my erection, but they barely looked up at me.

"We're going in the bedroom for a while," said Elektra.

"Cool, babe," said Rocket Man.

"Dig it," said Gypsy Dave.

Fairchild finished drawing on her reefer, and, speaking without exhaling, she said, in a hoarse constrained voice, "Beautiful."

We went into another room. She didn't turn on the light, but there were large windows letting in some light from a street lamp outside. I had a never seen such a messy room. Clothes all over the floor. Clothes and books. Books and clothes. And an unmade double bed.

"It's messy," said Elektra. "Do you mind?"

"No," I said.

"Really?"

"No," I said, "I mean, yes, I don't mind –"

"I could never see the point of making a bed." She brought herself up close to me again. "Do you make your bed?"

"No," I said. "But my mother does."

She drew her dress up over her head and let it drop to the floor. She had been wearing no underwear.

"What do you think?" she said.

"I think I should close the door," I said.

"Go ahead."

I turned and closed the door. She went over and got into the bed.

"Come here," she said.

I went over, and stood there. I wasn't quite sure of the protocol at this point.

"Oh, wait," she said, she leaned over and opened a drawer on the night table that was there. In the dim light I could see an overflowing ashtray, some cosmetics jars and bottles, a paperback book – *Siddhartha*, by Herman Hesse; never heard of him. She scrabbled around in the drawer, her breasts moving with a life of their own, and she came up with a Trojan in its wrapper.

"You don't mind, do you?" she said.

"Oh, no, not at all," I said, it seeming less a sin this way, if it was a sin, which it was seeming less like anyway each passing second.

"Good. Now take off those swimming trunks and that t-shirt and get in bed."

I did as I was told.

Perhaps life didn't have to be so difficult after all. Perhaps I had been denying myself life itself all my life in the service of some random superstition. After all, what if I had been born a Hindu, or a Pygmy, or a Hottentot —

"Now get on top of me," she said.

I obeyed her instructions.

I've always been good at following instructions, at taking orders.

And if I wasn't sure what she meant I wasn't too proud to politely ask her to repeat herself, or to elaborate.

At one point she ceased her instructions, and after a minute or so I asked her:

"Is this okay?"

"Yes," she said. "Just keep doing what you're doing."

Even I had to admit that all of this was perfectly natural after all.

Which makes sense I suppose, or else none of us would be here.

I was pleasantly surprised to find the activity so much more enjoyable than masturbation. But then how enjoyable had masturbation ever been really, with my mother usually in the next room; or even worse, in the army, with other guys grunting and groaning in the darkness all around me. No, this was definitely better, and the more I did it the more absurd it seemed that this act should be considered a mortal sin.

But suddenly I stopped.

Something about that mortal sin thought. The thing was:

How could I know for sure?

But while I had stopped she did not. She grabbed tightly to my shoulders, her nails digging into me as she stared with those dark eyes straight up into mine.

And then, as if I had swum to the top of some great cresting wave on my way back in to my own private beach, I came rushing and crashing in on the wave and into her.

Then we lay there together, me on top of her, the both of us sweaty and panting.

Once again I was not familiar with the protocol at this stage, but she helped me, shoving me gently off of her. After a minute she even removed the Trojan for me. I looked away in my modesty, but I think she tied it up and tossed it under the bed.

"That was good, Arnold," she said.

"Yeah," I said.

I gazed out the window. The leaves of a tree were thrashing in slow motion in the breeze, silhouetted by the street lamp's light.

Jesus floated into view again, right outside the window, smoking a cigarette. He was smiling.

"*Well,*" he said, "*now was that so horrible, Arnold?*"

Chapter 17

I confess I turned away from Jesus, and my eyes closed of their own accord.

I fell asleep.

I suppose I woke up an hour or so later. I lay there for a bit. Elektra slept quietly on her side, facing the other way, breathing heavily and slowly, as one would imagine a small child to breathe. The sheet had gotten bunched up around her hips. I drew it up to her shoulders and she unconsciously tugged it over her breasts.

I couldn't hear anything from the other room.

On the one hand I wanted to go home — well, to my aunts' home, to my little attic room in my aunts' house; but on the other hand I wanted to avoid the embarrassment of seeing Rocket Man and Gypsy Dave and Fairchild. I knew that there was no real need for embarrassment, these people were free spirits, bohemians: but I, alas, was not. I swear that if we had not been on the second floor I would definitely have just climbed out the window.

Of course I could have just gone back to sleep, I was weary from my busy day after all (a day which seemed to have begun a thousand years ago with me accompanying my cousin Kevin to Wally's cigar shop), but then if I overslept and didn't get back to my aunts' house before my mother awoke she would assume the worst, that I had drowned on my swim, perhaps purposely, in which case I would burn forever in that special place in Hell reserved for that most despicable regiment of the damned, the suicides.

So I got up, as quietly as I could, found my t-shirt and bathing trunks and flip-flops, and got dressed.

I went to the door and opened it; thank God, the lights were out in the living room. I stepped in and closed the bedroom door gently behind me. Fairchild was sleeping on the couch, under some sort of oriental printed sheet. I would have tiptoed were I not wearing flip-flops, but instead I trod quietly and slowly through the room, found the outside door, crept down the stairs and out to the rear of the house. I looked up at the porch where Elektra and I had stood and kissed. Yes, women were as great a mystery as ever. I walked around the house to Jackson Street.

I turned down Washington Street. It was empty. I had made my successful getaway.

The air was cool and clean and fresh, the ocean wind smelled alive with the grace of the universe, of seaweed and salt and bushels of glistening fresh oysters, and so naturally I had to have a cigarette. I stepped into the entranceway of Smythe's Book Shoppe to light one up. In the lighter's glare I saw a book in the window, *The Waste Land*, by T.S. Eliot. I thought, now there's a book I'll have to read.

And then I thought, "Oh Christ," because there he was again, reflected in the window.

"Got a light, buddy?" he said.

I turned.

Was I never to be set free?

What the hell, I gave him a light. He had his own cigarette already in his hand.

"Thanks, Arnold," he said.

"You're welcome," I said.

"Shall I walk you home?"

"I'd prefer you didn't," I said.

"Arnold, old boy, do you know how many millions of Catholics would give their right arm just to experience what you're experiencing now?"

"Okay, I'm going," I said, and I started walking again.

Jesus stayed by my side. He was getting to be a real pest.

"I think you made great progress tonight," he said.

"Yeah, swell," I said, quickening my step.

"That Elektra's a pretty hot number —"

"Okay."

I stopped.

"This proves you're not Jesus," I said. "Jesus would not call some girl a 'hot number'."

"I just did, Arnold."

He was smiling.

"Oh — you're impossible, Mac," I said.

"Mac?"

"Pal. Joe. Buddy."

"My friends call me Jesus."

I started walking again.

"Nice Jewish girl, too," he said, still by my side. "You know, we *are* the Chosen —"

I stopped again. We were at the corner of Washington and Perry.

"Okay, Jesus — if that's your name — you know what I'm gonna do? I'm gonna close my eyes again, really hard, and when I open them again, you're gonna be gone. Got it? I'm tired of this, pardon my language, crap."

"Oh, come on, Arnold, loosen up. I'm just here to tell you that it's really all right, for you to — you know —"

"I'm closing my eyes now," I said, and I did.

"– for you to — how can I put this and not offend your delicate Catholic sensibilities —"

"What?" I said, and I opened my eyes against my own will.

"Your delicate Catholic sensibilities," he said.

"But *you're* Catholic!" I nearly screamed.

"*Not so loud,*" he whispered.

"*You're Catholic!*" I hissed.

"Arnold," he spoke quietly. "I'm Jewish. You know that."

Okay, fine.

I closed my eyes again.

"My eyes are closed," I said. "They're closed. And this time, when I open them, you'd better be gone. And I really mean it this time —"

"Hey, buddy."

It was another voice.

Great, now what?

I opened my eyes.

It was a cop, in his patrol car. Just great.

"You okay, buddy?"

"Uh, yeah," I said.

"Had a little to drink?"

"Uh, yeah," I said. Furiously improvising, "I had a few too many, I guess, and I, uh, fell asleep at a friend's house, and, uh —"

"Where you staying, pal?"

"Right up the street, officer."

He paused, looking at me.

"You want a lift?"

"No, I'll be fine officer, honest, I live right up on North Street there, just one house down from Perry."

He seemed to think it over for a few more seconds.

"Okay, go right home, pal. And no more talking to yourself."

"Right. Thanks, officer."

He drove off up Perry Street, and I quickly headed that way too. Fortunately I was alone, at least for the time being. I made it to my aunts' house, and let myself in at the side door. I took off my flip-flops and tiptoed up to my room in the attic.

Chapter 18

I awoke next morning feeling odd. Well, I should say, odder than usual. I lay there and realized that one odd thing I was feeling was not hungover. So that was one good thing about marijuana.

I got into my stale bathing trunks and t-shirt, and went down to the kitchen where breakfast was being laid out as usual.

"Where did you go last night, Cousin Arnold," asked my young cousin, Kevin.

My mother and my three aunts all perked up at that.

"I went for a swim," I said.

"Yeah, but you didn't come home all night."

Now I might mention here that my mother and aunts go to bed at around nine o'clock. They had already been up for several hours that morning, having gone to their daily seven o'clock mass and already performed God knows how many chores. So normally they never had any idea when I went to bed.

"Obviously I came home," I said, cutting my scrapple.

"Yeah, but you must've come home really late."

"Your cousin Arnold is a grown man," said my Aunt Elizabetta. "He can come home at whatever time he wants."

"Yeah, but he must've come home really late."

"You shouldn't question your elders, Kevin," said Aunt Greta.

"It's very bad manners," said Aunt Edith.

My mother held her peace, but my cousin Kevin could no doubt see he that he was no match for a gang of tradition-bound old German women, so he cut out the third degree, at least for the time being.

After breakfast I went up and took a shower, shaved my face, and changed into a clean polo shirt and Bermuda shorts.

I went out onto the porch with a fresh cup of coffee and my cigarettes and one of my notepads. Kevin was already out there, reading his comic books.

It was horribly hot out already, the sort of day which is not conducive even to my sort of creative activity, but I had a poem I needed to write if I was to meet my weekly deadline with the *Olney Times*.

I sat there smoking. It occurred to me that perhaps I could wrangle a poem from the previous night's activities. Not to be immodest, but I had no doubt that I could — after all, there was no need for it to be a good poem — but I wondered if such a poem would be deemed suitable by my venerable editor at the *Olney Times*, Mr. Willingham.

People were slowly walking along the bright street, in their bathing suits, carrying their umbrellas and beach chairs and blankets and towels, in this stifling and blazing heat. They were quite mad, to go to the beach on such a day. But then of course it was their vacation and they wanted to get their money's worth. But they were mad nonetheless. They would broil on that merciless beach like so many lobsters. Even I was not that insane.

"How come you're not working on the railroad any more, Cousin Arnold?" said Kevin, out of nowhere.

"I was sick," I said. "I'm on a leave of absence until I recover fully."

"You don't look sick."

"Well, believe me, I'm still a little sick."

"I don't get it."

I decided to change the subject.

"Hey, Kevin," I said. "You want some more comics?"

"More comics?"

It was an alien and exciting concept for him to buy a new batch of comics when the old batch was only a day old. Normally he would buy a batch and read them over and over again for several days or even a week until he managed to scrounge up the money for a new shipment.

"Yeah, sure," I said. I stood up. "Grab those old ones and we'll trade 'em in."

He quickly gathered all the comics off of the porch floor and bounced to his feet.

"This isn't a trick, is it?" he asked.

"No," I said, "no trick. Just stop asking me questions."

"Sure, Cousin Arnold. I didn't really care anyway."

"As well you shouldn't," I said.

So we walked in that deadly heat over to the entrance of Wally's cigar store and pool room. I took a dollar out of my pocket and gave it to Kevin.

He looked from the bill to me, back to the bill, then to me again.

"You want change, right?"

"No, you can spend it all."

"Oh wow, and no strings attached?"

"Just that you can't ask me questions about myself. Especially at the breakfast table. It might upset the aunts and my mother."

"Got it. No personal questions. But I can ask you other stuff, right?"

"Like what?"

"Like, how fast does a train go."

"Okay, that kind of stuff's okay. Just no personal questions."

"Okay, but — what if like I wanted to ask you if you ever saw a dead person."

"All right," I said, "it's too hot for this. Go in and buy some comics."

The cigar store Indian was standing there in that unforgivingly hot sunlight. He looked bored and sullen.

"You're not coming in?" asked Kevin.

"No. I'm gonna take a little walk."

"It's too hot to walk."

This was so true. My torso was already covered in sweat, my polo shirt was heavy and wet.

"I'm gonna visit some friends."

"I didn't know you had any friends."

"Okay, go inside," I said.

"Right, see ya."

And he went into the dark store, with its bald unpleasant proprietor sitting like a disgruntled toad behind his cigar counter.

The cigar store Indian had not changed his bored expression.

I thought I would just take a stroll up Jackson Street and visit my friends' jewelry shop.

Chapter 19

I opened the door of the shop, and Gypsy Dave was behind the counter, talking to a middle-aged couple in bright clothes. Jazz music was playing from a hi-fi behind the counter. The store was very nicely air-conditioned.

Gypsy Dave waved at me and I waved back. He was showing the couple some rings.

"Very lovely," said the lady. She had a flat sort of accent. Like mid-Pennsylvania, Stroudsberg or Intercourse. "And you make these all yourselves?" she asked.

"Yes, ma'am," said Gypsy Dave.

"I think that's just wonderful. Don't you, Clyde?"

"Yep," said Clyde. "Real clever."

"Maybe we'll stop in later and pick up something for our daughter."

"Great," said Gypsy Dave. "But I'll tell you what, you people are so nice, just go on and take that ring for your daughter. Our compliments."

"Oh no we couldn't," said the lady.

"Go ahead," said Gypsy Dave. He took her pudgy hand and pressed the ring into the folds of her palm, like a baker pressing a currant into a wad of pastry dough.

"We just couldn't," said the lady.

"I insist," said Gypsy Dave. Even his accent had now become gallant, he sounded a little like Errol Flynn.

"Are you serious?" said Clyde.

"Absolutely. It's not every day I meet such nice people in here."

"Well, okay, then," said Clyde.

"My pleasure," said Gypsy Dave. "Tell your daughter to wear it in good health. 'Bye now. Hi, Arnold!" he said to me.

"Hi," I said.

"Come on over, buddy."

I walked over toward the counter. The middle-aged couple were still standing there. The lady was tugging on her husband's orange short sleeve, and she whispered something in his ear.

"So, how ya like our shop, Arnold?" said Gypsy Dave, smiling.

"It's very nice," I said. I was having trouble addressing him as "Gypsy Dave", so I just skipped an appellation entirely.

The middle-aged man took out his wallet, took a ten dollar bill out of it.

"Here, sir," he said to Gypsy Dave. "I'd like you to take this."

"Oh, please, of course not," said Gypsy Dave, "now you two people have a great day, and I hope your daughter likes the ring. Bye, now!" He turned again to me: "So, Arnold, I'm so glad you stopped by. Here, let me show you our stuff."

He proceeded to show me the wares in the display cases: rings, bracelets, necklaces, brooches. It was all very pretty.

The couple had a whispered confabulation together while Gypsy Dave was showing me the stuff. Then they left the store, like a tiny herd of two, each of them throwing a little wave. Dave waved back and so, slightly, did I.

He walked back down toward where they had been standing near the glass counter. He picked up a ten dollar bill and showed it to me.

"And that, my friend," he said, "is salesmanship."

He banged on the cash-register and deposited the ten.

"Was that a good price for the ring, Dave?"

Somehow I felt on safe ground just addressing him as "Dave".

"Oh, sure," he said. "The stone was a Cape May Diamond we found on the beach along with about a thousand others. The metal was scrap metal. If the four of us work together we can turn out ten of those babies in an hour from scratch. Come on, I'll show you the operation."

He lifted a wooden flap between two of the glass cases and I followed him through a door into a back room. It was a workroom, and Fairchild, Rocket Man and Elektra all sat at a big table, making jewelry. They had little saws and lathes, vises and soldering guns and various other tools, piles of metal and pebbles and seashells and what not.

Along with the smells of solder and cigarette smoke I could smell marijuana in the cool air. On the walls were paintings, drawings and posters, and through two big windows a world of light tumbled and sparkled in from the flowery back yard.

Everyone said hello to me and I said hello back.

"Well look who the cat dragged in," said Elektra. She had a many-colored bandanna on her head, holding all that wild black hair away from her busy fingers.

They invited me to sit and watch them work. We smoked cigarettes, and a reefer was passed around as well. I did not decline it when it came my turn.

"Hey, shouldn't someone be in the shop?" I said, always the good German boy.

"Don't sweat it," Rocket Man said. "A bell goes off if someone comes in the front door."

So we sat and talked. Every so often the bell did sound and one or the other of them would go out into the shop.

Once when Rocket Man was in the shop I asked Gypsy Dave about this one colorful pagan poster on the wall, and he told me all about the Buddha and the Bodhi tree. It was quite interesting. But I couldn't quite help thinking that all these years of wandering, and of asking questions of wise men, and of sitting under the tree, that even all that was probably not enough, not nearly enough in fact. I thought of all these millions and millions of Buddhists over the centuries, wasting their precious time seeking enlightenment when they might have been spending their time more profitably learning a foreign language or how to play the flute or simply talking nonsense with their friends. {*See Arnold's poem "Escaping the Heat" in the Appendix. — Editor}*

I guess I'd been there an hour or more, and suddenly Elektra said to me, "Arnold, let's step out and get a cup of coffee."

"It's awfully hot out there," I said. To tell the truth I was pretty engrossed despite my doubts in what Dave was telling me about Buddhism.

"The coffee shop is air-conditioned," she said. "Come on, you can buy me a piece of pie."

"Well, okay," I said, but reluctantly.

She led the way out the back way. Out the same door I had crept from the night before. The back yard was filled with greenery, with brilliant zinnia and azaleas and sunflowers.

"Wow, what a nice garden," I said.

She shook her bandanna off her head, her dark shining hair blossomed in the sun. She tied the bandanna around her neck.

"Come on, big boy," she said.

We walked over toward the Cape Coffee Shoppe on Washington. She was even prettier in this harsh sunlight. Somewhat smaller than I remembered her, her skin gleaming like honey, wearing a sleeveless dress with yellow and blue designs like a kitchen table on it, and rope sandals.

The coffee shop wasn't far. It was busy, but we found adjacent stools at the counter. I could feel her moist warmth. The coarse sunburnt hairs of my arm brushed the silky golden down on hers, and an electric shock jolted between us.

"Wow," I said, "Did you feel that?"

She just looked at me.

We each ordered coffee, and she ordered the peach pie, which is pretty good there. Although not as good as my mom's.

She had a bite or two and then she said, "Look, Arnold, I like you, but I want you to know I don't want to be your girlfriend."

"Oh, of course not," I said.

"Of course not?"

"Well, why should you?"

"Well, I don't know. You seem like a nice guy. Why shouldn't I?"

"Well, I'm recovering from a breakdown, for starters," I said.

"That's true," she said.

"And also, a pretty girl like you, you could do far better than me."

"Well, the thing is, Arnold, I don't really want a man, anyway."

"Oh, I see," I said.

"You do?"

"Well, why should you want a man?" I asked.

"I don't know. To have kids with?"

"But, do you want to have kids?" I asked.

"Not yet," she said.

"Well, there you go," I said.

"Yeah, I guess so," she said.

"It's like that Buddha guy," I said.

"Like the Buddha?"

"Yeah," I said. "I mean, when he was wandering all over seeking enlightenment, and sitting under the Bodhi tree and all, he wasn't worrying about getting a girlfriend, was he?"

"No, I guess not," she said.

"Or having kids," I said.

"That's true," she said.

She looked at me. She had such beautiful brown eyes. And such a nice body under that dress. I wondered if not being her boyfriend would preclude me from having sex with her again. After all, she was a beatnik.

"I've said it before," she said, eating her pie. "You are one strange man."

"I know," I said.

I considered telling her about my recent visits from Jesus.

But I decided not to.

Chapter 20

I insisted on paying the tab, despite Elektra's protestations.

We stepped out into that enormous heat. For some reason or for various reasons we stopped as soon as we got outside. She looked at me, silently. I have no idea what she was thinking about, and all I was thinking about was what she was thinking about. Was she in turn only wondering what I was thinking?

I thought of lighting a cigarette but it was too hot. Mary Star of the Sea church loomed right across the street, and I noticed one or two people going up the steps. It was Saturday, confession day.

"Okay, walk me to the shop," she said.

So we walked back down Washington and then down Jackson. Outside the shop she said:

"You can stop by any time, Arnold."

"Okay," I said.

"But not too often, okay?"

"All right," I said. "How about tonight?"

"No," she said. "I'm afraid you'll wear me out. Do you know what I mean?"

"I know all too well," I said. "I wear myself out, every day."

"Where do you live?" she said.

"At Perry and North. The big white house one down from the corner there."

"With your mother."

"Yeah," I said. "And my three maiden aunts. And my young cousin. And a bunch of boarders who come and go."

"It sounds bizarre," she said.

"It is," I said.

"Maybe I'll come by and visit you."

"I'm there quite often," I said.

Then she put her hands on my shoulder and gave me a kiss, which surprised me with its degree of concupiscence. Well, everyone always said women were a mystery, why should Elektra be any different?

And kissing her in that bright sunlight, that intense heat, both of us already moist with sweat after being outside for only three minutes, it felt almost as if we were in the intimacy of her bed together again...

But as I came up for air I noticed my aforementioned relations marching across Jackson Street on Washington, a small stolid squad of four old women and one young boy, my Aunts Elizabetta and Greta in the front rank, my mother and Aunt Edith in the middle, and young Kevin picking up the rear. Kevin was flopping along in that way young kids do, like mentally retarded people, and turning his gaze at random he saw me, and stopped, cocked his head, but then continued on.

"Okay, see ya, man," said Elektra, and she opened the door and went into the shop.

I was possessed of a slight erection, so I walked slowly back up to Washington. Even in this almost unbearable mid-day heat there were still lots of tourists wandering to and fro. They were insane. But who was I to talk?

I was about to turn left to go home when I remembered confession. I had never missed Saturday confession in my life, even when I was in the army overseas, nor even when I was in the nut house. I considered just going home, what the hell, everything had changed, at least in my little life everything had changed.

But somehow I could not break the habit just yet, so I turned right towards the Star of the Sea.

My mother and aunts walk so slowly, they and Kevin barely beat me into the church. I didn't feel like dealing with them right away, so I lit a cigarette. Two or three other Catholics stood at the foot of the steps, smoking one last butt before going in to have their sins annulled.

I finished my own cigarette, tossed it into the street, and went up the steps.

The shadowed stained-glass dimness of the church was a blessing after the inferno outside. I dipped my fingertips in the cool holy water, made the sign of the cross, and then went through the foyer into the nave, its smell of wood and marble, the sparkling of gold and candles. I genuflected and went on up to Father Reilly's confessional. I knew that my aunts and mother always went to Father Schwartz, farther down over on the other side, and I could see my mother and my Aunt Greta kneeling in a pew. No one else was in line for Father Reilly, but the red light was on, so I slipped into a pew myself and knelt down. Just then young Kevin popped out of Father Reilly's confessional like a jack-in-the-box, saw me, and immediately squirreled his way onto the kneeler next to me.

"Was that lady your girlfriend, Cousin Arnold?"

He had his hands folded as if he were praying.

"No," I said. "Now quit talking and say your penance."

"Wow, you have a girlfriend. I saw you kissing her."

"All right, excuse me," I said, and got up. "I have to go to confession."

"Are you gonna confess kissing her?"

"Say your penance," I said, and pushed past him to get out of the pew.

I told Father Reilly about the previous night's incident with Elektra. His silhouette behind the screen perked up a bit. I'm sure he recognized my voice by now, and this was the first time I had confessed anything more grave than daily self-abuse.

Because he was a priest after all I ran the whole Jesus thing by him, about Jesus encouraging me. And then, I don't know, maybe I was crazy from the heat, maybe it was the marijuana I had smoked (or of course, maybe I was just crazy), I started rambling on about whether fornication should or should not be a mortal sin. I think he lost patience with me after a while, because he rather abruptly absolved me and sent me packing with only three Hail Marys, which by the way is the exact same sentence he always gave me for my usual confession to seven or eight or more of the sins of Onan. {*See Arnold's poem "Dialogue in the Confessional", in the Appendix. — Editor*}

I left the confessional, knelt down in a pew and said my penance. Then I looked up. Kevin, my aunts and mother had all left the church. A few other penitents knelt scattered along the aisle seats of the pews.

Well, at least I was free of sin now, according to the Catholic church.

For the time being.

Chapter 21

The great thing — or I should say one of the many great things — about being unemployed is that I am never bored. Before I stopped working I had never quite realized just how boring work is. Oh, sure, I know that I performed a useful service all those many years, doing my bit in facilitating the high speed hurtling of great steel cars groaning with cargo and people safely and efficiently hither and yon all over the eastern seaboard, but, save for my pitiful two weeks' vacation each year — vacations that themselves were a form of work, as I tried to cram a year's worth of recreation into fourteen days and invariably achieved only an excruciating state of anxiety that was mercifully quieted only by my return to the grind of work — I had never known real, open-ended freedom.

I wonder now if it was not work itself which caused me to go insane, and not (depending on which of my doctors was speaking, and his mood of the day) repressed sexuality (either of the hetero or homo kind), or excessive religiosity, or alcoholism, or genetic pre-disposition. Perhaps it was only that eternal five-day-a-week prison sentence of honest labor that had driven me around the bend.

The boringness, the sameness, the inescapability of it all.

But then if work was the cause of my insanity, one would think that the absence of work (and an absence at half-pay, thanks to the Reading) might lead to a return to sanity.

And it is true that I do feel saner.

Except for the Jesus thing.

Let's face it, I know what my erstwhile doctors would think if I were to tell them that Jesus has appeared to me not less than three times recently, and smoking Pall Malls no less.

So either I am still slightly nuts, or Jesus smokes Pall Malls, there can be no other explanation.

Perhaps all those years of servitude formed a sort of pustule of aggregated tedium in my brain which one day simply burst.

The pus may have drained all away by now but the hole in my brain where the boil had been remains.

Or, Jesus has indeed been visiting me in person, and therefore I am not a madman but, *ipso facto*, a living saint.

But would a saint have extra-marital intercourse with a Jewish beatnik girl?

Speaking of Elektra, I decided to heed her advice, and to leave her alone for a day or two.

The next day I did my usual things. I went to Sunday mass, for whatever that was worth. I read comic books on the porch with Kevin. I ate. I napped. I read my cheap paperback thriller in the afternoon, took my long swim in the evening

I didn't go to see Elektra that day, or the next day, nor the day after that.

I wrote one poem in this period {*See Arnold's "Dialogue in the Confessional" in the Appendix. – Editor*} but added nothing to these memoirs, as nothing seemed particularly demanding to be added.

On the evening of the third day I went for a particularly long swim. It was quite dark when I got back home. As I walked down the street I could see that the lights were out on the ground front floor, where my aunts and mother and Kevin all live. But as I got closer I saw that apparently one of the boarders was sitting on the dark porch, smoking a cigarette. The street lamp voluptuously bathed its light in the merry garden that lapped in the breeze up against the rails of the porch — dark but for that pulsing red pinpoint. I went through the wobbly old gate, determined to get by with only a polite "good evening" to whoever it was, as I had no desire to be drawn into idle chitchat. I had bought this poem *The Waste Land* and I was anxious to dive into its mysteries.

"Just 'good evening'?" she said.

I stopped at the side of the porch. There, above an expansive rhododendron, was Elektra.

I came around the front, and up the steps. She was sitting in the rocker that I usually sit in. I sat down in the other rocker, the one Kevin treats as his own. She wore a loose silky dress, white with blue cornflowers, her shoulders and arms bare except for thin white straps, her thick hair pulled back. Her fingers were touching a small white plastic purse on the table next to her.

I lit a cigarette.

"I've missed you," she said.

"Really?" I said.

"Why didn't you come visit me?" she said.

"Well, I was thinking of stopping by tomorrow, actually."

"Why wait so long?"

"I didn't want to bore you," I said.

"Really?"

"Sure."

"So, you did want to see me?"

"Of course. Why wouldn't I?"

Even in these shadows she was beautiful to look at in the glow of her cigarette and the pale gleam of the street lamp, bathed in the odor of gently stirring chrysanthemums and tiger lilies, of rhododendrons and forsythia.

"I've never met a man who chose to forgo my company out of fear of boring me."

"Men are very selfish," I said.

"As are women," she said.

She put her cigarette out in the ashtray on the little wicker table.

"I think we should go to the Ugly Mug and have a beer," she said. "Then we should go to bed together. What do you think?"

I was thinking that Jesus was going to show up at any second, cigarette in hand, but instead the screen door opened and Kevin came out onto the porch. He was wearing a t-shirt and his BVDs.

"Hi, Cousin Arnold. Hi, lady."

"Hello, man," said Elektra.

"I'm not a man," said Kevin, staring at her. "I'm a boy."

"Cool," she said. "What's your name?"

"Kevin Armstrong."

"My name's Elektra."

He came closer to her, so that he was standing right in front of her, almost touching her bare knees.

"Are you Cousin Arnold's girlfriend?"

"No. I'm his friend."

"Oh. I saw you kiss him."

"Friends can kiss."

"Oh."

"Kevin," I said. "Go to bed."

"I don't want to go to bed. I want to talk to her."

"Why?" I said.

"Because she's pretty."

"Kevin?" This was my mother's voice, from inside the house.

"Uh-oh," said Kevin.

My mother opened the screen door. She was in her nightgown.

"Arnold?" she said.

"This is Arnold's girlfriend," said Kevin. "Her name's Electric."

"Kevin, get in here and go to bed, or you can't buy comic books tomorrow," said my mother.

You can believe Kevin went in through that door double-quick.

My mother stood there in the doorway, holding the door open.

"Mom," I said. "This is my friend Elektra."

"Hello," she said. "I"m Mrs. Schnabel."

"Hi, Mrs. Schnabel."

Elektra waved her hand.

"Well, I'll leave you two," said my mother.

"I love your garden, Mrs. Schnabel," said Elektra.

"Oh, thank you. But it's mostly my sisters' accomplishment. I do like to work in it though."

"It's lovely," said Elektra. "I want to come by and look at it in the daytime."

"Come by any time, dear."

"See, Arnold," said Jesus, who was sitting on the porch rail, a lit cigarette in his fingers, "they're completely hitting it off. Your mother's not even gonna care that Elektra's a Jew. Hey, and ya know what, if it does bother her, the hell with her."

I glared at him. He really was determined to drive me back to Byberry permanently. Or so it would seem.

Chapter 22

I was not about to sit there listening to his nonsense, so I stood up.

"Well, Mom," I said, "Elektra and I were going to go out for a beer."

"In your wet bathing suit?" she said.

"I don't mind."

"Oh, Arnold, go up and change."

I realized if I didn't I'd hear about it for a week, so I assented.

"I'll be right down," I said to Elektra.

"Take your time, Arnold," she said.

"You should take a quick shower," said my mother. "Get that salt off."

I went in past her, through the dark living room to the stairs. Kevin popped out of his little room at the far end of the hallway.

"Cousin Arnold, Cousin Arnold," he whispered.

"Go to bed, Kevin," I whispered back, and headed up the stairs.

On the second landing I stopped, because the little rascal was following me.

"What is it?" I was still whispering, because this floor, as does the third, holds tenants' rooms.

He bumped into my legs.

"She's pretty," said Kevin.

"Yeah, I know."

"My father said you didn't like girls."

To tell the truth I didn't care what Kevin's father thought. He's an oaf. But I couldn't tell Kevin this. He was stuck with the oaf for a father. I didn't think it was my place to undermine the fool in front of his son, so I said:

"I used to not like girls. Now I do."

"Oh," said Kevin.

"Now go to bed, you'll wake the aunts up."

I continued on upstairs.

I took my mother's advice and showered, quickly, then just as quickly changed into fresh Bermudas and a polo shirt, and headed back downstairs. As I got down to the first floor I could see my mother, still in the doorway, but she let the screen door close and came into the living room as soon as I reached the bottom step. She has the preternatural hearing of a cat.

She stopped me in the middle of the dark living room, her hands on my chest.

"She's very pretty, Arnold," she said softly.

"Yeah," I said. "Kevin thinks so too."

"It's time you met a nice girl."

"Um."

"And got married and settled down. Then you wouldn't have any more nervous breakdowns."

"I just met her, Mom."

"Don't lose her. Nice girls don't grow on trees."

"Mom, she's a *Jude*." I used the German word, as she tended to use German when referring to members of what are for her the more doubtful religions and races, but this brought her pause for only about one quarter of a second.

"I was hoping she was *Italienisch*," she said.

"She's Jewish," I said, hoping this would get her off her prospective-mother-in-law hobbyhorse.

"That's okay," she said, indomitably. "I know lots of nice Jewish people. As long as she agrees to bring the children up Catholic."

"Okay, Mom," I said, "good night."

"Don't drink too much," she whispered.

Elektra and I walked over to the Mug. Jesus had disappeared while I was upstairs, thank God. Wait, that last phrase makes no sense. Because if who I saw was Jesus, then he *was* God.

At any rate we made it to the Ugly Mug without further incident. We drank beer and Elektra told me about her life. It seems that everyone has one. A family, a past, a life. Then you meet someone and this other life becomes part of your own life.

I hadn't fully noticed the last time how funny Elektra could be, but she was, and is, and, oddly, she laughed at many of the things I said.

My whole life it seemed that whenever I said something I thought was funny I would be met by bewildered stares. Conversely, the coarse humor of my comrades in the army and on the railroad had always left me cold, and thus I knew I had a reputation as (in the regrettable parlance of the American regular guy) a tight-assed son of a bitch.

"You're the only person who's ever laughed at my witticisms," I said, on about the third mug of beer.

"People are stupid, Arnold," she said. "Don't you know that?"

I don't think I mentioned before that she's from Brooklyn, and has a moderate Brooklyn accent. On the other hand she has a Master's Degree in English literature from Columbia.

"Listen," I said. "I have to tell you something."

"Okay."

"I'm not fully recovered from that breakdown I told you about."

"I didn't think you were entirely. Why, are you going to get psychotic all of a sudden?"

"No. But, well, I'll just come right out and say it, I have these — visions."

"No kidding? What kind of visions?"

"Well — Jesus appears to me."

"Jesus Christ."

"Yeah," I said. "Him."

She stared at me. Then she gestured to the bartender. She asked him for a couple of shots of whiskey. He asked what kind. She asked me. I said bourbon was fine, Early Times if they had it. He asked if Old Hickory was okay and I said it was.

"So," said Elektra. "Jesus."

"Yeah," I said. That whiskey was seeming like a good idea now.

"And do you think it's really him?"

"Well," I said, "he seems very real."

"What's he look like?"

I paused while the bartender poured our shots and then took my money. Then:

"He looks like what you'd expect," I said. "Good lookin' fella. Long hair, beard, robe."

"Right. And what's he sound like?"

"Well, it's funny, he sounds — American."

"Uh-huh."

"And —"

"What?"

"He smokes Pall Malls," I said, pointing to my own pack lying on the bar there next to my lighter.

She had just swallowed her shot, and she held her hand over her mouth to keep from spitting it back out again. I took a sip of my own shot.

"Arnold," she said, after clearing her throat. "You're insane. You're absolutely nuts."

"Well, I guess that's what I'm telling you," I said. "I'm not quite right in the head yet."

"Yeah, but you're lovable. All right, I gotta go to the ladies' room. Try not to have a beatific vision while I'm gone."

"I'll try," I said, and she went off. The place was crowded, even though it was a Tuesday night, around midnight. It was the height of the tourist season after all. Some sort of rock and roll song played on the jukebox, and it went like:

> *Walk right in, sit right down*
> *Daddy, let your mind roll on*

Jesus sat himself down in Elektra's seat. He had a mug of beer in his hand and his eternal Pall Mall. Except now his hair was shorter, he didn't have a beard, and he was wearing a pale pink polo shirt and madras Bermuda shorts instead of robes.

"So how's it going, buddy?" he asked.

"You're the son of God," I said. "You tell me."

"Arnold," he said, smiling. "You crack me up. You make me glad I have the job I have."

Suddenly he started singing along with the jukebox tune:

> *Walk right in, sit right down*
> *Baby, let your hair hang down*
> *Walk right in, sit right down*
> *Baby, let your hair hang down*

I sighed. Soon Elektra would be back, and he would have to get out of her seat. Jesus continued to sing along with the record:

> *Everybody's talkin' 'bout a new way of walkin'*
> *Do you want to lose your mind?*
> *Walk right in, sit right down*
> *Baby, let your hair hang down*

A guitar solo came on, and he shut up, although he continued to nod his head enthusiastically to the music, and to slap one hand in time on the bar-top.

"Listen," I said, whispering, with my hand over my mouth, "if you really want to help me you'll just disappear. For good."

"Arnold: two things," he said. "First, stop whispering; it looks weird. I can hear what you're thinking, buddy. Second, if it wasn't for me showing up now and then and giving you a little honest advice and encouragement you'd be lying at home on your narrow little army cot right now with your dick in your hand instead of waiting for that cute little number to get back from the can."

"But you're driving me insane," I said, or, rather, thought.

> *Walk right in, sit right down*
> *Daddy, let your mind roll on*

He was singing along again, and he slapped my shoulder.

> *Walk right in, sit right down*
> *Daddy, let your mind roll on*
> *Everybody's talkin' 'bout a new way of walkin'*
> *Do you want to lose your mind?*

I determined to turn and stare stolidly across the bar until Elektra came back, and that's just what I did.

Chapter 23

Soon enough there was a tap on my shoulder. It was Elektra, sliding onto the stool that Jesus had apparently vacated. She was smiling, young and alive.

"What were you thinking about, deep thinker?"

Should I tell her? That Jesus had been keeping her seat warm? No. I didn't want to scare her.

"Oh, nothing," I said.

"Should we order more beers?" she asked. My mug was empty, hers was almost. Now normally I'm always ready for more beer. Call it the German in me. Or call it the dissatisfaction with my life in me.

"Y'know what?" I said, "let's take off."

"Ooh, a take-charge guy."

"That's me," I said.

In the summer of 1945, after we had won the war, for a while they put me in charge of several hundred German prisoners, repairing bombed-out rail yards. I was only a twenty-three-year old buck sergeant, but I spoke enough German to give orders, so I was given this job. The German prisoners were all starving, and usually they had to sleep out in the open in their filthy uniforms. Every few days or so one or two of them would die, and there was nothing I could do about it except try to keep their work to a minimum without winding up in the stockade myself for disobeying orders. In September I got shipped back to the States and I was discharged from the army. I went back to work at the railroad as a brakeman. Occasionally through the years I would be offered a promotion, but I always said no.

As we walked over to her place I guess I was thinking about the war, so I said, "Hey, Elektra, I'm sorry about what my people did to your people."

She stopped.

"But you're American, Arnold."

"I know. But I'm German. I mean both my parents were from Germany."

"The six million Jews weren't your fault. And besides, you fought in the war, right?"

"No, I never fought. I was an engineer in the army."

"It's the same thing. You were on the right side."

I thought of those starving German prisoners, and of the cities I had seen that had been bombed into rubble.

"Well, I was on the better side," I said.

She looked at me. We were standing near the corner of Washington and Jackson, the street was fairly quiet now. That delicious night-time ocean breeze rustled through the trees, and Elektra moved her body up against mine. She smelled like butterscotch and her skin in the light of the street lamp was that color too.

"What's up, so serious?"

"Well, um, while you were in the ladies' room I saw –" I hesitated. It's not an easy thing to say, that you've just seen Jesus. "I saw him again."

"Jesus."

"Yeah," I said. "He sat in your seat. I didn't want to tell you, but —"

"Because I'm a Jew you had to tell me?"

"Well, I just wanted you to know."

"And what was he like this time?"

"Very annoying," I said.

"In his robes still?"

"No. He had a polo shirt on, and Bermudas. And his hair was short this time."

"Still smoking Pall Malls?"

"Come to think of it, I don't think he lit one up this time. But I'm sure he had them on him."

"Arnold, you know you're wearing a polo shirt and Bermudas, don't you?"

"That's true," I said.

"Darling, you're just imagining him. You know that, don't you?"

"Well, I'm sure that's the case, but you see, my knowing that doesn't make it any less — disconcerting for me. I'm afraid I might go completely round the bend again."

I have to mention here that despite the supposed seriousness of the conversation I was in the process of getting an erection, and of course Elektra was aware of this, as she was causing it by pressing herself close to me.

"It seems to me one part of you is healthy," she said.

"Oh. Yeah," I said, as usual the very soul of wit.

"So do you want to come up to my room for a while?"

"All right," I said. "But only for a while. If I'm not back in my attic before morning my mother will have a heart attack."

"I don't think she will. I think she's one tough cookie."

"She is. But she worries about me. Since my breakdown. She worries I'll — hurt myself."

"Did you ever try to hurt yourself?"

"When I was in the mental hospital apparently I did, but I don't recall any of it."

"She's gonna have to let you go, Arnold. She wants to let you go."

"I know. But I should still go home after a while, just so she won't worry."

"Okay, so come on already," she said, and she put her arm in mine.

Once again I had to walk slowly because of my awkward erection. Despite my misgivings it seemed to be pulling me along behind it.

As we headed down Jackson Street to her house I saw him standing in the darkness of an elm tree farther down the block. He was pretending to stop so he could light a cigarette, but he was obviously observing us with a lowered and sideways gaze. I could see his face clearly as he lit his cigarette with his lighter.

I leaned my head a little towards Elektra's and whispered, "Do you see that guy down there, with the cigarette."

"Sure," she whispered back. "What about him?"

"That's him," I said.

"Arnold," she said, "that's just some guy. I've seen him around town."

"Well, then why does he pretend he's Jesus?" I asked.

"Oh, Christ," she said. She pulled her arm free and started walking quickly down the block toward him.

Great.

I continued walking also, but slowly. I didn't know what else to do.

Elektra was lovely to watch from behind, walking down that sidewalk with her determined stride, clutching her purse. I wondered what she kept in it?

I stopped outside her shop, but she continued on after the guy, who had started walking down Jackson Street after lighting his cigarette.

She caught up with him, and then I felt so abashed that I turned my eyes away.

I lit a cigarette, and waited, looking in the dark shop window. There was nothing to look at, as Elektra and her friends put the wares away at night.

A minute or so later she came back. I turned and looked at her.

"His name's Steve," she said. "Steve Smith. He's not even Jewish."

Chapter 24

I'll say this for Elektra, she didn't make a big deal out of it. She just said, "Well, come on," and we went around to the back and then up the stairs.

Fairchild and Rocket Man and Gypsy Dave were all sitting around their little living room again, listening to an old man singing with a guitar. As usual, or as usual as it could be for me, seeing as this was only the third time I had met them, they were smoking marijuana and drinking red wine. I was still saying hello to them all when Elektra pulled me by the arm towards and into her room.

Without much further ado, we were in her bed, and soon enough I was bidding farewell to the uneasy state of grace I had enjoyed since going to confession Saturday. But then, in the midst of the sin of fornication it occurred to me that I had committed the equally un-venial sin of self-abuse several times since my confession and thus was already in a state of mortal sin. You could only be damned once after all. And so I set to it with abandon.

The afterwards part again was nice. Neither of us talked. I could hear the old man singing in the next room. I let myself look toward the windows, but there were no divine apparitions.

After a while I said I should probably go home before I got too comfortable and fell asleep. She said okay, and turned on the light, so that I could find my clothes. She lay there and watched me as I got dressed.

"I still haven't seen any of your famous poems, Arnold."

I forgot to mention, she pronounces my name *Ahnold*.

"I'll show you some sometime," I said. "I keep them in scrapbooks."

I'd already told her they weren't very good. No point in overdoing the modesty bit.

"Write a poem for me," she said.

"Okay," I said.

"Just like that?"

"Sure," I said. "I've written poems with far less provocation, believe me."

"I look forward to it," she said.

"It will be on your desk the first thing tomorrow morning."

"I don't have a desk."

"I know."

"I like it when you're funny, Arnold."

"So do I," I said.

"Kiss me good night."

I did, we did, then I left.

In the living room they were all still there, and the old man was still singing.

"Come have a toke," said Gypsy Dave, holding out a smoking reefer.

"Okay," I said.

We chatted. It turned out the old man was not an old man, but a sturdy looking bearded young fellow named Dave Van Ronk.

After a little while I said good night to them all and left this room also.

When I came around the house to the front I lit a cigarette and looked up and down the street. I was looking for Jesus, or for that Steve Smith guy. I had this light feeling, and it wasn't entirely the marijuana I think.

I stood there. Elektra, the woman I had been with, lay in her bed in her room up there above my head. The windows of her room were dark, so I supposed she had gone to sleep, or perhaps she was lying awake. It occurred to me that she may well have been thinking of me. How very odd to think that someone other than my mother would spend any time thinking about me; I was always trying to think of anything else but me. Trying and usually failing, I'm afraid.

I headed home.

I realize now that I love walking home at night in Cape May, even when I'm somewhat or completely drunk. The fresh ocean air, the rustling foliage, so different from back home in Olney, especially since going home there meant basically going home to the Heintz plant across the street from us, with its stacks belching foul smoke even as the bars are letting out at two in the morning.

My mother was wise in making me come here. I hadn't wanted to come. No, why should I leave my little bedroom in our little house across from the factory, the same bedroom I'd had when we first moved there when I was just a boy.

I had gotten better here. It's true, I still had visions, but I felt better, and, amazingly, I had even found a young woman who liked me, for her own reasons.

I got to my aunts' house. Still no Jesus. But then I didn't feel like going up to my small attic room after all. What was the hurry? I wasn't sleepy. In fact I was as wide awake as I had ever been. I turned back, went down Perry Street and then up Washington.

When I reached the entrance of the Ugly Mug I hesitated, and then for no particular reason I went around the corner and went into the Pilot House.

The bar was still crowded with vacationers, and Freddy Ayres and Ursula were performing on the little stage. Freddy was singing "I've Never Been In Love Before".

I saw that Steve Smith fellow at the bar. He was drinking what looked to be a Manhattan, smoking a cigarette, leaning with one elbow on the bar, smiling and nodding his head in Freddy and Ursula's direction.

Of course the only empty stool in the joint was the one right next to him. I sighed and went over.

I ordered a Manhattan. I had a feeling I would need it.

"Hey," said this "Steve Smith", "didn't I see you on the street earlier tonight, with that gorgeous dark-haired girl?"

"Yeah," I said.

"She asked me my name, 'cause she said you thought you knew me."

"Yeah," I said. "Sorry."

"Oh, I didn't mind. She's some looker."

"Yes, she is," I said.

"Your girlfriend?"

"Well, sort of, I suppose," I said.

He seemed to study me appraisingly. He was about thirty-three; slim, sandy hair, somewhat balding. He gave no indication that we had been talking together at the Ugly Mug earlier that same night.

The bartender put down my Manhattan and Steve patted a little pile of money he had on the bar.

"Please, let me," he said.

"Okay," I said, "thanks."

The bartender took some money and I took a sip of the Manhattan. "Steve" continued to study my baleful countenance.

"Y'know," he said, "I couldn't help but wonder why you just didn't come over and speak to me yourself?"

And I wondered what kind of game Jesus was playing with me now. I don't know why, and I didn't know then, but I played along.

"I'm shy," I said.

"Oh," he said. "A shy guy."

"Yeah," I said.

"May I be perfectly honest?" he asked.

"Sure," I said.

"I was sorta kinda *hoping* you were *cruising* me there on the street," he said. "You know, getting your lady friend to do the groundwork."

"I don't understand," I said.

"Oh," he said. "Um, what's your name again?"

"You mean you don't know?"

"I think she said – what's your little lady friend's name by the way?"

"Elektra."

"Elektra – how exotic! Anyway, I *think* she said your name was – Arthur?"

"No."

"Alex?"

"No, it's –"

"Andrew?"

"It's Arnold," I said.

"Alan?"

"Arnold," I said.

"Arnold?"

"Yes," I said, wondering why I had sat down here, why I hadn't just turned around and walked out when I saw him.

"I'm Steve," said Steve, or Jesus, whoever he was, extending his hand. "Steve Smith."

"Hi – 'Steve'," I said, shaking his hand, which he kept clasped to mine for an unusually long quarter of a minute.

"Very pleased to meet you, uh –"

"Arnold."

"*Arnold.* So, where's your lady friend now?"

"In bed," I said.

"Ah ha. I'm sure you left her quite satisfied."

See, this is why I don't like drinking with a lot of guys. They always get crude. But on the other hand he had bought me a drink.

"I'll bet you really swing," he said. "Keep the ladies happy."

"Oh, probably no more than you do, Steve," I said.

"Oh, me, oh my goodness no, I'm hopeless with the ladies."

I finished the rest of the drink and in an attack of madness I motioned to the bartender.

"Two more here, please," I said, and I brandished my five dollar bill.

"Oh, thank you, Arnold, I don't mind if I do," said my new friend, or my old one. "*So* – and please don't take this the wrong way – but may I just come right out and ask you, and slap me silly if I'm being offensive, but do you by any fantastic chance swing both ways?"

"Which ways?" I said.

"Well, you know, like AC/DC."

"Steve," I said, "if that's what you would like me to call you –"

"Oh, please do!"

"Okay, look, 'Steve', can we stop playing this game?"

"I'm sure I don't know," he said. "Shall we?"

"Yes," I said. "Look, I know you were in the Ugly Mug earlier tonight. And I know you were watching us on the street."

"And you're very observant yourself."

"So you can just, you know, stop the game."

"Do you mean — you're interested?"

He spoke very low now.

"What?" I said. "No, I'm not interested. I would like it if you would stop following me around."

"But," he smiled, seemingly apprehensively, "I *haven't* been following you, Arthur. I did notice you at the Ugly Mug tonight, after all you two were sitting right across from me at the bar. But I left the Mug because, quite honestly I was cruising some other guy who had just left; but he didn't give me a second glance out on the street, so I just had a cigarette, and, hey, sure, I admit I was looking at you, strolling along with the lovely Agatha, but honest to goodness my dear chap," he was slipping into an English accent, "I have *not* been following you! Scout's honor, old boy."

The bartender had laid the fresh Manhattans down and taken his money. I picked up mine and took a drink.

"So you're saying you didn't talk to me earlier tonight?" I said.

"I don't *think* I did," he said. "But I'm so delighted we're talking now."

"Wait a minute," I said.

"Yes?"

"Don't take this the wrong way," I said, "but — are you — um —"

"Yes?"

He had just taken a sip of his drink, and he smiled again, as if hopefully.

I was wondering if he was homosexual, but I didn't want to offend the guy, especially if it turned out he wasn't either homosexual or Jesus.

"Sorry, I said. "Never mind."

"A little inebriated, are you?"

"Sort of," I said, although I wasn't really, not by my standards.

"So, tell me about *Alexandra*," he said, slipping back into an American accent.

"Who?"

"Your lady friend, what is it, Anoushka? No –"

"Elektra."

"Elektra, yes, she's quite stunning you know. Like a young Ava Gardner. What is she, Greek?"

"Well, no –"

"I knew she must be Greek, or maybe Italian –"

"Actually, she's –"

"I'll bet you *really do* satisfy her."

"What?"

"You know what I mean, old bean." He was speaking in an English accent again now. "Strapping fine chap like you."

"Um," I said.

"Yes," he said, looking me up and down. "I daresay you satisfy the young lady ever so well, don't you?"

"I, uh, do my best –"

"And that's what you have to do, Arthur." He had switched back to an American accent now. "Listen. I have many women friends, tons of them, and what they all want is a man who satisfies them."

"Yeah, I guess so," I said. If he was Jesus, he sure wasn't giving away anything. But why would he pretend to be some guy named Steve? Foolish question, if he was Jesus, his ways were perforce beyond my puny comprehension.

"In the sack," he said.

"Pardon me?" I said.

"On the springs, Arthur. *That's* where you need to satisfy them."

"Oh, right," I said.

"They tell me things, my girlfriends. Do you want to know what they tell me?"

"Sure," I said. "Fire away."

So he told me what his girlfriends told him women wanted, and we drank our Manhattans and then had another round. Most of what he told me took me by surprise, especially this thing he called yodeling in the valley.

"I can't believe you've never tried it," he said. "Go ahead! Try it and she'll be your slave."

"Okay," I said. "I will."

What the hell, if he had all these girlfriends, he must know what he was talking about, even if he wasn't Jesus.

"Promise me," he said.

"Promise what?" I said.

"That you'll go yodeling in the valley!"

"Oh, okay," I said. "I promise."

It was after last call, Freddy and Ursula had packed up their instruments and gone, the bartender had turned the lights up, everyone was drifting out of the bar, and Steve and I did too.

Outside we shook hands.

"Sure you wouldn't like to come up to my place for a nightcap, Arthur?" he said.

"No, thanks, uh, Steve," I said. "I'd better hit the hay."

"I understand. Your lady friend is waiting for you I'll bet."

It seemed easier just to say yeah, so I said, "Yeah."

He was still shaking my hand.

"Do it once for me, Arthur."

"Okay, I will," I said, although I wasn't quite sure what he was talking about.

He let go of my hand, turned abruptly and walked off, staggering and reeling a bit.

So maybe he wasn't Jesus after all.

I went home, drank two glasses of water with a couple of aspirin, went up to my room, and got into bed with *The Waste Land*.

"April is the cruelest month…"

Okay, this T.S. Eliot was losing me right there. This man had obviously never experienced a January in Philadelphia.

Chapter 25

No surprise, I had a mild hangover when I awoke the next morning. But here's yet another great thing about being on leave of absence (dear God, or dear Steve, whomever, may this leave of absence extend until I myself am absent from this world!): it really doesn't matter if I'm a little hungover because I have absolutely nothing to do all day.

Back when I was working I was far too responsible ever to have more than a couple of beers on a night before a work day, for fear of endangering hundreds of innocent lives on the railroad the next day. I would only really get my load on if I knew I was off the next morning; but now I was off every day of my life, and the only one I had to worry about endangering was my own fool self.

So the hangover was no problem, but as I went downstairs for breakfast I suddenly remembered my mother. What would be the result of her seeing me with a woman for the first time after forty-two years of my existence?

But here again I have to interpolate yet another way in which my life is now better.

I remember one time a few years ago I almost fell out of the cab of an engine as we were crossing the overpass by the Oak Lane stop. It had been snowing, I lost my footing on the slippery top step and I was halfway out the door and flailing when the engineer grabbed my arm, he pulled me in, and I didn't die, which I surely would have done if I had fallen.

It's funny, but serving with the engineers from D-Day plus one till V-E day, eleven months in a theatre of war, I never came close to being even scratched. But this one time on the train I almost died.

And so afterwards I always tried to think of this incident, and to be glad that I was alive, or at least not dead.

But so often I failed to be glad, like, say, roughly speaking, about ninety-nine percent of the time. Until in due time I felt not glad roughly 99.99% of the time. And then I went insane.

But here's the thing, after going completely insane for a week, and then only gradually regaining some modicum of mental health, I find now that things that might have seemed earthshaking problems to me in the old days seem piffling now.

I've already experienced about the worst I can imagine experiencing short of some really horrible physical illness or crippling accident or death.

And so an awkward conversation with my mother, even the prospect of an infinite number of awkward conversations with her, is certainly nothing that would stand between me and my enjoyment of a hearty breakfast.

So.

No matter how late I stay up the night before I have an unerring instinct for getting up and making it downstairs just as breakfast is being laid out.

My aunts serve breakfast for me and Kevin at nine, which is completely for our convenience, since, as I mentioned before, the aunts and Mom wake up very early. On this particular morning not only had they gone to seven o'clock mass and performed innumerable chores around the house but they had also gone to the butcher's and bought some excellent fresh sausage.

"Ah, sausage," I said.

"Yes," said my Aunt Elizabetta, "and Charlie Coleman brought us some strawberries this morning, and four chickens from his yard."

"Good old Charlie," I said.

"And some good tomatoes and corn," said Aunt Greta.

"And those peaches," said Aunt Edith, "I'm gonna make some good pies."

"Great," I said. I sat back as my mother put a big plate of sausage and eggs and home-fries in front of me.

"Cousin Arnold's gonna get fat if he eats all that," said Kevin.

"Cousin Arnold is a grown man. He needs his food," said Aunt Elizabetta.

"I want that much," said Kevin.

"No, you'll get sick," said Elizabetta.

We sat and ate for a while, or Kevin and I ate. My aunts and mother tend never actually to eat a meal, *per se*. One of them will eat half a slice of toast, say, and then pass it on to one of her sisters. If it's a big holiday meal, forget it, they won't even sit down for more than a minute at a time. There's no changing them. And yet they're all rather solid, and strong, albeit very short. They're almost like the remnants of some race of immortal and stoutly-built dwarves who have emerged from the darkest depths of the Schwarzwald to dwell for a time among men.

As Kevin and I dug in, my aunts and mother chatted about the things they chat about, including this latest batch of Charlie's eggs, as they passed around a bread-plate with the scrambled equivalent of one egg on it, of which each of them took one small appraising forkful, using the same fork, so as not to have to waste water washing more forks.

But of course Kevin had to bring it up, even though I had asked him to (bribed him to) please refrain from talking about my personal affairs.

"Cousin Arnold's girlfriend is pretty," he said.

A moment's silence fell, as if we were on TV and the sound had suddenly gone off because of technical difficulties.

Then the sound came on again.

"Do you want some more sausage, Arnold?" said Elizabetta.

"Yes, thank you," I said.

"She smells good, too," said Kevin.

"Of course she smells good!" said Greta.

"She smells really good," said Kevin.

"Arnold wouldn't go out with a girl who didn't smell good," said Edith. Edith is slightly dotty to tell the truth. "Arnold would only go out with a nice, clean girl."

Elizabetta forked me out another nice big sausage.

"Some more eggs?"

"No thanks," I said.

"Have some more toast, Arnold," she said.

"Okay," I said, and I grabbed another piece of buttered toast from the toast plate.

My mother, who had been hovering about, sat down to my right and picked up her own piece of toast.

"She's a very nice girl," she said.

"Of course she is," said Elizabetta, and she sat down on my left, just as Greta and Edith finally sat, on either side of Kevin.

"And it doesn't matter that she's Jewish," said Greta.

"Not at all," said Edith. "We worked with some awfully nice Jewish girls at the phone company. Remember Ginger Goldberg? She always smelled nice."

"As long as she lets the kids grow up Catholic," said Elizabetta.

"Are you sure she's not Italian, Arnold?" asked my mother. She passed the toast over my plate to Elizabetta. They would do their round robin with the toast now.

"She's Jewish, Mom."

"Well —" she said.

"Hmm," said Elizabetta, chewing her toast.

"That only means she'll go to limbo" said Edith. "Unless she converts, of course."

"She's still one of God's children," said Greta.

"She might convert," said Elizabetta.

"What is a Jew anyway?" said Kevin.

"It's another religion, Kevin," said Edith. "Jesus used to be one before he became a Catholic."

"Oh," said Kevin, already bored with the subject. "Who cares what religion she is. She's pretty and she smells nice."

I was finished with my sausage.

"Well," I said, "that was great. I'm going to sit outside with my coffee now and have a smoke."

I pushed my chair back.

"I'm done too," said Kevin.

"You leave Cousin Arnold in peace," said Elizabetta.

"I'm not going to bother him. Cousin Arnold, can I sit with you? I'll just read my comics, I promise."

"Sure," I said. Why fight the inevitable?

I stood up. My mother's fingers grazed my arm, just barely, as if a caterpillar had fallen down on me from a tree.

"Arnold, she seems very pretty and very nice. We don't care if she's Jewish."

"Swell," I said.

"If you ever want to have her over for dinner we'd be glad to have her."

"Okay," I said. "But you'll have to get your meat from the kosher butcher."

"Really?" said my mother.

"Yep."

"We don't have a kosher butcher in Cape May!" said Elizabetta.

"I think there might be one in Wildwood," said Edith, her face compacted in mental concentration.

"I'll ask Mrs. Fuchs," said Greta. Mrs. Fuchs has the house next door.

"There's a kosher butcher right down on Fifth Street back home," said my mother. "I could take the train up, and —"

She half-rose, as if ready to run off to the train station straight away.

"Mom, I was kidding," I said. I was already heading to the door with my cup and saucer.

"But it's really no problem," said my mother.

"Just kidding, Mom."

I went out the screen door and onto the porch. It was going to be another beautiful hot August day. I sat in my usual rocker, the one Elektra had sat in the night before. Kevin came out and sat in his usual rocker, next to mine. He had a stack of comics with him.

I put my cup and saucer on the little table next to my chair and lit a cigarette. I was still wearing the smoky clothes I'd worn the night before. It seemed like I could smell Elektra on them, this sort of burnt sugar smell she has.

"Cousin Arnold, you can read this one," said Kevin.

He handed me a very old *Tales From the Crypt*, its pages yellowed and autumnal, but its cover still alluring: a scantily clad young woman in danger of being trampled by an elephant. I held the cover sideways, comparing the cover girl to Elektra in my mind. Elektra was definitely better-looking. Then I remembered that Steve guy and his advice about the yodeling technique. I would have to do some research; I decided that after I had read the comic and had a shower I would head over to the library and see what books they had on hand *in re* the subject of human biology, and specifically the female anatomy. I could also take out some new mystery novels.

Chapter 26

We sat reading our comics for a while and then Kevin spoke.

"Cousin Arnold."

"Yes," I said.

"How would you like to take me fishing?"

"Fishing? You mean in a boat?"

"No, off the rocks."

"Oh, well, you don't need me for that."

"You don't want to go fishing with me?"

"No, not really."

Oddly enough he didn't pursue the matter. If he had I would have explained that I didn't fancy sitting on a rock all day in the hot sun. But he let it go. And then came up with this a couple of minutes later:

"What about going to see the ducks?"

"The ducks?"

"At that lake on Cape May Point. We could go look at the ducks."

"You want to go look at some ducks."

"Yeah," he said.

And I was the one who was supposed to be mentally ill.

"Maybe," I said.

"When?"

"I don't know."

"Let's go today."

"I have to go to the library," I said.

"I'll go with you."

"All right," I said.

I finished the comic, then went up, took my shower, and changed.

Kevin was on the porch when I came down. He had a stack of library books on his lap, and I had four or five of my own under my arm.

The library is in the basement of the city hall, a ten minute's walk.

We turned in our books at the desk, and Kevin immediately headed for the children's section. Normally I would have gone straight for the section with books about guys caught in a deadly whirlpool of violence and sin, but I asked the librarian where the biology books were. She told me, I found the section, the whole single shelf of it, and I set to work.

Nothing. Nothing I could use. Then I had a brainwave: the encyclopedia. Fortunately the library had a complete *Britannica*, only a few years old. I went right to the first volume and "Anatomy". The human body charts with the overlapping clear plastic pages were there, but they told me nothing new. I already knew where the vagina was (but at least I was finally able to see the difference between the vagina and the uterus). I checked the "C"s but there was no mention of this thing the clitoris. Same thing with the "V"s. Not even a word about the vagina, let alone a six-page article.

And this was supposed to be the world's greatest encyclopedia? A search for an entry under cunnilingus also proved futile.

I made my way to the table with the Webster's Unabridged Dictionary, and, after looking all around to make sure there was no one spying on me, I looked up and at last I found those mysterious words, but all the dictionary gave me were definitions – no pictures, no instructions, no help.

I was on my own.

As I headed for the mysteries and thrillers I consoled myself with the thought that thousands of generations of men had been at least as ignorant as I on this subject. Perhaps the thing to do was just to ask Elektra. Presumably she knew where this alleged little man in the boat was, if he indeed existed and Steve had not been pulling my leg.

I found a book called *This Sweet Sickness* which looked good. Kevin came over, his arms full of books.

"Now can we go see the ducks?" he whispered, because we were in the library, and he had been well-trained.

"The what?" I whispered back.

"The ducks, at the lake. You said maybe we could go see them."

I didn't want to see the ducks, but the boy looked so pathetic standing there that I was visited by a feeling of pity.

"I'll take you to see the ducks," I said.

"For real?"

"Yes," I said. "Now let's get out of here."

When we got home we put our books away, got two old bicycles out of the garage and headed out.

We biked in the hot salty sunlight along Sunset Boulevard with the lush woods on either side, and I had to slow down and stop occasionally until Kevin caught up. We turned left down Light House Avenue and there was the lake, Lily Lake I think it's called, or maybe it's Lake Lily.

We set our bikes down, and I sat in the shade of an oak tree while Kevin crept down and crouched at the edge of the lake to stare at some ducks that were floating quietly on the shimmering surface of the greenish water. The ducks looked bored, but then it was a hot day.

Insects buzzed, and one of the ducks emitted a half-hearted squawk. Yellow lily pads lay motionless on the water by the banks. I was as damp as a lily pad myself from the bike ride. No one else was around.

I got out my cigarettes and lighter and lit up a Pall Mall. I had always enjoyed a smoke in the fresh air. Not that I didn't enjoy one indoors, either.

I had stuck *The Waste Land* in my back pocket. I opened it and resumed where I had left off the previous night, i.e., the first line.

The next five or six lines got better, but then came this line: *"Summer surprised us, coming over the Starnbergersee"*, which a footnote informed me was a lake south of Munich, a city I had been stationed in, and in the summer, in 1945.

Here again Eliot was losing me. Why should summer surprise anyone? What would be surprising would be if summer did not come.

I closed the book over my finger. There was Kevin, squatting staring at the bored ducks. Then he took a wadded handkerchief out of his pocket, opened it up and began to toss bread crumbs onto the water. Sure enough two or three of the ducks skimmed over, squawking, and began poking their bills down at the floating crumbs.

The ducks were no longer bored.

The quacking word got out to all the ducks on the lake, a dozen or so of them.

Kevin slowly doled out his crumbs, one by one. He seemed to be trying to be fair, making sure all the ducks got an equal share of crumbs.

Finally the crumbs were all gone, and Kevin told the ducks this. After a few minutes they seemed to understand, and they swam away about their business, already looking bored again.

Kevin stood up, shook his handkerchief out, shoved it back into his pocket, and walked back to where I sat.

"Okay," he said. "I'm finished. We can go now."

The funny thing was that now I felt like watching the ducks. But I could see that Kevin had had his fill. I stubbed out the butt of my cigarette into the moist earth.

"Okay," I said. I field-stripped the butt and flicked the little pieces of what it had been into the warm thick air. "Let's go."

And then we got on our bikes and headed back home.

Who says my life is not exciting.

Chapter 27

After digesting my supper and reading some of *This Sweet Sickness* —
an excellent book by the way; I must say I made much quicker headway in it
than I'd been making in that *Waste Land* poem — I went for my usual
evening swim.

It's amazing how strong I've gotten. This time I swam down toward the
lighthouse, where I saw the last of the sun sinking down over the bay. Then,
just for a laugh, I swam out to the concrete ship on the other side of the
point.

This is some old ship, made out of concrete during a steel shortage in the
First World War, which for some reason unknown to me had finally been
run aground out here. It sits there a hundred yards or so from the shore,
looking forlorn.

It was very odd to swim up to it. I felt as if I were approaching a ghost
ship, even though as far as I knew no one had died on the ship. I considered
trying to climb up onto it, but that seemed just too creepy.

Doggy-paddling, I put my hands against the concrete hull of the ship. I
felt as if I were touching something that was not meant to be touched, and I
pushed myself away.

I felt oddly frightened, even though I knew there was nothing to be
afraid of, it was just some old abandoned ship made out of concrete. But I
turned and swam away.

I began to feel a little tired, so I headed in toward the shore, and fetched
up on the beach in front of the St. Mary's convent.

I walked up from the surf and then sat down to catch my breath, facing
the waves and the gleaming dark water where the bay opens up into the
ocean, the faint glow of the lights of Delaware on the far horizon.

After the scariness of the concrete ship it was soothing just to stare out
at the restless water. The lighthouse was behind me and to my left, and every
five seconds or so I saw the reflection of its beam out on the waves.

Then a woman's voice gently said hello.

I turned.

It was a nun, fairly young.

"Hello," I said.

"Are you all right, sir?"

She seemed more curious than frightened.

"Yes," I said. "I was swimming but I got tired, so I just came in to rest."

"Okay."

Then I remembered. I got up.

"I'm sorry, sister. I forgot this was private property."

"I figured you just didn't know."

"Oh, no," I said. "I knew. I just got tired and I didn't think."

"You really shouldn't be swimming all alone at night," she said. Even though it was dark now the paleness of her face seemed to glow within its frame of white linen, with that great scoop of a white bib-thing on her chest, and the long black folds of her habit moving and breathing in the breeze.

"Oh, I'm a very good swimmer," I said.

"But still. What if you got a cramp?"

This was an excellent point, and it occurred to me that maybe one of the reasons I had started swimming at night was that I was courting just such a cramp.

"You know, you're right," I said.

"You should walk home."

"Well, I will, but I left my flip-flops and towel and stuff down the beach there a mile or so." I pointed toward Cape May. "I can swim there easily now that I'm rested."

"Oh, please don't swim there," she said. "I'll worry."

It felt odd to be talking to a nun in her full habit while I was standing there wet in my swimming trunks.

"Please tell me you'll walk."

Her face seemed like any pleasant woman's now.

"Okay," I said.

"Promise me."

She even spoke the way ordinary women spoke.

"I promise," I said.

I noticed a couple of other nuns standing in the light of their porch up there. This was their vacation. What did they do all day? Did they swim, or play cards or Monopoly?

"Did the other sisters send you down to investigate?" I asked.

"I volunteered," she said.

"You're very brave, sister."

"Are you Catholic?"

"Yes," I said, although as soon as I said it I realized that I wasn't a very good Catholic any more. I was in a state of mortal sin after all.

She had been holding her hands inside her habit, but now she did a funny thing. She brought out one hand to shake mine.

"I'm Sister Mary Elizabeth," she said.

"I'm Arnold," I said, shaking her hand. "Pleased to meet you, sister."

Her hand was soft, and feminine, but what else would it be?

So odd, standing there on the dark beach in my wet trunks, shaking hands with a nun.

The lighthouse light flashed over our heads.

We said so long and I walked back down to the end of the fence that borders the nuns' beach. I turned on some strange impulse to wave back at her, but she was walking back up the beach to the convent and to her friends on the lighted porch.

I went around the fence, the surf rushing against my calves, and I headed down the beach of the cove.

I walked past the massive bulk of the abandoned World War II bunker, and when I had gone far enough so that I was sure the nuns couldn't see me I went back into the water, and I swam the rest of the way back to the Cape May end of the beach.

I had broken my promise to the nun, but what she didn't know wouldn't hurt her.

I made it back to my spot without further incident, toweled off, put on my t-shirt and flip-flops and started back home.

It was nice to walk along the boardwalk, and to see people. And when I got to Perry Street it was good to see Congress Hall there to the left, all lit up, not dark and abandoned.

I crossed Beach Drive and headed up Perry Street. I hadn't yet determined if I should go to see Elektra tonight. I wanted to, but I didn't want to start boring her.

I wanted to try this yodeling thing, that is if it was okay with her.

According to that Steve guy, she would be delighted.

Well, we would see about that.

Chapter 28

I took my shower, went up to my attic room and changed. I decided to go visit Elektra after all, even though I had seen her just the previous night.

I went downstairs quietly and crept out the side entrance so as to avoid my aunts and mother and Kevin, but unfortunately Kevin was sitting on the porch and he saw me trying to make my escape.

"Cousin Arnold! *Combat!*'s coming on!"

I hesitated, tempted. Sure enough the proud theme of *Combat!* blared from the Philco in the living room. But I stuck to my guns.

"I'm going out for a while," I called.

"Are you going to see Electric?"

I just kept going.

As I walked it occurred to me that I didn't even know Elektra's phone number, assuming she and her friends had a phone in their apartment. It also occurred to me that I didn't even know her last name.

I went around to the back of their house, behind the shop. I hadn't noticed it before, but there was a buzzer-button to the side of the door. I pressed it and waited. There was no response. I pressed it again. Nothing. I stepped back and looked up. Light came from the upstairs windows, but that meant nothing with this wild and wooly Bohemian crew.

I headed over to the the Ugly Mug. If they were there, fine; if not, well, beer was there and that was fine too.

Sure enough the four of them were all sitting in a booth with a pitcher of beer.

I walked over.

"Hello," I said.

They all said hello back to me, but it was awkward, there wasn't room for a fifth in the booth.

"Well," I said, "I think I'll go have a beer at the bar."

I found an empty stool, and ordered a Schaefer. A song about some guy named Louie was on the jukebox.

Just as the bartender was putting down my mug Elektra came up next to me.

"Hello, you."

"Hello," I said.

She had that mass of dark hair piled up high on her head in some strange fashion.

"Did you write that poem about me yet?"

"No," I said. "But I will. I hope."

{Arnold did indeed write the poem the following week. See "You Asked For It" in the Appendix. — Editor}

"Where have you been all day?"

I told her about my trip to the library, leaving out my search for solid information, and if possible pictures, concerning the female genitalia. I told her of my trip to the duck pond with Kevin, of my swim, the concrete ship, the nun. I left out the part about my writing a poem, as I didn't want her to feel slighted because it hadn't been about her.

"So you've had a pretty full day?"

Her dress was printed with red and black polka dots on a white background, and its scooped *décolletage* revealed the swelling of the upper part of her breasts, which, because she was standing and I was sitting on a barstool, were that much closer to the level of my eyes. I could feel the warmth of her body, and I found myself not answering her question but saying:

"Let's go to bed."

"Well, aren't you romantic?"

"Sorry," I said.

"Finish your beer," she said.

I finished it in two more gulps. It was then that I noticed that fellow Steve, on the other side of the bar, sitting near a group of young coast guardsmen. He was waving merrily to me. I nodded and got off my stool.

Elektra went and got her purse, said a quick goodbye to her friends, and we were soon out the door.

She put her arm in mine as we walked down Washington Street. She looked up at me.

"You know, Arnold, I don't usually behave this way."

"That's good," I said.

I hurried her along. I wouldn't put it past Steve to come tripping after us.

"I don't want you to think I'm just ready to jump into bed with you whenever you feel like it," she said.

"No, of course not."

"But luckily for you I feel like it too."

"Good," I said.

I'll skip ahead here...

"Arnold," she said.

"Yes?"

"What are you doing?"

"I want to try this yodeling thing," I said.

"Yodeling? Is that what it's called?"

"So I've been told," I said.

So I blindly gave it the old college try. (Not that I ever went to college.)

After a minute she said, "Arnold, that feels good."

"Really?" I said. I have to admit I didn't mind doing it, although I wasn't sure how long I could continue.

"But, baby, stop making that noise."

"You mean the yodeling?"

"Yes, the yodeling. It was funny at first but it's distracting already."

"So — I'm not sure I understand. You want me to stop?"

"No, keep doing it, just stop making that noise."

"Oh, okay. So don't actually yodel."

"No, wiseguy, don't actually yodel."

Well, you really can learn something new every day.

"But wait," I said.

"Yes?"

"Where exactly is this little man in the boat?"

"You really don't know?"

"No," I said. "I tried to, um, look it up in the library, but —"

"Okay, here."

She touched it with her finger.

"Ah," I said.

"Wiseguy," she said.

[The next nine lines of Schnabel's holograph have been completely cross-hatched out, in one of his occasional instances of apparent self-expurgation. — Editor]

Finally she said, "Okay, stop. Stop."

I stopped. I rested my head on her thigh. I dozed for perhaps a minute, then woke up, raring to go.

"Wait," she said. "Let me rest a minute, okay, baby?"

"Sure," I said.

I lay there next to her. Soon she was sound asleep, on her side.

This was a predicament. I wondered if she would mind if I just went ahead while she was sleeping, but on second thought that seemed rude.

After a while I got up and got dressed in the dark, and left quietly, gently closing her door behind me.

I walked home without incident.

I still didn't know her last name, and I still didn't know her phone number. But at least I'd gotten to the bottom of this yodeling thing.

Up in my room I turned on my electric table fan and read a few more lines of this *Waste Land* poem. I wasn't too impressed until I came to this line:

"I will show you fear in a handful of dust."

That was a line I wouldn't mind having written. I quit while I was ahead, closed the book, and put out the light.

The leaves of the oak tree in the yard jittered and whispered outside my little casement window, as if they wanted to come in.

I imagined Elektra's body, her smell, her smells, the sounds she made, and while doing so I went ahead and committed what is allegedly a mortal sin. Not that one more mattered at this point.

And then I too slept.

Chapter 29

I was awakened the next morning by the sound of rain. I got up and looked out through the adjustable screen in my small dormer window, the rain thrashing down and shaking the leaves of the oak tree out there and clattering on the tiles of the roof, splattering onto the window screen.

Then I lay back for a while, listening to the noise of the rain and the wind, to the quiet whirring of the electric fan.

It occurred to me that if this were a couple of weeks ago I would dress now and go off to early mass. But now I no longer went to daily mass. I had gone on Sunday, but that had been *pro forma*, something to keep my mother and my aunts unworried, or no more worried than they had to be.

It appeared that I had lost my faith. This despite the fact that I seemed to have had several conversations with Jesus over the past week or so.

I smelled scrapple cooking, even three stories below, so keen is my sense of smell. I got dressed and went down to breakfast.

There was the expected small talk from my mother and aunts on the subject of the northeaster we were now in the midst of. I was merely thinking of how I would spend this rainy day. It would be nice just to spend it reading, but there was the problem of young Kevin. I didn't relish having to listen to his absurd questions for the entire day. It might be best to buy him a new batch of comics, just to keep him occupied.

"What do you say, Arnold," said my Aunt Elizabetta.

"About what?" I said.

"About having your lady friend over for dinner."

"He hasn't even been listening," said Aunt Edith.

How observant she was!

"They want you to invite Electric over for dinner," said Kevin.

"What kind of name is Electric, anyway?" said Edith.

"It's not Electric, Aunt Edith," I said. "It's Elektra."

"That's a funny name," said Aunt Greta. "What is it, Greek?"

"*Sie ist ein Jude,*" said Edith.

"I know she's Jewish, but the name sounds Greek."

"Is she Greek, Arnold?" asked Edith. "Greek Orthodox is practically Catholic."

"Invite her for dinner, Arnold," said my mother.

It occurred to me that I was again living in a madhouse. It's true, these women were not raving screaming lunatics such as some of my fellow patients at Byberry had been, but they were only just a few steps away. Give them just the tiniest push and they'd be howling at the moon with the best of them.

"Arnold?" said my mother, looking worried.

"Yes?" I said.

"Wouldn't you like to invite Electric over for dinner?"

"It's Elektra," said Kevin.

"Don't interrupt," said Greta.

Everyone looked at me.

"Uh, I just met her," I said, to one and all.

"All that matters is she's a nice girl," said Edith. "After all, the Blessed Mother was a Jew. And she was a lovely person. Look at how she took care of the baby Jesus in that stable. Joseph, too, he was a Jew. He seemed like a really nice man."

"I'll think about it," I said.

"Ask her," said my mother.

"Okay," I said.

I finished my breakfast quickly, wondering what it was with people always wanting to meet other people. It was so much more pleasant usually not to meet people.

After breakfast I took Kevin through the downpour to Wally's to buy him some comics. It was the only way I knew to make sure he'd stay out of my hair for at least a part of the day.

I gave him three quarters and left him in the dark store under the watchful hostile eye of the trollish proprietor.

I was tempted to take a walk in the rain, but it was just too stormy, and my umbrella kept threatening to explode.

Should I go to the jewelry store and visit my new friends? No, I didn't want to make Elektra think I was coming on too strong, to have her and her friends think I had nothing else in my life, even though that was pretty much the case.

So I went to the Cape Coffee Shoppe, sat at the counter and ordered a cup, took out my notebook and Bic pen and began to make notes for the previous section of this memoir.

The shop was busy on this rainy day, what else was there to do for poor vacationers? Well, at least this was one day when they wouldn't have to lie in the blistering heat of the beach, their flesh burning, their children wailing.

They could drag themselves and their families into places like this and eat pie and ice cream.

What joy.

"Writing your memoirs?" someone said.

I looked up.

It was that Steve Smith guy. He was wearing what looked like the same pink polo shirt he'd worn the first time I had met him, except now it was wrinkled and stained. He hadn't shaved, and his skin was somehow flushed and pale at the same time.

"May I?" he said.

Well, there was an empty stool there and I didn't own it. He sat down. He had an umbrella, and he tried to lean it against the wall of the counter, but it fell over, and he left it there on the floor. He wore the same madras Bermudas he had worn the other night, or a similar pair, but these, like his shirt, were wrinkled and stained.

"So what are you writing, Arthur?"

"My memoirs," I said.

"No, seriously," he said.

"Seriously, I'm making some notes for my memoirs."

"Fascinating. I would like to write my memoirs. Coffee, darling," he said to the counter girl. "How is the pie here?" he said to me.

"It's not bad," I said. "I had some peach pie here the other day."

"I adore peach pie. I am so hungover. This has been the most drunken vacation I've ever had. Did I see you in the Mug last night?"

"Yes," I said.

He took out cigarettes, Salems, and offered me the pack.

"No thanks," I said. "I smoke Pall Malls."

"You're such a he-man," he said, lighting himself up with a trembling hand after clicking his lighter about ten times. He coughed. "I am so *intensely* hungover," he said.

The waitress had brought his coffee. He put his cigarette in the ashtray, then added a lot of sugar and some cream to the coffee. He lifted the cup and saucer with both hands, drank some coffee. He paused, then drank again. It was air-conditioned in here, but I noticed that he was sweating. He took another drink of coffee, then put the cup and saucer down again.

"Oh, dear God in Heaven," he said. "I think I need to see a psychiatrist, Arthur. I truly do. Sometimes I think I should just jump in the ocean. Just — go out really far. Like on a fishing boat. And just leap. But knowing me I'd just get involved in some absurd conversation with the fishermen, and —"

He waved his hands again, and then stopped suddenly and said, "Oh! Did you try the yodeling?"

"Well —"

"No, tell me you didn't, you rascal!"

"I did," I said.

"Bravo! And did she love it?"

"Well, she didn't complain," I said.

"Well done, old chap! And I'll bet she showed you something then, didn't she?"

He lifted his cup and slurped, all the while looking at me with wide mischievous eyes.

"Well, she fell asleep," I said.

Steve sprayed coffee all over the counter top.

Chapter 30

"Oh my God, I love this song," said Steve.
He began to sing along to the jukebox:

> *You don't own me*
> *I'm not just one of your many toys*
> *You don't own me*
> *Don't say I can't go with other boys*

He seemed oblivious to the mess he had just made all over the counter, so I grabbed a bunch of paper napkins out of the metal dispenser and wiped it up.

Steve just kept singing. At least he was on pitch.

> *And don't tell me what to do*
> *And don't tell me what to say*
> *And please, when I go out with you,*
> *Don't put me on display, 'cause*

He turned and pointed a finger at me:

> *You don't own me*
> *Don't try to change me in any way*
> *You don't own me*
> *Don't tie me down 'cause I'd never stay*

The people on either side of us had stopped talking and were now staring at Steve, but he didn't care. He closed his eyes and clenched his fists and sang:

> *I don't tell you what to say*
> *I don't tell you what to do*
> *So, just let me be myself*
> *That's all I ask of you*
> *I'm young and I love to be young*
> *I'm free and I love to be free*

To live my life the way I want,
To say and do whatever I please

An instrumental part came on, and so he finally shut up. The people kept staring at him though. He looked at me and shrugged.

"Arthur," he said, "I think I need a hair of the dog, and pronto. Will you join me for a cocktail at the Ugly Mug?"

"Well, Steve," I said, "it's a little early for me."

"Oh, pish, come on, we're on vacation, ness pa?"

"Ness pa?"

"It's French. At least I think it's French. Like, N, apostrophe, E, S, T, um, dash, uh, C, E, I think."

"Oh. *N'est-ce pas?*"

"That's it; you speak French, I'm so impressed."

"I don't really speak it," I said. "I took a course in the army, and I was in France for a while in the war, so —"

"I'll bet you were very brave."

"I was an engineer. I never fired a shot."

"I'm sure you were frightfully brave. Come have a drink with me."

"No," I said, "I should go home and have lunch."

"Let me buy you lunch, Arthur. You're the only friend I've made in this town."

That was sad.

"Come on," he said. "Don't make me drink alone. I'll buy you a tremendous cheeseburger."

I felt sorry for him. And also I wanted to get out of there because people were still giving him glances, waiting for him to break into song again.

Steve insisted on paying for my coffee. We got our umbrellas and walked down the block in the lashing rain to the Mug.

It was barely noon, but even so the northeaster had almost filled the place up with people desperate for some sort of good time on their vacations.

There was one empty booth and Steve made a beeline for it.

We sat down, we got out our cigarettes and lighted up. A young waitress came over.

"A pitcher of Schaefer, please, darling," said Steve. "Oh, and two Manhattans, up, and *arctically* cold."

"No Manhattan for me," I said, "I'll just have a large club soda please."

There was a boring part here, with Steve trying to talk me into having a Manhattan with him. Finally the waitress just looked at me, wanting to get on with her life.

"A club soda," I said. "No Manhattan for me."

"Okay!" she gave a strained smile and went away.

This song about people came on, people who need people being the luckiest people in the world, and Steve started singing again.

"Steve," I said. "Steve. Steve."

"What?"

"Steve, you have to stop singing."

"But I *love* Barbra!"

"Then let her sing."

"Oh, okay. Thanks so much for having lunch with me, Arthur."

"Steve —"

"Yes?"

"My name is Arnold."

"Arnold?"

"Yeah."

"Oh my God I'm so sorry."

"It's okay."

"Arnold. Arnold Arnold *Arnold*. I'll remember that now. So! Arnold, tell me the story of your life."

I paused for just a moment and then went ahead and started to give him the highlights. After a few sentences I could tell he was getting bored, and so was I.

The waitress came over with her tray. She laid down the pitcher of beer and two empty beer mugs, a Manhattan, and a large club soda.

"Would you like to order some food?" she asked.

There were menus on the table, but we hadn't opened them.

"I'll have a cheeseburger," I said. "Medium rare, with French fries. Please."

"Anything for you, sir?" she asked Steve.

"Oh, no, darling, I'll drink my lunch."

She went away again.

"Do continue with your life story, Arthur, I mean Arnold," said Steve, probably just to be polite. He picked up his Manhattan and sipped it.

I decided to get right to the dramatic stuff, and so I briefly told him about my breakdown and hospitalization, my failed attempt to go back to work, the railroad putting me on an indefinite paid leave of absence, my mother taking me to Cape May to stay at her sisters' boarding house.

"That brings us up to date," I said. "That's the story of my life."

Steve paused, still holding his Manhattan in mid-air. Then, no more sipping, he drank it all in two gulps.

He sighed.

"You don't know how *therapeutic* that was," he said, obviously referring to his Manhattan and not to hearing the story of my life.

He lifted the pitcher and filled his beer mug, then went to fill the other one. I put my hand over the mug.

"None for me, Steve."

"Oh, all right." He took a drink of beer. "Wait, did you say you write and publish a poem every *week*?"

"Yep. Every week. But don't worry, they're not very good."

"I *knew* you were the artistic sort. I could tell. Did you ever read *The Fountainhead*, by what's her name?"

"No," I said.

"Anne something. *The Fountainhead*?"

"Nope, never read it."

"Oh, you must read it. It took me more than a year to finish it, but I was *riveted* by that book. *Riveted*. What's another good book I've read? How about *Ship of Fools* by Katharine Anne, um — I haven't quite finished that one. So, a mental breakdown. Very interesting. Personally I think the world is mad. I would like to read your poems. Do you want to hear my life story?"

"Sure."

He told me his life story.

Boy, and I thought my life was dull.

Listening to him really made me want to drink some of that beer, and so finally I broke down and poured myself a mug.

Why had I come here with Steve?

I kept nodding my head as he went on and on.

I had felt sorry for him.

Now I felt sorry for myself, stuck here with him.

Fortunately my cheeseburger and fries arrived, so my lunch occupied me for a while. They make a good burger there.

But soon enough the burger and fries were gone, but Steve was still there. He'd ordered another Manhattan, and another pitcher of beer. He also tried to order me a Manhattan, but I stood firm on that score.

Steve went on with his life story, but I wouldn't be able to put down more than a few scraps of it here even if I wanted to, because, just as he had no doubt barely been listening to my own life story, I was probably even more barely listening to his, and after a while I realized I was falling into, or rising into, one of those episodes of mine, becoming detached from the world and myself. I could see Steve's lips moving but I couldn't make out any words at all. Oddly enough though I was hearing, as if from another room, that song that had been playing earlier, the one about people who need people.

I hate these episodes. There's always the fear that the episode will never end. And so the thing to do is to try to force it to end, by doing something, anything.

"Excuse me, Steve," I heard myself say. "I have to go to the – you know –"

I got up in a sort of panic and made my way to the men's room.

There was no one in it.

I stared at my face in the mirror.

"Okay," I said, "snap out of it. Snap out of it." I didn't like my face. I was tired of my face. "Snap out of it."

In desperation I started to say the first few phrases of the Hail Mary over and over again, a ploy that has worked for me before in these situations. But then I began to think about how absurd it was to pray to the Blessed Mother, because why should she help me, even if she did exist? And thinking about this, about the absurdity of saying the Hail Mary, and not even the whole Hail Mary but just the beginning part over and over again, I felt the panic subside, and I felt myself relaxing into myself again.

I took a deep breath.

Maybe the Blessed Mother really had come to my rescue. I had no way of knowing.

Then I actually did have to pee, so I peed.

I felt better now.

I rinsed my hands and went back out.

"Are you okay?" said Steve. "You looked a little I don't know what just then."

"I'm fine," I said. I sat and filled my mug. It was only my second one.

"So, I've been boring you," said Steve.

"Oh, no," I lied.

I looked at him. He did look somewhat like Jesus, although without the beard and long hair and robe. Could he actually be Jesus? No, that was insane.

Chapter 31

Steve raised his Manhattan glass to his lips, but, after upending it over his gaping mouth and shaking it vigorously, he finally realized that the glass had been emptied before he raised it. He lowered the glass and stared into it for a moment, then suddenly thrust the glass aloft and looked around for the waitress.

"Steve," I said, "you really shouldn't have another."

"Oh, my goodness, are you flagging me?"

"You haven't eaten," I said. "You should go home and take a nap."

He stared at me as if he were about to argue, but then he brought the glass down, but at an angle and a force which would have caused it surely to break, so I quickly reached over, took it from his hand and set it down on the table. And then suddenly he seemed to slump within himself.

He stared at the table and then sheepishly peered up at me.

"I'm such a hopeless alcy," he said.

"Let's pay up and I'll get you home."

"Okay, Arthur. But you must let me pay."

He strugglingly got out his wallet, and fumbling it open he spilled bills all over the table.

I wound up letting him pay for the check, just because it was easier that way, and I paid the tip, but as we were leaving he forced another ten dollars into the waitress's hand.

When we were at the door and opening our umbrellas I said, "That was an awful lot of money you gave the girl, Steve."

"Arthur," he said, "when you're as big a drunk as I am you learn to be very generous to waitresses and bartenders now let's go."

He was stopping at the Chalfonte, just a few blocks away, but the rain was really coming down now, the storm blowing in hard from the ocean. We tried to keep our umbrellas aimed into the wind, but they still blew inside out a couple of times each.

Once Steve fell, and I had some difficulty getting him to stand up again, but after no more than two minutes I did.

We made it to the Chalfonte. It's a nice old-fashioned hotel, broad but not tall, white wood, a long porch with rockers.

We went into the lobby, lots of people were sitting around reading or chatting, playing board games.

"Should we drop in at the bar for a quick one?" asked Steve, with a slight hopeful smile.

"No, go to your room now, Steve. Can you make it all right?"

"Sure. Absolutely," he said, but not in a very emphatic-sounding way.

He was drenched. His umbrella was blown-out, useless. He fumbled in his pocket and brought out a key attached to a numbered tag.

"See," he said. "I've even got my key."

"Great. Go right to bed, and when you wake up, eat something, Steve."

"Right. I guess you're going to see — your lady friend?"

Actually I had no definite plans to see her, but I didn't want to get stuck agreeing to meet him for a liquid supper that night, so I said, "Yeah."

"Good. She's very lovely."

"Okay, see ya later, Steve."

I held out my hand. Steve looked at his right hand; it held the hotel room key. He didn't seem to know what to do with it.

I patted him on the shoulder and turned to go.

"Wait! Arthur!"

"Arnold," I said.

"Arnold!"

"Yeah, Steve."

He looked over both his shoulders. In fact the desk clerk and several other people in the lobby were staring at us now.

He put his hand to the side of his mouth and whispered:

"Don't forget to yodel!"

"Thanks, Steve," I said. "I won't."

I went out the screen door to the porch, and opened my somewhat operable umbrella.

I still had the afternoon ahead of me. It would be nice to change out of my damp clothes and lie in bed and read for a while, maybe take a nap. I set out through the rain.

I decided to go down Jackson, just perhaps to peep into the window of my friends' shop. Maybe I could at least say hello if Elektra was behind the counter. Or maybe not...

I came to the shop, and I paused under the awning. Sure enough there she was, so was Rocket Man, but the shop was busy, there were six or eight people in there, and Elektra was talking to a customer over the counter. I walked on.

I'd gone down to in front of the next house when I heard Elektra's rain-muffled voice behind me, calling my name.

I turned and went back, she pulled me in under the awning, and we stood off to one side of the entrance.

"You don't say hello?"

"Well, you looked busy," I said.

"They can wait."

I held my open umbrella awkwardly off to one side.

"You're all wet," she said. "What are you doing walking around in the rain?"

"Well, I met that Steve guy in the coffee shop, next thing I knew he was dragging me into the Ugly Mug for lunch. Except all he did was drink, and then I had to walk him home in the rain, because he was drunk, and our umbrellas kept turning inside out."

She looked at me.

"You realize he's queer, don't you, Arnold?"

"Oh," I said.

"You really didn't know?"

"Well, I thought maybe he was just — eccentric."

"Uh-huh. Okay, no matter. Listen, lover, I owe you."

"Really? What for?"

"For last night."

I suppose I looked befuddled. Which I was.

"I mean *because*," she said.

"Because," I said, to say something.

"Because I fell *asleep*," she said, and I now at last I got it.

"Oh," I said. "Well, I figured you were tired."

She looked at me, and then pulled my wet shirt away from my chest with her fingers.

"Go home and get out of these wet clothes," she said. "You'll catch your death."

"Okay."

"Do you want to have dinner tonight?"

"I have dinner every night."

"With me, wiseguy."

"Sure." And then, I have no idea why I said this: "My mother and aunts want to have you over for dinner."

"You're kidding me."

"No."

"I'd love to have dinner with your mother and aunts."

"There's also my young cousin Kevin."

"He's cute. I like him."

"I don't think you'd have very much fun," I said.

"Why?"

"Well — they're already talking about us getting married."

"Old women are the same everywhere, Arnold. Tell them I'll come over tonight if it's okay."

"We eat really early," I said. "Six o'clock or so."

"Just like my parents. I'll get out of the shop early and be over at six."

"All right," I said. "You've been warned."

"I've been warned. Go home and get out of those wet clothes."

She gave me a kiss on the cheek. I'm not sure, but I think this may have been the first time she did this. Kiss me on the cheek, that is.

I walked home through the rain, and then I told my mother and aunts about Elektra coming to dinner. They bombarded me with questions. Among other things they wanted to know her dietary requirements. I told them she didn't have to have kosher food and that as far as I knew she ate anything.

I escaped upstairs and got out of my wet clothes, went back down to the third floor bathroom and took a bath. I brought *The Waste Land* with me. I still hadn't made much headway in that poem, and after a few lines, the sense of which pretty much escaped me (except for a general feeling of gloom), I reached out my arm and laid the book down on the toilet seat.

I lay back and listened to the sounds of the rain and the wind, the clattering and thrashing, the moaning and the singing of the storm.

It occurred to me that I still didn't know Elektra's last name.

Chapter 32

After my bath I went to bed, in my little attic room with the electric table fan blowing the warm humid air over my naked corporeal host. I switched on my table lamp in the dimness and duly read some more of *The Waste Land*, making scarce head or tail of it.

I did like this one part:

> *Unreal City,*
> *Under the brown fog of a winter dawn,*
> *A crowd flowed over London Bridge, so many,*
> *I had not thought death had undone so many.*

It reminded me of dear old Olney, that bridge that goes over the Heintz factory, the burnt metal smell.

The whiskey reek when you walk by the taprooms, etc.

So I put down *The Waste Land* and picked up *This Sweet Sickness* again, and that I quite enjoyed. It's about a madly obsessive young man who seems to all intents and purposes normal but who is actually insane. A good rainy day book. After a while I laid it aside and pulled the little chain on the lamp. I turned on my side away from my little window and closed my eyes, listening to the rain crackling and popping on the roof right above me, the crashing of waves of rain against the front of the house.

I fell asleep.

After an unknown amount of time I woke up and I saw Jesus sitting at my table with the desk lamp on, smoking a cigarette and reading one of the scrapbooks in which I keep cuttings of my poems.

I tried to speak but I couldn't get any words out.

He looked up and smiled. He was wearing that pink polo shirt again, and the madras shorts, just like Steve's shirt and shorts. He did look a little like Steve, but then I realized he looked like a lot of people, like Alan Ladd, and Jeffrey Hunter, and even Tab Hunter, and other people I couldn't identify.

"I know," he said. "Man of a thousand faces!"

I think I made some sort of sound, somewhere between a groan and a sigh and a yawn. I won't try to write it out phonetically.

"Hey," he said, "didn't mean to upset you, just thought I'd stop by." He closed the scrapbook and laid it on the table. He flicked off the lamp, just an old gooseneck desk lamp. "Go back to sleep!"

I still couldn't say anything.

Even though the light was out he still seemed illuminated in the rainy day dimness, as if his skin and clothes and his hair were phosphorescent.

"Hey, I like your poems, by the way," he said. "They really got better after your little breakdown, didn't they?"

I tried to talk again, but I just couldn't. I felt like my mouth was paralyzed with Novocain.

"So look," he said, and he stubbed out his cigarette in the butt-filled tin ashtray on my table, "I'll go, didn't mean to disturb your nap."

He stood, up, stooping a little because of course my room is right under the gabled roof.

"Have fun with Elektra tonight. And don't forget to yodel!"

He chuckled and went to the door. There was a black umbrella leaning against it, he took it, opened the door and went out, closing the door quietly behind him.

I closed my eyes.

I slept.

I woke up with a rush again.

Had I really just seen Jesus? No, I was dreaming. It's okay to have insane visions as long as you're dreaming.

I fell back to sleep.

When I awoke again I felt much better, very rested. The rain was still coming down, but much more lightly now, and the wind had settled too. The green of the leaves on the oak tree outside my window sparkled dully, like seaweed in clear water.

I remembered my dream vividly, if it was a dream, but I wasn't scared. To tell the truth it was beginning to feel normal to be visited by the son of God.

I got dressed and went down to the bathroom, taking my book with me. I peed, and then I brushed my teeth. I went downstairs and into the kitchen where all three of my aunts and my mother were fussing with various foodstuffs. My mouth watered. Aunt Elizabetta was rolling and cutting noodle dough. I peeked in the oven, and there was a roast beef in it. A duck simmered in a pot on the range. I went over to where my mother was stirring chocolate batter in an enormous bowl. She told me to get away and not to spoil my appetite. I said okay and got a cup of coffee from the percolator.

I went out through the dining room and into the living room, Kevin was in there watching *Clutch Cargo* on the TV. He said not a word to me, nor I to him, I speak of Kevin of course, not Clutch Cargo, and I went out onto the porch and sat down in my usual rocker. The afternoon's gale had lessened into a windy steady rainfall.

Jesus stood across the street, under his black umbrella. He waved with his free hand. A blue and white Tastykake truck hissed slowly by, and, when it passed, my alleged lord and savior had disappeared, into thin air, or rather into thick rainy air.

So, there you had it.

I was still insane. Or I was sane, and Jesus was my friend.

I continued to stare out at the street and then I saw another vision in the rain, off to the left, Elektra coming down Perry Street, holding up another black umbrella, wearing a pale blue dress, carrying a paper bag of something.

When she got near the front gate I stood up, and then, realizing she wouldn't have a free hand for the gate I ran down to get it for her.

When I closed it behind her she turned and held the umbrella over both of us.

"Hi, lover."

"Hi."

"Brought you wine."

She handed me the bag. I peeked into it, and it indeed contained a large bottle wrapped in straw, and filled apparently with liquid.

I looked up into Elektra's face, and it was beautiful in the wet grey light, with the rain rattling on her umbrella.

"What are we eating?" she said.

"Duck soup with noodles, and roast beef," I said. "And chocolate cake."

"Beef and duck and cake. Let's go, big boy."

Over her shoulder I could see Jesus again, standing across the street under his black umbrella, waving at me. Well, at least he didn't seem to be inviting himself to dinner. So I had that to be thankful for.

Chapter 33

So we went up the steps and onto the porch. Elektra partly closed and then snapped open her umbrella quickly a few times to flick the water on it over the rail.

It was odd, but just watching her do something so simple as shaking the water off of her umbrella made me want to go to bed with her.

She looked at me.

"What are you thinking about, Arnold?"

I glanced across the street, but Jesus had disappeared again. Should I tell Elektra that I had just seen him? No, even I could tell this was not a good time for that, if there ever was.

"I'm just thinking I'm happy to see you," I said, which was not a lie.

I wanted to put my arms around her, but this wasn't the time or place for that either, and anyway I was holding the wine in the paper bag, it would have been awkward.

"So shall we go in or just stand out here all night?" she said.

"I'd rather just go back to your place."

"Come on, Arnold."

She touched me on the face with her fingers, which made something inside me go hollow and then fill up again.

"Okay, let's go," I said.

We went over to the doorway, she put her umbrella in the wicker umbrella stand, the only kind of umbrella stand that's there, I opened the screen door for her and we went inside. Kevin was still there, sitting on the floor, watching the TV.

"Hi, Electric," he said.

"Hi, Kelvin," said Elektra.

"My name's Kevin."

"My name's Elektra."

"Hi, *Elektra*," he said, rolling his eyes.

"Whatcha watchin', Kevin?" she asked.

"*Astroboy.*"

"*Astroboy.* I don't think I've seen that."

"It's good. You wanta watch it with me?"

"I think I should say hi to the ladies first," she said.

"They're in the kitchen," said Kevin, turning back to the show. "Cousin Arnold'll take you."

"Okay. See ya."

"See ya," he said, but he was concentrating on Astroboy again.

I took her back to the kitchen. It was hot and moist and meat-smelling, and all the women stopped what they were doing and looked at Elektra.

For a strange moment there was silence. Elektra squeezed my arm, I snapped out of it, and introduced her to my aunts and re-introduced her to my mother.

Just then Charlie Coleman came in from the side-door hallway, wearing a wet rubber slicker and a rubber hat and rubber boots. He had an armful of lettuce and other greens, and a half-gallon mason jar of what I think was cream and a plastic container of butter. I hadn't even heard his truck pull up.

He cheerily said something I couldn't decipher, and my Aunt Elizabetta took the stuff off him, put the lettuce and greens in the sink, the jar and the container on the counter. Then my Aunt Greta dug into her apron and gave Charlie a few crumpled bills and some coins.

He thanked her, then he said something to me — I couldn't make it out, I thought he was saying something like, "Who got the gravy."

"He wants to know who the lady is, Arnold," said my Aunt Edith.

"Oh, this is Elektra, Charlie," I said. "Elektra, this is Charlie. Charlie helps my aunts out around the house."

"Hi, Charlie," said Elektra.

"Charlie brought us the duck earlier, too, Arnold," said my mother.

Charlie said something else, God knows what. He went on for quite a bit. Elektra nodded several times back at him.

Then Charlie left and the older women went back to staring at Elektra.

"Elektra brought some wine," I said, and I took the bottle out of the bag.

All four of the older women said variations of "You shouldn't have," Elektra said it was nothing, the old women said again she shouldn't have, she said it was no big deal, then they all said the same things one more time, but before they could go through it again I asked where the corkscrew was.

My mother and aunts don't really drink, but I was ready for one. My mother found me the corkscrew, and I opened the bottle. Elektra said she wouldn't mind one, and I could see a glance going around the old ladies, but under the glance I heard them thinking, *"She's Jewish, they probably drink wine all the time, like Italians."*

There were no wine glasses so we drank out of a couple of my aunts' Flintstones jelly glasses.

The old women got back to work on the food. Elektra asked if she could help with anything, but they all said no. Elektra asked again, they said no again. Then one more time around, and Elektra went over to the stove and started to engage in conversation with my Aunt Elizabetta, something to do with a gravy she was making.

I stood there like a lump by the kitchen table, drinking my wine, sweating in the kitchen heat. Elektra was speaking with the old women, the old women were speaking to her and to each other, and all of them were doing things with food and pots and pans.

My jelly glass of wine became empty. I refilled it.

Elektra came back over to me and touched my back with her fingers.

"How are you doing, Arnold?" she said in a low voice.

"Fine," I said. To tell the truth I was feeling just a little bit crazy, but I figured I'd probably be okay after I finished this glass of wine.

"What did that man Charlie say right before he left?" she asked.

"I have no idea," I said.

"He said he brought over the best duck he had," said my Aunt Edith. I hadn't realized she was listening. She was holding a bowl of dark red blood. "And then he said he also raises chickens and pigs, and he has a cow, and if you ever want to buy any chickens or ducks or pigs or eggs or cream or fresh butter he would give you a good deal. Then he said you were really pretty and that it was about time Arnold married and settled down."

"Oh, okay," said Elektra.

"Do you want to help me make the duck's blood soup?" said Aunt Edith.

"Um, okay, sure," said Elektra.

The old ladies had slit a living duck's throat, but thank God I had not witnessed the execution. I had stood witness once as my aunts killed a duck and then held it upside down to let it exsanguinate into a bowl. It was not an experience I wanted ever to repeat.

Come to think of it, I didn't particularly want to watch this next bit either, which involved some mysterious process of mixing the duck's blood into the simmering and fragrant duck broth.

I don't mind eating the duck's blood soup, I just don't want to watch any of these gruesome preliminaries.

Elektra was holding a wooden spoon and standing attentively next to my Aunt Edith who held the bowl of blood in her small but sturdy hands. Elektra only stands about five foot four or so but still she seemed to tower over tiny Aunt Edith.

I said I was going to go in to the living room and watch TV with Kevin until dinner was ready.

All of them, including Elektra, told me to go on in.

"Go on, Arnold," she said, waving the spoon.

She didn't have to tell me again. I topped off my glass, went on out through the dining room and into the living room and just caught the beginning of a Popeye cartoon, one of the good ones, with Bluto.

Chapter 34

As soon as *Popeye* ended, with Popeye in the passionate embrace of Olive Oyl, it hit me for the first time in my life:

"Kevin," I said, "Did it ever occur to you that Olive Oyl's name is a play on words?"

"What do you mean?"

"I mean her name is a joke."

"What's so funny about it?"

"Well, her name is the same as olive oil, the oil, like cooking oil. Except it's spelled differently."

"What are you talking about?"

"Olive oil. You know, oil made from olives."

"What about it?"

"Well, there's this oil made from olives, and it's called olive oil. And Olive Oyl in the cartoon has the same name, except it's spelled differently."

"Oh."

"I had never realized that before now," I said.

"Uh-huh."

"Had you?" I asked.

"No. Because I had never heard of olive oil before. What do I know about olive oil?"

"Good question," I said.

"If her name was Crisco Oyl maybe then it would mean something to me."

"Right," I said.

John Facenda {*A popular Philadelphia TV news anchorman of the era. Known as "the voice of God". — Editor*} came on with the news. We watched it for a bit. Some gang in England had robbed a train of 2.6 million pounds. {*The "Great Train Robbery" of August 8, 1963. — Editor*}

"When I grow up I'm gonna be a train robber," said Kevin. "No offense; I know you used to work on the railroad."

"No offense," I said. I had almost finished my topped-off jelly-glass of wine, and I felt much better than I had when the glass was full.

My mother came in and called us to dinner, so I got up and turned the TV off.

Normally we eat in the kitchen, but now because we were having company we were eating in the dining room, which is just a cramped uncomfortable room in between the living room and kitchen, with a table that's actually no bigger than the kitchen table.

The ladies had brought out the good china, which I find annoying to eat off of. It's got all this fancy imitation gilt along its scalloped edges which when you wield your knife and fork upon it makes for an awful scraping noise like desperate mice trapped behind a chalkboard.

Kevin and I sat down. He always sits immediately to my left when we eat. Or is it I who always sits to his right?

I noticed a black leather woman's purse on the table, and I realized it was Elektra's. I hadn't even noticed before that she was carrying a purse.

That's me for you in a nutshell, I amble through life noticing only things like the smell of steam coming up from a sidewalk grill, or the rainbow colors in a puddle of gasoline in a gutter, or worms in the grass on a rainy spring day, and yet I fail to notice that my inamorata is carrying a black leather purse.

There was a bit of fuss about Elektra wanting to help bring in the food, but the old women kept telling her to go on and sit down.

Finally she did sit down, to my right. And thank God she had brought the Chianti bottle in and put it well within my reach. The old ladies had opened all the windows now that the rain had lessened, and they had turned on two dueling oscillating black fans on tables on opposite sides of the room, but it was still hot in there from all the cooking in the kitchen next door.

Elektra put her hand on my leg. I was wearing Bermuda shorts. Her hand felt very warm. I glanced into her eyes, and she smiled. I could feel the warmth of her body, and she smelled like French toast with maple syrup. Embarrassingly, I started to get an erection.

Thank God again, my Aunt Greta brought out the big wooden salad bowl, and Elektra took her hand off my thigh before my erection could reach its full enormity.

The salad was dished out, or at least for me and Elektra and Kevin it was dished out. My aunts and my mother did their usual business of just sharing one plate, and either not sitting down at all or sitting down and then getting right up again.

My Aunt Elizabetta asked Elektra what she did for a living. Elektra told her about the jewelry shop, and Edith asked her if her family was in the jewelry business.

Oh, great, I thought, this is going to lead to her Jewishness. But fortunately Elektra's father was in the scaffolding trade, so that held Edith off at the pass.

Under further questioning Elektra revealed that she had gone to NYU and majored in English, and then had gone on to complete her master's degree in English Literature at Columbia. All four of the old women looked at her as if she were speaking Chinese.

"I'll probably go back for my Ph.D, but I felt like taking a year or two off first," she said.

This meant nothing to the old women. She might as well have been explaining Einstein's theory of relativity, not that I myself would have understood the latter either.

Aunt Greta asked her where she was from. Elektra said she was born in Brooklyn, but moved to the Upper West Side of New York City with her family when she was eight. My aunts and mother had all lived in Brooklyn when they first came to America, so this precipitated a conversation about the old Brooklyn neighborhoods. My aunts and mother had lived in Bushwick, Elektra's family had been from Williamsburg.

I'll say one thing, at least I was finding out some things about Elektra that I hadn't known before.

By this time we were on the duck's blood soup with noodles, and I have to say it was delicious.

However, I guess the hammer had to come down eventually, and so it did.

"Your neighborhood was really very clean," said my Aunt Edith.

"Oh," said Elektra, "yes, I suppose so –"

"The Jewish people are clean," said Aunt Edith.

"Um," said Elektra.

"Not like the Irish," said Edith.

"Uh," said Elektra, and she put her hand on my thigh again.

"Or the *Schwarzen*," said Edith.

Elektra squeezed my thigh.

"Bushwick was a very clean neighborhood," said Elektra.

"Not any more," said Aunt Edith. "Nothing but the *Schwarzen* there now."

"Okay, Edith," said Elizabetta, who has certain liberal tendencies, as well as sounder ideas, or ideas at all, about acceptable dinner conversation.

"What?" said Edith.

"Help me bring the roast beef in," said Elizabetta.

"Okay," said Edith.

I refilled my Flintstones glass.

"Don't forget me," whispered Elektra and I filled her up too.

"I want some grape juice," said Kevin.

He tried to reach for the bottle but I moved it away.

He accepted the deprivation without comment, and took to quietly singing the theme song to *77 Sunset Strip*.

My Aunt Elizabetta came in with the platter of roast beef, and my Aunt Edith followed with the gravy. My mother brought in the potatoes, Greta brought in the greens.

Elektra removed her hand from my thigh, which was good because I was starting to get another erection.

We made it through the meal. I felt sorry for Elektra, continuing to try to talk to my aunts and to my mother, something I never tried to do. Normally I just ate my food while they talked among themselves and I paid no attention, indeed I often brought a book to the table. It was a sore point with Kevin that he was not allowed to bring comic books to the dinner table, although this was permitted at lunch by some obscure loophole in familial law.

At the end of the meal there was a tedious discussion about letting Elektra help with the dishes, and while it was going on I went out to the porch with another topped-off jelly glass of wine and my cigarettes. It was almost twilight now, the rain had abated to a salty thin spray that seemed not to fall but to shimmer in the air. The air smelled of honeysuckle and gladioli, of wet dirt and the ocean. I sat down in my usual rocker, lit up a Pall Mall, and stared out at the street, covered like a forest floor with gleaming green leaves and fallen brown twigs.

Kevin was inside watching TV again. I could hear the theme song: *The Many Loves of Dobie Gillis*.

After a few minutes Elektra came out. She had a glass of wine too, and her leather purse. She sat down in the rocker next to me, put her glass down on the little wicker table between us, and took out her cigarettes. I gave her a light.

"Well, that was interesting," she said, quietly, blowing the smoke out the side of her mouth.

"I'm supposed to be the one with mental problems," I said. "And yet you volunteered for that."

"It wasn't so bad. You don't understand women. We're always submitting ourselves to absurd situations. It's our lot in life. Besides, your aunts and mother are nice."

"They're prejudiced," I said.

"I know. But they don't know any better."

She smoked, staring out at the street. The rain had stopped. The sky and the air had been grey all day, but now, just as the day was ending, an illumination fell across the street through the moist air, as if floodlights mounted on the gables of our house had all at once been switched on. I stared at Elektra's face and remembered I hadn't written her a poem yet.

"Oh, no," she said. "Will you look at who's walking down the street?"

Sure enough, coming down Perry Street was who at first I thought was Jesus, but then I realized it was just that Steve guy, unless of course Steve really was Jesus, which was still a possibility I supposed. He wore a light green sport shirt this time, and matching shorts. He wasn't carrying an umbrella.

He crossed the street and turned left on North, towards us. My aunts' house is one house in from the corner.

He gave no sign of knowing we were there until he was right abreast of us, then he stopped and stared.

"Arthur!" he said. "And your lady friend! *Quelle surprise*! May I come up and say hello?"

Chapter 35

What can you do when someone just invites himself up? Say no?
We were trapped.

I started to say, "Sure, come on up," but I hadn't got past the "sh" sound in "sure" before Steve was already working on the gate latch, which after only about half a minute he managed to lift up.

Next thing I knew he was on the porch, bending over and giving Elektra a kiss on the cheek.

"Don't tell me your name!" he said to her.

"Okay," she said.

"Athena!" he cried.

"No."

"No?"

"Nope," she said.

"Okay, uh — Jocasta?"

"No."

"Am I warm?"

"A little."

"Is it Medea?"

"Nope."

"Hmmm, let me think. *Lysistrata?*"

I couldn't take it any more.

"It's Elektra, Steve," I said.

"*Elektra!* I knew it! Thank you, Arthur!"

"Arnold," I said.

"Arnold! So what are you two up to?"

"Uh, well, uh," I said.

"Is this where you live, Arnold?"

"Well, uh –"

My mother opened the screen door, holding a tray with cups of coffee, saucers and spoons, a little cream pitcher, a sugar bowl.

"Hello, madam," said Steve.

"Hello," said my mother.

"My name's Steve. Here, let me take that tray." He took the tray from her. "And who might you be?"

"I'm Arnold's mother. Mrs. Schnabel."

"Are you? Arnold's only my best buddy, you know."

"Really?"

She looked at me in puzzlement.

"What a fabulous house you have, Mrs. Schnabel," said Steve.

"It's my sisters' house," said my mother.

"Yes, but *still*," said Steve.

"Can I have a cup of that coffee, Steve?" said Elektra.

"Of course, darling."

He went over and bent down with the tray; she took a cup and saucer, and with a gentle wave of her hand indicated she didn't want sugar or cream.

"Arnold?" said Steve.

I took a cup, black also.

"Would you like a cup, Steve?" asked my mother.

"No, thank you, I've just had a gallon of coffee."

"Can I get you something else?"

"Oh, no thank you, very much, I've only popped up to say hi really. Don't want to wear out my welcome."

"You're very welcome, Steve," said my mother. "Any friend of Arnold's is welcome here."

"So kind of you to say that."

He handed her back the tray.

Kevin came and opened the screen door.

"Hello, little man," said Steve. "And who might you be?"

"Kevin Armstrong," said Kevin.

"My name's Steve."

"Hello."

My Aunt Edith appeared behind Kevin. This was getting insane, and this time it wasn't all me.

"Hello," said Steve.

"Hello," said Aunt Edith.

"My name's Steve. Arnold's friend."

"I'm Edith. Arnold's aunt."

"Hello, *Aunt Edith*, and aren't you just as cute as a button?"

At this Aunt Edith retreated back indoors but Kevin just stood there in the doorway.

"So!" said Steve. "I should be going. Arthur I mean Arnold, where is this *VFW club* I've heard so much about?"

"Just go right down the street here till you get to the next corner, Congress Street, then go right and it's another block and a half or so on the right-hand side. You can't miss it."

"Care to come?" He looked hopefully at me, then at Elektra, then back to me again, with a sad half smile on one side of his face.

"Uh, no, Steve, thanks," I said. "we, uh —"

"We just ate an enormous and delicious meal," said Elektra. "I think we're just going to sit here for a while, Steve."

My mother still stood there, holding her tray, and Kevin remained in the doorway.

"I should probably eat something," said Steve, wistfully. "Do they have good food at this VFW?"

"It's okay," I said. "Go for the meatball sandwich."

"Steve, why don't you let me fix you a plate?" said my mother.

"Oh, no, I couldn't, Mrs. Schnabel."

"You wait here, I'll bring you out a tray. Would you like a glass of wine?"

"A glass of wine? Well, that would be nice."

"Sit down and I'll be right out."

"I really shouldn't."

He looked at me for guidance. I surrendered.

"Go ahead, Steve," I said. "Pull up a chair."

"I'll only stay for a quick glass of wine. No food."

"No," I said, possibly with a note of firmness. "Bring him some food, Mom."

"I'll heat a dinner up."

"Oh, please don't, Mrs. Schnabel," said Steve. "Just something cold is fine."

"Would you like some roast beef?"

"That would be lovely, thank you."

She went in, shooing Kevin in front of her.

"May I pull that over?" Steve said, pointing to another rocker on the other side of the doorway.

For some reason or a host of reasons I couldn't even answer him. And it didn't really matter anyway.

He went over, picked the chair up, brought it over and set it down across from us, but closer to my chair than Elektra's. The porch is not all that deep, and so his knees were only about a foot from mine.

The light that just a few minutes before had brightly colored the street had now fallen away. A silence fell, or was allowed to resume, but it was still rather windy out, so this was the silence of wet leaves hissing in the trees, of fallen leaves scudding along the street like flotsam in a river, and, from seemingly far away but only a few blocks away, the ocean endlessly crashing at the edge of the continent.

Then Steve started prattling again.

Twenty minutes later he had devoured a roast beef sandwich and downed a jelly glass of wine, all the while talking, although I've already forgotten about what, even though I am writing this the next afternoon. Evening had fallen, the street lamps had come on. It was just me and Elektra and Steve on the porch now.

"Well, I really should be going," Steve said, at last.

I just couldn't bring myself to say what I know you're supposed to say when someone says that, which is "No, stay", and neither did Elektra.

"Are you sure you two wouldn't like to have a drink with me at the VFW? I'm buying."

"Steve," said Elektra.

"Yes, darling."

"Lean closer."

She gave him a come-hither wiggle with her index finger.

Steve rose from his seat and leaned closer to Elektra, holding his cigarette up and away.

"Arnold and I want to go to bed," she said, quietly but distinctly.

Steve's mouth made an *O*, then his head snapped back and the *O* became a thin line.

He stood up.

"Can you ever forgive me?" he asked. At first he was facing Elektra but then he looked at me.

"Forgive me, Arnold."

"I forgive you, Steve."

"Okay, give me directions for that VFW place again."

"Steve," I said, "do you really want to get drunk all over again?"

He said nothing for a couple of moments, blinking in the twilight.

"But what else is there to do? This is my vacation."

"You could — take a walk?"

"Oh please."

"You could see a movie."

"Arnold, this is my *vacation*. *You* understand, Elektra, don't you?"

"Sure."

"You two are lucky. You have something to do besides drink. But who knows, maybe I'll get lucky."

"At the VFW?" I had to ask.

"Stranger things have happened, old boy."

"Be careful there, Steve."

"You mean don't get beat up?"

"Well, yeah."

"Arnold, for me getting beat up is an occupational hazard, so don't you worry."

He asked me again for the directions, I gave them again, and he went away, walking quickly.

"So that's your Jesus," said Elektra.

I hesitated, but now that she had brought the subject up I felt honor-bound to say something.

"I had a few more of those — hallucinations, today," I said.

"You mean you saw Jesus again?"

"Or something like him."

"Did he look like Steve?"

"A little," I said.

She looked at me. She had been smoking a cigarette, and now she stubbed it out in the ashtray.

"How would you like to go to my place now?" she said.

"I would like that," I said.

"I have to say good night and thank you to your family first," she said. "You stay here."

Steve had left his plate and wine glass on a tray on the table. Elektra filled the tray up with our cups and saucers and our empty wineglasses, and took them inside.

I sat and waited, smoking a cigarette. I could hear the theme music of *I'm Dickens, He's Fenster*.

The street became darker, the street lamps came on.

I finished my cigarette, and after a couple of minutes I lit up another one.

I didn't mind waiting. After forty-two years there was no hurry now.

Eventually Elektra came out. She got her purse off the table, took up her umbrella, put her arm in mine, and off we went.

We still had the whole evening ahead of us.

Chapter 36

It started to rain again as we walked up Perry Street. Elektra opened up her umbrella over both of us. I was having one "first" after another these days, and in my forty-two years this was the first time I had shared an umbrella with a woman who was not my mother. I took the umbrella, it seemed the gentlemanly thing to do, walking on the street side of the pavement, as I had somewhere heard the gentleman was supposed to.

I felt as if we were in our own private world under the umbrella, with her bare arm in mine, and I found this feeling strangely exciting, in nearly every way one can imagine being excited, including sexually.

Neither of us said a word as we walked; I can't account for Elektra but for me it felt redundant and meaningless to add anything to the sound of the rain drumming on the umbrella, the murmuring of the wind.

As we turned down the stone path to the side of her house I felt overcome by the wet beauty of the rose bushes, the ivy crawling up the side of the house, the glistening grass, the caramel smell and the touch of this woman who for her own reasons was choosing to share my baleful broken presence, and as we turned the corner to go into the rear entrance I couldn't control myself, and with my one free arm I embraced her and kissed her.

A minute later she said, "Whoa, tiger."

I had dropped the umbrella. It lay upside down on the ground, filling with rainwater. We were both streaming wet.

"I can't help it," I said.

"I don't want you to help it," she said.

"Should we go up now?"

"Yeah," she said.

Fortunately none of her friends seemed to be home, and we went right into her room.

She told me to stand still, and then she

(The next page of Arnold's copybook has unfortunately been torn out, probably by Arnold himself in one of his occasional retrospective acts of modesty or prudence. We continue mid-sentence with the next extant page. — Editor)

breathing heavily and slowly, and, I confess, coughing a bit. She laid her dark head in my damp armpit, and sure enough, after a minute I heard the steady childlike breathing of her sleeping.

I looked at the illuminated dial of my watch: it was after ten, which meant that we had been doing what we had been doing for approximately two hours. She seemed so sound asleep I decided to get up and go. Once again I found my clothes and put them on. They were damp, but I didn't care.

As I was pulling my Bermudas on she woke up and said, "You're going?"

"Yeah, I guess so," I said. "Unless you want me to stay."

"Your mother will worry, won't she?"

"I doubt it. She's probably in bed by now herself."

"You can go, Arnold. I'm exhausted and I want to sleep."

"Okay."

I felt it incumbent upon me to kiss her, so I leaned over and did so. She seemed to fall back to sleep even as I raised my face from hers.

I was lucky in leaving; her friends were still out.

I was also lucky in that the rain had stopped again, although it was still rather windy out.

I felt emptied of madness, I felt content, and wide awake. I had no idea why this woman was allowing me to make love to her. It didn't seem to me that I was any bargain.

I walked along, breathing in the rich air smelling of water and life, feeling as if my feet were barely touching the pavement, but just as I put my hand on the front gate of my aunts' house I thought of poor Steve at the VFW.

I hesitated.

He wasn't my problem, just some random lonely drunken queer fellow, but, don't ask me why, I felt sorry for him.

I thought I'd just walk down to the VFW anyway. If he was still there maybe I could get him to go back to the Chalfonte before he got in trouble. If he wasn't there I'd have a quiet beer and then go home and try to read some more of *The Waste Land* till I got sleepy, which, if that poem continued as it had been, would be after three or four lines.

The VFW is off the beaten track, and generally speaking only locals go there. I've stopped in there off and on over the years, although I've never officially joined the post. It's not really my cup of tea. I prefer the more touristy bars like the Ugly Mug, the Pilot House, Sid's, even the Top of the Marq. I suppose I prefer those places because I feel more anonymous in them. If I go into the VFW it's always the same locals I've seen there every other time I've been there on my yearly vacations, and unfortunately they know who I am, because my aunts are year-round residents and everyone in town knows them because everyone in Cape May knows everyone else.

Now why does this bother me, I wonder? Shouldn't I like it that everyone knows me? But no, I don't like it. If I must go into a bar, and apparently sometimes I must, I prefer to slip in quietly, the unknown quiet man quietly drinking his beer or Manhattan. The last thing I need is a bar full of hearty fellows clapping me on the back and asking me how it's going.

It took me a long time but eventually I've come to realize that I am not a regular guy. I can imitate one passably sometimes if I'm with casual strangers, but the more people know of me the more they know how hopelessly irregular I am.

Oh, sure, back home in Olney I would sometimes go with the other ushers to the Fern Rock Diner on Fifth Street after noon mass on Sundays, but the only ones that ever made any attempt to advance our ecclesiastical friendship tended to be even more hopeless and boring than myself. So I would drink my coffee and eat my fried mush and eggs and scrapple and go home.

Same thing in the army. Same thing on the railroad.

Same thing with the Catholic Youth Organization and the Community Service Corps, even those hotbeds of chaste Catholic bachelors: the only guys who wanted to be friendly with me were just the ones whose conversation made me (no Steve Allen or Jack Paar myself) want to run out screaming in the streets from the excruciating tedium of it all.

I digress, but after all this is my memoir and no one will ever read it anyway, probably not even its author.

I walked down the windy dark empty street, turned right at Congress, made my way up the block and crossed at Park Boulevard and came up on the lit-up small parking lot of the VFW post. It's just a plain one-story stuccoed building, dull and brown, it's windows made out of filmy glass bricks like ice cubes. I opened the door and went in. The first thing I heard was Steve's distinctive tenor, singing along to a song on the jukebox called "Be My Baby". And there he was in the middle of the crowded bar, waving a beer mug in time to the music.

Amazingly, it didn't look like anyone wanted to beat him up, at least not yet anyway.

I thought, *Okay, now I want to go,* but of course Steve saw me, stopped singing, and began waving energetically at me, calling out my name. Or rather calling out the name Arthur, which I suppose is close enough.

Chapter 37

Reluctantly but resignedly I walked over to where Steve sat. A quietly stunning girl who looked vaguely familiar sat on the stool to his right, a nice looking clean-cut guy sat to his left. On that guy's left was a local mechanic I know named Buddy Kelly, and on the other side of the girl was an older guy.

"Arthur! Come meet my friends!"

"Hi, Buddy," I said, to Buddy.

"Hiya, Arnold."

"Oh my God, I keep calling you Arthur," said Steve. "And I don't know why. Can I just keep calling you Arthur?"

"Yeah, why not," I said.

He introduced me to the others. The girl was named Daphne and the older man was introduced as Mac, her father. The other fellow was named Dick Ridpath.

Dick asked me if I would like a drink, and I said I'd take a beer. I started to reach into my pocket, but he insisted on buying. What the heck, I let him buy me a draft.

There weren't any empty stools nearby, and so I stood there sipping my beer. I tried not to stare goggle-eyed at this Daphne girl, who seemed a little young to be in a bar, but what the heck again, she was with her father.

The man Dick was movie star handsome, as was Mac, who was a sturdy man in his late forties I suppose. Both of them were also unusually well-spoken. Buddy on the other hand is a short troll-like kind of guy, but a genial enough fellow.

"I'm so glad you came!" said Steve. "Where's — um — Alexia?"

"Elektra," I said.

"Where is she? You should see her!" he said to all the others, swiveling his head and practically bouncing on his stool like a six-year-old. "She's *incredibly* beautiful. This lustrous dark hair, deep brown eyes, the most lovely olive complexion!"

"Steve," said the girl. She had a rather deep voice for such a young woman, she couldn't have been more than nineteen, and yet she seemed almost supernaturally self-possessed.

"Yes, sweetheart?" said Steve.

"Don't you know you should absolutely never extol the beauty of one woman in front of another woman?"

Steve clapped his hand to his mouth, and said something, but it was unintelligible.

"Take your hand away from your mouth, Steve," said Daphne, smiling slightly.

He did.

"I'm so terribly abashed," he said.

"I forgive you."

"But let me just say, darling Daphne, do you know how beautiful my friend Arthur's lady friend is?"

"No, how beautiful is she, Steve?"

"She's almost as beautiful as *you* are, darling Daphne."

"Now you're on the right track," she said. "Dick, buy Steve another beer."

Dick did this, and when the bartender laid the beer down Steve reached for it greedily.

The bar was packed. The storm had driven all the fishermen onto shore, and by the way they were shouting and drinking it looked like the fishing fleet wouldn't be going out again at first light, if at all.

There was one empty table and Dick suggested we move to it so we could all be more comfortable, although he obviously meant so that I could be more comfortable, since I was the only one standing.

A couple of minutes after we moved to the table Steve laid his head on his arms and fell asleep, while the rest of us chatted.

Dick was a lieutenant commander in the navy, and he seemed to be some sort of family friend to this Mac fellow, whose last name I eventually divined was MacNamara, and whose mother-in-law owned a house not far from my aunts' on Windsor Avenue. The girl Daphne was at Bryn Mawr College, and I slowly recognized her as a pretty but somewhat somber face I had seen around town in past summers, each year a little taller and a lot more — what's the word? Imperious? Or even like the way the Blessed Mother looks in some old pictures, beautiful and calm but somehow somewhat bored or even miffed about something.

Let's put it this way about my new companions: except for Buddy – and I had no idea what he was doing in such a group – these were people who not only had gone to college but who had gone to good colleges, people who read magazines like the *New Yorker* and *Holiday*, not the *Olney Times* or the *Catholic Standard and Times* or dare I say *True*.

But they were all friendly to me, and Dick asked me about myself.

I just didn't feel like going into it all, but I didn't want to lie, so I said I was on a disability leave from my brakeman job the railroad, leaving out the fact that the disability was entirely mental.

As I sat and chatted with these nice people that floating feeling I had felt on leaving Elektra slowly seeped away, and was replaced by a pleasant drowsiness.

I finished my beer and said I should be going.

I felt responsible for Steve, so I shook his arm, figuring I'd get him up and try to walk him home. At first he wouldn't wake up, but then a new song came on the jukebox and suddenly his head popped up and he began to sing in a loud falsetto voice:

> *Big girls don't cry*
> *Big girls don't cry*

Then he fell out of his chair and onto the floor.

"Oh dear," said Daphne.

"Well, I'd say Steve has had enough for one night," said Mac.

"Do you know where he's stopping, Arnold?" Dick asked me.

"Yeah," I said. "The Chalfonte."

"Give me a hand. My car's outside. You good people stay here and Arnold and I will get young Steve home."

Steve was very light, he felt like a straw man as Dick and I lifted him up and threw an arm over each of our backs and then frog-marched him out the door to the guffawing cheers and hoorahs of the fishermen and dockworkers at the bar and tables. Steve even moved his legs a little bit, like a marionette handled by a drunken puppeteer, and if he didn't exactly help us he didn't hinder us in his removal.

I expected Dick to have some fancy sports car but it turned out to be a Volkswagen, sitting there pale blue in the light of the parking lot. We deposited Steve in the back, and I got in the passenger seat and Dick got behind the wheel. We both rolled down our windows to let in the cool salty air.

"So, where is this alleged Chalfonte?" he said.

"Turn left out of the parking lot and I'll give you directions," I said.

He stuck the key into the ignition but instead of turning it he took a rumpled looking cigarette out of his shirt pocket.

"You wouldn't mind if I smoked a reefer, would you, Arnold?"

He had already brought a lighter out of his Bermuda shorts pocket.

"Uh, no," I said.

He lit it up, took a big drag, and held it in.

Without letting out the smoke he said, in only a slightly strained voice.

"Would you like some?"

"Okay," I said.

I took the reefer and took a drag. What the hell. Maybe it was normal nowadays for naval officers to smoke reefers. Maybe it always had been.

"I get just mildly intimidated around Mac," he said.

"Really?"

Dick didn't seem like the sort of guy who would be intimidated by anyone.

"Yeah," he said, at last letting out the lungful of smoke. "I'm madly in love with his daughter, for one thing."

"Daphne," I said, exhaling my own lungful.

"Right," he said, taking the reefer back from me.

He took another big draw, and then, handing the reefer back to me, he turned the ignition key, put the car in gear, and pulled out of the parking lot.

Dick silently drove down Congress. Neither of us said anything until we approached North Street.

"Turn left up here, Dick," I said, and he did.

I should mention that we continued passing the reefer back and forth as Dick drove.

"Thing is," he said, after a few more moments, and as though we had never interrupted our conversation, "I'm afraid she thinks I'm just some boring older guy, some quote unquote friend of the family."

"I doubt that," I said.

"Really?"

We were passing my aunts' house.

"Go right this corner," I said. "No, Dick, I think she likes you. Even I could tell that by the way she was looking at you. And I'm pretty unobservant."

"Well, thanks, buddy." He made the right turn on Perry. "It's Arnold, isn't it?"

"Right," I said.

"So, how do you like being a brakeman?"

"Well," I said, "go left up here, on Washington, by the way. I liked it okay, being a brakeman. It's all I've ever done really, except for when I was in the army. But now I don't feel like a brakeman any more."

"Really? What do you feel like?"

"I don't feel like anything," I said. "But I kind of like not feeling like anything."

"I think I know what you mean," said Dick. "Like, I never really felt like 'naval officer' defined me. Although I don't know what would."

"Just human being is enough I think," I said.

"Yeah," he said, after a pause.

As we went by the Ugly Mug we saw drunk people piling and tumbling out onto the street.

"I write poems," I ventured.

Dick turned and looked at me.

"*Really?*"

"I know," I said. "It's embarrassing."

"A brakeman poet."

"That's what they call me actually. Some years ago the *Philadelphia Bulletin* wrote an article about me, and they called me the Rhyming Brakeman. Because every week I publish a poem in the *Olney Times*."

"Don't think I've seen that paper."

"It's just my neighborhood weekly. I've published a poem a week in it every week since I was eighteen years old."

Of course I was very "stoned" on the "pot" or else I never would have been making all these humiliating confessions.

"That's great, Arnold. Y'know, I'm a lifelong Philadelphian myself, and I don't think I've ever even been in Olney, except maybe to go past it on the way to somewhere else."

"There's not much reason for anyone ever to go into Olney."

Dick took another pause here, knitting his brows.

"That's not *entirely* true, Arnold. I have a cousin who used to go up there to go to Zapf's music store."

"I stand corrected," I said. "Turn right on Howard here and it's just a few blocks to the Chalfonte. Where did you grow up, Dick?"

"Downtown. My family has a house at 19th and Panama."

Probably one of those nice old townhouses, with dark gables and towers and spiked black fences. But I can't say I envied Dick, and I don't know why.

We were quiet, and then then came the Chalfonte looming up on the left all large and white and dark-roofed.

Dick pulled up in front of the lobby entrance and turned off the motor. We had smoked the reefer down to a stub. Dick tapped it out with his fingertips, and then dropped it into his shirt pocket.

"Well, let's do this," he said.

"Right," I said.

It took a while, and Dick even gently slapped him once or twice, but then all at once Steve's eyes popped open, and he seemed very quickly to grasp the situation. I suppose he was used to this sort of thing.

"Well, here I am," he said. "Home sweet Chalfonte."

He managed, with our help, to get out of the car and to stand up on his own two feet.

"I can make it from here, guys, thanks."

But when we let go of his arms he wobbled a few steps forward, then stopped, swaying, and holding his arms outstretched to right and left like a tightrope walker.

"*Help,*" he said, in a quiet voice.

We rushed up and each grabbed an arm.

I'll spare myself a detailed description of the rake's progress that then ensued, but suffice it to say that Steve became intermittently resistant, with several attempted escapes, in between spells of complete collapse. Fortunately there was no one at the desk or in the lobby. It's that kind of an old-fashioned hotel. After approximately ten grueling minutes Dick and I at long last got him up the stairs to the second floor and into his room, which looked like a gang of burglars had just ransacked it looking for hidden jewels.

We got him into his bed, pulled his shoes off but otherwise left him dressed, and then we left the room and went back downstairs. On the way through the lobby Dick pointed to the right.

"Is that a bar down there?"

"Yeah," I said.

"Let's get a drink."

"Okay," I said.

So we went down the hall to the King Edward Room, which fortunately was still open.

Chapter 38

This was a Cape May bar into which the gods of drunkenness had never guided me before, and it was nice, as bars go, small and dark and quiet. No jukebox, no television, just the sound of talking from a small groups of people drinking at the bar and at some dark wooden tables.

Dick and I took stools at the bar and Dick said, "Y'know, after that ordeal I think I could use a Manhattan."

Ah, the sacred brotherhood of the Manhattan.

I knew I shouldn't but I let Dick order one for me. He explained nicely to the bartender that he didn't want a cherry but would the man please just cut a fresh bit of lemon peel, just the yellow part but not the white pith, and could he twist a bit of the lemon oil into the drink.

I told the bartender I'd try it that way too, even though I'd always had a cherry for a garnish the six thousand other times I had had a Manhattan.

As the bartender mixed our drinks we took out our respective coffin nails. Dick had his in an engraved metal case, of the kind that holds twenty cigarettes. He gave me a light with his lighter.

"So how long have you known old Steve?" he asked.

"Not long. I met him at the Ugly Mug a couple of nights ago," I said. "But it feels like a lot longer."

"He seems very fond of you."

"Yeah," I said.

"You do know he's shall we say homosexually inclined."

"Yeah," I said. "My lady friend told me."

"You couldn't tell?"

"I'm not very quick about these things," I said. "Or about a lot of things."

"Ah well," said Dick.

The bartender brought us our drinks, all deep ruby, glistening and beaded. We clicked our glasses and drank our magic potion.

Dick was silent, and so I decided to try to be a good conversationalist.

"So what do you do in the navy?" I asked.

Dick sighed. He tapped his cigarette into the ashtray, and then said, without looking at me, "I work in *matériel* allocation. Very boring. Shuffling papers."

"I understand," I said.

He looked at me.

"Really?"

"Sure," I said. "It's boring. You'll get a more interesting job someday."

Or not. What the heck did I know?

He looked away again. I seemed to have touched a sore spot. Oh well. Most men liked to talk about their boring jobs, but maybe Dick was different.

"If you don't mind my asking, Arnold," he asked, "what was your disability?"

"My disability?"

"You mentioned you were out on a disability. From your railroad job."

"Oh."

Now *he* had touched a sore point.

I decided not to lie. After all, anyone with eyes could tell that except for my occasional slight smoker's cough I was physically as healthy as an ox.

So I very briefly told him about going insane, the hospital, my failed attempt to go back to work, my mother bringing me down here.

"Well," he said. "You seem fairly recovered now."

A couple of women burst into shrieking peals of laughter down at the other end of the bar.

"I'm better," I said. Just saying what little I had said had worn me out, so I skipped the part about my visions of Jesus, and my occasional flights of what my doctors gently call disassociation.

"I'm sure you'll be able to get back to work soon," he said.

He was trying to be nice, and I should have left it alone I suppose. There's a reason people talk almost entirely in clichés. (In fact there's probably a whole host of reasons.) But instead I said, "Actually, I don't want to go back to work."

"No? Why not?"

"Well, one reason is: what if I lose my mind again on the job? God forbid I might cause a train accident."

"Good point."

"And I'm also afraid that just going back to work in itself might drive me permanently insane. For years I went to work every day and just accepted it as my fate. But now, the thought of it just — I don't know — all those years on the trains, all those hours, all those days —"

"I understand," said Dick.

"You do?"

"Sure. It sounds boring to me."

"It is!" I said.

"I don't know how people do it, work these absurd jobs all their lives. Not that being a brakeman is *absurd*," he hurried to add.

"No," I said. "A brakeman serves an important function," I murmured, halfheartedly.

"But just doing the same thing every day," he said. "Christ!"

"Yeah," I said. "But didn't you say your job was boring?"

"Oh, right, I did."

"So how do you cope?" I asked. I really wanted to know.

Dick finished his drink and motioned to the bartender for two more.

"Arnold, I can't lie to you. Actually my job is pretty interesting. The only thing is, it's classified. I just *tell* people I'm in *matériel* allocation."

"Oh. Classified."

"Yeah. I'm not supposed to talk about it. Strictly speaking I shouldn't even talk about how I'm not supposed to talk about it."

I finished my own drink.

So what is Dick's job, I wonder. Swashbuckling on the high seas. Meeting double agents in back alleys in exotic ports. Fine if you liked that sort of thing.

"So what would you like to do if you don't go back to work for the railroad?" he asked.

"You know, Dick, I've lain in bed at night trying to think of jobs which I wouldn't consider boring, which wouldn't suck the soul right out of me, and for the life of me I haven't thought of one yet. What I'm hoping is the Reading will forget all about me but keep sending me checks."

"I see."

"If not, I think I'll take my pension." This was the first time I'd talked to anyone about all this. "I have more than twenty years in, and my mother and I live very cheaply. We own our house back in Philly, and I even have savings invested in government bonds."

"You're awfully young just to retire, though," said Dick.

"But my days seem very full to me now," I said.

"Really? And how do you fill them?"

"Well, I read, and take walks. And every night I take a long swim. Plus I still write a poem every week."

"That's good."

"Not that they're good poems."

"But still."

"Also, it's a little embarrassing to say, but I'm writing my memoirs."

"Really? Life on the railroad?"

"No," I said, "And I don't know why, but so far I've written practically nothing about the railroad."

"So what do you write about?"

"I write about the things I do every day. The things I think. The things that happen to me."

Dick just looked at me. I think he was wondering just how crazy I still was, and now that I look over what I've just written, I can't say I blame him.

The bartender laid down two fresh sparkling cold ruby-red Manhattans.

"Oh, no," I said.

"Oh, yes," said Dick. "Come on, buddy, one more and we're gone."

"Okay," I said, "but I should go home after this."

"Sure."

We clicked our glasses and drank again.

"So, Arnold, tell me about this lady friend of yours."

Shamelessly I did so.

"She sounds great," said Dick.

"Yeah, I suppose so," I said.

"What's the matter?" he said.

"I just remembered I keep forgetting to ask her last name."

"Well, no matter."

"I've never had a girlfriend before, Dick. Don't you think that's odd?"

He paused, drawing his lower lip inward, then he sighed again and said, "Well, yes, technically I suppose it's odd. But I don't think it's anything to beat yourself up about."

Suddenly I realized that this couple sitting one stool away from Dick had heard what I'd just said, and Dick's response. I felt the fool, more so than usual that is.

I think Dick also realized that the couple had overheard us, and he read the abashment on my face.

He polished off his drink and said, "Hey, drink up and let's breeze."

As we were leaving the bar I realized that I had let Dick pay for all the drinks. But it was too late now. We went through the lobby, and out the doors, and then I felt myself floating down the porch steps instead of walking down them.

"Oh, Christ."

"What is it, Arnold?"

Dick was floating there beside me.

"Dick," I said.

Our feet were about two feet off the ground.

"Yes?"

"Do you notice anything funny right now."

"No. Do you?"

"Yes. Can't you see? We're floating in the air."

"I don't think so, Arnold."

"No?"

"No. You've just had a bit too much to drink." He put his hand on my shoulder. "Take a deep breath."

I did.

"Now let it out, slowly."

I did this, and as I exhaled I felt my feet returning to the earth, and Dick with me.

Dick's hand was still on my shoulder.

"Are you okay now? Feet on the ground?"

"Yeah," I said.

"Do you want to sit for a bit?"

"No," I said. "I think I should go home."

"You felt you were floating. In the air."

"Yes."

"I've had that feeling. Do you want a cigarette?"

He offered me one of his, a Chesterfield. I took it because it seemed like too much effort to extricate my own.

He lit us both up with his lighter.

"Although in my case," he said, "the floating has occurred only when I've taken LSD."

"What's that?" I asked.

"It's a drug. I first took it as part of some tests the, uh, government was conducting. I still like to take it sometimes."

"Why?"

"Well, it opens up a whole other world. I see things. I see things I wouldn't see normally, and I see them in a way I wouldn't normally see."

The street was quiet, except for the wind, the sound of the ocean, the hushing sound of the geraniums below the Chalfonte's porch.

"I see Jesus," I said. "Or rather I imagine I see him. I even thought Steve was Jesus."

Dick looked me in the eye.

"But you're okay now?"

The thing was I did feel okay, right then.

"Yeah," I said.

"Come on, I'll drive you home."

We got in his Volkswagen and drove quietly back to my aunts' house.

Before I got out Dick shook my hand and said, "Stop over at Daphne's grandmother's place tomorrow night. We're having a cook-out if it doesn't rain. Bring your lady friend."

I almost wanted to say "Why?" As in why would he want me to come to their cook-out?

"It's just a couple blocks down there on the corner of Windsor Avenue, big green house with a widow's walk, and turrets and steeples. 200 Windsor."

"I know the house," I said. "But I usually go swimming in the evening."

"Come after your swim. We'll be at it all night. Do you play croquet? Mac sets up these lights and we play croquet on the back lawn."

"Well —"

"Or badminton."

Yep, that was two games I'd never played.

"Don't be a stick in the mud, Arnold."

I wanted to say I'd "try" to make it, but that seemed absurd. It wasn't as if I had a demanding social schedule laid out for the next day without a minute's free time.

"Tell ya what, Arnold," he said, gently. "Stop by if you feel like it. I'd like to have you there. I so rarely meet someone I can talk to."

I said okay and good night, got out, closed the car door, and Dick took off down the street.

And I thought *I* was strange.

Chapter 39

I went right up, tiptoeing so as not to arouse family or boarders.

I did stop in the bathroom on the third floor, to pee, and to brush my teeth.

When I came out though I saw a woman standing right outside the door. She wore a long pale gown, and in the 25-watt light of the wall sconce outside the bathroom her long hair gleamed like dark gold.

My immediate thought was, *"Oh, great, now it's the Blessed Mother, this is all I need."*

And I was ready to walk right past her or through her without a word, but she said, "Hello."

"Hello," I said.

"You're Arnold, aren't you."

"Yes," I said, trying not to sigh.

The whole Holy Family had it in for me, or so it seemed. And where was Joseph?

"I'm Gertrude."

This took me aback.

And then it occurred to me that this was actually an ordinary mortal woman. (Although as it turned out I was wrong in this assessment.)

"Oh, hi," I said.

"I just took the apartment down the hall today. It looks like we share this bathroom."

"Uh, yes," I said, the soul of wit. "Um," I added, for good measure.

"Your aunt told me you write poetry."

"Yes," I admitted.

"I'd like to read some of your poems."

"You say that now," I said.

"I'm a writer myself."

"Oh really."

"Gertrude Evans?"

"Yes?"

I confess I felt awkward. I had never spoken to a woman wearing a nightgown in a dimly lit hallway before. Excepting my mother of course.

"I thought perhaps you might have heard of me. Gertrude Evans. I've published two novels."

"Unless they're mysteries I doubt I would have heard of them, I'm afraid," I said.

"But you're a poet. You must read poetry."

"Well —" I said.

"Who's your favorite poet?"

I said the name of the first one that came to my mind, even though I'd only read a couple of pages of his poem and hadn't understood any of it:

"T. S. Eliot."

"I love Eliot."

Now that I thought about it, she really didn't look anything at all like the Blessed Mother. Not that I knew what the Blessed Mother looked like.

"Well —" I said, but then I couldn't think of anything else to say. To tell the truth I wanted just to go up to my little attic and go to bed, but she was standing in my way in the narrow hallway.

"I've come here to get away and try to finish up my latest book," she said.

"Well, good luck," I said.

"You're shy, aren't you?" she said.

"Yes," I said.

"You shouldn't be. Your other aunt told me you had a nervous breakdown."

"Uh, yeah, sort of," I said.

"So how are you now?"

"Better, thanks."

Especially now that I was pretty sure she wasn't the Blessed Mother.

"I had to be hospitalized once myself. Well, not exactly hospitalized. I signed myself into a rest home for a month. It was my present to myself for finishing my second novel. I'm really hurt that you haven't heard of me, Arnold."

"Don't feel bad," I said. "I haven't heard of practically anyone."

"But still. And your other other aunt told me you have a lady friend?"

"Yes, I suppose so."

"Your mother told me she's very pretty. Are you going to marry her?"

"I've only known her for about a week," I said.

"I have to use the bathroom, but would you wait out here a minute?"

What an odd request, but I have never known how to say no to a woman, so I said okay.

She went in, and I walked the few steps down the hall to stand by the window. I lighted up a cigarette, exhaling the smoke through the screen out into the night air. I had no idea what this woman wanted. I suppose I should mention here that she was an attractive woman, in the physical sense.

Eventually I heard the toilet flush, with its usual cacophony of a truckload of kitchen appliances dumped down a deep dark pit, and in due course Gertrude Evans came out. She motioned to me, beckoning with her upturned index finger. I came forward.

"Wait here," she said. "I want to give you something."

She went down the hall to the door of the apartment on the right, opened it and went in, leaving the door open. A minute passed. My cigarette had burned down, and I went into the bathroom and dropped the butt into the toilet. I wanted to flush it, but I knew this toilet, it wouldn't be flushable for at least another two minutes, so I left the butt there and went back out into the hallway and waited.

I did my best to stay sane as two more minutes passed, and then this Gertrude came out of her room. She had a book, a thick hardback. She handed it to me.

"Here," she said. "This is my first novel. I inscribed it for you."

"Thanks," I said.

"You don't have to read it right away. And you don't have to say you like it if you don't. But now you'll have to show me your poems."

"Right now?"

"Tomorrow."

"Well, okay. But really they're not very good. It's just a hobby of mine."

"But your mother told me you get your poems published."

"Yes, but only in our neighborhood paper, the *Olney Times*."

"You've been drinking, haven't you?"

"Yes," I said.

"With your lady friend?"

"Well, not most recently," I said.

"You're a very mysterious man. I like you. Good night, Arnold."

She put out her hand like a man. I took it and we shook hands like men. Except her hand didn't feel like a man's. It was small and soft and to my embarrassment I felt a tingle of concupiscence in my organ of at least prospective procreation.

I mumbled good night, turned and went back down the hall and up to my attic room.

I got undressed and I knelt down by my bed, something I hadn't bothered doing in a week. And then after crossing myself I remembered why I hadn't been saying my prayers. If there was a God I doubted he wanted to hear my supplications and prevarications, especially after having had sinful and perhaps perverted relations with a woman only a couple of hours before. So I crossed myself again, just to cover my bases, and got into bed. I had the bedside light still on. This Gertrude woman's book was on the night table. I examined it for the first time. It was titled *Ye Cannot Quench*. By Gertrude Evans. The dust jacket drawing showed a young woman in a nightdress not unlike the one Miss Evans herself had just been wearing. She lay in a bed, with one leg up, the nightdress had slid down, exposing the leg. The girl in the drawing was smoking a cigarette and looking out the window at what looked much like the Heintz factory from my own window back in Olney.

I opened up the book, and on the first page she had written, "To Arnold, mon semblable, mon frère! Best wishes, Gertrude Evans".

I skipped to the inside back cover, where there was a black and white picture of Miss Evans. She seemed to be looking right at me.

I closed the book and pulled the chain on the light.

This had been a very long day, and all I really wanted to do now was sleep, but too many thoughts were milling about inside my head. I almost wished I had one of those awful deadening sleeping pills that the doctors used to give me. But then I remembered I had something better than a sleeping pill. I picked up *The Waste Land*, read a dozen or so very beautiful if incomprehensible lines, and sure enough I soon was fast asleep, lulled by the whishing sound of the leaves of that old oak tree outside my window and by the enormous and never-ending shushing of the ocean.

Chapter 40

I awoke with a slight hangover. That second Manhattan. Someday I'll learn.

I lay in bed for a while, thinking it all over. Fresh warm sunlight swam through the leaves of the oak tree outside and dappled through my little casement window, casting shadows like the reflections of the ocean over my bed.

What did it mean, all these new people in my life?

After a few minutes of pondering this I saw the basic fallacy of such a question. I remembered what Elektra had told me, that all the thousands of religions of mankind had only been invented so that people could try to make some sense out of the randomness of life. But who said anything had to mean anything more than just what it was? Well, of course lots of people said just that. But what did they know? They all had conflicting theories anyway, and since they couldn't all be right, maybe they were all of them wrong.

But on an even deeper level, why was I asking myself of all people such a question, as if I could possibly know the answer. Who was I, Bishop Sheen? Dr. Albert Schweitzer?

And so thus concluding that there was no possible way I could make any sense out of this influx of new people into my little world, and I wouldn't trust myself for one second even if I did come up with some cockamamie theory, I relaxed back into my pillow, breathed in the morning air smelling of warm wet flowers, and then at last tossed aside my sheet and swung my legs out of bed.

But wait.

It did all mean something.

It meant that I now might actually have to deal with other people instead of just staying holed up as usual in my head and in my little protective family unit.

I confess I sat there in my boxer shorts and entertained some overwhelming thoughts. For instance I realized that I had managed to live forty-two years without making any close friends, and without even once reaching a first-name basis with a woman whom I was not related to by blood. When I looked at these bald facts clearly in this warm morning light I realized that I must always have been, if not completely insane, then definitely weird.

It's not as if I had lived the life of a hermit. I had a job, I was active in parish activities. I coached the CYO boxing team. I stopped in various of the neighborhood taverns, admittedly rotating my visits so as not to be even a weekly communicant at any given one. And although it's true that Olney does seem to boast an enormous population of quiet bachelors such as myself who still live in their parents' homes, I made no friends even with any of this celibate army. There had always been an invisible wall between me and all these other people I came up against every day. And the final proof of my weirdness was that I somehow never thought myself weird. Because in truth I never met any fellows that I really wanted to be friends with, while women seemed to me like creatures from another planet.

Perhaps my losing my mind last January was simply the ultimate efflorescence of this lifelong oddness. And could it be that my meeting Elektra and her friends, and Steve, and now Dick Ridpath and his friends, and even this Gertrude Evans – could it be that all these new people in my life were proof that I had left my old zombie life behind for something slightly more human?

If only I could stop having these visions of Jesus.

If only I would stop floating two feet off the ground at random moments.

Oh, well, you can't have everything in this life, that much I knew.

I blinked myself out of this reverie, and the first thing I noticed was that book by Miss Evans, *Ye Cannot Quench*, sitting on my bedside table. I picked it up and flipped through it. I guiltily realized I hadn't even read a line of it the night before.

I turned to the first page of the novel.

A young girl named Emily gets off a bus at the Port Authority Terminal in New York City. There is quite a bit of description of her walking out of the terminal and to Times Square. All the teeming crowds of people and the soaring tall buildings and the honking traffic. She goes into a coffee shop and orders a coffee. An old lady starts talking to her. The old lady's name is Martha, and she's a rag-and-bones merchant. She tells Emily that she, Emily, will find her fortune, and love, in New York City.

This last bit gave me pause. How could this old rag-and-bones woman be expected to know whether this random girl would find her fortune and love in New York or not? If she was that prescient, why was she selling rags and bones for a living? You'd think she'd at least get a job in a carnival or something.

But this silly girl Emily picks up her bags and walks back out onto the street actually wondering if it was true what the old woman said.

Oh well, maybe this was why I preferred mysteries. They were definitely less frustrating than these literary sorts of books.

I got dressed and went downstairs to get some breakfast, bringing Miss Evans's book with me, and as usual my built-in clock was unerring; my mother was just laying out breakfast for me and Kevin.

I sat down to my pancakes.

My mother sat next to me and sipped some coffee.

My aunts were all elsewhere, doing their little duties.

Kevin was reading an old *Brain Boy* comic.

I opened up *Ye Cannot Quench* again. I had to be able to tell Miss Evans something about it when I saw her again.

"Elektra is very nice," said my mother.

"She's pretty," said Kevin.

"Yeah," I said, "she's nice."

My mother didn't say anything more, although I'm sure she would have liked to. I went back to my pancakes and to *Ye Cannot Quench*.

Some days it would seem there is no need to go to the world, the world will come to you.

So it was this day.

After breakfast I sat out on the porch with my cup of coffee and book. Kevin of course came out as well, and we both sat and read, he his comic books, I Miss Evans's novel.

In short order Emily finds a room in a small women's residency hotel and starts a job at a publishing company. The publisher's son is named Julian Smythe and he seems a bit of a rake. His description made him sound to me like a dead ringer for Rock Hudson. One of the other girls in the office invites Emily to a bar after her first day of work, and they sit next to an intense looking young man writing intently in a notebook. Emily's friend strikes up a conversation with him by asking him for a light. It turns out he's a poet named Porter Walker. He works as a cab driver to support himself while he writes an epic poem about the city of New York. His description reminded me of the young Montgomery Clift.

I closed the book over my finger. So, who was it to be, Rock Hudson or Montgomery Clift in the end? It was hard to tell at this point.

Then Miss Gertrude Evans herself came walking around the side of the house. She carried a folded canvas beach chair, a big canvas carry-bag with towels in it and who knows what else.

She was wearing a black one-piece bathing suit, with a long sleeved white shirt like a man's shirt over it, but the shirt wasn't buttoned.

"Hello, Arnold," she said, through the side railing.

Oh, she also had a big straw hat on and she wore sunglasses.

In the sunlight her hair was much lighter than it had been in the dim hallway the night before, and microscopic gold sparkles rippled through it as the warm breeze touched it.

She took off her sunglasses. Her eyes were bright green in the shade of her hat.

"Is that my book?"

"Yes," I said.

"Do you hate it?"

Hate is a strong word, and so I didn't precisely have to lie.

"No," I said.

"Good. I'm going down to the beach."

"Have fun," I said.

"Hello, Kevin," she said across me.

"Hello," said Kevin.

Apparently they'd already been introduced.

"And what are you reading, young man?"

"*Brain Boy.*"

"Is it any good?"

"It's okay."

"Are you the *Brain Boy*?"

"No."

Now she did an odd thing, she reached through the side porch rails and touched my bare leg with her sunglasses. (As usual I was wearing Bermudas.)

"Don't you go to the beach, Arnold?"

"I don't like it during the day," I said.

Her hand and the sunglasses retreated back across the porch floor and out of the railing.

"I hope to do some writing on the beach," she said. "I have this strange ability to write among crowds. It's as if I draw energy from all the humanity surrounding me."

Here's the awful thing. Even as she said this I felt a stirring down below. It was because she was wearing a bathing suit. I can barely hold a conversation with a fully-clothed woman. If she's only wearing a low-cut bathing suit I can pretty much forget about sparkling repartee.

Fortunately I had her book still in my hand, so I held it open over my recalcitrant lap.

What would Porter Walker — the Montgomery Clift poet — say?

She stood there seeming to await some response.

"The energy of humanity feeds my own poems," I said. "Just as the sun and the rain nourish my aunts' garden here. My poems are like flowers. All I can do is to tend them, to try to let them grow in the most beautiful fashion possible."

She stared at me, and then put her sunglasses on.

"I hope to see you later, Arnold," she said.

She then went around the porch to the front, down the bluestone path to the gate, out through the gate and down toward Perry Street and the beach. She left the gate unlatched.

Kevin and I watched her walk away in the sunlight, carrying her chair and her big canvas bag.

When she was out of earshot Kevin said, "What was that crap about flowers all about?"

"Sorry," I said.

"Don't worry, she bought it. I'm only a kid and I could tell that. Ladies love you, Cousin Arnold."

I ignored this last remark and went back to Miss Evans's novel.

The Montgomery Clift poet guy asks Emily for her phone number, and she gives it to him.

Chapter 41

One night at her women's residence hotel Emily gets called to the phone in the corridor. It's Porter Walker, the poet. He asks her if she would like to go out and dig some jazz with him the next night. She says okay.

But the next day at work the young publisher Julian Smythe (the Rock Hudson guy) stops by her desk and asks her if she likes to read. She says yes, and that she was an English major back at the University of West Virginia, graduating *summa cum laude*, and in fact she's had a short story published already in the *West Virginia Quarterly*. Good, he says, and he lays a massive typescript on her desk and asks her to read it for him and hand in a report.

The book she has to read is none other than the first volume of Porter Walker's epic poem of New York, titled *The Brawny Embraces*.

I decided to take a break, and I checked the back cover of Miss Evans's book and read the critics' raves.

"A stunning achievement."

"An important new voice."

"Not just a great new woman novelist, but a great novelist full-stop."

"A bemusing amalgam of Virginia Woolf, Dawn Powell, and Emily Brontë, with just a healthy soupçon *of Edna Ferber."*

Oh well. I went back to where I had left off, and next up there was a long transcription of the opening of Porter's poem:

Off the docks I leapt, salty seabag in hand, and I breathed
that sour thick greasy dirty and glorious smell
of the City, the smell of sewage and sweat, of blood
and despair, of longing and defeat, but also of joy
and Seagram's 7, of moldy paperbacks read by candlelight
in cold water flats, and of drunken young girls
with laughter the color of gasoline in a cobble-stoned
gutter. Farewell to the sea! Farewell to my farting
coarse shipmates, to your boring endless stories repeated
endlessly and to your unfunny jokes! Hello, Metropolis!
Accept your returning sailor to your redolent bosom
and let him drink deep of your warm milk!

There was a page or two more of the poem, and I confess I skimmed it.

I have to confess also that if I'm honest with myself I know that most of my own poetry is just as absurd as Porter's, except that my stuff always rhymes and my poems are always short. But what I didn't know was whether Porter's poem was supposed to be bad or not. Emily didn't seem to mind it. But maybe Emily was supposed to be an idiot.

Dostoyevsky wrote a novel about an idiot {which I tried to read once but couldn't finish — *Marginal interpolation in Schnabel's holograph.* — *Editor*}, so this wouldn't be the first time this sort of thing had been done.

Anyway, Porter comes and picks up Emily after she gets off work, and Emily feels an electricity from Porter's intense eyes, and her palms inside her white gloves start to perspire, but right then who should come walking up North Street from the right but Dick and Daphne.

At first I felt shy about calling hello. I'm just not the calling hello type. But as it happened Dick saw me and waved.

"How's it going, Arnold?"

"Okay," I called back.

They weren't dressed for the beach; so I noticed with my eagle eye. Nevertheless they both looked magnificent, wearing almost matching outfits of white shorts and polo shirts, a pink one on Daphne and pale blue on Dick.

"Who's your young friend, Arnold?" asked Daphne.

"Kevin," called Kevin. He does seem to like the ladies. Oddly so for a ten year old, or however old he is.

"Are you Arnold's son?" asked Daphne.

"No," said Kevin. "He's my cousin."

"My name is Daphne. This big lunk is Dick."

"Hello," said Kevin.

"Hello, young fella," called Dick. "Arnold, you *are* coming to the cook-out tonight, aren't you?"

"Maybe," I said.

"Oh, please come, Arnold," said Daphne. "And bring Kevin."

"I want to go to a cook-out," said Kevin.

Sometimes it's best just to abruptly change the subject, so I said, "Where are you two headed?"

"Dick's taking me to Frank's Playland."

"I want to go!" said Kevin.

"Come with us," said Daphne.

Kevin looked at me.

"Can I go, Cousin Arnold?"

Why was he asking my permission? But then his parents had left him here, so I suppose I was in charge of him almost as much as my aunts or mother were. When I was his age I just would have gone off without asking permission of anyone. I suppose things are different now. (Or maybe he's not quite ten years of age. Maybe he's only eight years old.)

"Sure, go," I said.

Sotto voce he said, "I need some money."

I reached into my pocket, dragged a dollar bill out of my wallet and put it in Kevin's outstretched greedy little paw.

"Come with us, Arnold!" called Daphne.

"No, thanks," I called back, feeling more awkward than usual to be having this shouting conversation back and forth from the sidewalk across the lawn and garden to the porch. I told them I still had to take a shower and shave, which was true enough, but not the real reason I didn't want to go, which was that I had not the least desire to go to Frank's Playland, and that if anything I had a desire not to go there. Kevin of course didn't care less whether I came along or not, and after shoving my dollar bill into the pocket of his shorts he bolted down and joined Dick and Daphne. After a round of see-you-laters, the three of them walked away, Daphne holding Kevin's hand.

I picked up Miss Evans's book again, and Emily and Porter were walking down the city street, it was a warm summer evening, and her palms got even sweatier, so she takes off her gloves and puts them in her purse. She feels Porter's male vibrations emanating from his lithe body. Then all at once I realized that I was letting my young charge go off with a couple of people I had only met the night before.

How tiresome this all was.

I could see Dick and Daphne and Kevin walking past the house down at the corner of North and Perry. I put my book down and went quickly off the porch and down to the sidewalk. I caught up with them right before the corner of Washington Street.

"Arnold," said Dick, "I thought you were going to take a shower."

"I changed my mind," I said.

"He's afraid we'll lose young Kevin," said Daphne.

She was was still holding his hand, or vice versa. The little lecher was in seventh heaven.

So we walked up to the boardwalk and Frank's Playland. I hadn't been in Frank's in I don't know how many years. After I had been on the railroad for a couple years and we had some money I would go with our little family to

Cape May on the train for weekend getaways. As the only surviving man of the household I would take my brothers and sister to Frank's. I remember enjoying it all: the skee-ball; the pinball machines; those glass boxes which took your money so that you could desperately try to grasp and extricate some cheap toy or doll with a horrible mechanical claw; the fortune-telling machines; the peep boxes. The counter in the back, overlooking the beach and the ocean, where you could buy cotton candy and Cokes and hot dogs.

Nothing much had changed, except there were a few newer pinball machines, and some electric rifle- and machine-gun-shooting machines I didn't remember from the old days.

And presiding over it all was the all-powerful short and squat Frank himself, with his change dispenser and his roll of precious coupons and his wet cigar.

And here he was still, older but as formidable and as frightening as ever.

What little youth I had once had now seemed farther away than ever.

I used to find this place amusing, indeed I had looked forward to coming here.

Now I found it all rather frightening.

All these wild-eyed children yapping.

I felt like a ghost wandering through a carnival swarming with mad midgets.

I'll say this, Daphne and Kevin seemed to be having a jolly good time. Dick on the other hand seemed to be just along for the ride, like me, although seemingly less painfully so.

Under duress, I joined in a game of skee-ball. But I felt like I was tossing handfuls of my soul away, down into that little black hole.

It all started to get to me after a while, the noise of the machines, the kids shrieking and babbling, the parents telling the kids to shut up and behave. The smells of suntan lotion and boiling grease.

At one point Frank stared straight at me. I realized that I was standing there alone, and that Dick, Daphne and Kevin were twenty or thirty feet away, gathered around a new jet fighter machine.

I decided to go outside for a smoke.

After the tempest of the previous day the sun was out in full force now, beating down on the boardwalk and the vacationers walking distractedly back and forth, blazing all over the beach and the hordes of half-naked broiling people swarming around on it. The ocean glistened and flashed, indifferent to all this madness.

I was standing there holding my unlit cigarette when all of a sudden Dick was beside me.

He gave me a light.

"You're a good guy, Arnold."

"Really?"

"Yeah. This is agonizing for you, but you're putting up with it for Kevin's sake."

"It was only guilt that made me come, Dick."

"You're still a good guy."

{The next five lines of Arnold's holograph are rigorously crossed out. — Editor}

Then we both ran out of things to say. We finished our cigarettes and stubbed them out into the cracks in the boardwalk. I wondered if I should say something, but I drew a blank in that blazing sun and heat. Then it was over, Daphne and Kevin came out, they'd had their fill.

"Heading back to the house?" Dick asked me.

"Oh yes," I said.

"We're going back too. Big canasta game. Want to play?"

"No thanks," I said.

We strolled back, Dick and I walking in front. Daphne and Kevin walked hand in hand behind us, chatting away about something or other. Dick and I were silent.

At our gate Dick took my hand.

"Hope to see you tonight, Arnold. Bring your girlfriend."

"Okay, I said. "I'll come."

"I want to come," said Kevin.

"No, Kevin," I said, "I'm not going until late, after my swim."

"Jeepers."

Jeepers?

"You can come over some other time, Kevin," said Daphne. "You and I can play."

"Neat. Can we throw rocks?"

"Sure we can throw rocks."

Sometimes I really don't know if Kevin is abnormal or not. But who am I to judge?

Daphne kissed him on the forehead.

He made a little jump.

"Kiss me again!" he yelped.

She kissed him on the forehead again while Dick and I watched. This kid was making out like a bandit.

Dick and Daphne walked off down shady North Street, and Kevin and I went through the gate and up to the porch.

Kevin immediately sat in his usual rocker and began to read *Brain Boy* again.

I went upstairs at long last to take my shower and to shave.

Chapter 42

It was now time for me to do my daily writing.

Ever since the weather started getting really hot I've taken to writing either on the porch or in the back yard, depending on who was around and likely most to disturb my lofty ruminations; Sometimes I go to the coffee shop or to the library.

I figured Kevin was probably still on the front porch re-reading his latest batch of comics for the twentieth time, so I took my notebook and my pen and went downstairs, out through the side door and to the back of the house, where the coast was fairly clear, only Miss Rathbone at her easel, painting the little cottage. That is she was painting a picture of the little cottage, not painting the cottage itself. She and her mother have taken the little red cottage in the back for the month. I said hello to her and ensconced myself at the grillwork iron table under the shade of the oak tree, the one the hammock's hung on.

I still had to write this poem for Elektra. But after staring at my poetry notebook for about five seconds I knew I wasn't ready yet. This is the way it is for me with my poems. I can write one every week, but I have little control over what I'm going to write about. So instead I had the idea to write a poem about my recent conversations with Jesus {*See Arnold's poem "My Invisible Friend" in the Appendix. — Editor*}.

And so I did.

"I've been watching you, Arnold."

This was Miss Rathbone.

I'd just finished the poem, after my usual method of writing and furiously rewriting, tossing crumpled notebook pages aside so it looked like a summer snow had fallen all around me, and smoking most of a pack of Pall Malls in the hour-and-a-half I'd been working.

I turned and looked up at her, standing a few feet to my left.

"I've never seen anyone so concentrated on their work."

"Yeah, well, someone's gotta do it," I said, closing my notebook. I have no idea why I said this, by the way.

"Were you writing one of your poems?"

"Uh, yeah," I said.

"May I read it?"

"Okay," I said.

I long ago gave up being shy about my bad poetry. People tend to be impressed or at least to act impressed by the mere fact that I write poems at all and publish them, even if it is only in the *Olney Times*. Miss Rathbone stood there and read the poem, and then she apparently read it again a few more times. In the meantime, because I don't like to be a litterbug, I got up and picked up all my crumpled notebook pages from the grass, then I sat down again, smoothed the pages out, shoved them back into my notebook, and waited for this present social interaction to play itself out.

I have been a bad memoirist I notice. I haven't described Miss Rathbone. The problem is, I already know what she looks like, and since no one will ever read this rubbish anyway, why do I have to describe her? But for what it's worth, she's slender and distinguished looking, I guess she's forty or so, maybe thirty-five, very well-spoken. She teaches art at a girl's school called the Shipley School. She wore a sort of smock, pink, and all decorated with tiny paint splotches. Her legs were long and bare under it, and she was barefoot. She wore a very broad pink straw hat with a red ribbon around it. I shall now resume my narrative.

"This is really quite a beautiful poem," she said, handing me back my notebook.

"Thanks, Miss Rathbone." It occurred to me that I hadn't stood up when she first came over to me. And usually I'm so polite that way. So now I half-stood and gestured to one of the other grillwork metal chairs. "Would you like to sit?"

"Well, just for a moment. I should get back to my painting before I lose the light."

I thought, *the sun is still blazing away up there*, but what did I know?

She sat down across from me and removed her hat. She has long light brown hair, and at this moment it was tied up in a round bun at the top of her head. I offered her a cigarette, but she preferred her own, pastel pink Vogues. I gave her a light.

"I'm told you publish your poems in your neighborhood weekly."

"Yes," I said. "The *Olney Times*."

"Have you ever tried to publish your poems anywhere besides the *Olney Times*, Arnold?"

"No," I said.

Come to think of it her fingernails were pink, too.

"I think you should try to get your poems published in book form."

"You're kidding."

"No, I'm absolutely serious."

"But most of my poems are really bad," I said. "Even I know that."

"I can't believe that. Not after the poem I've just read."

"Well, that one might not be too bad," I said, and I remembered what my friend Jesus had said. "I think maybe they've gotten a little better, uh, in recent, er –"

"Since you had your breakdown."

"Yes," I said.

Even though she and I had barely ever spoken to each other I was not surprised that she knew about my breakdown, and the reason for this is that my mother and my aunts, with particular emphasis on Aunt Greta, are incapable of meeting any other female and not telling them at once my entire life story.

"May I read some more of your poems?"

"Sure."

"I would like that very much."

"Okay."

"You'll get them to me today?"

"Sure," I said. "Well, I guess I'll be going now."

"Where to?"

"I'm hungry."

I stood up.

"I could make you something."

"But don't you have to paint?"

"Oh bother my painting."

"But what about the light?"

"I could take five minutes to make you a sandwich. I should make Mother something anyway," she said, gesturing with her head behind her.

I hadn't consciously noticed her before but old Mrs. Rathbone was now sitting across the yard reading at the umbrella-table in front of the cottage. The old lady must have very acute hearing, as it seems most of the women around here do, because she called across, "Nonsense, Charlotte, I'll make Arnold a sandwich."

All of a sudden she was up and limping with her cane across the yard toward us. Surprisingly quickly she was standing in front of me. Another little old woman, my life was filled with them.

"What would you like to eat, Arnold?" this one said.

"Um, liverwurst?"

"I don't think we have liverwurst."

"Uh, ham?"

"How about bacon, lettuce and tomato?"

"That'll do," I said.

"What will you drink?"

"Iced tea?"

"What about a nice Sawn Sair?"

"Well, I don't know what that is, but sure."

"Okay. Anything for you, Charlotte?"

"Just some Sawn Sair for me, Mother."

"You never eat, girl."

"And I'm not about to start now, Mother."

"All right. One bacon, lettuce and tomato, and I'll bring out the Sawn Sair."

"You should eat something, Mother," said Miss Rathbone.

"I'll have half a rasher of bacon. Sit down, Arnold, I won't be a jiffy."

I started to sit, but Miss Rathbone said, "Wait, don't sit, Arnold."

I stood straight again.

"Let the poor man sit," said Mrs. Rathbone.

"I want him to bring me his poems, Mother."

"Oh, well, in that case," she said. "I've heard you write poetry, Arnold."

"Yes," I said.

"And what's this about you squiring about this attractive young Jewess?"

So they knew about Elektra, and had probably heard all about last night's dinner.

"Um," I said.

"Mother," said Miss Rathbone.

"What?" said Mrs. Rathbone.

"Don't grill Arnold about his private life."

"I wasn't grilling him."

"Hobble along and make his sandwich, Mother."

"Do you see, Arnold?" said Mrs. Rathbone.

"Uh, what?" I said.

"How she treats me?"

"Oh," I said. "Uh —"

"Don't forget the Sawn Sair, mother," said Miss Rathbone.

"My daughter likes you, Arnold," said the old lady. "That little Jewish wench of yours had better watch her step."

I smiled, probably pathetically, and at last Mrs. Rathbone turned and started back to the cottage.

After her mother had gotten safely through the screen door Miss Rathbone said, "Sorry about that. She's a little bit cuckoo you might have noticed."

"Oh, she's nice," I said.

"She is a great millstone round my neck and always has been, but somehow I've never quite been able to extricate myself from her. Not that I don't love her desperately, in my way. How do you do it, living with your mother?"

"It's all I've ever done," I said. "Except when I was in the army."

She ground out her pink Vogue in the scuffed tin ashtray that was already overflowing with my Pall Mall butts.

"My time in the WACs during the war was the happiest time of my life," she said. "Loved every minute of it. How did you like the army?"

"Not much," I said. "I hated it, actually."

"Best years of my life," she said. "Well, why don't you go get those poems?"

"Okay," I said.

I took my notebook and pen and went back to the house.

It seems that every day I realize more and more clearly that I am absolutely not the only insane person around here.

Chapter 43

I went back up to my attic room and got my latest scrapbook of poems. I can't remember if I've mentioned it before but I put cuttings of my poems from the *Olney Times* into these big scrapbooks that I buy at the 5&10. *{In fact Arnold has mentioned this before, in Chapter 32. — Editor}* I stood at my table and flipped through the book. It was true, my post-breakdown poems were perhaps less bad than the others, although one or two of the poems immediately preceding the complete loss of my marbles were not too bad either.

I headed downstairs and once again I ran into Gertrude Evans on the third floor. This time she was coming out of the bathroom. She was wet, and wearing a white fluffy bathrobe, carrying a white towel and some bottles and jars of toiletries, another white towel wrapped around her head. Fresh from the shower as she was her lips nonetheless were bright blood-red with lipstick.

"Oh. Arnold," she said.

"Hello, Miss Evans," I said.

"Call me Gertrude."

"Okay," I said.

"But please don't call me Gertie."

"Okay."

"Or Trudy."

"All right."

"What's that, a photo album?"

"No," I said. "It's a scrapbook of my poems."

"Oh, I want to read them."

"Well —"

"What? Don't you want me to?"

"It's not that," I said. "But Miss Rathbone just asked me if she could read them."

"Oh. Miss Rathbone. The painter."

"Yes."

"I wouldn't have thought she was your type, Arnold. And does your girlfriend know about her?"

"No," I said.

"You're such a rogue, aren't you? Let me see. Take these bottles and let me take a look at these *poems* of yours."

Awkwardly we performed a hand-off, me taking her bottles and jars of creams and unguents, and also her towel, she taking the book. I stood there holding her stuff while she looked through the big stiff pages. I didn't really mean to, but I could see into the opening of her robe, and one of her breasts was almost entirely visible. I looked away, but there wasn't much to look at in that hallway. There was a faded color picture of Our Lady of Lourdes on the wall so I looked at that.

"Very interesting," she said.

I looked back at her. She didn't look up. She was reading one of my poems to herself, moving her lips. But what was disconcerting was that even more of her one breast was showing now, like the moon dipping out from behind a white cloud.

I don't know how long I stood there. I kept turning to look at the Blessed Mother, but I also kept turning back to look at Miss Evans, or I should say at Miss Evans's breast, faintly outlined by what looked like a light but not painful sunburn.

Finally at long last she closed the book and cocked her head and looked at me.

"I don't know if you're a genius or insane," she said. "And what's that?"

I hadn't realized it, but I had suffered an erection, and it was this to which she referred.

"Oh, sorry," I said.

"No need to apologize. I consider it a compliment. Come with me."

She turned and walked to her door, still carrying my scrapbook. She opened the door and looked back at me.

"I'm not going to bite you," she said, and then she went in.

She had my scrapbook, and I had her creams and unguents and her towel. What could I do? I followed her into her room.

Her apartment is a studio. It has a small kitchenette, with a table, and she laid the scrapbook on it.

"Close the door, Arnold."

"I can't stay," I said.

With one movement of one hand she took the towel from her head and dropped it over the back of a chair. Her wet golden brown hair fell about her neck and shoulders.

"Close the door. And put those things down over here."

I closed the door with my foot, then went over and put the towel and bottles and jars on the table.

"I really should go," I said.

She took a step closer to me, and she pointed a finger at the bulge in my Bermudas.

"Don't you find it difficult to walk with that?"

"It" had started to subside somewhat, but as she said this it revived.

"I'm supposed to bring Miss Rathbone my poems," I said. "And her mother is making me a sandwich."

She took another step closer. She put her hands on my arms.

"You're very strong," she said. "A workman. A workman poet. A mad workman poet. Do you like gin?"

"Yes," I said. "But I really should go."

"You can't walk out with that thing showing."

She had a point.

"Have one drink with me."

"Just one," I said.

Universes collapsed, stars exploded and disappeared, new galaxies burst into creation, gods and entire races lived and died as she went into her little kitchenette and took a bottle of Gordon's gin and poured healthy drams into two of the Flintstones glasses that my aunts had supplied the apartment with. She came up to me and handed me one of the glasses.

"I don't have any tonic. Oh, did you want ice?"

"It doesn't matter," I said.

"My kind of man. Cheers."

She drank hers down in a gulp. Her eyes expanded and then seemed to shrink and then resume their normal size, albeit slightly glazed. I drank half my drink. She put her empty glass on the table and dropped her arms to her sides. I tossed off the rest of my own drink.

And then I did a strange thing. I put my glass on the table and grabbed her by the waist and kissed her on the neck, my nose in her wet hair.

"Oh," she said.

I pulled her robe down over one shoulder and kissed her shoulder.

"Ah, ah," she said.

She put her hands on my chest and pushed.

"What about your sandwich? What about Miss Rathbone? What about your girlfriend?"

"Oh," I said. "I forgot about all that."

"You passionate man."

She lowered her hands to my side.

"I should go," I said.

"Why?"

"Miss Rathbone and Mrs. Rathbone are waiting for me."

"With your sandwich."

"Yeah," I said.

"I suppose you'd better go then."

She withdrew her hands. I picked up my scrapbook.

"Oh, by the way, how do you like my novel so far?" she asked.

"Very much," I lied, without a moment's hesitation.

"Thank you."

I turned and walked out, closing the door behind me. I walked gingerly over to the bathroom, went in, closed the door, unzipped my Bermudas, and splashed cold water from the tap onto the offending portion of myself.

Chapter 44

After I had doused the damnable thing with several gallons of cold tap-water it grudgingly gave up and surrendered and I put it away and zipped up my Bermudas. I cracked the bathroom door and peeked down the hall; I couldn't put it past Miss Evans to appear yet again, and I was already feeling pangs of guilt. After all, how long had I been seeing Elektra? Just a week or so? And already I was kissing another woman? That couldn't be right.

I heard music coming from Miss Evans's room: opera.

At last I crept out of the bathroom, holding my scrapbook of poems, and tiptoed past her door. Well, I was wearing my flip-flops, so I suppose I wasn't exactly tiptoeing, but I walked or shuffled as quietly as I could.

I successfully made it downstairs and out the side door, but just then I saw Steve coming down the sidewalk. If I had left the house just thirty seconds sooner I might have avoided him, but no such luck.

He waved weakly to me from the other side of the picket fence that borders our yard. Even from here he looked pale and pathetic. I walked around front and down the stone path to where he stood by the gate, although he made no motion to open it.

"Arthur I mean Arnold," he said, "I just came over to apologize."

"Oh, that's okay, Steve."

"I feel horrible."

"You shouldn't feel horrible. All you did was get drunk."

"No, I don't mean I feel horrible about getting drunk, although I do, what I mean is I feel horrible *physically*. I don't think I've ever been so *sick* in my life! I threw up all over my bathroom at the Chalfonte, and then I passed out in it. Fortunately I woke up in the cold light of dawn and was able to find some Mr. Clean and a sponge under the sink and clean the disaster scene up before the maid came in. Anyway I wanted to come over here and apologize, and to thank you for getting me home."

"Well, Dick helped too," I said.

"I know. I don't deserve friends like you guys. What's that big book you have there?"

"It's a scrapbook of my poems. I'm supposed to show them to this lady who's staying here."

"Oh. Well, I won't keep you."

Suddenly I had a brainwave. After that disgraceful Miss Evans incident I was feeling rather wary of this lunch with Miss Rathbone, even with her mother there as chaperone. Maybe if Steve was there he could act as a sort of buffer, or at least prevent things from turning into a complete orgy on the grass.

"Come with me, Steve," I said. "I'm just going out back."

"I don't know, Arnold. I was thinking of just going back to my room and lying down some more. Staring into the yawning abyss of my soul. But it *is* so *hot* in that room! I feel like Albert Guinness in that movie about the soldiers building that bridge? What was it called? *The Bridges of Tokyo Rose*?"

I opened the gate.

"Come on, Steve."

"Well, if you insist. I hope this lady isn't going to expect me to speak coherently. Or God forbid, *cleverly*."

"Don't worry about it."

So Steve went with me around the house and out back where Miss Rathbone and Mrs. Rathbone sat at the metal table under the oak tree.

"Oh, no," he muttered. "They have *wine*."

"You don't have to drink it," I said.

"What a bizarre concept," he said.

"Miss Rathbone," I said, when we got closer, "Mrs. Rathbone. This is my friend Steve."

"Is he what kept you so long, young man?" said Mrs. Rathbone. "We were afraid you had died in your room."

"Sorry," I said. I tried to think of some excuse for taking so long and drew a complete blank. Fortunately Steve came to my rescue.

"Are you a painter, Miss Rathbone?"

She was still wearing her paint-splattered smock-dress.

"I dab and daub," she said. She and her mother were already drinking from a bottle of white wine on the table, out of the jelly glasses that my aunts traditionally provide all their tenants. These were Jetsons glasses.

"I wish I could have been a painter," said Steve. "I'm so envious of artistic people like you and Arnold."

"Sit down, Steve," said Miss Rathbone. "Would you like some wine or a sandwich?"

"Oh, God, no, thank you," he said. "No. No wine. I'll just have a cigarette, thank you very much. No. No wine for me."

"Well, sit down anyway. Here's your sandwich, Arnold."

It was sitting there on a plate, with sliced pickle and potato chips, a neatly folded pink paper napkin on one side and an empty Jetsons glass on the other.

"Thanks," I said.

Both Steve and I pulled up chairs.

"Have some Sawn Sair, Arnold," Miss Rathbone said, raising the bottle, which I saw was actually called *Sancerre*.

"Oh, I don't know," I said. As bad as I am I'm still not much of a daytime drinker. Especially with a blazing August midday sun hanging up there in the sky like a balloon full of molten lava ready to burst all over us. And I had just had that rather large shot of gin up in Miss Evans's room.

"Just half a glass," she said, and she three-quarter filled the empty Jetsons glass.

I ate my sandwich quietly while Steve and Miss Rathbone chatted about their respective jobs, about where she and her mother lived and where Steve lived. Their words passed into my ears and out again, leaving only the vaguest impressions on my brain. Steve smoked a cigarette. He seemed much more subdued than I'd ever seen him in our brief acquaintance, so I guess he really was hungover. When Miss Rathbone asked him again if he wouldn't like something to drink he said he would take some water if she didn't mind. She went back into their cottage.

Mrs. Rathbone asked Steve if he was married.

"No," he said. "*Hardly.*"

"A good-looking young man like you. You must have all the girls after you."

"Oh, sure," he said. "Beating them off with a billy club."

"You know Charlotte's single."

"Charlotte is Miss Rathbone?"

"My daughter, yes. How old are you, Steve?"

"Thirty-three."

"You should ask Charlotte out for a date."

"I'm sure Charlotte could do *much* better than me," said Steve.

"She scares men away because she's very independent. You're not afraid of independent women, are you, Steve?"

"Not at all," he said.

I pushed my empty plate away and got out my cigarettes. This was working out better than I could have expected. Working out better for me, anyway.

Miss Rathbone came back carrying a flowered plastic pitcher of ice and presumably water and another Jetsons glass.

Chapter 45

Miss Rathbone sat down and poured Steve a glass of what apparently was ice water.

He thanked her, lifted the glass and drank it all, his Adam's apple palpitating like a small creature trapped in his throat.

He put the glass down.

"Oh my," he said.

Miss Rathbone opened up my poetry scrapbook and began to read.

"I wish I could write poetry," said Steve.

"Are you ready for some wine now, Steve," said Mrs. Rathbone.

"Oh, please, Mrs. Rathbone, no, thank you."

She topped her own glass off.

"Don't mind if I do," she said. She took a drink. "Don't you drink, Steve?"

"Oh, boy, *do* I drink," he said.

"Hungover, huh?"

"I'm afraid so," he said.

"You need a woman, Steve," she said. "Arnold here, he's got a woman. Nice Jewish girl, hey Arnold?"

I suddenly realized that the old girl was drunk. That she'd been drunk all along and was now getting even drunker.

"Hey, Arnold?" she said again.

"Mother," said Miss Rathbone, barely looking up from my poems. "Leave Arnold alone."

She took a drink of wine herself, again barely looking up from my deathless verse.

"Arnold can take care of himself," said Mrs. Rathbone. "It's Steve I'm worried about."

Miss Rathbone turned a page.

"Leave Steve alone as well."

"He needs a girl."

"I'm sure he doesn't," said Miss Rathbone, while reading another one of my poems.

"*You're* a girl," said Mrs. Rathbone.

"Nominally," said Miss Rathbone.

"Ask her out, Steve," said Mrs. Rathbone.

"Mother, be quiet," said Miss Rathbone.

"I'll ask you out, Miss Rathbone," said Steve.

"What?" she said. Seemingly reluctantly she looked up from my book, putting a pink fingernail on her place.

"I'd like to ask you out, Miss Rathbone."

"Are you mad."

"Perhaps. Will you go out with me?"

"Where?"

"I was invited to a cook-out tonight. Will you accompany me?"

"I was going to make bluefish for mother and myself. We got two nice fresh ones from this Charlie Coleman fellow who works here."

"Go to the cook-out, Charlotte," said Mrs. Rathbone. "I can broil myself a bluefish. I'm not a complete cripple."

"But the other one will spoil."

"I'll freeze it."

"I don't know."

She went back to reading my poem.

"I'd love it if you would accompany me," said Steve. "Miss Rathbone."

"Call me Charlotte," she said, not lifting her eyes from my book of masterpieces.

Chapter 46

"*Charlotte,*" said Steve, smiling as if mysteriously.

Miss Rathbone said nothing to this, not smiling but not frowning either, and continued to read my poems.

"Well," said Mrs. Rathbone, "I'm impressed. You're not a *cad*, are you, Steve?"

He poured himself another glass of water from the flowered plastic pitcher, his cigarette between his lips.

"*Now* you ask me, Mrs. Rathbone?" he said.

"You treat her right or you'll have me to deal with."

Steve took another big drink of water.

"Thrash me with your cane?"

"I'll thrash you soundly with my cane."

"Then I assure you I will be the perfect gentleman."

"I wish you two would stop talking nonsense while I'm trying to read Arnold's poems," said Miss Rathbone.

"You shouldn't read in front of guests, Charlotte," said her mother. "Put Arnold's poems away and read them later."

"How about if I strike you over the head with this book, you old bat."

"Ha," said Mrs. Rathbone.

"Now let me read."

"Are you still sure you want to go out with her, Steve?" said Mrs. Rathbone.

"Oh, *positive.*"

"You like them with spirit, huh?"

"Yep."

"What about you, Arnold?" she said.

"Pardon me?"

"Do you like a girl with spirit?"

I thought about this for a moment.

"Yes?" I said.

"You men have it made," she said. "The world is your oyster. We women have to content ourselves with being the oyster."

Miss Rathbone made a snorting sound but I didn't know if she was snorting at what her mother said or at one of my poetic phrasings.

"Hey, excuse us!"

This was someone calling from our neighbor's driveway on the Perry Street side. I turned and saw it was group of men who had just pulled up in a long white Cadillac convertible. They were all wearing sunglasses, and one of them was a Negro.

"Can you help us out?" called the guy from behind the wheel.

"Yes?" I said.

Steve put his hand on my arm, I didn't know why.

"We're looking for Windsor Avenue, 200 Windsor Avenue?"

"Oh," I said. This was the address of where Dick and Daphne and Daphne's father Mac were staying. I thought I remembered Dick saying it was Mac's mother's house or something like that. "It's right down North Street," I said. "The corner after the next corner."

"Next corner after the next one," said the guy.

"Yeah," I said, "just back on out and go that way," I pointed to the right. "Not the next corner but the one after."

"Great, thank you very much. We have a cook-out to go to."

"Have fun," I said.

The guy waved, backed out, and drove off down the street.

Steve only now took his hand off my arm.

"Do you know who that *was*?" he asked me.

"No," I said.

"It was *Frank Sinatra*!"

Miss Rathbone looked up from my poems.

"What?"

"It *was*," said Steve. "And that was *Sammy Davis, Jr.* in the car with him, and *Dean Martin* and *Joey Bishop*!"

"Who was the other fellow?" said Mrs. Rathbone.

"I'm not sure who the other guy was, but I *think* I might have seen him on TV or in the movies."

"Was it, what's his name, *Peter Lorre*?" said Miss Rathbone.

"You mean Peter *Lawford*," said Steve. "No, it wasn't him." He dug into his pocket and took out a VFW matchbook, opened it up and read something on its inside. "I knew it. 200 Windsor." He held out the open matchbook for everyone to see. "*That's* where we're *going* tonight, Charlotte. The *cook-out*."

Mrs. Rathbone took the matchbook out of his hand and held it close to her eyes.

"I'll be hornswoggled," said Mrs. Rathbone. "You're sure that was Sinatra?"

"Of *course* I'm sure."

"I don't know how I feel about Charlotte going to a party with Negroes."

"I'll protect her," said Steve.

"In my day the races didn't mix."

"Your day is gone, Mother," said Miss Rathbone.

"You behave yourself there, young lady, with these movie stars and Negroes."

"I fully intend to dance the Watusi with the first Negro I see there. With Steve's permission of course."

"Oh, I wouldn't have it any other *way*, Charlotte," said Steve. "What do you think, Arnold?"

"About what?" I said.

"About Sinatra and those guys going to the cook-out?"

"It's okay with me," I said.

"Are you coming tonight?"

"Well, I told Dick I would. I guess I'll stop by."

"You *have* to come. Are you bringing Alicia?"

"Elektra."

"Are you bringing Elektra."

"I don't know. I didn't ask her."

"You *must* come."

"All right."

Mrs. Rathbone had lowered her chin to her chest and was now apparently sleeping. Steve reached across and took his matchbook out of her fingers. Miss Rathbone had gone back to reading my poems. I suddenly felt very sleepy myself.

"I think I'm going to lie down," I said.

"Are you going up to your room?" asked Steve.

"No," I said. It would be too hot up there. I found I could barely talk I was so sleepy. "I'll just — *hammock*," I mumbled.

As in a dream I got up from the chair and climbed into the hammock that hangs between the oak tree and a hook at the back of the house. {*See the Appendix to read Arnold's classic poem "The Hammock". — Editor}* I laid my forearm over my eyes. I felt myself suspended between the heavens and the earth.

I breathed in the warmth of the day.

I could hear Steve and Miss Rathbone quietly talking, but their words made no more sense to to me than the sound of the rustling oak leaves above my head.

I fell asleep.

Chapter 47

I dreamt that I was walking along the roofs of an enormously long train, trying to reach the locomotive.

This is a recurrent dream, and indeed in the waking life of my brakeman career I have walked along the roofs of thousands of hurtling railroad cars. How odd that I got so used to it. To this day I am afraid of heights, but after a year or so as a brakeman I was striding back and forth along the tops of moving trains as nimbly and as naturally as a monkey.

With the new trains we don't have to walk along the roofs any more except in certain rare circumstances. A brakeman's job is so much easier and less dangerous nowadays.

But this dream.

The usual dream I have is that I'm trying to reach the locomotive but I'm never able to. More and more cars magically appear and prevent me from ever reaching the locomotive.

And then there's the variant dream where I'm walking along the roof of a train and all of a sudden a tunnel appears out of nowhere. I lay myself down on the roof of a car and the dark tunnel rushes over me, just inches above my head, and I lie there holding onto the bare metal, and the tunnel keeps rushing and swooshing darkly above me, and the tunnel keeps going on and on and on in darkness.

I'd have to say the tunnel variant is by far the more disturbing dream.

So anyway I was dreaming the first variant, marching smartly along above the train, but I couldn't even see the locomotive it was so far away, and I kept walking along, leaping from one car to another, and then all of a sudden the second variant kicked in, and a tunnel in an enormous mountain came rushing toward me.

I decided that for once I wasn't going to lie down and be stuck in this endless tunnel, and so I just leaped up, and the most wonderful thing happened, I kept flying up and up, up the side of this green and rocky mountain, and then I was at the top of the mountain, and I just touched down on a big rock at its peak and then pushed off and up again, flying down the other side of the mountain, and I saw the train snaking out of the tunnel on the other side, except the train was so long that I still couldn't see its locomotive, even though I was about a mile above it, the train just went on and on over this green and rolling countryside and disappeared in the far-off hazy green hills.

I flew along, above the train. I didn't know where I was flying to. But I kept flying.

Then I woke up, and Elektra was standing there, her arm folded across her chest, smoking a cigarette.

"Hello," she said.

For a moment I couldn't speak, but I felt like I was still floating in the air. I flapped my arms, the hammock turned over and I fell out onto the grass.

I sat up.

She crouched down next to me.

"Dreaming?" she said, one hand steadying the swinging hammock.

"Yes," I said.

She was wearing a flowered shirt tied at the waist, with a white bathing suit under it. She had a canvas bag slung on her shoulder with an orange towel bulging out of it, and I realized I'd never seen her in a bathing suit before.

"Do you mind me coming by?" she said.

"No, not at all."

I looked over at the metal table. Steve and Miss Rathbone and Mrs. Rathbone were gone, God knows where.

"Looking for someone?" she said.

"Oh. Steve was here," I said.

"Him again? I think he's in love with you."

"Yeah, maybe," I said.

I stood up, went over to the table and got my cigarettes and lighter.

"I took off a little early," she said. "I thought maybe you'd like to take a swim with me, Arnold."

"Oh," I said, lighting up my usual post-nap cancer stick. "But I usually go for my swim in the evening."

"So can't you adjust your little schedule? Or do you have writing you want to do?"

"Oh, no, I've already done my writing for the day."

"Did you write me my poem?"

"Uh, no. I'm afraid not. But I will."

She came forward and stood close to me. I could feel the warmth of her.

"I wonder," I said.

"Wonder what?"

She was so close to me I had to blow the smoke up over her head.

"I wonder if we can take a swim later," I said.

"Do you want to go up to your room?"

"Oh, we couldn't do that."

"Oh, right. I guess your aunts and mother would never let you hear the end of it."

"Maybe after a million years," I said.

"All right, let's go," she said. "But get your bathing suit so we can take a swim afterwards."

I said okay, and I walked her around front. Kevin was still on the porch. He was now reading some old Tom Swift book that he'd gotten from the library.

I left Elektra there and went upstairs, very quietly, and changed into my bathing trunks. I grabbed a towel and went down to the third floor, again stepping as lightly as humanly possible, but unfortunately I did have to go to the bathroom. I went in and peed as quietly as one is ever able to pee. And then I flushed, creating the usual racket of an entire cellblock of convicts attacking the bars of their cells with tin cups in protest. I brushed my teeth, then I drank some water from the tap, cupping it into my mouth with my hand as the metallic symphony slowly subsided. Then I went back out into the corridor, and, sure enough, Miss Evans popped out of her room.

"So, there you are," she said. She wore a yellow-and-black polka dot sundress, and she seemed hot and sweaty. Well, it was a very hot afternoon.

"Hi," I said.

"Going for a swim?"

"Uh, yeah."

She took a thick strand of her hair and wound it around her index finger.

"How was your sandwich?"

"My sandwich?"

"The sandwich Miss Rathbone made you."

"Oh, it was her mother who made it, actually. But it was fine."

She let go the coil of hair and it fell to her neck.

"And did Miss Rathbone like your poems?"

"I guess so," I said, and started to walk by.

"What's the hurry, Arnold? The ocean's not going anywhere."

"It's just that my friend's waiting," I said.

"Oh, your lady friend?"

"Uh, yeah."

"I want to meet this paragon. I'll go down with you. I was just going down to read on the porch."

And it's true, she had a book in one hand.

I let her lead the way down the narrow stairs. "I want to read those poems when the Rathbone is finished," she said over her shoulder.

"Sure," I said.

"Have you read this?"

She stopped and I almost fell over her. She held up the book. *The Fountainhead*, by Ayn Rand.

"No," I said, "but I think this friend of mine was talking about that book."

"Elektra?"

She even knew her name.

"No," I said. "This guy Steve."

"Steve," she said.

"Yes."

"Hmmm. I've hardly ever met a man who likes Rand. I'd like to meet this Steve."

Somehow it seemed inevitable that she would.

"Oh, but your friend is waiting," she said.

"Yes," I said.

She turned and went down the stairs, and I followed her.

Normally guests will leave by one of the side entrances on the ground floor, but, since I knew that Elektra was waiting on the porch, I took Miss Evans through the front section of the house. We had to go through my aunts' kitchen, and as bad luck would have it all three of them and my mother were in there performing various kitchen activities. I immediately knew I had made a mistake by taking Miss Evans this way.

I could never describe the complex of emotions, hidden but obvious, conversation, superficial but fraught with meaning, all of it somehow managing to be deeply boring but completely unmemorable, which ensued in the next three minutes of chatter among the old women and Miss Evans.

Miss Evans seemed to have completely forgotten that I was there, so I started to sidle out of the kitchen.

"Where are you going, Arnold?" she asked, as if I hadn't told her just a few minutes before.

"Uh, swimming?" I said.

"Oh, right, your lady friend is waiting," she said. "His lady friend is waiting outside," she said to the ladies.

"Invite her in, Arnold," said my mother.

"Is she coming to dinner again?" said Greta.

"We've got plenty of sauerbraten," said Elizabetta.

"They're getting serious," said Edith.

Sometimes you just have to get tough if you don't want a one-way ticket back to Byberry.

I held up a hand.

"Elektra won't be coming for dinner," I said. "In fact, don't hold dinner for me. I'll get something out. 'Bye."

I turned and headed for the front door.

Miss Evans followed on my heels.

"*Wait* for me, Arnold," she said.

I crossed through the dining and living rooms and came out onto the porch. Elektra was there, leaning back against the rail, apparently chatting with Kevin.

"Well, there you are at last," she said.

"Yes," I said.

I awkwardly held the screen door open for Miss Evans.

"So," she said, "you must be Elektra."

"Hello," said Elektra.

"Elektra," I said, "this is Miss Evans. She's staying here."

"Gertrude," said Miss Evans, and she walked over and extended her hand. Elektra took it.

"You're a very lucky girl," said Miss Evans.

"Am I," said Elektra.

"Such a talented handsome man. What was it first attracted you, his poetry or his physique?"

"Neither. But the physique didn't hurt."

"You have a lovely figure yourself."

"I could lose some weight."

"Not at all. Men like a girl with some meat on her bones. Well, don't mind me, I'm just going to read my book."

She sat down in the rocker next to Kevin, the one I usually sit in.

"And your name is Kenneth?" she said to him.

"Kevin," he said. "Kevin Armstrong."

"And what are you reading?"

"*Tom Swift and his Electric Rifle.*"

"Have a good — *swim*," said Miss Evans to me.

"Okay," I said.

"Nice meeting you, Elektra."

"Nice meeting you, Gertrude," said Elektra.

We went down the steps, down the bluestone path, through the gate and onto the sidewalk. We turned down North Street and crossed it at the corner.

As we reached the other side Elektra said, "Who is that madwoman? With her Ayn Rand?"

"She's a novelist," I said.

"Oh." She put her arm in mine. "She wants to go to bed with you, Arnold."

Chapter 48

I said nothing. What could I say? That just that afternoon I had drunk a large shot of Gordon's gin with Miss Evans, and kissed her bare neck and shoulder? No, even I knew that wouldn't do.

We walked up to Washington Street and turned. People were starting to come back from the beach, blistered-red, sweating and weary, looking as if they had been through a battle. Even the little children hobbled and staggered as though on a death march, or else were carried by their sandal-dragging parents or brave older siblings.

"If you want to go to bed with her, don't let me stop you," said Elektra.

"With Miss Evans?" I said.

"With Gertrude. Yes."

"Oh. But I don't I want to," I said.

"Why not? She's attractive."

"Well —"

I didn't say anything else though, because I wasn't sure of the answer, or answers.

She put her hand on my arm, stopping me.

I looked into her eyes, they seemed so cool and welcoming in the midst of the tired hot world all around us.

"Why not?" she asked again.

"Because I'm trying not to go completely insane," I said.

"Do you think she's that nuts?"

"I guess I should know," I said.

She looked at me but now it was her turn to say nothing.

{Once again Arnold Schnabel's modesty appears to have gotten the best of him, because the next seventy-two lines of his copybook holograph are vigorously crossed out. — Editor}

...lay on my back, halfway on the bed and half off, panting and sweating. She lay on the rug near my feet, and for a full two minutes we both lay where we were, saying nothing. Anything we could possibly have said would have been inadequate.

Finally she got up, climbed over me and lay down on the bed.

We listened to each other's quieting breathing, to the whirring of the electric table fan blowing warm air over us, to the sound of people's voices from the street below, that other world.

After a while she said, "Ask me anything."

I thought about it for a while and then I said, "What's your last name?"

"Ross," she said.

"Ross," I said.

"Yeah."

"And your real first name is Betsy?"

"Right."

"So your parents named you Betsy Ross."

"They wanted to give me an American name. But believe me, it gets to be a real drag telling people your name is Betsy Ross. So one night I was high on reefer with my friends and I changed it to Elektra. Now Elektra seems a little pretentious to me, but I'm kind of stuck with it."

{Arnold's modesty strikes yet again here. The next three lines are crossed out. — Editor}

"Arnold, listen."

"Yes," I said.

"Why don't you stop swimming alone at night? I'm afraid you're going to drown."

"Okay," I said.

"Really?"

"Sure," I said. "But I can still swim on the quiet beach, can't I?"

"Well, okay. But just be careful."

"Okay," I said.

And it was funny, a little more than a week ago I didn't really care too much if I drowned or not. But now I did care.

"Let's go swimming now then," she said.

"Sure," I said.

And so we went down to my beach together and took a swim in the soft late afternoon light. We swam out together, and after a bit Elektra said, "Okay, this is enough for me." The waves lifted her up and down, her dark hair was as sleek as oil. "I'm not in your condition, tough guy. I'm going in."

"Do you want me to come in, too?" I said, not really wanting to come in yet.

"No, you go ahead, Arnold." She tossed a wet thick rope of hair out of her face, turned and swam in.

I didn't want to scare her, so I didn't go out much farther. I simply swam up toward the Point, following the curve of the beach. When I reached the old shore-defense bunker I turned around and swam back and then in.

Elektra sat on her towel smoking a a cigarette and watching me.

She handed me my towel, I dried myself off, laid the towel down next to her, sat down and lighted up a cigarette.

"So," she said, "have you seen Jesus lately?"

I had to think it over for a moment, but then:

"Not today," I was able to say, truthfully enough. "But wait, I just remembered a funny thing. I spoke with Frank Sinatra today."

"Arnold," she said. "Please don't joke. Or don't joke if I can't tell if you're joking or not."

So I told her about the Sinatra incident.

"And you say you know these people who are having this cook-out?"

"Yeah. In fact they invited me to come, and to bring you, too."

"Tonight?"

"Well, yeah."

"And are you going to go?"

"I'll go if you want to go," I said.

"But you won't go if I don't want to go?"

"I can take it or leave it," I said.

"Don't you want to meet Sinatra?"

"I already did meet him, sort of," I said.

"You don't really care, do you?"

"About going to the cook-out?"

"About Frank Sinatra."

Well, let's face it, when you've got Jesus himself turning up on a fairly regular basis Frank Sinatra isn't so special.

We walked back to her place, to her door in the back yard. Evening was coming on.

"So can we go to this cook-out?" she asked.

"Sure," I said.

"All right, let me take a shower and change. I'll come over in about an hour."

I sidled off, and home. I wanted to slip upstairs quietly, but my mother was sitting on the porch, saying a rosary. She asked me if I wanted some sauerbraten, but I told her I was going to a cook-out. She seemed amazed by this, understandably.

I went upstairs, resigned to running into Miss Evans again. I took a shower and went back to my little attic room. I took out my memoir copybook and wrote for a while. Before I knew it almost an hour had passed, so I went down, wearing a clean pair of Bermudas and a fresh polo shirt.

I heard opera music coming from Miss Evans's door again, but nevertheless I stepped as quietly as I could. But as I got abreast of her door I heard the sound of sobbing.

Now I felt bad.

I wanted just to go on downstairs, but somehow I couldn't. I knocked on the door and called hello a couple of times.

The sobbing stopped, I heard the scritching sound of the phonograph needle being lifted, the music stopping in mid-note.

The door opened. Miss Evans was wiping her eyes with a handkerchief.

"Oh, Arnold, how nice."

She was still wearing the polka dot sundress.

"Are you okay?" I asked.

"Am I okay? Of course I am. Why?"

"I heard you crying."

"Oh. That was me listening to Callas. *La Traviata*. I always cry listening to opera."

"Oh," I said.

"But it was so thoughtful of you to check. Would you like to stop in?"

"No, I'd better not," I said.

"You're such a tease. I thought I wanted to come down here to Cape May to be alone, but right now I don't want to be alone. But I suppose you're going to meet your lady friend."

"Well, she's coming here," I said.

"I still want to read your poems."

"Miss Rathbone still has them," I said.

"I must get them off her. Pry them from her hands."

"Well, I'll see you later," I said.

"I'll take a walk perhaps. By the ocean. Buy some cotton candy."

"That sounds nice," I said.

"Would you like to kiss my neck and shoulder again?"

She lowered one of the straps of her dress.

"I don't think I'd better," I said.

She put the strap back up.

"Oh well."

A tear came to her eye. She dabbed it with the handkerchief, which I now noticed was sopping wet.

"Don't mind me," she said. "I shouldn't listen to so much opera. There's a Rock Hudson movie at the Beach Theatre. Perhaps I'll go see that."

"Well, okay then," I said, trying to escape.

"Elektra is lucky," she said.

"Listen, Miss Evans," I said, "I'm a loony tune. I — I have visions of Jesus. I imagine myself to be floating in the air. I live with my mother. You're not missing much."

She looked at me for a moment, then said, "Well, have a good time, Arnold."

And she closed the door.

I stood there for a few moments, I don't know why. But then I heard the scritching noise again, this time of a phonograph needle being dropped onto a record. The opera music began again.

I went downstairs.

Chapter 49

I made my way out the side entrance in a successful maneuver to avoid my mother and aunts. Evening had fallen and the porch was empty except for a couple of guests, a young married couple named DeVore, sitting in rockers and reading magazines by the porch light.

I said hello and went up and over to the other side of the porch to my usual rocker. Miss Evans's novel was still sitting on the little table, so I picked it up for something to read while waiting for Elektra.

Porter Walker takes Emily to a bar in Greenwich Village called the Kettle of Fish, and they drink beer and listen to a jazz trio.

"Can't you hear what those cats are *doing*?" he asks Emily.

Emily listens for a minute and then says, yes, she can hear it.

Then the old rag-and-bones lady shows up again and comes over to the table where Porter the poet and Emily are sitting and drinking cheap beer.

"I told you you would find love," the old lady says.

The rag-and-bones lady goes away, and then, after talking about the meaning of the universe and about himself, Porter finally asks Emily about her new job, and she wonders if she should tell him that she is reading his epic poem for her job, but she decides not to.

They hit a couple of more bars and eventually wind up at one called Bob's Bowery Bar. It turns out Porter's apartment is just around the corner from the bar, and Emily decides to take up Porter's invitation to spend the night at his "pad", but strictly on a platonic basis, supposedly.

They go up to his pad, it's just the one room, with a narrow bed but no couch. Porter says he'll sleep on the floor. Emily gives him a hard time about this. He says he's used to sleeping on floors. It goes on like this, and then all of a sudden Emily kisses him. It started to get pretty hot and heavy here, and I felt embarrassed reading it on the porch.

"What are you reading?" called Mrs. DeVore.

"Um, it's called *Ye Cannot Quench*," I called back.

"Isn't that the novel Miss Evans wrote?"

As I have said, everyone knows everyone's business around here.

"Yes," I said.

"You must lend it to me when you're finished," she said.

"Well, it's not my book," I said. "Miss Evans lent it to me."

"Oh, she must like you. And what about your lady friend?"

See what I mean? How did they even know I had a lady friend?

"I hear your lady friend is a real hot ticket, Arnold," said Mr. DeVore.

Already we were on a first-name basis, and I'd never done more than say hello to these people.

"Jewish girl, isn't she, Arnold?" said Mrs. DeVore.

"She is a member of the Israelite tribe," I said, and I have no idea why I said that, but it, or the way I said it, somehow seemed to take them aback and they smiled and went back to their magazines, she a *Ladies' Home Journal*, he a *Saturday Evening Post*.

I went back to Miss Evans's book and the steamy scene. They were now on Porter's bed, and Emily's bosom was heaving and she was running her hands over his slim lithe muscles and breathing in his "musk of the city and manhood". And just when you think she's about to — you know — she goes into a long remembrance of a date she had with a high school boy back in West Virginia, on a night "scented with honeysuckle and sweet warm sweat". The boy, named Cletus, or "Clete", takes her out to a remote mountain spot in his Model T —

But meanwhile I'm thinking, why is this Emily all of a sudden daydreaming about this old boyfriend of hers while she's busy kissing and running her hands along the lithe muscles of this Porter guy?

But I kept reading anyway, thinking there was still a chance it might make some sense.

And then all of a sudden Steve was standing there, saying, "Aren't *you* engrossed?"

At first I wasn't sure if this was Steve himself, or maybe an apparition of Steve as Jesus. He was carrying a bouquet of calla lilies, so that made me suspicious. I glanced over at the DeVores, and they were both looking at Steve, although seeming to be trying to pretend that they weren't blatantly staring at him. So this made me think it was probably really Steve. If things have gotten to the point where other people are seeing Jesus too, well, then we're all in big trouble.

"Hi, Steve," I said.

"So you're coming tonight, right?" he said.

"Where?" I asked.

"To the cook-out."

Once again I'd forgotten all about it.

"*You* know, he said. "The one with Frank Sinatra. And the Rat Pack. Swimming pools. Movie stars?"

"They have a swimming pool there?" I asked.

"I have no idea," he said. "But you *are* coming, aren't you?"

"Yes," I said. "I'm waiting for Elektra."

"When is she supposed to be here?"

I checked my watch.

"About a half hour ago," I said.

"Primping, I'm sure," he said. "I feel so much better now myself. Had a beauty nap. How do you think I look?"

He was wearing white loose trousers and a long-sleeved white dress shirt of some very light-looking material. He also wore white shoes I noticed.

"You don't think the white bucks are a bit *de trop*?" he asked.

"No, not at all," I said.

"And the calla lilies?" he asked.

They did seem odd to me, but I didn't say so.

"She told me she likes calla lilies," said Steve.

"Who?" I asked.

"*Who?* My date! Charlotte."

It all came back to me now.

"What do you think of her?" he asked. "May I sit?"

"Sure," I said.

And he sat down in the rocker to my right. He leaned over toward me and spoke lowly, as if he didn't want the DeVores to hear him, and in fact I could see them over his shoulder, pretending to read their magazines, but straining their ears to catch our every word.

"Tell me true, what do you think of her?"

"She seems nice," I said.

"I think she's divine," said Steve. "Magnificent. She reminds me of Deborah Kerr. With just a bit of Katherine Hepburn. Or Bette Davis. Just — *fabulous*. And her mother — isn't her mother a scream?"

"Yeah," I said.

"So what do you think of her and me?"

"Miss Rathbone and you?"

"Yes. I certainly didn't mean *Mrs*. Rathbone and me."

He had gotten progressively louder, but now I spoke in a very low voice.

"Do you mean — for you to — go out with her?"

"Yes! What d'ya think?"

It was full dark now, the street lamps were on, and inside the house in my aunts' living room *Route 66* was playing on the TV. The DeVores were still trying to eavesdrop.

"Steve," I said in my lowest voice, "I was under the impression that you — didn't like girls."

Steve whispered, "You mean I'm queer as a three dollar bill?"

"Well, yeah," I whispered back.

"Well, what if I am?" he asked, in a normal voice, or normal for Steve. "Does that mean I can't go out with a woman?"

"But — why would you want to?" I asked.

"Oh, so just because I'm not interested in — in *ravishing* her — does that mean I can't go out with a woman?"

"I —"

"Arnold, can't you get your mind out of the gutter for just one minute?"

"I'm sorry," I said.

"There are more things to life than sex you know."

I really couldn't think of anything to say to this.

Steve sat back and took out his cigarettes. I felt bad, so I gave him a light.

"Thank you, Arthur," he said. So now I was back to being Arthur again, but I didn't have the heart to correct him.

I lit up one of my own, and we sat in silence for half a minute.

Bugs were starting to come out for their evening's adventures. Little gnats, and probably mosquitoes soon enough.

"I'd like to get married too," said Steve, although no one had mentioned marriage. "I don't see why I can't have all that, like everybody else. A nice wife. Maybe even a brat or two."

This was all too confusing to me, to be honest. I thought homosexuals were not supposed to like women. Why would a homosexual man want to be married to a woman then?

"You think I would be living a lie?" asked Steve.

He was speaking normally again, normally for him that is, in other words not quietly, and I could see that the DeVores were hanging on his every word. Steve saw me looking at them, and he turned his head around to look at them also.

"Would you like me to speak louder for your benefit?" he asked them.

They both immediately picked up their magazines and buried their faces in them.

Steve stared at them for a few more seconds, then turned back to me, and shrugged.

"Why can't I have my cake and eat it too?" he asked me. "I think I would make a marvelous husband. I wouldn't be pestering her for you-know-what all the time. Oh, I know what you're thinking, what if she *wanted* to be pestered?"

Actually I wasn't thinking that. I didn't know what I was thinking.

"Well," he said, "I venture to say I could rise to the occasion. You know, close my eyes and think of England."

"Why would you think of England?" I asked.

"It's just a saying, Arthur," he said. "Look, you're my best friend. Give me your blessing."

"Okay," I said. After all, what did I know about any of this?

"Thanks, buddy. She likes you, you know."

"Miss Rathbone?"

"Yes. Charlotte. She's simply mad about you. Or mad about your poems, anyway. After you fell into your deep plummetless slumber she and I sat together for a full hour while her mother snoozed too, and most of that time Charlotte spent reading your poems. I dare say she'd prefer you to me. Well, I guess I should get back there; she's waiting for me. You *are* coming tonight, aren't you?"

"Um," I said.

"I'm as excited as a schoolgirl on prom night. I just want my slice of the pie, Arthur. My piece of the American dream. I don't want to grow old in some fussy old parlour with some other old queen. I'd like a proper wife to go home to. And I can always have my fun on the side, can't I?"

"Well, that wouldn't be right, Steve," I said, in a low voice.

"Oh, Mr. Morality! Get with it, Arthur, don't you know how many husbands fool around on their wives? And not only just with other *women*?"

"That still doesn't make it right, Steve," I said, in my quietest voice.

He paused here, looking at his white shoes.

"You're right," he said. "It's not right. That's why if I do marry Charlotte I'll just have to — to change my ways. That's what I'll do."

"Steve," I said, "don't you think maybe you're jumping the gun a little here?"

He looked at me.

"Like maybe we should go out on a first date before we register at Lit Brothers?"

Just then Miss Evans came walking around the side of the house. She stopped at the side of the porch.

"Hello, Arnold," she said.

She was still wearing the polka dot dress, except now she carried a white pocket book, and she had a white sweater over one arm.

"*Arnold!*" said Steve. "And here I was calling you Arthur again! Hello," he said to Miss Evans.

"Hello," she said.

"My name's Steve. My friend Arnold has such barbaric manners."

"My name's Gertrude. Gertrude Evans. Are you the friend who's read *The Fountainhead*?"

"Yes! By Ann what's-her-name?"

"Ayn Rand."

"I loved that book!"

"You have excellent taste. And I see you're still reading *my* book, Arnold?"

I was still holding the book in my hand.

"Yes," I said. "I'm —" I tried to think of a way not to lie outright. "I'm amazed," I said. Amazed at how absurd the book was.

"Well, thank you very much, Arnold," she said.

Steve had leaned over and looked at the cover of the book, touching it with two fingers.

"Oh my God," he said. "You *wrote* this?" he asked Miss Evans.

"Yes," she said.

"I'm so impressed. Arthur I mean Arnold you'll have to let me read it when you're finished. May I, Gertrude?"

"Of course," she said.

"Where are you off to, may I ask?" he asked her.

"I'm going to the movies," she said.

"Oh really? To that Rock Hudson show?"

"*A Gathering of Eagles*, yes," she said. "I'm sure it's terrible, but I'm a sucker for Rock Hudson."

"Honey, I hate to tell you, but it's very boring. It's just Rock flying B-52 bombers all around."

"Really?"

"Really; now if it was *Lover Come Back*, or *Pillow Talk*, or even *The Spiral Road* it would be a different story. Why don't you come to the cook-out with us?"

"What cook-out?"

"Some pals of ours are having a cook-out down the street. They told us to bring friends. Frank Sinatra's going to be there."

"Frank Sinatra?"

"Yes," said Steve. He turned around to look at the DeVores again and said, loud and clear, "*Frank Sinatra.*"

They raised up their magazines again.

"I don't know," said Miss Evans.

"Wait here," Steve said to her. He stubbed his cigarette out in the ashtray and stood up. "I have to go back and get my date."

Steve went down the steps with his calla lilies, around the porch and past Miss Evans, saying, "Go on up, darling! Wait on the porch with Arthur."

Right then and there I finally decided that Steve was definitely not Jesus. Or at least most likely not.

Chapter 50

Miss Evans came around to the front of the porch, put one foot on the first porch step, but hesitated.

"I wonder if I should just go to that movie?" she said in my direction.

"I love Rock Hudson," said Mrs. DeVore.

I'd almost forgotten that Mr. and Mrs. DeVore were still sitting there. But they were still there all right, not missing a word anyone said.

"He's divine," said Miss Evans.

"So handsome," said Mrs. DeVore. "And tall and dark and strong. Darling," she said to her husband, who was under medium height, balding and blond-haired, and thin except for a pot belly, "should we go see the movie?"

"Is it a war picture?"

"Is it a war picture?" Mrs. DeVore asked Miss Evans.

"I don't *think* so," said Miss Evans. "But I believe Rock Hudson does play a bomber pilot."

"I love men in a uniform," said Mrs. DeVore. Should I describe her? What can I say, she was the sort of woman who produces no visual impression whatever. "Should we go, darling?" she said to her husband, in a voice which was like a million other voices.

"Okay," said Mr. DeVore, sounding if not quite enthusiastic then reasonably open to adventure.

"The only thing is Arnold's friend Steve said it wasn't very good," said Miss Evans.

"Oh," said Mrs. DeVore. "Now I don't know what to do."

"Well, that's just *his* opinion," said Mr. DeVore.

"I know," said Mrs. DeVore, "but —"

"Mr. 'Frank Sinatra' there."

"Oh, my God, that's right!" chirped Mrs. DeVore. "Arnold, is Frank Sinatra really going to be at that cook-out?"

The problem here was that listening to them all talking had driven me slightly insane again. I felt like they were all part of some boring movie that I had been transported into, except that I was still a real person and they were just projections on a screen. I suddenly realized that my cigarette had burnt down almost all the way to my fingers, and I dropped it into the ashtray and tapped it out with my fingertip.

"Arnold?" said Mrs. DeVore again.

"Argyle," I said.

"What?"

"Aardvark."

"What?"

"What did he say?" asked Mr. DeVore.

She turned back to face him.

"Argyle," she said, sounding a little frightened. "And aardvark."

Miss Evans came up the porch steps and over to in front of where I sat.

"Are you okay, Arnold?" she said in a low voice.

I took a deep breath.

She put a hand on my shoulder, and this helped. Her eyes were kind. I came back. Or the world came back to me.

"Yes," I said. "I'm okay." I took another breath and, trying to sound normal, I turned to the DeVores and said, or croaked, "Yeah, Frank Sinatra's supposed to be there."

Mrs. DeVore smiled in a nervous-looking way at me, her teeth bared and clenched tight. Mr. DeVore beyond her leaned forward and also smiled, in the way one smiles at a possibly rabid dog.

Miss Evans continued to hold her hand on my shoulder.

"So, should I go to this cook-out, Arnold?" she said.

"I don't know," I said.

"I *would* like to meet Frank Sinatra," she said. She ran her hand from my shoulder down to the upper part of my arm. "Wouldn't you?"

I thought about this.

"I did meet him," I said. "He asked me for directions."

I glanced down at her hand touching my arm, and I saw that she saw me do so. She caressed my arm once more, then took her hand away.

"What was he like?" she said.

"Well, just like anybody else," I said.

"You really talked to him?" said Mrs. DeVore. "Where is this cook-out? Is it around here?"

"It's on the Street of Dreams," I said.

"What?"

"Love laughs at a king," I said. "Kings don't mean a thing on the street of dreams. Dreams broken in two can be made like new. On the street of dreams."

Mrs. DeVore stared at me. Her husband leaned forward in his rocker and stared at me.

The husband tapped the wife on the shoulder, beckoned her to lean toward him as he leaned toward her. He whispered something in her ear, something no doubt to the effect of, *"He's crazy. Better leave him alone."*

They both settled back in their rockers and lifted up their magazines.

Miss Evans leaned down toward me.

"Wasn't that a Frank Sinatra song?" she asked in a low voice.

I nodded. And I wondered, had I quoted those lines to Mr. And Mrs. DeVore because I was still at least somewhat in the grip of an attack of madness, or had I simply wanted to make them stop butting in?

But then Steve came around the side of the house, arm in arm with Miss Rathbone, who wore a long gauzy ivory-colored dress and carried a small pink purse with sparkles on it. She had made her hair into a sort of billow above her forehead, with silver or silver-colored barrettes above her ears guiding it in waves behind her bare shoulders. She carried what looked like a pink silk scarf draped over her forearms and behind her back.

"Arnold," said Steve, "Gertrude! Look how marvelous my date looks!"

"Oh be quiet, Steve," said Miss Rathbone, but she let him guide her around to the front of the porch, her arm in his.

"Hello, Miss Evans," said Miss Rathbone.

"You look wonderful," said Miss Evans.

"Thank you. You don't look bad either."

"Great," said Steve, "everybody looks fabulous, now let's get this show on the road!"

"But Arnold's waiting for his lady friend," said Miss Evans.

"Oh, I forgot. Well, we'll see you there then, Arnold. Come on, darling," he said to Miss Rathbone.

He tried to pull her arm, but she wouldn't budge.

"I loved your poems, Arnold," said Miss Rathbone. "I devoured them. I found them extraordinary."

"Are they really?" said Miss Evans.

"Extraordinary," said Miss Rathbone.

"Oh, God, Arnold, the women love you!" said Steve. "That's it, I'm going to start writing poems tomorrow!"

"I'm afraid it's not quite that easy," said Miss Rathbone. "Arnold has honed his craft. And he has suffered."

"I can *hone*!" said Steve. "And God knows I've suffered!" Mr. and Mrs. DeVore were paying attention again, indeed how could they not, and Steve said to them, "Really, I *know* about suffering!"

Once again they smiled uncertainly and picked up their magazines.

Thank God, or whomever, I saw Elektra coming along Perry Street.

Steve was speaking some nonsense, I don't know what.

I watched Elektra crossing North Street.

In the light of the street lamp it was as if she was walking on to a stage. She wore a dress I hadn't seen before, all splotched with silky red and black, and she carried a small shiny black purse on a long thin strap hanging from her bare shoulder.

Mid-street she stopped, and she looked at this group of people sitting on the porch and in front of it.

Then bravely she continued toward us.

Chapter 51

"Well, look at *you!*" called Steve. "Don't you look *gorgeous!*"

Elektra raised her arms and did a twirl, her red and black dress flying around her and then settling on her figure as she strode toward us.

"Oh my goodness, Miss Elektra, I've never seen you quite this dolled up before!" yelled Steve. He had disengaged his arm from Miss Rathbone's, and he clapped the fingertips of his hands together.

I noticed that Miss Rathbone rolled her eyes, while Miss Evans stared at Steve with her head slightly cocked.

Mr. And Mrs. DeVore stared quite blatantly from Steve to Elektra and back again.

I stood up.

"Excuse me, Miss Evans," I said, and went over to the steps and started down them, Steve still yelling compliments to Elektra, but just then I heard my small cousin behind me, saying:

"Cousin Arnold!"

I turned on the second step.

"Yes, Kevin?" I said.

He was standing in the doorway, holding the screen door open. Behind him I could see my Aunt Greta and my mother leaning forward on the couch and staring out the door.

"I want to say hello to Electric!"

"Oh," I said.

This kid was getting a little obsessed. Not that I could blame him.

I went down the steps, Elektra came through the wooden gate, we met on the stone path, and there, for the first time in my life in front of witnesses I was kissed on the cheek by a woman whom I was not related to.

The next few minutes were very confusing, complicated, and somewhat boring, involving Elektra and myself going back onto the porch and Elektra being introduced to everyone she hadn't been introduced to, and re-introduced to everyone else, and Kevin babbling up at her as she leaned forward to listen to him, one hand holding back a mass of her shining black hair, and giving him a look at her breasts that will probably give the boy material for self-abuse for untold years ahead.

The one good thing about this scene was the fact that after a minute Elektra put one of her hands on my arm, and kept it there.

Steve was right, she did look swell. Now that she was close to me I saw that the red and the black print of her dress was made up of large red roses on a black background. She wore red lipstick, and had make-up on her eyes that made them seem even darker and larger than their normal dark largeness. Around her neck she wore a necklace of varicolored Cape May diamonds. Her dress was low-cut and molded around her breasts and I confess that, just as Kevin stared at her bosom shamelessly as she leaned over to chat with him, so also and maybe just sightly less shamelessly did I.

Finally Steve seemed to get bored with it all.

"Okay! Let's go while the night is young! Gertrude, you *are* accompanying us, aren't you?"

She also had come down to the foot of the steps.

"I feel like a fifth wheel," she said.

"Every car needs a spare, honey. Come on! *Frank Sinatra!*"

So, soon enough we were all filing down the path to the sidewalk in awkward disorder.

Kevin suddenly ran down off the porch and grabbed Elektra's arm.

"Electric! Take me with you!"

"Sorry, Kevin," I said. "This is a grown-up party. Go back and watch TV."

Reluctantly he let go of her, and Elektra and I followed the others out through the gate, and as I closed it I saw Mr. And Mrs. DeVore staring outcast at our little band, left with no one to bore but themselves and possibly Kevin; but no, not even him. He turned and quickly scrambled up the steps and back into the house, anxious no doubt not to miss any more of *Route 66.*

Steve led the way, with Miss Evans on his right arm and Miss Rathbone on his left.

I deliberately let some space open up between our two groups as we walked, and I stopped Elektra with my hand.

"Hello," I said.

"Hello, Arnold."

I realized then that she was the nicest thing that had ever happened to me.

"You don't really want to go to this, do you?" she asked.

"Not particularly," I said.

"Let's just go for a little while. I know it's stupid, but I want to see what Frank Sinatra looks like. Then you and I can split."

"Okay," I said.

So our little band walked along, past Congress to Windsor.

The house was a great turreted three-story affair with the front entrance around the corner, with screened porches on both the first and second floors, gardens and lawns filling the space between the house and the sidewalk. Down past the sides of the house we could see lights and people in the back.

Steve led the way through the gate and up a flagstone walkway that went through the gardens and then around either side of the house. We went to the left, and then at last came to the back yard where the party was. Colored paper lanterns with electric lights in them were strung around the yard. Women wore dresses that looked like tissue paper, and the men mostly wore short-sleeved shirts and light-colored trousers. A couple of young maids in black uniforms walked around with a tray.

Dick Ridpath excused himself from a conversation with an older woman and came over and greeted us warmly. Steve introduced Miss Evans, and Dick not only was gracious to this uninvited guest but knew of her work and said he was looking forward to her next novel.

With Dick's able help, soon we had drinks in our hands and were mingling with the pleasant men and women there.

I was mildly surprised that one by one Dean Martin, Joey Bishop, Sammy Davis, Jr. — and, finally, even Frank Sinatra — came up and introduced themselves to me and Elektra.

And then, while Frank Sinatra was chatting with Elektra, asking about her jewelry store, it finally dawned on me: it was she who was attracting these stars of stage, screen, and television, and not the odd fellow she was with. I'll say this for Frank Sinatra though, he was a gentleman; because after chatting with Elektra for about five minutes (during which time she kept her arm in mind, while I stared off into space and occasionally at Mr. Sinatra's hairpiece) he said to me, "And what do you do — Arnold is it?"

"Yes," I said. "Well, I write poems, Mr. Sinatra."

"No kidding. Do they rhyme?"

"Oh, always," I said.

"Did you ever think of writing song lyrics?"

"No," I said.

"If you ever want to give it a try, I'm always looking for new material. I could give the lyrics to Jimmy Van Heusen, say, see if he could turn them into a good song for me."

"Well, I doubt I could do that, Mr. Sinatra," I said.

"Call me Frank. Why not, Arnold?"

"Well — Frank — it's the things I write about."

"Like what?"

"Like — I don't know. Worms on the pavement on a rainy day. The scariness of an amusement arcade. Having a conversation with Jesus, or with an hallucination of Jesus. Fighting off demons while you're trying to watch TV. That sort of thing." {*Cf. Arnold's poems "The Day of the Worm", "Frank's Playland", "My Invisible Friend", and "The Schaefer Award Theatre", in the Appendix. — Editor*}

"You don't think you could just write me a love song?"

"I've asked him to write me a poem," said Elektra, "and he still hasn't done it."

"But I'm determined to do it," I said.

"Don't rush him, honey," said Frank. "You got a real poet on your hands here. Most bums would jump at the chance to work for me. I'd like to read your poems, Arnold. You got any books out?"

"No," I said. "Just a lot of clippings from the papers the poems have appeared in."

"Yeah, how many?"

"Oh, a lot," I said. Like thirteen hundred, but I didn't want to boast.

Frank reached into his back pocket and took out a thick worn old wallet. He was not a big man at all. Like me he was dressed in Bermuda shorts and a polo shirt, except he wore white shoes with no socks, whereas I wore white Keds with white socks. For a second I thought he was going to give me some money. But instead he pulled out a visiting card with gold edging. He handed it to me. All it had on it was a phone number, embossed in gold and black.

"This is my number, kid. You ever think you've got some good material for me, give me a call. Collect."

"Thanks, Mr. Sinatra."

"Frank."

"Thanks, Frank." I looked at the card, wondering if that was real gold on it. "I doubt I'll come up with anything suitable though."

"You let me be the judge of that," he said. "Something about love is always good."

"I don't know," I said.

"Or like loneliness. Loss. Late at night with the deep-blue blues. Maybe that's more your style."

"You're probably right," I said.

"Just nothing about worms," he said. "Or Jesus. Or demons."

Steve was working his way toward us, with Miss Rathbone and Miss Evans.

Frank pointed to the card that I was still holding up between thumb and forefinger, as if I were about to hand a movie ticket to an usher.

"Put the card in your wallet, Arnold. I don't want you to lose it."

I took out my wallet and did as he advised.

I didn't think I'd ever call him, but I didn't want to make the guy feel bad.

Chapter 52

It was all very interesting chatting with Frank Sinatra, I suppose, but to tell the truth I was getting hungry, so I was glad when Dick came over and told us he had a brand-new batch of burgers ready to go.

Elektra and I excused ourselves from Frank and went over to the charcoal grill with Dick. He gave us burgers on paper plates and suggested we sit at a wooden table nearby in front of a long gingerbread pavilion. The table was loaded down with big bowls of pickles and potato salad and coleslaw and beet salad. Little wicker baskets held silverware and paper napkins.

We sat and ate and drank our beer (Schmidt's) and looked at all the people milling about. Filtered flood-lights had been set up, and so the yard was fairly well-lit. Some people were playing badminton (among them Dick's beloved Daphne, laughing and pouncing around like a child, but she didn't look like a child), others were playing croquet. But mostly people just stood around drinking and talking.

"So, what did you think of Frank Sinatra?" asked Elektra.

"He seemed nice," I said.

"Yeah," she said. "You should write him a song, Arnold."

"Would that I could," I said.

"You don't think you could write a song lyric?"

"No," I said. "Not one that Frank Sinatra could sing."

"Is that really what your poems are all about," she asked, "demons and worms and — talking to Jesus?"

"I write about what I know," I said. "I used to write about things like Mother's Day, or the first snowfall of the year, or how good it feels to walk home from church. But that all changed with my breakdown, I'm afraid."

"You still haven't shown me your poems."

"You'll have to get in line. Miss Rathbone has them now, and Miss Evans said she wants them next."

"So I'm sleeping with you, and I don't get special treatment?"

"I promise to put you next on the list after Miss Evans."

"How do you feel?" she asked.

"You mean do I feel crazy at all?"

"Yeah."

"Well, I felt a little crazy on the porch, right before you came over. Something about the way Mr. and Mrs. DeVore were talking was just driving me around the bend."

"They would drive me crazy."

"But then Miss Evans noticed something was wrong with me, and she talked to me, and touched my arm. And that made me feel better."

It occurred to me by the way she looked away that she didn't like my mentioning Miss Evans. And I remembered what Daphne had said about extolling the virtues of one woman in front of another. I had much to learn, everything to learn.

I plunged ahead.

"But I felt really better when I saw you come walking down the street," I said.

She turned her head to look at me.

"Really?" she said.

"Yes," I said.

We continued to eat and drink, and then Elektra said, "You know I'm probably going away at the end of the summer, don't you, Arnold?"

"Well, I assumed you would, since the jewelry store wouldn't do much business after the season's over."

"Yes. We'll probably close up at the end of September."

I didn't say anything, I was concentrating on my food.

"So you're not upset, that I would be leaving you?" she asked.

"I never expected you to stay with me," I said. "I'm lucky you're here with me now."

"Will you go back to Philadelphia?"

"I have no idea," I said.

"So you're just taking it one day at a time."

"Yeah," I said. I had finished eating, and I took out my trusty Pall Malls. "In the group therapy meetings at the hospital they used to talk about taking it one day at a time. Each day is the first day of the rest of your, you know, whatever."

I lit my cigarette. Elektra took out her Marlboros and I lit her up too.

I suppose my face was giving away something, because she looked into my eyes and said, "What?"

"It's hard to explain."

"Try."

I tried. It felt as if someone else were talking, a character in a book or a movie, but I tried.

"For quite some time before my crack-up I felt like each day could be the last day of my life. And then when I cracked up I kind of wanted each day to be the last day of my life. And then when I got a little better I didn't care if it was the last day of my life. But now it's different. I still feel like each day might be my last, but this feeling just makes me want to live life even more."

She blew out some smoke and looked at me, and then she looked over my shoulder and I turned and Sammy Davis, Jr. was standing there with two full beer bottles in one hand and another one in the other.

"Arnold, man," he said, "excuse me for eavesdropping, but I just want to say that what you said just now was deep. Very deep. I brought you two some fresh beers."

We thanked him and invited him to sit with us.

"So Frank tells me you're a poet, Arnold," he said, after he sat down on the bench across from us.

Like Frank and me he wore Bermudas and a polo shirt, except he wore sandals with no socks.

I admitted that I was a poet (leaving out — as I had with Frank — the adjective "inept").

"I can see you're a very deep cat. Listen, would you two care to blow some reefer?"

"Sure," said Elektra immediately.

"Follow me," he said, and he got up.

"Um, I think I'll take a pass," I said.

"Come with us, Arnold," said Elektra, and she put out her cigarette in a big seashell that was serving as an ashtray.

Of course I said yes. I would follow her anywhere. Anywhere within reason. Within my definition of reason. Which left me a lot of room. I put out my own cigarette and stood up.

We took our beers and went all the way to the back of the yard, out of the glare of the floodlights, by a white-painted wooden fence that was bordered with rhododendrons and azaleas and some bushes I couldn't give a name to. A greenhouse ran along one side of the yard back here, its glass sparkling, its windows and doors open, and inside its dimness it looked like a jungle was trying to get out.

Sammy pulled a reefer out of his shirt pocket, gave it to Elektra, and lit her up with a fancy gold or gold-plated lighter.

I was thinking how odd it was to think that I had seen this man on TV and in movies and now I was seeing him in person. I don't know why, but I hadn't really thought about this when I was talking to Mr. Sinatra, but now I thought about him, too, all the movies and TV shows I had seen Frank in. And now I had just seen him in person, and he was just another little middle-aged guy with a toupée. And Sammy was another even smaller guy, with very shiny black hair, horn-rimmed glasses, a glass eye, and a broken nose.

Sammy and Elektra passed the reefer back and forth and talked about jazz.

I was remembering Sammy from a TV series I had liked, called *The Magic Carnival.* He did a guest appearance on one episode where he played a carnival barker for this sideshow that purported to contain the secret of life. I found this episode very disturbing at the time, and in fact I still sometimes have nightmares about it.

I was about to ask him about this particular show when I'm afraid to report that my *bête noir* appeared once again.

Yes, it was he, Jesus, standing there smiling by my side, smoking his traditional Pall Mall.

"Yes, Arnold, it's me again."

I said nothing, because I didn't want Elektra and Sammy to see and hear me talking to an apparition of Jesus.

Please go away, I thought, as loudly as I could.

"That's not a very nice thing to say," he said.

I don't care, I thought. *Are you trying to drive me insane?*

"Wow," he said. He looked away, smoking his cigarette. He had a new outfit on, new for me, anyway. A white long-sleeved shirt, white trousers, white shoes. He turned back to me. "You're not being very friendly," he said.

I'm not? I thought.

"Not really," he said. "I mean, considering who I *am* –"

Okay, Mr. Jesus, I thought, *if you are Jesus, what the h--l do you want?*

(I may be a railroad man, but I never use language like this. This is why, even as I thought this rude sentiment, I mentally substituted dashes for the offending letters.)

"I just want you to love me, Arnold," he said, with raised eyebrows, as if he were offended.

Okay! I thought. *I love you! Fine! Now leave me alone.*

He sighed.

"You say you love me, but you don't act like it. You should be glad to see me."

Well, I'm not! I yelled mentally.

"We've talked about this before," he said, tapping his ash down onto a yellow rhododendron. "Most Catholics would kill to have a vision of me. You act like it's some great *hardship*. Like I'm persecuting you. Oh, no. Don't do that again. That eye-closing thing."

I was closing my eyes tight. This had worked that one time. If I just kept my eyes tight shut for a while, then when I opened them again he would be gone. Such was my plan, anyway.

"Why can't you just let me stick around, Arnold?" he said. "Why can't you accept me?"

What am I supposed to do? I yelled internally, keeping my eyes shut. *Fall down at your feet?*

"Oh, no, I hate that sort of thing. Just, you know, accept me into your life. Believe in me. Walk with me," he said. "Worship me."

Do you know how egocentric that sounds? I screamed inside. *Worship you? Are you that desperate for adoration?*

"Well, I *am* the son of God, Arnold."

So that automatically means you have to be worshipped?

I don't know where all these ideas of mine were coming from. But anyway, after a pause he said:

"Wow, I never really thought about it that way."

Well, think about it! I thought, again keeping my eyes shut.

I could hear Sammy and Elektra talking, about trains and miles the way these jazz buffs seem to do. Jesus was silent for a moment, so I supposed he was thinking about what I'd said.

"Arnold, now I feel like a big jerk," he said.

Right. So now I was supposed to feel sorry for him.

"Arnold, open your eyes."

I did, because it was Steve talking.

"Are you *that* high?" said Steve, who was standing right where Jesus had been. "Say, I'll have some of that, Sammy," he said, and Sammy nodded and passed him the reefer.

Steve took a big drag and held it in, then he took a couple of smaller drags and held them in. Then he let all the smoke out in a great whoosh, passing the reefer to Elektra.

"Anyway, Arnold," he said, "I feel like *such* an enormous big jerk."

Jesus, or my brain, had done it again. All I could do was sigh and ask Steve what the problem was.

"It's Charlotte," he said. "And Gertrude. Trouble. I need your help, Arnold."

How odd, I thought.
That anyone would need my help.

Chapter 53

Elektra had taken another drag from the reefer and passed it on to Sammy.

"Steve," she said, "you are too much, man."

"I beg your *pardon*," he said. I noticed he was holding a bottle of beer. But at least it was only beer. He didn't seem drunk at all. Not yet. "But *Alicia* —"

"Elektra," she said.

"*Elektra* – you're a woman, maybe *you* can help me."

"I doubt that, Steve," she said.

Sammy had taken his own series of drags off the reefer and he passed it on to me.

"You got woman trouble, man?" Sammy asked Steve, seeming just slightly surprised.

"Oh, brother, do I!" said Steve. He tugged once at my short sleeve. "Arnold, Charlotte's mad at me. And after I brought her the calla lilies, too."

"Did you — extol the virtues of Miss Evans in her presence?" I asked.

"Yes! How did you know?"

"I just guessed." I was starting to learn a thing or two.

"She told me to drop dead," said Steve. "And now she's off talking to *Joey Bishop*."

"Joey's cool, brother," said Sammy.

"Oh, I'm sure he's *very* cool, Sammy," Steve said, "but *I* happen to be *very* fond of *Charlotte*."

"I dig," said Sammy, but he still looked somewhat puzzled.

Right around then I realized that despite my earlier decision to abstain I was standing there smoking the reefer as blithely as if it were one of my trusty Pall Malls.

"Arnold, let someone else have a puff of that," said Steve, and he took the reefer out of my hand and started taking his own distinctive series of long and short drags from it.

"Steve," said Elektra, "I thought you were queer, man. What the hell are you doing fooling around with women?"

"I beg your pardon, Miss *Missy*," said Steve, still dragging away. "Someone has obviously not studied her Kinsey Report."

"What the hell are you talking about?" said Elektra.

"Dr. Kinsey said that *most* people swing *both* ways. Or at least they *can* swing both ways." He finally let the smoke whoosh out in a great cloud. "If you had gone to a boys' prep school like me you'd know *exactly* what I'm talking about."

"Whatever, man," said Elektra. "But now *you're* bogarting the joint."

"Oh, sorry, darling," said Steve, and he passed it to her.

"No big thing," said Sammy, and he brought another reefer out of his shirt pocket.

"So what should I *do*?" asked Steve, to one and all.

"Just be cool, man," said Sammy. "She's just putting you in your place."

Sammy lit the new reefer with his lighter, which I now belatedly realized seemed to be studded with diamonds or little sparkly things that looked like diamonds. His initials were engraved on it: *"S.D.Jr"*. The diamonds sparkled in the light from the lamps flooding over the party-goers in the yard closer to the house.

"Yeah," said Elektra. "Just be cool, Steve."

"But I've *never* been able to be cool! Just look at her, chatting away with Joey Bishop, and here I am *heartbroken*. Women are so *complex* compared to men."

"You got that right, brother-man," said Sammy, nodding.

"You guys are so full of crap," said Elektra.

"Oh, *you*!" said Steve.

"Women are no more or less complex than men," she said.

"You big *liar*!" said Steve. "At least with men you don't have to mind every single word you *say*!"

"Oh, give me a break, Steve," she said.

Elektra was hanging onto what was left of the first reefer, and I realized that Sammy had handed me the new one, and that I was duly smoking it.

"Where's that other goofy broad, anyway?" Elektra asked Steve.

"You mean Gertrude?" said Steve. "She was talking to Frank last I saw. Why? Don't you like her?"

"I'd like her better if she kept her eyes to herself."

"What *ever* do you mean?"

"I mean she has eyes for Arnold." She took a drag from the tiny butt-end of the reefer, held it in for a moment, and then exhaled the smoke in Steve's direction. "Not that I care," she said, shrugging one shoulder.

"Oh yes you do, *Miss Jealous*," said Steve. "And that roach is about to singe your delicate little fingertips."

"Oh," she said. She let the minuscule reefer-end fall to the grass, then stepped on it with her sandaled foot.

I noticed that her toenails were painted red, sparkling in the flood-lamp light. Had they always been painted red? I had no idea. And my eyes traveled up from her feet to her legs, shiny pale caramel, then the silky red roses swimming in the shimmering blackness of her dress, her glowing pale caramel arms, her small strong hands tipped with red fingernails — no, I couldn't remember if they had been red before — her gleaming shoulders and neck, her red lips, and her dark eyes gazing at the moment at a profusion of pulsing white chrysanthemums.

I wanted to kiss Elektra's lips right then and there, but of course I knew I couldn't. But this denial of what I wanted to do made what I wanted to do so much more precious.

(We may thank the reefer for the above observations of course.)

"Ow," said Steve, and he slapped a mosquito on his inner arm below his biceps. "Ew." He flicked away the dead mosquito.

"Is any one else being eaten *alive?*" he queried.

I suddenly realized that a mosquito was sucking my own blood out of the soft flesh behind my knee. I slapped at it but the little engorged bugger got away.

"I am," I said.

"Yeah, me too," said Elektra, expertly swinging down and tapping dead a mosquito that had alighted on her ankle.

"Let's go inside," said Sammy. "Why don't you slide me that muggles your digits are glued to, Arnold?"

"Pardon me?"

"The reefer, brother. Slip it on over and I'll save it for later."

"Oh, okay."

I handed it to him, and he rubbed out the lit end with two callused fingertips.

"Groovy," he said. "Now let's find a quiet place where the mosquitoes ain't biting."

"Should I try to get Charlotte to come?" Steve asked Sammy.

"Sure, brother," said Sammy.

"If she just gives me one last chance I'll never let her down again."

"And what if she doesn't give you another chance, Steve?" asked Elektra, touching his chin with her finger.

"Well — there's always *Gertrude*," he said, and he lifted Elektra's finger off his chin and kissed its tip.

I remember thinking right then: This is going to be a long night.

Chapter 54

We headed back to the main part of the yard, and I had the strange sensation that I was a movie camera being rolled forward into the midst of the party-goers. Elektra had her arm in mine, and it felt as if she were guiding me along.

"How're you doing, lover?" she asked me.

"Okay," I said.

Just this brief exchange of words was enough to transform me from being a movie camera on a track into one of the actors in the movie. I couldn't tell if I was the star, though, or a supporting player.

Our little group headed towards where Miss Rathbone stood chatting with Joey Bishop.

Steve lost no time in going right up to them. Joey and Miss Rathbone were talking about Joey's TV show.

"Excuse me – Joey?" asked Steve.

"Yeah?" said Joey.

"Could I talk to Charlotte for just one second?"

Joey looked at Miss Rathbone questioningly.

"What is it, Steve?" said Miss Rathbone.

"I'm really really, really really, *really* sorry, Charlotte. I was an unthinking boor. Please forgive me."

Miss Rathbone looked at him with pursed lips.

"Should I take a hike?" asked Joey.

"Please forgive me, Charlotte," said Steve. "Wait, don't move."

He raised his hand, as if to slap her.

"Are you insane?" she asked.

In one swift motion he slapped at her hand and squashed a mosquito that was sitting on the outside of her thumb.

"Got him!" said Steve, and he flicked the dead bug off her hand.

"Oh. My hero," said Miss Rathbone.

"Dude strikes like lightning," said Sammy. "Hey, people, we were just gonna go inside to get away from these little beasties. Wanta join us?"

"Okay, I'll come," said Miss Rathbone, rubbing her hand. "Would you care to join us, Mr. Bishop?"

"No, thank you very much. I'm going to mingle a bit."

"You don't have to worry about Steve, Mr. Bishop," she said.

"Oh, no, I'm not worried," he said. "I just gotta — you know —"

"It's cool, man," said Sammy.

"I'll catch you good people later," said Joey. "Really nice meeting you, Miss Rathbone."

He went off, and Miss Rathbone said to Steve, "See, you scared him away."

"I did not!" said Steve.

"It's very cool, man," said Sammy. "Come on, let's breeze."

We all went around to the front of the house and up the steps to the porch.

"This is nice," said Miss Rathbone. And it was. The porch was screened in, and there was even an Igloo cooler with ice and cans of beer in it.

"I know someplace nicer," said Sammy. "And with a bit more shall we say *privacy*." (He pronounced privacy like *privvacy*, with an English accent.) "Follow me."

We went into the house, through the living room, and into the dining room where an old lady sat playing cards with a few other older people of both sexes.

"Well, hello, Mr. Davis," said the lady.

"And hello to you, milady," said Sammy and he went over and kissed the lady's hand.

The room, like the living room we'd just passed through, was very modern. Well, 1930s modern. It was like one of those sleek large rooms in an old Fred Astaire movie, which was odd, because the house was a Victorian that must have been at least as old as my aunts' house (which was a hundred and four years old.)

Sammy introduced us to the lady and her friends. Her name was Mrs. Biddle, and I was just barely able to put it together that she was "Mac" MacNamara's mother-in-law, in other words the grandmother of Daphne, the young girl that my new friend Dick was in love with. The other old people's names went into my ears and right out again at the speed of sound.

"We just thought we'd head up to the second-floor porch, Mrs. Biddle. Get away from the mosquitoes."

"Great idea, Sammy," she said. "Those dreadful mosquitoes. I've phoned the mayor to have more trucks come by and spray DDT but he said it was too dangerous. I suppose he'd rather have us die of malaria."

While saying this she took a cigarette out of a box on the table and screwed it into a shiny jet-black holder. Quick as a shot Sammy had his lighter out and he gave her a light.

"Politicians," said Sammy.

"They're all a bunch of bums," said Mrs. Biddle.

"We'll just head up then."

"Stop in the kitchen and take some beer out of the ice box. There's plenty. Mac always goes overboard for these get-togethers. Or mix yourself some cocktails."

"You're too kind, Mrs. B.," said Sammy.

We were all herding on out when Mrs. Biddle lifted up a rattan cane that had been leaning against the table and grabbed my arm with its hooked handle.

"What is your name again?" she asked me.

I told her my name.

"Don't your aunts have the house on North Street over near Perry?"

"Yes," I said.

It never fails. Everyone in this town knows everyone else's complete family tree going back four generations at the very least.

"Tell them I've quite admired their garden this summer."

"I will," I said.

"Their gladioli are extraordinary."

I didn't really know what to say to this. And I realized that the rest of the crew had left the room, leaving me alone with Mrs. Biddle and the other old people.

"How *are* you?" she asked.

So of course she knew all about my breakdown.

"I'm — I'm doing okay," I said.

"Was that your lady friend, that dark-haired girl?"

I mumbled an assent, and waited for the reference to Elektra's Jewish heritage, but instead Mrs. Biddle only said, "Very pretty."

I stood there a moment, and it occurred to me that I had never actually seen anyone smoke a cigarette using a holder before. Not in real life, anyway.

She seemed to be appraising me. I half-expected her to ask me to leap about and cut some capers for her, but instead she said only, "Do you play canasta?"

I confessed that I did not.

"I suppose poker is your game?"

"I'm afraid I have no game," I said.

"And you a railroad man?"

It's true, railroad men play a lot of cards, but I never did. Never shot craps, either. I was not, never had been, and undoubtedly never would be a regular guy. And it was too late to start now.

"How is your poetry-writing coming along?"

"Not bad," I said.

"I don't know why, but you intrigue me," she said. "Come by and visit me and we'll talk."

"Okay," I said. What else could I say?

"Don't make me come looking for you."

I told her I wouldn't.

"A man of few words," she said. "I like that."

"Still waters run deep," said an old man at the table. He looked like Edward Everett Horton, and the way things were going this night, he might well have been Edward Everett Horton.

"Are you deep, Arnold?" asked Mrs. Biddle.

"Sammy thinks I am," I said.

"Oh, then you must be. Well, go join your friends," she said, and she picked up her hand of cards.

I left the dining room and went down a hall. I saw a stairway which one might reasonably have expected would take me to this second-floor porch, but I also saw a large kitchen, and I remembered what Mrs. Biddle had said about helping ourselves to some beer. That sounded like a good idea.

Chapter 55

I had just gone into the kitchen and was headed for the refrigerator when all of a sudden that girl Daphne came bursting into the kitchen through an opposite doorway and practically ran into me.

"Oh, hi!" she said. "Arnold."

"Hello," I said. "Daphne."

"I'm so glad you came tonight. Dick was very impressed with you, you know. And he hates everybody. I'm sorry I didn't get to say hello before, but I was absolutely obsessed with playing badminton. Do you play?"

Here we go again.

"No, I'm afraid I've never played," I said.

She was wearing yellow shorts and a matching yellow sleeveless top, and she was sweaty.

I suppose she noticed me giving her the once-over, because she asked me if she looked horrid.

"No," I said.

"Should I change out of these sweaty clothes?"

"Are you going to play more badminton?"

"Possibly. I'm very competitive."

"Don't change then," I said.

The ends of her brown hair were wet. She took one damp strand between finger and thumb, ran it away from her head and let it fall back to her neck.

"Was that your girlfriend I saw you with?" she asked.

"Well," I said, "we've only been seeing each other for about a week."

"So you work fast."

"Or else I'm worked on fast," I said.

"What are you doing in here? Looking for the bathroom?"

"No. I came in with Sammy and some other people, to get away from the mosquitoes, but then Mrs. Biddle —"

"She's my grandmother."

"Right; she stopped me and talked to me for a while."

"Did she *interrogate* you?"

"She asked me some questions."

"What did you tell her?"

"Only my name, rank, and serial number."

She opened her mouth, paused, then smiled.

"Funny man. So where are Sammy and the others?"

"They went up to the second-floor porch."

"Do you want a beer?"

"Well —"

"Let me get you one!"

She turned and skipped over to the refrigerator, which was a very large and modern one of the sort I'd only seen before in Doris Day movies.

She opened the doors and bent over, and I tried not to stare, even though (and because) she was facing away from me.

She twisted her head over her shoulder and said, "All we've got is Schmidt's in here."

"That'll do," I said.

She took out a bottle of beer and a bottle of Frank's orange soda.

"Want a glass?"

"No thanks," I said.

There was a bottle opener nailed to the wall, of the sort you see in taverns, with a metal cup under it to collect the caps. She popped the caps on our respective beverages and handed me the beer.

"Cheers, big ears," she said.

We each took a swig of our drinks.

"Tell me about going insane," she said.

"My friends will be wondering where I am."

"Briefly then."

"It was very scary," I said.

"So you knew you were going insane."

"Yes, I knew something was coming."

"And what was it like while you were insane?"

"I've blacked out a lot of it. But what I remember was like being in a dream. Or a nightmare."

"How horrible. Tell me more."

"I saw things. Or imagined them."

"Like what?"

"Well, one night I imagined that Jesus came to me."

"Oh my God, do go on." She put her soda bottle down on the red formica kitchen table and stepped closer to me, which made me feel awkward. I could smell her warmth. I took another good drink of beer. "What was he like?" she asked.

"Jesus?"

"Yes."

"He was — very comforting. Somehow. And the next morning I woke up feeling a lot better."

"But not completely better."

"No. And I'm still not completely better."

I took another drink.

"I really should join my friends upstairs," I said.

"I'm giving you the third degree," she said. "I'm worse than my grandmother. But tell me something. Do you still – see things?"

"Yes," I said, because at the moment I couldn't summon the energy to lie.

"Like what?" she said.

"Like Jesus."

"Oh boy, him again. Does he talk?"

"Does he."

"What about?"

"Well —"

"Do you suppose he's real?"

"No," I said. "I think he's a figment from a part of my brain that's still in the dream world even though I'm awake."

"But maybe he *is* real," she said.

"I doubt that."

"But what if whatever is in your brain is as real as what's in the physical world?" she asked.

"I'd rather not think about that."

I took a drink. She put her hand on my left arm.

"Tell me something else."

What the hell, I was already singing like a canary.

"Okay," I said.

"What do you think of Dick?"

This was a good break. I was glad to get off the Jesus subject.

"I like him," I said.

"He's not quite right in the head either," she said.

"Really?"

"Yes. And he's madly in love with me. What should I do?"

"Do you like him?" I asked.

"I'm madly in love with him, but I haven't let him know it."

"Ah."

I don't know if she was aware of it, but she was squeezing the crook of my arm, with surprising strength for a girl.

"May I confess something," she said. "Something personal."

"I'd prefer you didn't," I said.

"I'm a virgin."

I finished the beer in two more gulps and put the empty bottle down on the red table. Then I pried her hand off of my arm.

"Well, I should find my friends now," I said.

"I've made you uncomfortable."

"Yes," I said.

"So Dick's all right," she said. "In your opinion."

"For what my opinion's worth."

"To be my first man."

"Yeah. Well, see ya, Daphne."

"But wait." She put her hand on my arm again. "What if he *is* Mr. Right?"

She looked into my eyes, disconcertingly. I probably gulped before answering her.

"Isn't that what you want?" I said.

"Oh, sure, I suppose. But then if I *do* find out he's Mr. Right, that'll mean he'll be the only man I'll ever know."

"I see."

"So I'm wondering if maybe I should know some other men first," she said. She ran her thumb along my biceps muscle. "Build up some sort of a basis for comparison. Then after a few years I could give Dick a go. See how he measures up. What do you think of that as a plan?"

"What if Dick meets someone else in the meantime?"

She stopped rubbing my arm and tugged at the sleeve of my polo shirt.

"Dick is always meeting someone else, believe me; there are no flies on Dick. But he'll wait for me."

She tugged on my other sleeve with her other hand, as if to make sure they were even.

"How do you know he'll wait?" I asked

"He's told me he would wait for me."

She wet her fingertip on her tongue and began rubbing a place on my shirt, over my chest. I looked down. I had a mustard stain, and she was wiping it off.

A chorus of ancient laughter crackled in from the hallway, from the direction of the dining room. One of the card-players must have made a joke.

"I really should go up now," I said.

"I disturb you."

"Yes," I said.

Now she was playing with the collar of my shirt. I was drenched with sweat, as if I had just played a vigorous round of badminton myself.

"It's too bad you're Dick's friend," she said.

"Why?"

"Because if you weren't I might kiss you."

"Well, I'll be going now."

Once again I pulled her hand away.

Then I turned and reeled out of the kitchen.

I seemed to remember seeing a staircase, and sure enough I found it, and bolted up the steps two at a time.

What was it about insanity that women found so appealing?

Chapter 56

As I ran up between the narrow walls and veered around the first landing as if my life depended on it I thought, *Why now?* Why were all these females emerging from the woodwork only now? Where had they been hiding during all my former grey celibate years? Was I that much different now?

Suddenly in the middle of a flight, in the middle of a step, I halted, panting, sweating.

Yes, I was that different.

Who or what had I been before my breakdown?

I'll tell you what: a sort of walking mummy, mechanically clumping through the world swathed in the thick stale wrappings of a personality that wanted only to worship and serve some imaginary great father who had deigned to grant me this half-life I lived.

It took going insane for me to shed those stale wrappings. Perhaps something inside me had willed me to go insane in order to shed those foul rags. But shed them I did, and I walked out of that hospital like a naked child.

And I still felt like a naked child.

But I didn't want to go back to the old way.

If there was a God, if this Jesus who supposedly kept appearing to me was indeed Jesus, well, I was sorry but he was going to have to do without my worship. He'd had forty-two years of me, he wasn't getting any more.

I had continued to mount the steps during the latter stage of these lucubrations, and I found myself in a hallway.

Real life always comes back to bring us down to planet earth even in the midst of our most exalted philosophizing, and so it was that I realized that I had to urinate. Bolting that last beer with the terrible and beautiful Daphne had done the trick.

I went looking for a bathroom. I found one likely door and opened it, it was a bathroom all right, but an attractive woman with short red hair was sitting on the toilet, smoking a cigarette.

"Sorry!" I blurted.

She merely shrugged and smiled as I shut the door. Her face had seemed familiar to me, but I couldn't quite place her. I figured she must be another show-business person. A show business woman. Another woman.

Where were they all coming from? It was like an invasion from outer space.

But then I could think of worse invasions.

I went down the hall and up the stairs again, figuring a fine house like this would probably have at least one bathroom on the third floor. Around narrow landings and down a short hall I went and sure enough I found another bathroom, and, thank God or Steve or no one, it was unoccupied.

You can well believe me that I latched the door while doing my business. Lately it seemed that even the most casual trip to the bathroom could be fraught with adventure.

I felt much calmer after voiding my bladder. I flushed the toilet, washed and dried my hands, lit a cigarette, smoothed my hair, and managed to leave the bathroom without incident.

But then in the hall I thought about this female business again.

I thought about it but I didn't come to any conclusions. Perhaps women just were attracted to men who weren't mummies, even if they were insane. I walked along and went up some steps and out to a very small porch with a lovely ornately-carved white wooden railing. No one else was there.

I supposed they had all gone downstairs again. Oh well, I decided just to finish my cigarette in peace, staring out across the street at the rooftops across the way, at the starry sky leaping out above me and descending into the purple sea on the horizon. Treetops swayed beneath me like giant dancing girls shaking their hair and their thousands of little hands and fingers, the breeze smelled of scallops and seaweed, and, yes, of marijuana.

I heard a guitar, and then a woman's voice singing:

I met my love by the gas works wall
Dreamed a dream by the old canal
I kissed my girl by the factory wall
Dirty old town
Dirty old town

It suddenly dawned on me that this was Elektra's voice, and that she was singing somewhere below me. I looked around me and I realized that I was on the widow's walk on the roof of the house. Behind me was the attic tower. I had managed to overshoot not only the second floor but the third as well.

I sighed, and put out my cigarette on the underside of the rail. I field-stripped the butt, letting the little pieces of tobacco and paper fly away on the ocean breeze, and then I went back inside. At this rate I would be lucky if Elektra even remembered what I looked like.

Well, all I had to do was go down past the third floor and to the second and then find this second-floor porch. That should be within the realm of my capabilities.

As I went down the first flight of steps I could still faintly hear Elektra's ringing voice.

Clouds are drifting across the moon
Cats are prowling on their beat
Spring's a girl from the streets at night
Dirty old town
Dirty old town

Chapter 57

I went past the third floor and successfully made it down to the second. There were two doorways on the front side of the hall. The door to the first was closed, but the second one was open. I walked over, and I could hear Elektra's voice:

> Heard a siren from the docks
> Saw a train set the night on fire

Before I could go in however, a woman appeared in the doorway. She had red hair, cut like Peter Pan's.

"Oh, it's you," she said.

As with the woman I had surprised in the bathroom just a short while ago, I felt that I had seen this woman before, or at least that I had imagined seeing her before, I didn't know where or when.

"Hello," I said.

"The bathroom," she said.

"Oh!"

Indeed this *was* the woman I had intruded upon as she sat on the toilet smoking a cigarette.

She stuck out a hand.

"I'm Shirley," she said.

I shook her hand.

"I'm Arnold."

"Oh, Arnold. I've heard about you."

She held onto my hand.

She did look awfully familiar. I mean I seemed to know her from before the bathroom incident. She wore a pretty shiny green dress and she was very trim.

"I'm going down for more beer," she said. "Would you like one?"

"Sure, thanks," I said.

She stared at me, still holding onto my hand.

"You have an aura," she said.

"I do?"

"Yes. It's very slight, but I can see it. Around your head."

"Like a halo?"

"Sort of. It's like your head is giving off this shimmering glow."

With my free left hand I touched the top of my head. It felt normal enough.

"I can tell you're a very spiritual person," she said.

All I could think was, *Great, this is all I need: a halo.*

"Oh," she said, and she seemed saddened.

"What?" I said.

"Your aura's fading."

"Thank God," I couldn't help but say aloud.

She at last let go of my hand, but she continued to stand in the doorway, effectively blocking it. She seemed to be studying my eyes. I found this as disconcerting as when Daphne had done the same thing, and I looked over her head. The porch was out there. Someday I would reach it.

A harmonica had been playing but now Elektra's voice was singing again:

> *I'm going to make me a good sharp axe*
> *Shining steel tempered in the fire*
> *I'll chop you down like an old dead tree*
> *Dirty old town*
> *Dirty old town*

The harmonica came back in.

"Your girlfriend has a lovely voice," said Shirley. "And you have a very — radiant soul. I feel that you've been touched by God."

"You don't know the half of it," I said.

"When I was holding your hand I felt like you could pull me along up into the sky, into the stars."

"Oh, I doubt I could do that," I said.

"You mean I'm not advanced enough," she said.

"Oh no, not at all. I just mean I don't think I could do that."

"Have you traveled through the stars, Arnold?"

Forget about traveling though the stars, I was having a hard enough time just making it out to that porch.

Elektra started singing again:

> *I met my love by the gas works wall*

"But you're probably in a hurry to get out to your girlfriend," said Shirley.

"Well, I wouldn't say I'm in a hurry," I said, trying to be polite.

"Then help me bring the beers up," she said.

I was doomed. That porch was my promised land, my city of gold, and I would never reach it.

Next thing I knew Shirley had my hand in hers and she was leading me back to the staircase.

Dirty old town
Dirty old town

I thought of dear old Olney, the Heintz factory behind our house, the great stacks belching black smoke, the rattle of the 47 trolley, the beer smell of the taverns, the sneakers swaying from the telephone wires, the butcher shop smells of sawdust and blood, the sugary warmth of the bakeries, the wooden darkness of the confessional box...

But then I got a grip on myself. I halted, but Shirley kept going, holding onto my hand, until both our arms were outstretched, with Shirley already on the second step down. She turned her head.

"Come on, Arnold!"

"I should go see Elektra," I said. "My, uh –"

"Your girlfriend."

"Yes. She'll be wondering where I am."

"We'll only be a minute."

"Somehow I doubt that," I said.

"Why?"

"Something will happen."

"I'm not going to seduce you, Arnold."

"I didn't mean that," I said. Not necessarily, anyway. "I just meant that something else would happen. That would prevent me from getting out to that porch."

"Like what?"

"I don't know. Dean Martin will come in and want to hear my thoughts on Jesus and salvation."

"I doubt that. You don't know Dean."

"I just meant that as an example."

"You're being silly."

We were still holding hands at arm's length while all this was going on, with Shirley on the second step of the stairway. We were like a poster for some dramatic movie.

She had been smiling, but now her face turned serious, and she looked into my eyes.

"You can see the future," she said.

"No," I said. "But I can do what I can to ward off the possibility of certain historical trends."

"You really do have a deep soul."

"Thank you," I said. "Can I have my hand back?"

"Of course, Arnold."

She let go of my hand. Its palm was warm and sweaty.

"So," she said. "A beer for you? Or would you prefer a cocktail? A *cocktail*! Would you like a Manhattan?"

I told her that would be very nice.

Shirley went down the stairs and I turned back.

I realized that Sammy was singing now, and had been singing:

> *Oh, the train I ride on*
> *Oh the engine shine like gold*
> *Just like gold*

Chapter 58

When I got to the doorway I stopped and listened to Sammy sing:

Ah, stop your train, darlin'
Let a poor boy ride
Ah don't ya hear me callin'?

Then I went through the doorway. This was a bedroom, a night-table lamp was lit. On the opposite side of the room was a screen door, presumably opening onto the porch I'd been trying to get to all this time. I went on through the room, opened the door and went out.

At last.

A light in a blue fixture glowed in the ceiling, and Sammy sat in a rocker off to the left, with his back to the porch railing; he strummed a guitar and sang, turning his head and nodding to me:

Can't you hear me call?

Elektra, Steve and Miss Rathbone all sat in a white slatted wooden porch glider across from Sammy. A low and narrow glass-topped table was in front of the glider, with beer bottles and ashtrays on it. Elektra raised a hand in my direction, her eyebrows raised. I sat down next to her.

"Where were you?" she whispered in my ear.

"Uh, with Mrs. Biddle," I said, which was true enough, although not the entire truth, but I didn't want to get in a big conversation while Sammy was singing. I did whisper, though:

"I heard you singing. It was very pretty."

"Thanks," she whispered back.

And she rubbed my lower back with her hand.

I glanced across to Steve and Miss Rathbone. They were holding hands, or Steve was holding Miss Rathbone's hand. Each held a cigarette in his or her free hand, and their heads nodded slowly as they gazed at Sammy as he sang on:

Yeah, smokestack lightnin'
Yeah, hear me call

Hear me call

The porch was screened in, free of bugs. The trees I had seen from above now loomed before me, two stout oak trees, and Sammy seemed to be singing and playing in time to the brushing of their leaves against the screening in the soft and slightly salty breeze.

> *Let a poor boy ride*
> *Let a poor boy ride*

Elektra laid her head on my shoulder, and the four of us on the glider swung it gently back and forth.

Sammy's eyes were closed as he sang, and even though he was basically singing just the same few words over and over again with slight variations his voice and the words carrying on these simple ringing chords seemed as true and as beautiful to me as anything I'd heard before.

It occurred to me that I was happy.

How odd.

And, me being me, it also occurred to me that right that minute all over the world people were suffering, killing one another, starving, dying.

Was it right for me to sit here feeling happy while my fellow creatures suffered?

But then it occurred to me that all these suffering people would choose to be happy if they had a choice, so what sort of insufferable prig would I be to deny myself happiness if it fell my way?

"Sing the song, Sammy!" said Dean Martin, coming through the door holding a Manhattan in each hand and with a cigarette hanging from his lips. He was dressed as if for the golf course, in a green knit sport shirt and blue trousers.

"Drinks are here!" said Shirley, following Dean through the door and carrying a tray with five more Manhattans on it.

Dean and Shirley passed the drinks around.

"Cent'ann'," said Dean, and we all raised our glasses and drank.

Sammy asked Dean if he would sing "that cowboy song from *Rio Bravo*," and Dean said he would. He pulled around the one free rocker so that it faced between us on the glider and Sammy, and he sat down. Shirley sat down on his knee.

Sammy strummed the guitar, and Dean began to sing:

The sun is sinkin' in the west
The cattle go down to the stream

But still that familiar and horrible little voice in my head told me I didn't deserve this. I had always felt barely worthy even to buy a ticket to see a movie, and here I was being entertained by these famous performers and absolutely free of charge while far better people than myself would have to pay good money to see them at the Latin Casino or the 500 Club.

I told the little voice to be quiet and to go away, at least for now. The moist breeze blew through the trees and through the screen. Elektra had sat up straight when Shirley handed her her Manhattan, but now she laid her head on my shoulder again. I felt her hand on my hand and her bosom against my arm.

"Hey," she whispered, and I turned my head to look at her, into her dark eyes.

Dean sang:

Gonna hang my sombrero
On the limb of a tree
Comin' home, sweetheart darlin'
Just my rifle, pony, and me...

That was it, I felt like I was coming home, even though it was a home I'd never had, a home I had never been to. I had walked through hell to get here. But now that I was here, now that what remained of me was here, I was glad.

Sammy joined in:

Whippoorwill in the willow
Sings a sweet melody

Then Sammy and Dean sang together:

Ridin' to Amarillo
Just my rifle, pony, and me

The breeze tumbled a sweep of dark curling hair into Elektra's face. I cleared it away with my fingers and she closed her eyes.

No more cows to be ropin'

No more strays will I see
Round the bend she'll be waitin'
For my rifle, pony and me

Chapter 59

Next Shirley sang a song with Dean:

If our lips should meet, innamorata
Kiss me kiss me sweet, innamorata...

The words were pretty inane, but who was I to be critical? After all, just now I found on the floor a clipping of a sonnet I wrote last year, it must have fallen out of my scrapbook when I took it down to Miss Rathbone:

"First Communion, St. Helena's, 1962"

The little children pass all dressed in white,
their first communion gravely to receive,
that they might not dwell in eternal night;
the Good Lord has granted them His reprieve.
but what of the Hindu, Jewish, Moslem,
and Protestant boys and girls, whom, through no
fault of their own, God chooses to condemn
to at best an afterlife in Limbo?
He has His reasons for this I am told,
but still it seems a little harsh to me,
a bit arbitrary, a trifle cold;
and worse, some say that they might even be
sent to Purgatory or even Hell;
this seems far from fair to me, truth to tell.

What the — go on, say it, they can only damn me once — what the hell was I thinking?

It wouldn't be so bad if the above lines were a joke, but at the time I wrote them I was quite serious.

I'm becoming convinced that I didn't just go mad this past January, oh no, I think I was secretly quite mad for many years, perhaps since birth.

And for that matter how mad is my longtime editor at the *Olney Times*, Mr. Willingham? (An Episcopalian I might add.) He's the one who printed this rubbish. But then I've suspected for some time he only glances at my copy once or twice a year, if that.

So, yes, I had been a madman. But was I still a madman?

Frank Sinatra and Miss Evans came up and joined us. More songs were sung. Frank did a nice version of "The Lady is a Tramp"...

Then the guy who had been in the car with Frank and Sammy and Dean and Joey came through the screen door, the guy that neither Steve nor Miss Rathbone nor I had recognized.

He was a hearty, muscular guy of about my age, with a receding hairline and a face like a boxer's. He wore khakis and a pale blue alligator polo shirt, and he smoked a fine cigar.

He said hello to Sammy and Frank, Dean and Shirley, how-do to Steve and Miss Rathbone, to Miss Evans and to Elektra. Then he said to me that I must be this Arnold he'd been hearing about.

I said I was, and he put out his hand. The knuckles were scarred and gnarled.

"My name's Larry," he said. "Larry Winchester. Pleased to meet you, Arnold."

Chapter 60

I assured this Larry Winchester that I was pleased to meet him as well.

"And who is this lovely young lady sitting on your lap?"

Only then did I realize fully that Elektra was indeed sitting on my lap. The thing was that Miss Evans had squeezed onto the glider between Elektra and Steve, and so to make room for her out of politeness, or more likely so as not to be in too close propinquity to her, Elektra had slipped onto my lap.

This was categorically the first time anyone had ever sat on my lap in my entire life. Another big first for our hero.

Caught up in these reflections I forgot to answer Larry Winchester's question, but fortunately Elektra did.

"My name's Elektra," she said, and she presented her hand.

Mr. Winchester took her hand and brushed her knuckles with his somewhat scarred lips.

He and Elektra exchanged pleasantries having to do with her name and how she got it, and, as I so often do when people talk, and sometimes when I talk, I checked out mentally, thinking about anything but the present subject of conversation, and then I suddenly realized that Mr. Winchester was addressing me.

"You know," he said, "my mother is obsessed with your work."

"Really?"

"Yes. She cuts out your poems from the *Olney Times* and Scotch-tapes them to her refrigerator."

"Aww," said Elektra.

"She's going to be so impressed that I met you."

I didn't know what to say, which is not unusual for me of course. However, after many years of social doltishness, I've gradually realized that people are much more comfortable if you say something, anything other than saying a great resounding nothing, no matter how dull, so I scrabbled around on the littered floor of my brain and brought this gem up:

"So, you're from Olney, Mr. Winchester?"

"My mother lives there," he said. "I've mostly lived out in L.A. since the war. Now I'm based in Europe. But I was just visiting in Philly, and good old Mom is still cutting out your poems every week."

"Tell her I appreciate it," I said.

"Don't worry, I will."

That was it for me, I had exhausted my supply of sparkling repartée.

Sammy was still playing his guitar through all this, although no one was singing.

Mr. Winchester gazed at me, smoking his cigar.

Fortunately Elektra rescued me again.

"What do *you* do, Mr. Winchester?" she asked.

"Larry," he said. "Please call me Larry."

"Larry," she said.

"You too, Arnold. If I may call you Arnold."

"Sure."

"Sure, 'Larry'," he said.

"'Larry'," I said.

"I'm a movie director, darling," said Larry in answer to Elektra's question. "I've also done a lot of TV work."

"What movies have you directed," asked Elektra.

"Well, we just opened a picture called *The Return of the 300 Spartans*, with George Maharis –"

Elektra cocked her head and twisted her lovely lips.

"And earlier this year we had a little thing called *Stopover in Singapore*," tried Mr. Winchester. "With Dane Clark?"

"Umm," hummed Elektra.

"How about *Bayonets of Blood*? With Rory Calhoun?"

"I don't think so," she said.

"*Two For Tortuga*? With Lex Barker and Tina Louise?" said Larry. "*The Vacant City*? With Dennis Hopper?"

"Um, no," said Elektra.

"*Several Lonely People*? With Eddy O'Brien? *Mademoiselle 38*, with Mara Corday?"

"I've seen them all, Larry," I said. (Basically, if it's come to the Fern Rock Theatre on Fifth Street, I've seen it.)

"Well, that's gratifying" he said. "I was beginning to think my career was for naught."

"Oh, please don't go by me, Larry," said Elektra. "I just don't see too many movies."

"A sign of intelligence, my dear."

"I would rather read a book, usually."

"Who are your favorite authors?"

"Oh, I don't know. Dostoyevsky, Tolstoy. Proust I suppose. Henry de Montherlant."

(In honesty I have to say that the last two names she mentioned were gibberish to me, but afterwards I asked her to repeat them and spell them out for me.)

"Beauty *and* brains," said Larry Winchester. "You're not an actress by any chance are you?"

"No."

"A pity. I would cast you in a minute. With your looks, your presence."

What a racket I thought. I made a mental note that if there was anything to reincarnation I would become a movie director in my next life. It had to be a better job than being a brakeman. Or a poet. Or a madman, for that matter.

Chapter 61

Larry and Elektra continued to chat, and I checked out again, another one of my fade-outs into my own merry little world.

Occasionally I've gotten into a little trouble or embarrassment because of this proclivity.

One time in 1942 I was sitting around with some other railroad guys at Oscar's Tavern down on Sansom Street and they all started saying "All right! Let's go then!" And they clapped me on the back and said, "Let's go, Arnold!" And I, having no idea what they were talking about said, "Okay!" And followed them out the bar and down the street to the recruiting station where we all joined the army. But the thing was, as railroad men we were exempt from the draft, and all we had to do was keep working for the railroad and we wouldn't have had to go to war. Which would have been fine with me. But there I was with all the rest of them, volunteering, just because I hadn't been paying attention.

I lost my virginity that way, too. A few weeks after V-E Day I was sitting with some of my buddies in a café in Frankfurt, drinking peppermint schnapps and beer, dreaming of God knows what, when one of them said, "You up for it, Arnold?" And I said, "Sure." Next thing I knew I was being frog-marched into a brothel, gibbering with fright as if I were being dragged to the electric chair. And as terrified as I was going in I was even more terrified an hour later when I shuffled out, expecting a lightning bolt to strike me down at any moment and cast my wretched unshriven soul screaming hellward.

This daydreaming was also how I joined the Democratic Party, why I came to be the boxing coach of St. Helena's Parish CYO, and why I often found myself volunteering for extra shifts on the railroad or for extra masses as an usher. It's only by sheer luck that I have never been sitting obliviously woolgathering with some guys at a bar while they all agreed that we should tear off our clothes as one and run screaming out into the street naked or pull an armed robbery of the PSFS Bank or jump off the Benjamin Franklin Bridge.

So I knew that Larry and Elektra were chatting, I just had no idea what they were chatting about. Until Elektra tweaked my cheek and said, "Arnold, answer Larry."

"Um —" here we go again, I thought, desperately trying to tread water until I could figure out what the heck was going on.

"If you don't want to say," said Larry, "I understand."

"Oh, no, I don't mind," I said, thus throwing away the out he had just handed me.

"So?" he said.

"Well, I'd have to say —" might as well be affirmative — "I'd have to say yes."

"Ah," he said. "So tell me about it."

"Oh," I said.

"I mean if you'd like to."

"Sure," I said.

"Aren't you working on a memoir?" said Elektra.

"Yes," I said, wondering what this had to do with anything.

"So tell Larry about it."

"Well," I said, at long last realizing that he must have been asking me if I was working on anything special in the literary realm, "it's — it's just about my life, really."

"So you're writing your autobiography?"

"Well, I thought it was going to be like that at first, but mostly it's more like a sort of diary, I suppose. Just the little things I do all day."

"Like Jack Kerouac," said Larry.

"Uh, maybe," I said. I remembered seeing Jack Kerouac on Steve Allen, although I'd never read any of his books because they didn't have scantily-clad women with guns on the covers.

"Do you have a publisher yet?"

"Oh, no, no one would ever publish this stuff, Larry. I'm only writing it to —"

I stopped in my verbal tracks.

"To what, Arnold?"

"I don't know," I said.

"You're a true artist, Arnold," said Larry. "I'll be honest with you, I used to think your poems were — well, what do I know?"

"Oh, no," I said, "They were."

"Were what?"

"Bad?" I said.

"I wasn't going to say *bad* exactly."

"Mediocre?"

"Well, the point is, I looked at some of your most recent poems on my mother's Frigidaire, and I thought they were quite good."

"Thanks."

"Arnold, I think you and I might be able to work together."

"Doing what?"

"Writing movies."

"Movies?"

"Sure. Why not? I like to work with other guys. Somebody to kick around ideas with. Bang the typewriter keys when my fingers get tired."

"Well, I don't know."

"Oh, I get it. You feel you have to concentrate on your memoir. And your poems."

"Well, no, not really."

"Then what's the problem? There could be a few bucks in it for ya, kiddo."

"Really?"

"Sure. I don't write anything on spec. I get the contract, then I write the goddamn script, and not one second before."

Scripts, specs, contracts, it all seemed somehow so tedious to me.

"It's like I gotta shoot a picture in Paris next month, Arnold. I got the cast and a budget, but the script they want me to do stinks."

"Well, I don't know, Larry," I said. "Is there a murder in it?"

"Yeah, a GI on leave in Paris gets mixed up with a dame and a killing."

"I don't know."

"You're tough, Arnold. You're very tough."

"Arnold's tough all right," said Elektra, and she moved in my lap.

It was then that I realized that I had an erection.

Chapter 62

Fortunately Larry and Elektra began to talk, about Paris; I say fortunately because all I could think about was my erection, pressing up against Elektra's warm buttocks. It amazed me that she went on blithely talking about Parisian streets and cafés and film-makers and movies and books and writers I had never heard of as all the while this thing with its own mind pulsed up against her.

I realized that I had to do something to detumesce this annoying organ, and so I deliberately tried to think of the most unexciting things imaginable. I cast my mind back to the many dull sermons I had stood through as an usher at St. Helena's: old Father Peck's mumbling endless rambles, young Father Murray's tediously exuberant dithyrambs, Bishop Graham's somniferous basso dronings, but even after five minutes of this retrospective feast of boredom my erection still pulsed proudly and defiantly.

"Hey, pal, don't worry about it," said that familiar voice.

I looked over Elektra's shoulder, and there — where Steve had been sitting on the other side of Miss Evans — he was: Jesus, with his white shirt, white trousers, and white shoes. In one hand he held both a Manhattan and his usual Pall Mall, and in the other he held the hand of Miss Rathbone, who, like Miss Evans, seemed only to be listening to Larry and Elektra talk.

"It's not like this is some major torture for you, some big *problem*, Arnold," he said.

"I didn't say it was," I thought but did not say, wishing to keep my insanity or my visitation, whatever it was, to myself, thank you.

"Well, you're sitting there acting like it's some big problem, instead of taking part in the conversation like a sane person."

"Yes, like a sane person," I said (without speaking). "That would certainly be an accomplishment for me, wouldn't it?"

"Oh, boo hoo. You've got it so tough. Well, you know what's tough, buster? Getting scourged. After being betrayed by one of your supposed best friends. *That's* tough. And how about a crown of thorns for a *chapeau*? Oh, never tried it? Well, how about being cru-"

"Okay, I get it," I said.

"I hope you do."

"So I'll get back into the conversation."

"I'm not stopping you."

I turned away from him, and I looked at Elektra's beautiful face, lifted and in profile to me.

"I loved breathless," she said.

"Excellent movie," said Larry. "I've met Jean-Luc; nice guy, too."

"Who's Jean-Luc?" I said, making, as my mother has often advised me to do, an effort.

"Jean-Luc Godard," said Larry. (I got the spelling later from Elektra.) "He's a French movie director."

"Ah," I said, and as Larry named some of this Godard's movies (none of which I've seen, the Fern Rock doesn't show too many French movies) I became aware of one good thing my little colloquy with Jesus had brought about: my erection had gone away.

Chapter 63

Now however I had a new problem, *viz.*, my right leg had fallen asleep and the other one was heading there. And as much as I marveled at the impossibility made real of a young and beautiful woman actually sitting in my lap, the bald fact was that Elektra, although a small woman, was still nonetheless cutting off the circulation in both my legs.

Elektra and Larry had started talking about another one of this Godard's movies, I didn't catch the title.

I wanted just to lift her gently up off my lap, but of course I was too shy to do so, or to say anything. I might mention here that perhaps one cause of my paralysis of will was the fact that Larry had taken out a small porcelain pipe and filled it with what he said was hashish, and that I had partaken of it.

The pipe made its rounds and eventually Elektra handed it to me again, Larry lighted me up with an expensive-looking silvery butane lighter and I duly dragged away, wondering if it were possible to get gangrene from having a girl sit on your lap too long.

What would it be like if I had to have my legs amputated?

On the plus side I wouldn't have to go anywhere.

On the negative side I wouldn't be able to go anywhere, except in a wheel chair.

All in all therefore it seemed like a good idea to lift Elektra up, and after passing the pipe along to Larry I was gearing myself up to do this when I felt something on the side of my leg. At first I thought it was a bug, but looking down I saw that the fingers of Miss Evans's hand were caressing my thigh. I looked up at her face, but she was looking right past me, at Larry, apparently following the conversation he was having with Elektra. Looking past her I saw with some relief that Jesus had now transmogrified back into good old Steve, who suddenly said to me, "I don't like foreign movies! Do you, Arnold?"

"I never really thought about it," I said. And why would I have, since except for the odd Godzilla movie and some Hercules movies with Steve Reeves, and the occasional English Frankenstein or Dracula movie, I've hardly ever seen a foreign movie.

"You're such a philistine, Steve" said Miss Evans, who was sucking on the hashish pipe now.

"I am not!" said Steve. "I just don't like to *read* while I'm watching a movie. Is that so horrible?"

"You have no culture," said Miss Evans, now blatantly caressing the underside of my thigh with at least four of her red-tipped fingers. The funny thing was that I could barely feel her fingers because my thigh was asleep. "What about Ingmar Bergman?" she said. "He's one of the greatest artists of the 20th century."

"Oh my God," said Steve, grabbing the pipe out of her hand, "I saw one of his movies once. It was the dreariest thing I'd ever seen. I wanted to kill myself after it. Instead I just had a cocktail and then I was fine."

"You're an idiot, Steve," said Miss Evans.

"You're mean," he said sucking away on the pipe. "Charlotte," he turned to Miss Rathbone, who was vaguely staring at Sammy, who was singing a song about a new dawn and a new day. "Did you hear what she said?"

"What?" said Miss Rathbone.

"Gertrude says I have no class."

"I never said that," said Miss Evans. I could see that she was fully gripping the underside of my thigh now, but my leg was so numb it was like looking at someone else's leg.

Larry and Elektra were still holding their own conversation through all this, still talking about French movies.

"At least I'm not a pseudo-intellectual," said Steve.

"Steve," said Miss Rathbone, "you're not any sort of intellectual."

"Well, that's true," said Steve. "And look at your hand, missy," he said to Miss Evans, "all over or should I say under Arnold's leg."

"What?" she said. She looked down and saw her hand attached to my leg like a starving leech. "Oh." She let go. "Sorry," she said to me, "I was not aware."

Elektra twisted on my lap.

"What's going on?" she said.

"Gertrude was caressing Arnold's leg," said Steve.

"I was not," said Miss Evans.

"Liar," he said.

Elektra simply took the hashish pipe from Steve, turned back to Larry and continued her interrupted conversation as Larry lighted her up with his lighter.

Sammy sang his song.

"I love this song!" said Steve. "Sing it, Sammy!"

I listened to Sammy sing.

And this old world
is a new world
and a bold world for me

Both my legs were more or less completely numb now, my brain a little less so.

Chapter 64

Fortunately Elektra got up voluntarily from my lap soon after — she had to go to the ladies' room — and so I'm happy to report that I am not yet a paraplegic.

I stretched out my legs and wiggled my toes in my Keds.

Sammy had finished his "new dawn new day" song and now he asked Frank if he would like to sing another one. Frank said sure, they exchanged a few more words, Sammy strummed a few introductory chords, Frank cleared his throat, coughed gently, tapped his cigarette ash into a nearby standing ashtray, and sang:

> *Like the beat beat beat of the tom-tom*
> *When the jungle shadows fall*
> *Like the tick tick tock of the stately clock*
> *As it stands against the wall...*

"Why are you torturing me?" whispered Miss Evans in my ear.
"Pardon me?"

> *Night and day, you are the one*
> *Only you beneath the moon or under the sun*

"Torturing me. Sitting here like that, stretching your legs like some great panther."
"What?"

> *Night and day, you are the one*
> *Only you beneath the moon or under the sun*

"Showing off your muscular legs."
She ran her hand over my right thigh. I unstretched my legs, and tried to unflex their muscles as best I could.

> *Whether near to me, or far*
> *Its no matter darling where you are*
> *I think of you, day and night*

Larry had put away the hashish pipe, and had lit up another fine-smelling cigar. He was ostensibly watching Frank sing, but I noticed him looking at Miss Evans and me out of the corner of his right eye.

> *Night and day, why is it so*
> *That this longing for you follows wherever I go*

"Such sweet torture," said Miss Evans into my ear.
I made bold enough to lift her hand away and I dropped it on her lap.

> *In the roaring traffic's boom*
> *In the silence of my lonely room*
> *I think of you*

I noticed Steve staring at us wide-eyed, and even Miss Rathbone was observing our shenanigans from over the crest of her regal nose.

> *Day and night, night and day*
> *Under the hide of me*

I stood up, swaying slightly, from the drugs, from the alcohol, from sitting too long with Elektra on my lap, from everything.

> *There's an oh such a hungry yearning*
> *burning inside of me*

"Where are you going?" said Miss Evans.

> *And this torment won't be through*
> *Until you let me spend my life making love to you*

"I want a drink of water," I said.

> *Day and night, night and day*

"I want one, too," she said, and she too stood up.
I went over to the screen door, opened it and went through, and Miss Evans was right behind me.

I made it out to the hall and I was heading for the staircase when Miss Evans grabbed my arm.

She hauled herself in to me.

"Don't think I didn't see you looking at me," she said.

It's true, I had been shooting her the odd glance, but only in the way one would keep an eye on a large cat known for sudden attacks of hysteria.

"Um," I said.

"I know your type," she said. "You like to use your power over women."

"Pardon me?"

She looked to her left, saw a door. Without letting go of my arm she reached over with her other hand and opened the door. The room inside was unlit. She pulled me into it, swinging me around as she did.

Still without letting go of my arm she reached behind her and closed the door.

Frank and Sammy had started on "Old Man River", and I could hear Frank singing:

Tote that barge, you gotta heft that bale

Once again Miss Evans drew herself close to me, and now she gripped my other upper arm with her other hand (thus gripping both my arms, in case you're trying to keep track).

Some faint light came in from the porch. Her face was like an enormous close-up from some old black-and-white movie, the part where the heroine says something extremely dramatic.

"You're like Howard Roark, aren't you?" she said.

"Who's Howard Roark?"

"The protagonist of *The Fountainhead*. But that's right, you haven't read it."

"I did see the movie," I offered.

"Howard Roark is the Gary Cooper part," she said.

"You must be kidding," I said.

"False modesty will get you nowhere with me."

"I assure you my modesty is warranted," I said.

"Come to my room tonight."

"I don't think that's a good idea," I said.

"You find me unattractive?"

"No."

"Is it because of Elektra?"

"Uh, yes," I said.

"You don't sound so sure. Are you sure that's the only reason?"

"No," I admitted. "It's not the only reason."

"Then what's the other reason."

"Oh, nothing."

"Tell me."

"I'd prefer not to."

"Tell me."

Her long red nails bit into my biceps, like two small but powerful ferrets.

"Um —"

"Tell me!" she said.

"You terrify me," I said.

Finally, she let go of my arms. She straightened my polo shirt sleeves. She looked away, and then looked back to me, up into my eyes.

"You wicked man," she said. "You wicked, wicked man."

Chapter 65

I said nothing. Not because I was trying to be the strong, silent type, but because I couldn't think of anything to say, let alone something witty or profound.

Suddenly she grabbed the cloth of my shirt at my chest in both her hands and pulled me closer to her.

"Have you read Kierkegaard?" she asked.

"No," I said.

I had heard the name, but it lay stranded somewhere between Kant and Knut Hamsun on that long list of authors I intended to get to when I found the time in my busy schedule.

"He speaks of a great leap. A leap into faith. Don't be afraid to take that leap, Arnold."

"It's not the leap into faith that I'm afraid of," I said.

"What are you afraid of?"

She stared deep and questioningly into my eyes, even though I'd just finished telling her it was her I was afraid of; I've noticed in life that with some people you just have to keep telling them something, perhaps with slight variations, until at last they get it through their thick heads that you actually mean what you say.

But before I could answer she answered for me:

"It's me," she said. "Isn't it? You're afraid of me. Why are you afraid of me?"

I didn't quite know where to begin. But I did know there was probably no extremely gentle way to answer this question. So on the spur of the moment I decided to fall back on the time-honored recourse of babbling the first nonsense that came into my head.

"I'm afraid of your passion," I said. "I'm afraid to take that leap because I fear it would be like leaping into some great dark lake. No, some great dark sea. A great dark warm, stormy dark sea. In which I would drown."

"You're such a poet," she said.

"Well, I guess I'll go get that drink of water now," I said.

She hesitated only a fraction of a second before tightening her double fist-hold on my shirt front and pulling me around and then pushing me back and down onto a bed that I had only vaguely been aware was even there.

I lay back on the bed, looking up at her in the half-darkness. I became aware that Frank had started singing again, out on the porch:

Fly me to the moon
And let me play among the stars
Let me see what spring is like
On Jupiter and Mars

She stepped closer to the bed, between my legs. She lowered one of the straps of her sundress off her shoulder, and a soft pale crescent of bosom appeared.

Moving like an Olympic gymnast I lifted my right leg up and to the other side of her, sprang to my feet and quickly sidestepped around her, heading for the door.

She grabbed my arm, again, and pulled me around to face her.

"Tonight, then. My room," she whispered.

The loosened shoulder strap lay down at her elbow, and that side of her dress hung low, revealing more than enough of her to cause me to sigh.

Where was my friend Jesus when I needed him, I wondered.

"Right here, buddy," he said.

And sure enough he was standing behind her in the shadows, glowing in his white shirt and trousers. He popped a cigarette into his mouth from a pack of Pall Malls, and shoved the pack back into his shirt pocket.

In other words please be true
In other words...

"You don't have to look over my shoulder," she said. "Don't be afraid to look into my eyes."

"Yeah, don't look at me, Arnold," he said, taking a lighter out of his pocket.

I looked into her eyes. She put her hand on my cheek.

"Or I could come to your room," she said.

"Give her a break, Arnold," he said. He lit the cigarette, clicked the lighter shut, took a drag. *"Christ you can be a stick-in-the-mud."*

"Your poet's garret," she said. "I could creep away before dawn, and your mother and aunts would be none the wiser."

"Miss Evans," I said.

"Gertrude," she said.

"Listen, Gertrude," I said.

"I'm listening."

"I'm leaping, but I'm leaping in the other direction."

"So, tonight then?" she said.

It was as if I were speaking Chinese.

"You're not speaking Chinese," he said, with a grin. *"But you are speaking with a woman."*

> *In other words please be true*
> *In other words, in other words*
> *I love you*

I removed her hands, from my face and from my arm. Nevertheless she kissed me, warmly but briefly. She drew her face away from mine.

Her eyes were dark blue, gleaming and beckoning.

I noticed him smiling, nodding his head.

I turned, went to the door, opened it and went out.

I really needed a glass of water now.

Chapter 66

I moved quickly. I certainly wouldn't have put it past Miss Evans to come running out after me and grabbing me again, perhaps to throw me down on the hall carpet with a deft jiu-jitsu maneuver.

I headed for the staircase and descended the stairs two steps at a time, glancing up at the turning of the first flight just to make sure she wasn't following me.

Almost falling down the ground-floor flight I practically slammed into Daphne's father, Mr. MacNamara.

"*Whoa*," he said, holding one hand against my chest and hanging onto the bannister with his other hand.

"Oh, I'm sorry," I said.

"What's the rush, Arnold?"

"I, um —"

I suppose I looked like a lunatic. Which I suppose is what I should have looked like, since I was acting like a lunatic.

He removed his hand from my chest, then took another step up so that we stood at the same level, facing each other. He looked into my eyes.

He's a tall man, solidly built, the sort of man that the writers of the paperback novels I like to read would call "ruggedly handsome". He wore a madras sport shirt and tan shorts. His nose appeared to have been broken at one time, and his eyes were somewhat hooded, almost sleepy-looking, and yet somehow very watchful. He seemed to be looking into me, but I found this calming instead of disconcerting.

"Where you headed, Arnold?"

His voice was deep, and I found this reassuring also.

"I was going to get a drink of water," I said.

"Running like you had a hellhound on your trail?"

"There was — um — there was —"

"A woman," he said.

"Yeah," I exhaled.

He took out a pack of Chesterfields, gave them a shake and offered them to me.

I had my own Pall Malls of course, but I took one of his Chesterfields. He shook another one up and put it in his lips. Getting a hold of myself I took out my lighter and lit us both up.

I don't know why, but it didn't seem strange to be standing smoking in this narrow staircase with this man.

"I guess you've seen a lot," he said.

"No more than the average person," I said.

"I'm not talking about things you've seen in the physical world. Anyone can see that shit. I've seen that shit. You know what I mean."

"Yeah, I guess so," I said.

"But you know what, Arnold?"

"What?"

"There's even more to see."

"Really?"

"And I don't mean in the physical world."

That was what I thought he meant.

"Well," he said, "you'd better get that drink of water."

"Yeah," I said.

He patted my shoulder and continued up the stairs, and I went down them.

At the foot of the stairs I could hear the gentle, crackling-leaf voices of the old people in the dining room, playing their canasta or shooting craps or whatever it was they were doing. I turned right, down the hall and into the kitchen. I found a glass on a drainboard and at long last I filled it with cold water from the tap, and I drank, in great continuous gulps. This felt so good I repeated the operation, drinking another full glassful. I sighed, and stood there, staring at the steel sink. Putting my cigarette between my lips I rinsed out the glass and put it back in the dish rack.

I was ready now, or as ready as I could expect to be.

The kitchen was empty of other human beings, but I felt life all around me, as if even the walls of this house were alive.

Dick Ridpath walked into the kitchen.

"Oh, Arnold," he said. "How's it going?"

"Okay, Dick," I said.

"Having a good time?"

"Sure," I said.

"Ready for another beer?"

"I don't know if I should," I said.

"Why not?"

"I'm afraid of being hungover."

"How many have you had?"

"Um —" I tried to remember. Two beers in the yard? One with Daphne in the kitchen. A Manhattan on the porch. "I think I've had about about three beers and one Manhattan," I said.

"Oh, Christ, have a beer." He went to the enormous double-doored Frigidaire and took out two brown bottles. "It's only Schmidt's," he said.

He popped them open on the wall-opener and handed me one.

"Cheers, Arnold."

We drank. I had to admit it tasted good. And after all, what was a slight hangover in the great course of things? It wasn't as if I had anything to do the next day. Or any day.

"Daphne told me she had a chat with you," he said.

"Yeah."

"Did she say anything about me?"

"She said she's madly in love with you."

"Seriously?"

"Yes."

"Wow."

He stared at the linoleum tiles on the floor.

After half a minute he looked up, at me.

"Should I ask her to marry me then?"

For once I thought about what I was going to say before saying it, and then I said that he was asking the wrong person.

"Right," he said. "Right."

He was looking at the floor again.

There was an ashtray on the kitchen table. I went over and put out my cigarette.

"You can't change the things you've done, can you, Arnold?"

I turned and looked at him. He was looking at me now.

"No," I said.

"But we do have some say about the things we do now."

"Yes," I said, after thinking it over for half a minute.

"Right," he said.

He turned his head slightly, seeming to gaze out the kitchen window. I had no idea what was on his mind, or on his conscience. Sometimes it's hard to say enough, and sometimes I think it's easy to say too much. I've come to realize that some men's souls are like bombed-out cities. But even the most bombed-out city can be rebuilt, in time. I held my peace.

For some moments it was as if he had forgotten I was there. I could hear the leaves of some dark bush brushing against the window screen, the strumming of guitar strings and low voices from upstairs on the porch, and as if from another house I heard the ancient murmuring from down the hall in the dining room.

Then Dick turned to me.

"Why are we being so serious?" he asked.

"I have no idea," I said.

"Shall we go rejoin the party?"

"Sure," I said.

Chapter 67

"Where is everybody, anyway?" asked Dick.

"Well, there's a bunch of them up on the second-floor porch," I said.

"Ah. Do you want to go up?"

"Sure," I said.

"Your girlfriend's up there? What's her name, Eurydice?"

"Elektra," I said.

"Oh, right, Elektra. Real pretty girl, Arnold. I'm impressed."

"Yes," I said. "I'm not worthy."

He smiled at me.

"Let's go up."

"Okay. Uh, where's Daphne?" I asked as we headed out of the kitchen.

"Still playing badminton probably. Oh. Hello, Mrs. Biddle."

She was coming down the hall our way, moving quickly along with determined cracks of her walking stick. It hadn't registered with me before, but she was wearing a light-colored dress with winged collars and buttons down the front that somehow made me think she should be on a rubber plantation in Malaya or the Philippines.

"You two," she said. "What are you up to?"

"Heading upstairs," said Dick.

"To smoke reefer with Sammy, no doubt."

"Let's hope so," said Dick. "Why don't you join us?"

"My goodness," she said. "I haven't blown gage as we used to call it since the thirties."

"Come on up."

"No, I should stay down here with those living corpses in there. Besides, I'm winning at canasta. You, Arnold," she said to me.

"Yes?"

I successfully fought the impulse to click my heels and stand to attention.

"Don't forget to come see me," she said.

"All right."

"What are you doing tomorrow?"

Same thing I did everyday. Which was:

"Nothing."

"Good. Stop by around four. We'll have tea. You do drink tea."

"Copiously," I lied.

"I'll feed you. Come hungry."

"I'm always hungry," I said.

"All right, begone. I'm just going in to get some more ice and whisky."

And she brushed past us and into the kitchen, leaving a fugitive fragrance of dried roses and Scotch.

Dick and I headed up the stairs.

At the landing Dick stopped and looked at a painting on the wall. An actual real painting, and not a reproduction of one, or a photograph of the Pope or Bishop Sheen or Jackie Kennedy such as one would find in our own little house back in Olney. It was a sun-dappled picture of a bunch of people in top hats and bonnets and with parasols standing around near some lake.

I waited patiently while Dick stared at the picture; I've come to realize that when it comes to odd behavior I am in no position to be critical. And then suddenly Dick turned and said, "What do you think of the concept of the vision quest?"

"Um, I really don't know much about it."

"It's this sort of deliberately difficult journey that American Indian boys go on. To become a man and learn to appreciate nature. And the spiritual world. And this helps him decide in what direction to go in life."

"Ah," I said.

"A lot of cultures have this sort of thing. Some sort of rite of passage." He turned to me. "Do you think we miss something in our culture by not having that?"

"Beats me."

Dick was now looking at another painting on the adjacent wall of the landing. More of the old-fashioned people, staring out at an ocean or sea with a lot of boats sailing around on it.

"The navy has me studying all this sort of thing," he said. "I just got back from almost a year in Japan, checking out Buddhism. And I might go to Tibet."

"That sounds interesting," I said.

"Yeah."

There was a little wooden table in the corner, with a cut glass vase with some geraniums in it. Dick put his beer bottle on the table, then took out his cigarettes and offered me one. I shook my head no and took out my own. What the hell, it had been well over a minute since I'd finished my last one.

Dick lit us up with a battered old Ronson with the letters U.S.N. on it. He clicked the lighter shut and dropped it in a pocket.

"Daphne just told me that you've had visitations from Jesus," he said.

"Well, if you want to call it that."

"So what does he say?"

"Well, he gives me advice."

"Really? Good advice?"

"Sometimes I'm not so sure."

He took a drag of his cigarette. I suppose it was the kind of drag the authors I like to read would call contemplative.

"A lot of people would kill to be in your shoes, Arnold."

"Overall, it's pretty disconcerting, Dick," I said. "I could do without it."

He paused, then said, "So what do you think of all this Rat Pack business? Frank and Dean, and Sammy. Joey."

"They seem like nice guys," I said.

"So you don't think it's odd they're here. In Cape May."

"Now that you mention it."

"They're friends of Mac's. Daphne's father."

"Ah," I said.

"He seems to know everyone. But you don't really care, do you?"

"They're all just people."

"That's true," said Dick. "They wipe their asses just like the rest of us." He paused, staring at the floor. Then, "But look," he said, looking up, "you want to see something neat? Watch this."

He turned to the painting of the people on the beach front, put his cigarette between his lips and then pulled himself up and climbed down into the painting.

I saw him in there with all the other people.

He was waving at me and calling for me to come on in.

What the hell, I did as he had done. I put my beer bottle on the little table, grabbed the sides of the frame, and climbed up and down into the picture just as if I was climbing out of a window and into the outside world.

Except now I was standing on this sunny beach front and Dick was standing there before me with a broad smile on his face. He wore an old-fashioned blue sport-jacket over a white shirt and white trousers. He had a bright red cravat around his neck with a diamond stick-pin, and he wore a straw boater.

The seaside air was bright and warm and the breeze smelled of hibiscus and lemon.

"So, what do you think?" asked Dick. "Pretty neat, hey, Arnold?"

I looked down and saw that I was similarly attired in 19th century gentleman's fashion. I even had suede spats on over my two-toned shoes. Looking up I saw the shadowed underside of the brim of a straw hat.

"Yeah," I said. "Pretty neat."

Chapter 68

I looked around. We were standing on this terrace on some sort of bluff overlooking the water. It seemed to be late afternoon. On the landward side of the terrace was what appeared to be a small but smart hotel. The other people on the terrace paid us no mind. A white-bearded man and a woman with a parasol sat in chairs staring out toward this sea like green crushed velvet on which a strikingly large number of sailboats and steamships wended lazily this way and that. A younger couple stood near a trellis-work fence above what I assumed was a beach. The redolent hibiscus I had smelled blossomed deep gold along the fence with white and bright yellow chrysanthemums and some other bunchy pink and purple flowers.

The temperature I'd say was in the low 70s. You could hear people talking, but other than that everything was as muted as a dream.

"We seem to have left our beers behind," Dick said. "Care for a libation?"

"Sure," I said.

I figured as long as I was going to be utterly insane I might as well go ahead and have a drink.

"There must be a bar in that hotel. Let's go up."

We walked past a few more people strolling about or sitting at tables. I noticed that they were speaking French.

"Where are we, Dick?"

"I think it's Normandy. Or maybe Brittany. One of those places. Here we go."

We went up a couple of steps and through some open French doors, their glass frosted and etched in designs of various flowers and vines.

Sure enough, we were in a saloon, almost full with stylish people sitting at tables with white table-cloths and at a long mahogany bar.

"Table or bar?" asked Dick.

"Bar," I said, resignedly.

We walked over and grabbed a couple of empty stools. The bartender came over.

"Beer?" Dick asked me.

"Yeah, sure," I said.

He spoke briefly in French with the bartender. All I could make out was *bière* and *s'il vous plaît* and *merci*.

Dick turned to me and said, "He says they've got a pretty good *saison*."

"Great," I said, not that I knew or cared what a *saison* was, as long as there was alcohol in its list of ingredients.

Our cigarettes were burning down. Dick slid a large glass ashtray over and we both stubbed out our butts.

"Oh, jeeze," Dick said, "I hope we have something to pay for this."

He patted his pockets and from inside his jacket he brought out a rather large wallet. He opened it up, revealing a healthy-looking sheaf of colorful foreign currency.

"Well, this should do," he said, and he put the wallet back in his jacket.

"So, what do you think?" he asked. "About all this?"

"Oh, it's all really great, Dick," I said.

"I'm glad you like it."

The bartender loomed up just then with two large round glasses and a big bottle like a champagne bottle, with a rounded cork and a wire hood. He showed the label to Dick, and Dick gave him the go-ahead nod.

We both kept quiet while the bartender twisted off the wire and then worked out the cork. This is one reason why I've never liked to order bottles of wine on those rare occasions when I've taken my mother out to dinner. I hate that awkward eternity when the sweating waiter is wrestling the bottle open, and then that absurd ritual of him pouring a taste into my glass. I always want to say, *"Pour away, my good man, it's all the same to me, and after all it isn't as if I haven't ordered the cheapest bottle on the menu anyway."*

At last the barman filled our glasses, thank God dispensing with any taste-testing ritual, and then he went away.

"Now let's raise our glasses," said Dick.

I raised my glass. I did have to admit that the beer looked good. It actually had a decent head for one thing, unlike the Schmidt's or Ortlieb's I customarily drink.

"Cheers," said Dick.

We touched our glasses and drank, and in fact the beer was excellent, even better than the occasional German lagers I would permit myself to drink at the Schwarzwald Inn.

"Not bad, huh?"

"Yeah, it's pretty good," I said.

Perhaps complete insanity was not so bad after all. I wiped a bit of foam off my nose.

Dick was leaning sideways against the bar, looking at the people at the tables. Nearly everyone was chatting away, but still the place seemed oddly quiet. Then I realized that of course there was no radio or jukebox.

I also noticed that the air smelled different from what I was used to. A seaside and flowery breeze not unlike Cape May's wafted in from the terrace and mingled with the barroom smells of cigarettes and cigars, but under it all were hints of burning coal and just the faintest suggestion of compost.

"Oh my God," said Dick, interrupting my olfactory reverie. "Don't look now, but I swear that's the young Marcel Proust over there."

"Who?"

"Marcel Proust." He spelled out the last name for me. The young moustachioed man he was referring to was sitting by himself at a small table, apparently drinking tea and reading a book. "Famous French writer. Wrote an enormous seven-volume novel called *Remembrance of Things Past*. I've been trying to read it in French for years now, and I'm still only midway through the fifth volume."

"Oh," I said. If he had been talking about David Goodis or Richard Stark I might have been able to add a bit more to the conversation.

"Wow," said Dick. "He's awfully young. That means he hasn't started his masterwork yet. Look at him over there. He's reading his book, but occasionally he looks up. Observing. Just taking it all in. I wonder if we should talk to him."

Leave the guy alone I thought. But I don't know why I thought this. Maybe because I've never really liked it when people try to talk to me. Except when I'm drunk of course. In which case I only dislike it later, in the cold retrospective of hangover.

"Let's go chat with him," said Dick.

"You go, Dick, I'll just sit here."

"No, I can't go alone. He'll think I'm gay and I'm trying to cruise him."

I had no idea what Dick meant by this. I would think that appearing gay is an admirable quality. And I don't know at all what he meant by "cruising". I suppose it's some sort of sailor's slang.

Chapter 69

"Come on, Arnold," said Dick, giving me a pat on the arm. "Let's just go over and introduce ourselves. Just say hi."

"But — what will we say to him?"

It would be different if the guy was sitting right next to us at the bar, but it did seem odd just to go over to someone sitting by himself at a table.

"I'll think of something," said Dick. "Listen, Arnold, nobody goes to a café just to read a book. If they really wanted to read they'd sit alone in a quiet room. But everyone who reads in a public place secretly wants someone interesting to come up and ask them what they're reading, or ask for a light, whatever."

"Yeah, but —"

"No buts! Come on, buddy, this is Marcel Proust! He's like on the same level of Shakespeare! Well, almost. If it was Shakespeare you'd go over, wouldn't you?"

"Frankly, no," I said. But then I thought of certain embarrassingly gregarious episodes in my checkered past, and I had to add, "Unless I had a load on."

"Am I going to have to buy you an absinthe then? Has it come to that?"

I had some vague recollection of the concept of absinthe from when I was in France during the war, although I couldn't remember ever drinking it back then.

"Well — that's pretty strong, isn't it?"

"Damn straight that shit is strong. Let's have a couple."

"I don't know, Dick."

"Well, it's like this, Arnold. I hate to pull rank on you, but either we go over to Marcel and have a chat, or — and again, I hate to be like this — we're going to have to have a couple of absinthes, in which case you'll be so drunk you'll be absolutely flying over there for a chin-wag with young Marcel. The choice is yours, soldier."

"Well, sir, how about if I tell you to go take a running flying leap into that ocean out there?"

Dick smiled broadly, put his hand on my shoulder and squeezed it with little shaking movements.

"That's the Arnold I like," he said.

He stood up, taking his glass and the bottle, and flicked his head in Marcel Proust's direction.

"Come on, buddy."

I stood up as well, taking my glass, and we headed over to Marcel Proust's little table.

He was sitting near the open French doors, but, rather than facing the terrace and the dark green sea beyond, he sat sideways, facing in the direction of the bar, so that with a look to his right he could gaze on the saloon and its inhabitants, and by looking to the left he could gaze outside at the ladies under their parasols, the gentlemen in their straw hats, the bright green neatly-mown grass, the quietly stirring chrysanthemums, the sea with its toy-like boats in slow motion, and, off farther to the left, a grove of sighing lindens, and, under the trees, benches with people sitting at them, the women's dresses as colorful and exuberant as the flowers that exploded gently all about these sunny grounds.

We were standing by his table. He seemed rather self-consciously absorbed in his book, which he held propped up against a flowered teapot. He was a pale young man with skin as smooth as bone china, with shiny dark hair and a wispy black moustache.

"*Vous lisez* Ruskin, *monsieur?*" said Dick.

I could just barely understand what Dick was saying. I saw the name Ruskin on the spine of the young fellow's book. Of course I had no idea who this Ruskin was.

"*Oui,*" said Monsieur Proust, smiling and seeming not to mind the intrusion.

The next exchange between Dick and Marcel Proust pretty much went past me, although I got the impression that they were saying something about this Ruskin fellow.

Next thing I knew, Monsieur Proust was waving his hand, inviting Dick and myself to join him.

There was only one free chair, though, and I was about to go look around for one, but Marcel Proust simply snapped his fingers and a humble middle-aged waiter appeared at once. Marcel said something to him, the waiter bowed and slipped away and came back with a chair in about four seconds flat.

So, there we were sitting with Marcel Proust. Dick introduced us.

Monsieur Proust shook my hand, rising in his seat slightly.

"You speak Franch, Meestair Schnabel?"

"Not too much, uh, *pas beaucoup,*" I said. "*Je regrette.*"

(I think I've mentioned somewhere in these notes that the army had made me take a crash course in conversational before the Normandy invasion; I had attempted to use some basic French during the seven or eight months I was in France and Belgium during the war, but my ability to communicate in that language had never risen above that of a mentally retarded francophone two-year-old, and that was eighteen years and millions of destroyed brain cells ago.)

"I am zo sorry," he said. "My Eengleezh eez 'orrible."

Despite what he said — and his accent certainly was as thick as peanut butter — the book he was reading was apparently in English (it had an English title anyway) {*"The Stones of Venice, Vol. III"* — *Marginal insertion in Schnabel's holograph – Editor}*.

He had a small plate with some scallop-shaped little cakes on it in front of him, and he offered them to us. Dick and I both took one, and they were delicious, a little like the butter cake they make at Fink's bakery back in Olney.

He then asked us about ourselves, and Dick told him, in French, that he was an American naval officer, and I believe he told Marcel Proust that I worked on the railroad. But then he said something about me being a poet.

"*Un poète!*" said Marcel, his eyes lighting up.

Here we go. It's tough enough having one of these "oh you're a poet" conversations in English. Try having one with a French guy when you speak hardly any French and his English isn't so hot either. Let me tell you, it's impossible. After one or two eternal minutes of torture I thought I'd better change the subject. One thing that practically always works is to ask someone about what they do in life, or what they would like to do. With Dick's translating help I tried this now, and it worked.

At first I couldn't understand what Monsieur Proust said, but he made a scribbling motion, and Dick said, as if warm butter wouldn't melt in his mouth, "He wants to be a writer, Arnold. A novelist. Like Balzac or Flaubert or —" Dick said some names I didn't recognize and whose sounds left no corresponding sequence of letters on my brainpan.

Monsieur Proust said something I couldn't make out at all, and finished with a shrug.

"He says he has no idea what he'll write about," said Dick. "Because he doesn't really do much in his life and he says he has no imagination to create stories and characters."

"Tell him I've never let any of that stop me," I said.

Dick translated, and Marcel smiled and said yet another thing that was all Greek to me, although I could see he was asking me a question.

"He wants to know what you write about, Arnold."

Dick had asked me this same question the night before.

"Just the things I do all day," I admitted. I tried to put it in French. "*Les choses que je fait*," I said, bits of the language somehow tumbling back to me over the past two decades of life. "*Les choses que je vois.*"

"Zee sings you see?" asked Marcel.

"*Oui*," I said. "And the stuff I think. *Les choses, uh, dont je pense.*"

"*Les choses que vous faites*," he said. "*Les choses que vous voyez, et les choses dont vous pensez.*"

"Yep," I said. "I mean *oui*."

"*Formidable*," he said. He picked up one of the little cakes and absentmindedly broke a little piece off of it. Then just as absentmindedly he put the little piece of cake into his teaspoon. He dipped the teaspoon into his teacup, moistening the cake. Then, staring off toward the sea, he raised the spoon to his lips, taking a small taste of the tea and cake.

Suddenly he seemed as if paralyzed, staring off into the distance.

I looked at Dick, but Dick was staring at Monsieur Proust.

Finally, after about a minute, Marcel seemed to snap out of it. He smiled at us with his sad dark eyes, and put the teaspoon, still with a splash of tea and a morsel of cake in it, back onto his little ornate china saucer.

"*Formidable*," he said. "*Tout-à-fait formidable.*"

I didn't think what I'd said had been quite so formidable as all that, but what the heck, I guess writers are just strange people.

Chapter 70

We then experienced one of those silences that drift over the best of conversations. Young Marcel was gazing out toward the ocean, while Dick was smiling, looking around the room at the women with their billowy dresses and hats like sprouting topiary and the men with their top hats and waxed moustaches and Van Dykes.

I drank my beer.

If this was one of my psychotic episodes it was certainly one of my more realistic ones.

But then I thought, what if *this* were my real life, and if the life I remembered living before was a dream, some sort of crazed fantasy?

But if the latter were the case, why did I not have any memories of life here in the 19th century?

If I were indeed a 19th century man, then I was an insane 19th century man, because all my memories were of a 20th century life.

So either way, 19th century man or 20th century man, I was screwed: I was a nut.

Unless — unless Dick and I actually *had* travelled back in time and across an ocean. The very idea of which was of course insane.

I sighed and took another sip of the excellent ale.

"*Un ange passe, messieurs?*"

This was said by a very short bearded gentleman in a derby who was standing by our table, smiling.

Marcel stood up, and reaching down, shook the short fellow's hand. He introduced us, and Dick and I, joining in the old-school politeness, stood to shake the man's hand, which was normal-sized even if he was only about four feet eight inches tall.

I didn't catch his name. He and Marcel chatted a bit, and Marcel made a graceful hand signal to the passing faithful waiter. In a flash the waiter was right there with another chair for the short guy. The short guy said something to the waiter, and we all sat. The man said to me in much better English than Marcel spoke:

"So, you are enjoying your visit to France?"

"Uh, yeah" I said. "I mean yes. *Oui. Beaucoup.*"

"Marcel tells me you are a poet."

"Oh, it's just a hobby, really," I said.

"'Obby?"

"*Un passe-temps,*" said Dick.

It was weird, I was understanding more of the French as we went along. Especially when Dick spoke it. If these French people didn't have such strong French accents I would be in pretty good shape.

The little guy said something in French to Marcel that I couldn't make out, and then he turned again to me and said, "Monsieur, all art is an 'obby."

"Not if you make a living from it," I said.

The little guy laughed, and translated for Marcel, but then the waiter appeared again, with a tray on which were a bottle of something green, a carafe of water and some glasses, a bowl of what looked like sugar cubes, and a small plate with little slotted spoons on it, all of which he proceeded to lay down on the already crowded little table, and then he bowed and went away again.

I couldn't read French very well, but I could read what was printed on the label of the bottle of green liquid, and what it said was "absinthe".

This situation now had every possibility of getting really ugly really soon.

I could handle getting obliterated occasionally back home in Olney, or in Cape May. It had always been my policy that if I must get drunk I would try to do it within easy stumbling distance of my own humble abode. But getting obliterated in another century, in another continent, no, this was too much, even if I was crazy.

I polished off the beer in my glass and stood up.

"*Je regrette, monsieur —*"

"*Henri!*" said the little guy.

"Okay. *Je regrette, Henri, mais, uh, nous devons vraiment partir maintenant. Je regrette beaucoup —*"

"*Non, non!*" he cried.

It occurred to me that he was already two or three sheets to the wind.

"No, I'm really sorry, monsieur, *mais* — Dick, help me out."

"Come on, Arnold, one absinthe. One and done."

"No, Dick, remember? We have to go to, uh, that *thing*."

I stared poison daggers at him, but to tell the truth I'm sure that If Dick had pulled me firmly back down to my seat then I would have stayed there, and woken up the next day in some dockside alleyway in 19th century France. But he took pity on me.

"Oh, right," he said, "the *thing*."

"*La chose?*" said Marcel, seeming glad to repeat a word he recognized.

Dick said something in French, something about meeting some *jeunes filles*, and he finished his glass of ale and stood up. Marcel and the little guy stood up also, and hands were shaken all around. Dick said a few more words to Marcel, something about wishing him good luck with his writing. The little guy Henri had already sat down and poured himself about four fingers of absinthe, and he was busy now slowly dripping water over a sugar cube on a slotted spoon and into his glass, transforming the green spirits into a slowly swirling cloud of oblivion.

Dick and I both had one more quick handshake with Marcel, and we were about to go when Dick said, "Oh, we never paid for our beer," and he pulled out his wallet.

Marcel had sat down but now he practically leaped up again, waving his hand and saying, *"Non, non, monsieur! C'est à moi!"*

So we let Marcel pick up our tab, and we headed back out to the terrace. The sun was starting to set over the sea, or the English Channel, whatever it was, and the little boats and ships had turned into silhouettes, casting mirrored silhouettes onto the deep green water.

"Can we go back now?" I asked Dick.

Chapter 71

"Go back?" said Dick. "But we just got here." He patted his pockets and came up with a silvery cigarette case. He popped it open. "Oh, look, we even have cigarettes. Care for one?"

"Okay," I said. I picked one out. It was as thick as my little finger and as long as my ring finger. I patted my own pockets, looking for something to light it with. My trusty Zippo lighter was gone, but I found an ornate box of wooden matches.

I lighted up Dick and then myself. The tobacco was strong and harsh, and both of us coughed a bit. But I had to admit there was something about it I liked. You knew you were smoking something when you smoked one of these babies. You could almost feel the cancerous nodules popping up merrily inside your freshly blackened lungs.

We stared out at this pleasant seaside scene, Dick and I, for all the world two gentlemen in straw hats who actually belonged in this particular universe.

"You might have a point though," said Dick, picking a dark and horsefly-sized shred of tobacco off his lip and flicking it away. "About getting back, that is."

"Right," I said.

"Your girlfriend — Alexa?"

"Elektra. Her name's Elektra," I said wearily.

"Right, Elektra," said Dick. "She'll be wondering where you are."

"And Daphne will be wondering about you," I said, thinking this might give him a nudge.

"Arnold, as long as there's someone willing to be trounced by her at badminton I assure you I'm the furthest thing from her mind."

"Yeah, well, anyway, we should probably be moving along."

"Right," he said. "But look at these women. Fantastic."

In the day's waning light even more of the ladies had come out to sit or stroll on the terrace or to stand by the trelliswork fence gazing out at the sea which was now blazing up in the setting sun, and it's true that with their delicate parasols and their hats blossoming like mad flowers and their voluminous dresses of rich reds and blues and greens and purples and with their light singing voices on the breeze they seemed like a garden that had somehow become human.

"Don't you just sort of want to meet a couple of these babes, Arnold? I mean, you know, just to shoot the breeze for a bit?"

"I don't speak French well enough, Dick, and we really should get back."

"Yeah, I suppose you're right," he said, wistfully, probably wishing his companion wasn't a tight-assed old confirmed-bachelor usher from St. Helena's. "So, how do we get back?"

I almost dropped my fat French cigarette.

"Dick, don't you know?"

"Not really. It's not as if I drop into *Belle Époque* France on a regular basis."

"Oh, no."

I just wanted to sit down. I wanted to go back to that table with Marcel and the little guy and start guzzling absinthe hand over fist.

"Now, don't get upset, Arnold. We *got* here. There must be a way to get *back*."

"Oh, no," I moaned, ignominiously.

I thought: This is going to be just like when I first went nuts, except this time I won't come back from it.

"All right," said Dick. "Look, leave it to me. Here's what we do."

"What?"

"Um, uh —" He was looking around, looking up, looking back down. "Um —"

Great. He had no idea.

I looked out at that sea and at the blotchy orange sun sinking down into it. I started walking across the terrace and over toward the fence.

"Hey, Arnold, wait up."

I kept walking and Dick hop-skipped up until he was in step with me.

"Gonna check out the sunset, Arnold?"

I kept going. We reached the fence. Below it a rocky bluff sloped steeply down to a white beach with foamy surf lapping at it from the sparkling rich green sea. There was a gate over to the right, and it led to a zigzagging stone stairway going down the side of the bluff to the beach. I went over, opened the gate and went through. Dick followed me. We stood there on the other side of the fence, about four feet away from the verge of the bluff. I walked over and looked down. It was about a hundred foot drop to the beach and almost straight down.

"Are you thinking of doing what I think you're thinking of doing?" asked Dick.

"Yeah," I said.

Well, Miss Evans had been bugging me about taking a great leap.

"All right, then," he said. "Let's do it."

We both backed up to the fence.

"Count of three?" said Dick.

"No, let's just do it," I said.

"Okay then."

We ran forward and leaped off the bluff, swooping down at first but then leveling off above the beach and the surf and the ships and boats and then up into the purple sky above that big orange setting sun.

Next thing I knew I was back standing on the first floor landing in Mrs. Biddle's house, and Dick was standing next to me, still staring at the painting of the old-fashioned people, the sea and the boats.

"So, shall we go up?" he said.

"Yeah, sure," I said.

Dick picked his beer bottle up off the little table and headed up the stairs, and I followed him with my beer bottle and my cigarette.

It was a fat cigarette, with dark brown strong tobacco, and it was neither one of Dick's Chesterfields nor one of my own Pall Malls.

CHAPTER 72

Coming up the stairs we could hear the voices of people talking and laughing, the sounds of a guitar strumming.

When we got to the second floor I realized I had to urinate again, so I excused myself and went down the hall while Dick went through the doorway that led out to the porch. I came to the bathroom in which I had surprised Shirley on the toilet, but this time I took no chances. The door was slightly ajar, and the light was off, but I knocked anyway and called "Hello?"

Silence only responded, and so I went in, and after I clicked on the light I quickly made sure to turn the thumb-switch on the deadbolt. I really had to pee. Besides the booze and beer I had had on the porch and in the kitchen there had been that large bottle of excellent ale I had drunk with Dick in France.

I thought about it all as I urinated, the thick French cigarette still burning slowly between my lips.

Dick had said nothing about our little adventure through time and space. But then I had said nothing about it either. What if his reasons for keeping mum on the subject were the same as mine, i.e., not wishing to seem like a lunatic? Perhaps I should sound him out gently. Or, on second thought, perhaps not. If he wanted to talk about it — if indeed he had experienced it — then let him. Right then and there I just didn't feel like exposing yet another facet of my lunacy.

I finished, zipped up, washed my hands. I looked at my face in the mirror. Yes, that was definitely a foreign cigarette hanging out of my mouth.

Basically, what little world-view I could be said to possess was crashing to the earth. But at least I was back in my own time, or at least the time I was used to being in.

But how odd that it was even 1963. Part of me always felt as if it were still the 1930s, the time of my boyhood and young manhood. Since then a world war had happened in which I was the tiniest cog, the trains had gone electric, the airplanes had become jets, television had replaced radio, oil had replaced coal in our furnaces, and the world had changed even in the way it smelled.

I had just returned from an excursion into the past but in a sense I walked around every day feeling as if I had been transported into the future, a minor character in an impossibly long and plotless episode of *The Jetsons*.

It occurred to me that only small children lived in the present. The rest of us live in the past, our physical selves stumbling through a future that grows more unrecognizable with each passing day.

I dried my hands and went back out into the hall. I still had the not quite-finished bottle of Schmidt's and my staunchly glowing strong French cigarette. I could hear Frank singing again now:

> *Try to think that love's not around*
> *But it's uncomfortably near*
> *My old heart ain't gaining no ground*
> *Because my angel eyes ain't here*

I went back down the hall, through the doorway into the connecting bedroom, and back out to the porch. They were all still out there: Dick of course, and Mr. MacNamara; Frank and Sammy (who was accompanying Frank on the guitar), Dean, Shirley, Larry Winchester, Miss Evans, Steve, Miss Rathbone; and Elektra, whom it seemed as if I hadn't seen in hours, although in human time I suppose it had been less than half an hour. But this whole day seemed less like a day than a long season. And it wasn't over yet.

Elektra got up from the glider (she had been sitting next to Miss Evans, who was eyeing me as if I were some fascinating visitor from another planet). She put both her hands on my upper arms and said, in a low voice, "Lover boy."

"Hello," I said, in my own quiet voice.

"You ready to blow this popsicle stand?"

"Sure." Her eyes were dark and deep. "But let's wait till Frank's finished," I whispered.

It seemed rude to leave him in mid-song. We stood near the doorway and listened as he sang and as Sammy played the guitar. I noticed that Dick, who was standing over near where Frank sat, was gazing pensively at his cigarette, now burned down almost to the end. I couldn't tell if it was one of the French ones. As casually as I could I leaned over to an overflowing ashtray on a table near the door and stubbed out my own seventy-year-old cigarette.

> *Pardon me but I got to run*
> *The fact's uncommonly clear*
> *Got to find who's now number one*

And why my angel eyes ain't here
Excuse me while I disappear

There was a pause after Sammy strummed the final sad chord, then everyone clapped.

Frank, who seemed to have been staring intently into himself as he sang, now smiled, took a gold cigarette case from his Bermuda shorts pocket and said, "How'd all these people get in my room?"

Elektra and I said our goodbyes.

As I shook hands with Larry Winchester he said, "So, whaddaya say, kid?"

I had no idea what he was talking about.

"Um, I don't know, Larry."

"I can let you have a grand upfront."

"A grand?"

Did he think I was in financial difficulties, what with being put on leave of absence by the railroad?

"Larry," I said, "really, I couldn't."

"I knew you were tough. All right, two grand. But that's for a finished treatment."

Treatment? I looked around for help, but Elektra was saying good night to Sammy, and no one else seemed to be paying attention to us.

"Larry," I said, as definitively as I could, "really, I just couldn't."

Larry was smoking a cigar, and he drew contemplatively on it now.

"I have a feeling it's not just the money for you, is it?" he said.

"Uh, no," I said.

"So you wanta see if we're *simpático* first?"

"I don't know what that means, Larry."

"Like if we get along, if we click."

"Oh."

"So we'll get together and see if we click. But I can't let you do it on spec, Arnold."

Spec?

"Look, come by tomorrow. We'll kick around some ideas."

"Kick around ideas?" I was grasping at straws. "You mean, like a bull session?"

"Yeah, like a bull session."

"Well, I guess I could do that. You're staying here?"

"I have that honor, sir."

"Well, okay."

"I like to start early, but the way tonight's going, maybe we better sleep late just a little. Whaddaya say you drop by tomorrow around ten, ten-thirty."

This seemed quite early in the day for a bull session, but what did I know?

"Well, okay, Larry, sure."

"Great, I'll see ya tomorrow then."

Elektra had joined us.

"Good news, sweetheart," said Larry. "Your boyfriend's getting into the picture business."

"Wow, that's great, Arnold. So you're gonna help Larry write his screenplay?"

"Damn straight he is," said Larry.

It was all starting to come together now. Apparently I was agreeing – or almost agreeing – to write a movie with Larry. This didn't bother me. It wasn't as if I didn't have loads of free time anyway, and two thousand dollars was nothing to sniff at.

Chapter 73

It so happened while we were going through the laborious procedure of saying goodnight to everyone that Miss Rathbone and Steve got up to go also, and, sure enough, Miss Evans too.

So now we had to wait until this latter group said goodnight to everyone. I lit up another cigarette, one of my Pall Malls this time, even though my lungs and throat were still scorched and befogged from that French cigarette.

Frank came over to me.

"You got my card, right?"

"Got it, Frank."

"I appreciated how you didn't walk out in the middle of my song."

"My pleasure."

(Although it did occur to me that if we had slipped out quietly then we would have been a half hour gone by now.)

"I could see that your lady friend — what's her name, Ariadne?"

"Elektra."

"I could see Elektra was ready to go. She's got the hots for you, boy."

"Oh, I don't know —"

"Arnold, if there's one thing I know it's dames." Elektra was kissing Sammy goodnight on the cheek. "And believe me, that kid's got it bad for you. She reminds me of Ava."

"Ava?"

"Gardner. My second wife. Third wife? Whatever. She reminds me of Ava. God how we used to fight. And God how we used to —" He finished his sentence with a sigh. "So, Arnold, you gonna call me?"

"Well, I don't know, Frank."

"Call me any time. I want a lyric from you."

"Well, I can't promise anything."

"Yeah, I know. So I hear you're gonna work with Larry?"

"Um, maybe —"

"Good man, Larry. He could be an A-list director, but he's got a bad habit of telling studio heads to go fuck themselves, you should pardon my French. I've wanted to work with him for years. Maybe you could write me a part. What's the movie about?"

"Something about a young soldier on leave in Paris who gets involved in a murder, I think."

"Maybe it could be an older soldier."

"Well, I don't know —"

"Okay, I don't wanta be pushy. Oh, here she is."

Elektra came over.

"Take care of this girl, Arnold."

"Okay," I said.

It went on like that for a while, but at last we made it downstairs, with Steve and the Misses Rathbone and Evans in tow.

So now we just had to make it through the dining room and the valley of the old people and we were free. But even this maneuver took at least another twenty minutes. I assured Mrs. Biddle that I would indeed be there for tea the next day, and that in fact I had an appointment there tomorrow morning to get together with Larry Winchester to find out if we were *simpático* enough to write a movie together.

"Why do you want to write a movie?" said Mrs. Biddle. "They're such drivel. You should stick to your poetry."

"He's offering me two thousand dollars upfront," I said.

"Oh, that's different then I suppose. All right, I can see you're chafing at the bit, and your girlfriend is eyeing you ravenously, so go."

At long last we all made it out of the house. We went down the walk to Windsor and made the left on North Street, Elektra and I in front. I felt a tap on my shoulder.

"Arnold," said Steve, "I want to thank you! That's the most fabulous party I've ever been to!"

"Glad you liked it, Steve."

I noticed that he was swaying a bit, sort of like Popeye the sailor man, even though he had Miss Rathbone on one arm and Miss Evans on the other. Then I noticed that all three of them were swaying, although not in unison.

"Oh, by the way, who wants to go to the Ugly Mug for a nightcap?" said Steve.

Not me, that was sure, but about ten minutes later we were all milling about outside the Mug, and Steve and Miss Evans and Miss Rathbone seemed to have gotten even drunker on the way.

Elektra said she wanted to go home, she had to work in the morning. Me, I just wanted to be no more hungover than I was already fated to be. Steve was pulling on my right arm. Miss Evans grabbed my other arm. Elektra pulled her arm away. Miss Evans then yanked her own arm away from Elektra's grasp, accidentally hitting Miss Rathbone in the nose. Miss Rathbone sat down on the pavement. Miss Evans grabbed my arm again. Elektra told her to leave me alone. Steve went around to help up Miss Rathbone, but he tripped on the curb and fell. Miss Evans called Elektra a floozy. Elektra slapped Miss Evans, and then things got so chaotic that it wearies me even thinking of how to recount it all.

But another interesting thing happened during the ensuing brawl, which soon included several young coast guardsmen who had apparently just been thrown out of the bar, plus the bouncers and bartenders who had thrown them out.

What happened was I began to float up, slowly, to about twenty feet off the ground. I looked down on it all, at the tumbling and stumbling bodies, and as I did the shouts and screams faded away as if someone had turned the volume down on God's television set, or rather switched the sound to another channel, because all I could hear and very clearly was the gentle rushing and hushing of the ocean several blocks away. I rose myself up just a little higher so that I could see the ocean, enormous and dark and alive. And then I looked down again at the humans swirling all around and against each other, not like animals, not like insects, no, but like human beings, and one of them was me. I was trying to pull one of the coast guard boys off of Steve, and then one of the other coast guard guys socked me on the jaw.

I came down, and rejoined my body, sitting on the pavement, next to Miss Rathbone, who had still not gotten up.

She put her arms around me and kissed me.

Next thing I knew Elektra was pulling me to my feet and dragging me down Decatur Street. Then Miss Evans came running up and grabbed my arm for what seemed the eleventh time that night. Elektra hit her on the shoulder with her handbag, and now Miss Evans sat down, holding her shoulder and looking bewildered.

Soon enough, but not soon enough for me, we were at Elektra's house, at the rear entrance behind her shop.

She turned her back to the door and pulled me to her.

We were both out of breath, both sweating. My jaw was numb where the coast guardsman had punched me, but it didn't hurt, at least not yet. Elektra's warm butterscotch smell mingled with the moist scents of honeysuckle and ivy and roses and the clean sea-weedy smell of the ocean.

"My hero," she said.

I suppose modesty forbids me to go into what happened next. I could go ahead and write it out; after all it was interesting, and included some things

I had never done before, not to mention some things that had never before been done to me, but what's the point, I know I'll only end up crossing it all out. God forbid my mother should find it. But now that I think about it, even if I could be absolutely sure my mother would never see it, it seems to me perhaps that some things become lessened once I put them into words. And I wouldn't want that to happen.

Chapter 74

Suffice it to say we bade each other a fond goodnight, and I went on my way. Elektra didn't ask me to stay the night, although I was feeling so wild these days I think I might actually have done so had she asked.

But still I must admit I preferred just going home to my little attic room. This had been by far the longest day of my life, and I was ready for some quiet solitude. Speaking of which I decided to take an indirect route home; if the battle royal was still in progress and had spread farther down Washington Street I had no desire to get involved. Let them fight on without me until they dropped one by one. Henceforth Arnold Schnabel would be the Switzerland of human beings. So I walked down to the beach and turned right on Beach Drive. The ocean crashed obliviously and darkly and, tired as I was, for two cents I would have stripped down on the other side of Frank's Playland and gone in for a swim. But I remembered the promise I had made to Elektra, no more solitary night-time swims, and I couldn't bring myself to go against my word to her.

As I walked past Sid's Tavern I noticed it was still open and thriving, its front doors open and beckoning, the lights inside twinkling on a happy bar full of people, the jukebox playing a song about *let's dance, let's dance, let's do the twist, the stomp, the mashed potato, too.*

Again I was tempted. The siren call of oblivion, how often had I obeyed its summons, marching like a zombie into how many low dives? But I walked on and turned up at Perry Street, homeward.

After climbing the side stairs as quietly as I could I stopped on the third floor and stood by Miss Evans's door. If she was still out at the bars then that probably meant she would be all the more likely to stage an all-out assault on my room at three in the morning. If she were in and please God already asleep then maybe I wouldn't have to nail my door shut with railroad ties.

Fortunately I heard deep female snoring. Good.

I went up to my room, but you may be sure, dear reader, that I did bolt my door, although after thinking it over a minute I decided not to prop a wooden chair against the knob.

I got undressed and into bed and picked up *The Waste Land,* trying to find where I left off, not that it seemed to matter a whole lot. At the end of one passage was this:

'You! hypocrite lecteur!—mon semblable,—mon frère!'

— the last two phrases of which Miss Evans had quoted when she inscribed her book to me.

I read the footnote and saw that T.S. Eliot was quoting Charles Baudelaire; yet another famous poet I suppose I'll have to read some day. So Miss Evans might have been quoting Baudelaire directly. Or she could have been quoting Eliot quoting Baudelaire. Or both. This too did not matter; what mattered was that she was a nutcase. Contrary to what might seem logical, nut cases do not necessarily like to associate with other nut cases. I suppose I should only speak for myself, but I find my own insanity to be more than sufficient unto the day. I don't need any help.

I put *The Waste Land* aside for some other time and picked up Miss Evans's novel, *Ye Cannot Quench*. At least this I was able to understand. In the sense that I knew what was going on. On the other hand, after finding my place and reading about three lines I realized that although I could follow what the characters were doing I couldn't really understand the characters themselves because they behaved and talked so oddly, which is saying something coming from me. They seemed like characters in a movie, and it occurred to me that maybe I would enjoy the book more, or at all, if I tried to imagine the characters as movie stars. So I decided that the Rock Hudson-like guy would be Rock Hudson and that the Montgomery Clift-like guy would be Clift, the younger Montgomery Clift, like from around *A Place in the Sun*. The girl, Emily, I had to think about for a minute. Debbie Reynolds? No, she was not quite that innocent. Definitely not Doris Day either, even if it was a Rock Hudson movie. I settled on Natalie Wood, and that seemed to work. I also made the movie black-and-white, although some of the Rock Hudson parts seemed like they should be in Technicolor.

Even after I had worked all that out I still had trouble reading more than few lines further. I was mostly just lying there thinking about what I'd already read, or what I could remember of it, as it was already rapidly disappearing from my brainscape.

The Clift guy, Porter Walker, was still making out with the Natalie Wood girl, Emily. Boy, in the old days I wouldn't even let myself read these kinds of scenes. At least not ones that went on for so long. But then the sort of books I tended to read usually kept it to the basics. *"He drew her scarlet mouth roughly to his. She did not resist. Far from it." "She took the cigarette from my lips and flicked it out the window. I wondered if it landed on anybody.*

But I didn't wonder for long." "She turned and locked the door. She put the key in the top of her dress. I wondered if she was locking everyone else out or locking me in. I wondered but I didn't care." That sort of thing. But Miss Evans's scene really went on and on. I decided to save it for later and picked up the murder story I was reading, *This Sweet Sickness*.

I woke up around my usual time, eight or so, and all in all I didn't feel too much like squeezing myself through my small window and hurling myself from the roof. Fortunately I had had only the one Manhattan. In fact if I hadn't had that ale in 1890s France I would probably feel much better than I did. It's always that *just one more* that pushes you over the borderline, even if you did have it in a different century.

My jaw ached from where the coast guard guy had socked me, but I didn't seem to have any teeth loose.

I threw my legs resignedly over the side of the bed and as usual reached for my cigarettes and lighter.

And here something genuinely unusual happened. First off, after lighting up I went into a coughing fit, but this wasn't the unusual part. Well, maybe slightly unusual in that this fit was a bit more severe than usual, perhaps due to that powerful French stinkweed I'd smoked the night before.

What was unusual was that I finally decided that smoking was stupid unless you were planning to commit suicide in the very near future, and that I was quitting cigarettes now, after going through a minimum of a pack a day ever since I was overseas in the army. Amazingly I had never smoked before going into the service. But there I was in England going through all this boring training, everybody else smoked, I had lots of free time, so I started smoking. It was something to do. And here I was a couple of decades later, still puffing away.

The only thing was, I was just about to stub out this last cigarette forever when I was already missing it. So I took another small drag, and this time I only coughed a little bit. Well, all right, I'd start cutting down today. I would smoke this one, but it would be my last one till after lunch. Then I'd take it from there

I finished the cigarette, only coughing a few more times, stubbed it out, got dressed and went out, taking Miss Evans's book with me. It wouldn't do to be seen with another novel until I managed to get through hers, if I could get through it.

I stopped again outside her door and pricked up my ears. She was no longer snoring, but at least there were no other alarming sounds, no keenings or wailings or gnashings of teeth that I could hear.

Breakfast passed pleasantly enough. My bruised jaw went unmentioned and perhaps unnoticed, possible proof that I was not the center of the universe after all. Kevin kept his nose in his Tom Swift book, and I read *Ye Cannot Quench* while my mother and my aunts sat and drank their coffee. They probably knew I was hungover. They were talking gardening and I remembered that I was supposed to pass on Mrs. Biddle's compliments on their garden, but I was not quite ready for such polite conversation. The ladies must have heard about Frank Sinatra being at the party I had gone to, but none of them asked me about him. If it had been Bishop Sheen or President Kennedy or Lawrence Welk or Arthur Godfrey I think they would be impressed, but I don't think Sinatra means much to them.

Eventually Emily and Porter finished making love, and now, as Porter slept a "deep, poet's sleep", Emily picked up his copy of his epic poem from his night table and picked up where she had left off:

Slam bang goes the drummer slackjawed above his traps,
wang wang wang wails the sax man arching his back like a snake,
bwah bwah bwah goes the trumpeter straight up
at that smoky Heaven where churn the dreams of the damned
and the screams of the saved propelled by the
boomp boomp boomp of the bassman, and the
chinkle tinkle pinkle of the piano fellow
as I pound my beersopping table in glorious time –
"Hearken! Hearken ye fools, and dig
this crazy sound..."

Suddenly I remembered my appointment with Larry Winchester. I checked my watch. He had said ten or ten-thirty. I didn't know how long he wanted to work (or whatever it was we were going to do) and I had to meet Mrs. Biddle for tea at four; so, as this was Saturday, I figured as soon as I'd had my shower I'd better head right over to church and go to confession, which seemed to be another habit I wasn't quite ready to quit.

I managed to take my shower successfully, and I was coming down the third-floor hall after changing when, you guessed it, I ran into Miss Evans coming out of her doorway.

"Oh, Arnold," she said.

She was wearing a bathrobe, and nothing else apparent except for rubber flip-flops.

"Hello, Miss Evans."

"*Gertrude*, please, Arnold, for the last time."

"Gertrude."

She held some bottles of unguents and lotions, and she had a towel over her arm, even though my aunts provide clean towels.

"Where are you off to, Arnold?"

"Confession."

"How nice."

I didn't really know what to say to this. I said nothing.

"I wish I were Catholic," she said. "It would be nice to tell someone my sins and then to be cleansed. To start again. Anew."

She reached over and touched my polo shirt.

"Are you allowed to go to confession wearing a sport shirt and Bermudas?" she asked.

"The rules are relaxed in the summer, at the seashore anyway," I said.

"Perhaps I should go."

"Sure, give it a try," I said, and I started to pass.

"But what do I say? To the priest."

"Say, 'Bless me, Father, for I have sinned. It's been such-and-such a time since my last confession.'"

"But I've never been to confession."

"Oh, well, tell him it's your first time then."

"He won't think it's odd?"

"Priests are trained to deal with oddness."

"I'll tell him it's been a year."

"Okay."

"He won't be terribly cross with me?"

"Probably not. Go to Father Reilly, he's pretty easy-going."

"Okay, I will. Goodbye, Arnold. Perhaps I'll see you later in the day."

And the way things were going she undoubtedly would see me. Unless I was kidnapped by Communist agents or creatures from outer space.

I headed downstairs and out and out into the beautiful warm day, off to the Star of the Sea. Off to see Father Reilly with my own boatload of sins. It occurred to me that his easy-goingness was surely going to be challenged today.

Chapter 75

Luckily I got to the church shortly after confessions started at ten, and hardly anyone was there.

For a moment I considered not going to Father Reilly. It's true he was the most lenient and broad-minded priest here, but on the other hand, did he really deserve to have to deal with my nonsense two weeks in a row?

But, on another other hand, perhaps he, having been exposed to my madness in full flower last Saturday, would perforce be better able than one of his unblooded colleagues to give me spiritual guidance.

What the heck, I decided, this is what he gets paid for.

So I marched right up to his confessional and went in.

"Bless me, Father, for I have sinned, it has been one week since my —"

"Oh, no, it's you."

"Yes, Father."

He sighed.

"Should I go on, Father?"

He sighed again.

"I can leave," I offered. "I really don't mind. I can go to Father Schwartz, or, um —"

"No, no," he said. "Stay."

"Okay."

I settled down. I realized I wanted a cigarette. I had denied myself my usual luxurious post-breakfast smoke. Not to mention my briskly bracing post-shower smoke. Or my walk-to-church smoke, savoring that last good drag before flicking it into the always butt-littered gutter across the sidewalk from the church steps.

"Did you hear me?" his voice said, from the other side of that black screen.

"Pardon me?"

"I asked you if you would tell me your first name."

"Oh, sorry, Father —"

"You certainly don't have to."

"Oh, I don't mind. It's Arnold. Arnold Schna-"

"Just your first name."

"Okay," I said. "It's Arnold."

"Arnold," he said. "Good. My name's Jim."

"I know. Father Reilly. Hi, Father."

"Call me Jim."

"Okay. Father Jim."

"Just Jim."

"Just Jim?"

"Just Jim. I'm just a man. Just like you, Arnold."

I doubted this very much. But in order to move things along I ceded the point. I did have an appointment with Larry Winchester after all. So:

"Okay, Jim," I said.

"I remember you well from last week, Arnold. I felt bad about — about dismissing you so abruptly."

"I didn't mind, Father."

As indeed I had not. I'm always happy to be dismissed, abruptly or not, it's all the same to me, as long as I get to leave.

"Yes, but still. I feel I was shirking my duty. I apologize."

"Okay." I shrugged, but of course he couldn't see that. "Should I start my confession now?"

"Okay. Go ahead."

"Well, first off, I'm afraid I had sexual intercourse again. Outside the sacrament of marriage, that is."

"Oh. Uh, more than once?"

"Uh, yeah, I'm afraid so. It was, what? Three times? Four? Wait. No. Let me see —"

"Don't worry about the number, Arnold."

"Okay, and also we did some other things that weren't exactly intercourse I guess, but —"

"You touched each other impurely."

"Uh, yeah, you could say that, you see I —"

"That's okay. I don't need all the details."

"Oh, good."

"So, was this all with the same woman, Arnold?"

"Yeah. And actually that's another thing I wanted to ask you about, Father, because she's Jewish, and, well, not a practicing Jew, but, anyway, she doesn't think sexual intercourse outside of marriage is a sin."

"Uh-huh —"

"So I'm wondering if that makes it less of a sin for me. Since I'm not making another person commit a mortal sin."

"Arnold, according to Church doctrine it's a mortal sin either way. And it's a mortal sin for her even if she doesn't think it is."

"Well that doesn't seem fair. I mean, what about some — I don't know — headhunters in the Amazon — who never knew about Christianity? It's a sin for them too?"

"I'm afraid so."

"But they can't even get properly married in the first place because they don't have any priests to marry them."

"Oh. I see your point."

"I mean —"

"But forget about the headhunters, Arnold. The fact is, Arnold, that you, Arnold, are in a state of mortal sin."

"Okay. So, uh, I guess I didn't have too many other sins this week, no mortal ones anyway. Oh, I guess I masturbated a few times. That's mortal," I said. "Which is weird."

"What's weird, Arnold?"

"That you can get sent to hell for masturbating and it's the same punishment for extra-marital intercourse."

"Well, that's the way it is."

"Yeah. Okay. Uh, I got drunk two or three times."

"Okay. Anything else?"

"Oh, yeah, I forgot, the sin of doubt. I have to tell you, for this whole past week or more I've really had my doubts about religion. So, yeah, a lot of doubt. But what do I know?"

"Did you —"

"Yes?"

"Last week you said Jesus had appeared to you."

"Oh, right."

"Has he, have you, did you —"

"Yeah, I'm afraid so. He's appeared to me, uh, several times."

"And is he still telling you to go ahead and have extra-marital intercourse?"

"Well — uh — he's — uh —"

"Don't you think this Jesus could just be a figment of your imagination, Arnold?"

"Oh, yeah, definitely, but —"

"What?"

"I mean who's to say Bernadette of Lourdes wasn't just seeing things? Or those kids at Fátima?"

"Those were certified miracles, Arnold."

"Okay, but what if my Jesus sightings got certified? I mean, who's to say?"

He didn't say anything.

"Like what if I brought proof of a miracle."

"What kind of proof?"

I was thinking of that cigarette from 1890s France. But that miracle didn't have anything to do with Jesus. Or did it?

"Answer me this, Arnold. Has anyone else seen this Jesus of yours?"

"No. But, like, all these other saints that Jesus or Mary appeared to — Jesus or Mary always only appeared just to the saints, right? Not to everybody, but. Just. To the saints. That's why the saints are saints. Because they're the only ones who can see Jesus. Or Mary. Or whomever. Right?"

"So you think you're a saint."

"Hey, I don't know. That's not for me to say, Father."

"Jim."

"Jim."

"Listen. You're not a saint, Arnold."

"Well, okay, if you say so."

"But — what do I know, right?"

"Hey, that's your opinion. You're entitled to it, Father."

"Jim."

"Jim."

A pause ensued, a great echoing empty pause.

"So —" I said.

"So," he said.

Somebody started knocking on the wall of the booth on the other side of Father Reilly.

A muffled voice said, "Hey, Father Reilly, what's goin' on?"

"Wait your turn!" yelled Father Reilly.

"Sorry, Father."

"Kneel there and examine your conscience and I'll be with you when I'm ready."

"Sorry," said the voice.

"Now," said Father Reilly, to me, in his low, "confessional" voice, "where were we?"

"Well —" I did have that appointment with Larry, and I hate to keep people waiting — "I guess that's about it, Father. I mean Jim. I mean, that's about it for my sins."

"Okay. Are you going to try not to have sexual intercourse with this woman again, Arnold? This — Jewish girl?"

"Um, I don't know, Father. I really doubt that I'll try not to."

"I can't give you absolution unless you at the very least intend to try."

"Well, what about all those other weeks I came in and confessed to the sin of self-abuse? We both knew I was going to do it again, and you always gave me absolution for that."

"That's different."

"How's it different? They're both mortal sins."

There was silence. I could hear Father Reilly breathing. I almost fancied I could hear that other poor guy in the other booth breathing, or sighing.

"Is she pretty, this girl?" Father Jim asked, in a low voice.

"Uh, yes, Father. Very. Dark hair. Deep dark eyes. Smooth skin. And she smells — she smells like —" I tried to remember, but she had various smells, all of them good. "She smells like pound cake sometimes. Like, right from the oven —"

"Okay, look, I absolve you," he said abruptly. "*Ego te absolvo ab omnibus censuris, et peccatis, in nomine Patris, et Filii, et Spiritus Sancti. Amen.*"

"Oh. Thanks, Father."

"Three Hail Marys, three Our Fathers."

"Okay."

"Now go. Go now. Go and sin."

"Go and sin?"

"As I'm sure you will."

He slid the little shutter shut.

I got up and went out. Poor guy. And he still had Miss Evans to deal with.

I grabbed a pew, said my penance, crossed myself, and got out of there.

Chapter 76

Another beautiful day lay glittering and pulsing before me as I paused at the top of the church steps; happy or presumably happy vacationers walked up and down the sidewalks of Washington Street, going to the beach or wandering into and out of the shops, and even though I no longer unreservedly believed in Catholicism I still felt that old feeling of accomplishment on leaving confession, that feeling of starting anew, of attempting to get through at least the next hour before falling into a state of black sin all over again.

Contentedly I patted my pockets for my cigarettes.

Then I remembered that I had decided to try to start quitting today, that I had told myself I wouldn't have another cigarette till after lunch, and that, even more horrifying, in my insanity of good intentions I hadn't brought my cigarettes with me.

At once a tidal wave of nausea rose up from my stomach into my throat. I choked it back down and then I felt an overweight mouse inside my skull chewing greedily at my brain cells.

My spit tasted like used motor oil. I swallowed it down and at once was racked with another brutal surge of nausea.

I grabbed the cast iron rail and staggered down the steps, barely keeping in what had so recently been a quite enjoyable breakfast of scrapple and eggs, home-fries and breaded fried tomatoes washed down with my usual copious cups of strong black Chock Full o' Nuts coffee. My legs felt as if they were made of Silly Putty, and my Bermuda shorts and polo shirt had become soaked with icy sweat in a matter of seconds.

I found myself sitting on a wooden bench on the corner by the church, bent over, staring down at the shimmering sidewalk. Many wonderful cigarette butts lay like stubbed and trodden but still precious little tubes of ecstasy upon the concrete, jetsam of another beer-drenched summer Friday night at the shore. I saw one fat unfiltered butt, only half smoked at best, perhaps even my own brand, Pall Mall, although my eyes were so clouded I could not be sure. I reached down, almost vomiting again, and picked it up. Breathing heavily, licking my parched lips with my swollen leathery tongue, with trembling fingers I smoothed out the butt. It would do. It would do just fine, thank you very much. Just two or three drags, that sharp strong tarry smoke filling my mendicant ravaged lungs, and I would be whole once more, human once more, or at least as human as I could reasonably expect to be.

I patted my pockets again. But no, no, of course not, I had had to be a tough guy. I had left my lighter at home with my cigarettes.

The aforementioned vacationers marched to and fro before me, dressed in their hideous seaside attire of flaming dacrons and polyesters, strutting men with murderous scowls and frightened eyes, women with stiff sprayed hair like the headdresses of pagan priestesses, and screaming feral children veering dangerously off the curb, apparently intent on throwing themselves underneath the burning tires of an endless stream of enormous dirty belching automobiles packed with yet more family groups of Nazis, carnival hucksters, thieves, murderers, and maniacs.

All I had to do was bum a light.

Half the people going by me were smoking. Happily, contentedly smoking in the shining hot sunlight, the pale smoke swirling up and disappearing into the bright blue indifferent sky, into that great bottomless maw of a universe without meaning.

But then I sat up a little straighter and I thought: is it really true I can't go more than two hours without a cigarette? That I would stoop so low as to fish a butt from the sidewalk?

Then of course I remembered some other occasions when I had done just that, usually when stumbling home drunk, the only other passersby my fellow wretched inebriates wandering the haunted night-time streets like some exiled race of the damned.

I took a deep breath, and coughed only a little bit. My mouth had gone bone dry over the past few minutes, but now I could actually feel a drop of moisture in there, and it did not even taste of death and ashes.

The corpulent mouse was still ensconced in my head, but he had stopped chewing. I supposed he was full, and taking a post-prandial nap.

My breakfast had receded from my chest to a defensive position just below my solar plexus, nervously awaiting instructions from HQ.

I looked at the butt. It was an Old Gold, not my brand. I flicked it away.

I took another deep breath, and stood up. The world rocked and moaned but did not fly apart or implode.

I felt my soaked shirt drying on my shoulders and back.

I launched myself forth into the stream of ambulatory humanity, my legs once again feeling if not quite like legs then at least not like something you would find sticking out of a beached octopus or squid, and the pavement unfolded obediently under the soles of my Keds, with only the occasional slight ripple or tilt.

I thought it best to head straightaway for Mrs. Biddle's house and my appointment with Larry Winchester.

Chapter 77

When I came to Jackson Street I felt a longing in my heart. Right up the block was the pretty little jewelry shop in which Elektra worked with her charming Bohemian friends. I paused at the crossing, letting the sundazed vacationers walk all around me. How nice it would be to go visit her there, where she would be working either behind the counter or in that cool back room, twisting her metals and setting her soothing cool Cape May diamonds.

I wouldn't mind smoking a reefer now in that pleasant back room smelling of warm solder. And perhaps Elektra and I could —

But duty called. I crossed Jackson, headed down to Perry Street and then up Perry to North. When I came abreast of my aunts' house I halted again. Should I go in and get my cigarettes?

"I would if I were you."

It was him again. Or Him, as the case may be, leaning against a streetlight pole and smoking a cigarette in the hot sun.

"I really am trying to quit," I said.

"I know that. I'd quit too if I were human."

He was dressed very casually, in unpressed khaki trousers, a faded blue t-shirt, sandals. He needed a shave.

"I can probably bum a couple from Larry," I said.

"What if he only smokes cigars?"

"Oh."

"Tell ya what, take a couple of mine," he said.

He reached into his pocket and took out an open pack of Pall Malls. He gave them a shake and held them out to me, one cigarette protruding.

I took the cigarette.

He gave the pack another slight shake and two more Pall Malls poked out of the pack.

"Let's be real, Arnold. You're gonna need more than one to get you through the afternoon."

"No," I said. "I'll just take this one for after lunch. If I take two the second one will only drive me crazy thinking about it."

"That makes absolutely no sense," he said, "but, hey, suit yourself."

I stuck the cigarette behind my ear.

"Mind if I walk with you?" he said.

"I'd prefer you didn't."

"Lighten up, Arnold."

"All right," I sighed. And we walked off down the street together.

"So how'd it go with Father Reilly?" he asked.

"You don't know?"

"Arnold, I may be the Son of God, but even I have my limitations."

"That's not what I was taught."

"Church doctrine has changed continuously ever since they pulled me down from that cross a couple of thousand years ago, Arnold. It's changed constantly and it will continue to change and it will also be, until the end of time, more or less full of baloney."

"If you say so."

"I say so. So how'd it go with Reilly?"

"I think I bugged him."

"I'm sure you did. He give you absolution?"

"Yeah," I said, "but he was a little grudging about it."

"Asshole."

"He's just doing his job."

"I know. but I'll tell ya, Arnold, it's not easy getting good priests these days." We walked a few more paces and then he added, "But then it never has been easy."

"Oh," I said, "while I have you here. A question."

"Fire away, my friend."

"Something Father Reilly and I were talking about, regarding these visits I have from you —"

"Please, go on."

"Am I — and I know this sounds egotistic, but I'm just curious —"

"What?"

"Am I a saint?"

He smiled.

"That's entirely up to you, Arnold."

"But —"

"Okay, here we are, pal."

We were at the sidewalk gate to Mrs. Biddle's house on Windsor Avenue.

"You're not coming in, are you?" I asked him.

"No." He smiled again. "Why? Do you want me to?"

I looked at him, then gave him a little wave and opened the gate.

I went up the flagstone path to the porch and up the steps.

At the front door I looked back down the path. He was gone.

I touched my ear. The cigarette was there. Could this be adduced as proof of a divine visitation? I took the cigarette and looked at it. Just an ordinary Pall Mall. It wouldn't even get me through the front door of the Vatican. I stuck it back behind my ear and pressed the doorbell button.

After half a minute the old fellow whom I had seen in the dining room last night — the one who looked like Edward Everett Horton — opened the inner door and looked at me through the screen door.

"Oh! Mr. Schnabel! You're here bright and early." He pushed open the screen door. "Do come in. I'll fetch Mrs. Biddle."

"No, please don't bother her," I said, coming in. "I'm having tea with her later today, but I'm here now to meet Mr. Winchester."

"Larry! Lovely fellow."

The old guy was wearing an off-white suit, with white buck shoes and a blue-and-red paisley tie. He was smoking a strong fragrant cigarette, and his skin looked like old paper. His eyes seemed ancient, like pale amethysts, but his hair was a shiny dark brown. I think it might have been dyed. He led me from the foyer into the living room.

The room was cool, both sunlit and soothingly dark at the same time. No one else was around.

"Larry's out back I think. Shall I tell him you're here?"

"Don't bother," I said. "I'll just go back there myself if I may."

"Of course. I'm Tommy by the way, how rude of me."

He extended a slender and blue-veined hand.

"Hi, Tommy," I said.

"I'm a friend of Mrs. Biddle's."

"Pleased to meet you."

"Arnold — may I call you Arnold?"

"Sure," I said.

"May I say you don't look very well."

"I don't feel very well," I said.

"You look like you've been ridden quite hard and put up wet."

"Uh, yeah."

"Too much partaken last night?"

"A little," I said. "But the real problem is I've decided to give up smoking."

"Then what's that cigarette doing behind your ear?"

"I told myself I wouldn't smoke it till after lunch."

"Good God, smoke it, man."

"I'd rather wait."

He took a drag of his own cigarette, seeming to appraise me through the smoke.

"Wait here," he said. "Sit down. I'm going to get you something that will help."

He went away, the soles of his shoes seeming barely to touch the floor.

I sat down on the couch. On the end table was an ashtray with four or five butts in it, and a large bowl containing an inch or so of tan liquid. There was a book lying open face-down on the coffee table. Had Tommy just been reading it?

I picked up the book. It was an enormous volume, *Remembrance of Things Past, Volume One.* By that Marcel Proust guy. Tommy seemed to be about four-fifths of the way through it, which a cursory perusal convinced me was about four-fifths further than I would ever get. I put the book back down the way I had found it.

Tommy came back into the room, carrying a very tall glass of something dark and icy on an engraved metal tray. He sat down weightlessly next to me and put the tray on the coffee table.

He picked up the beaded glass and proffered it to me.

"Put yourself outside of that," he said. "I guarantee you'll feel better."

"Thanks," I said.

I took the glass and drank a little. It was iced tea of some sort, but with a peculiar bitter and thick taste to it.

"Drink some more," he said.

I took a good gulp this time and felt it go down, seeming to wash a metropolitan sewage-drain full of nastiness into my capillaries and out through the pores of my skin. I had started to sweat again during my walk over here, but now it felt as if all the accumulated toxins and tars of twenty years were oozing out of me and seeping down into the brocaded wool of the couch.

"Go on," he said.

I did so, and with each gulp I felt fresh life coursing through me, fresh life and pleasure and wisdom.

"Go ahead, finish it now, Arnold."

I did, and put the empty glass back down on the tray.

"Feel better?" he asked.

"Yes. Thank you very much," I said. Almost at once the sweating stopped. "What was in that?"

"Just strong black Assam tea, with honey, ginger and lemon juice. And ginseng root. And just the tiniest modicum of laudanum."

"Laudanum?"

"Tincture of opium."

"Oh."

I picked up the glass and rattled the cubes, took one last sip of what was left.

"Want some more?" he asked.

"Isn't this addictive?"

"Well, yes."

"I'd better not then. No point replacing one habit with another one."

"No, I suppose not."

He took a gold cigarette case from his jacket pocket. I hadn't noticed that his previous cigarette had disappeared. He took one out, put it in his mouth, lighted himself up with a gold lighter from his other jacket pocket, exhaled dreamily.

I passed the ashtray over to in front of him, and he nodded.

"Oh, hope you don't mind," he said. "If I smoke."

"Not at all."

"I doubt I'll ever quit."

I sat there. I thought that perhaps he was was going to say more, but all he did was stare into space, or into his memories. After a while he sighed and tapped his ash into the tray.

In my life I've found that if you are left alone with any human being for more than two minutes they start telling you their entire life story in excruciating detail. But apparently Tommy wasn't like most people. Who was he? Why was he here?

I'm afraid I was rather blatantly staring at him. He turned his head slightly my way, and smiled.

"Oh, but you wanted to see Larry."

"Oh, right," I said.

"It's probably easier just to go out the front again and circle round the house. You'll see him back there."

"Okay," I said. I stood up. I felt an inch or two taller than normal.

"I'll see you out," he said.

He floated up and we walked out of the room, back to the foyer and to the door.

I turned and extended my hand.

"Thanks for the iced tea, Tommy."

His wizened bird-boned hand wafted into mine.

"Just come back in if you want more," he said. "I have plenty. And I can always make more of the tea."

"Okay, thanks," I said, and I went out the door.

I felt as if my body were floating inside of me.

Chapter 78

I went down the porch steps and around to the left on the tilting and mossy stone path. It was shady along the side of the house, with an oak tree, some box elders, some other trees whose identities I failed to note or was ignorant of.

Places always look so different in the day if you've only ever seen them at night. Last night the house and its grounds with its lights and its party-goers had seemed mysterious and glamorous; now the house seemed mysterious but in a more prosaic way, like an old book lying open on a table in bright sunlight.

A big and sun-sodden old house, with peeling paint and the smell of damp wood, and all was quiet, all was still, even the leaves on the trees and on the bushes and flowers.

And I had a similar feeling to the one I'd experienced last night alone in the kitchen of this house, that the house itself was alive.

I paused and put my hand on the old painted wood. It was warm and soft, almost spongelike.

Through my fingers I felt and heard babies crying, children laughing, people talking, shouting, whispering. I saw old people dying. I saw and heard young men and women grappling in darkness, some not so young.

I took my hand away and continued on to the back of the house, and I saw Larry sitting at the same picnic table I had sat at with Elektra the previous night. It was shaded by a large elm tree. Larry was sitting there with a portable typewriter. He wore khaki shorts and a short-sleeved white shirt. He had a pair of horn-rimmed glasses on, and he was absorbed in reading a bound sheaf of papers. There was a plastic flowered pitcher of what looked like iced tea on the table and a couple of matching plastic glasses.

Someone had cleaned up the yard. You'd never know there had been a big party out here the night before. There was no one else about. No sign of Frank or Dean, Sammy or Joey, or Shirley, or Dick and Daphne, or Mr. MacNamara. Just Larry.

"Hello. Larry?" I said.

He looked up, and gazed at me for a moment as if he didn't know who I was.

"Oh, Arnold. You made it."

"I sure did," I said.

He stood up and took my hand. He was smoking a cigar, and he had a couple of back-ups in his shirt pocket.

"I'm so glad. Sit down."

He gestured to the other side of the table, and we both sat down. I noticed he also had a stack of blank typing paper on the table, a notepad, a couple of ball-point pens.

"So, you ready to do some work?"

"I'll give it a try," I said.

"Pour yourself some iced tea. It's good."

"Oh," I said. "I don't know. I just had some iced tea that Tommy made me."

"Oh. Was it his special iced tea?"

"Yes," I said.

"No wonder you seem so calm. He must like you."

"Well, he thought I needed something."

"Hungover?"

"Not especially. But I'm trying to quit smoking and apparently I looked like death warmed over."

"Oh. I see you've got a cigarette in your ear there."

"I'm saving it for after lunch."

"Do you want me to put this cigar out?"

"No, please don't. I think it helps actually."

"Fabulous. Here, have some iced tea. Don't worry, there's no laudanum in it. At least I don't think there is."

He poured me a glassful. There was still some ice in the pitcher, and the cubes made delicious little clunking sounds. I picked up the glass and drank. It tasted like the tea Tommy had given me, with the spicy ginger taste but lacking that murky thick flavor which I could now identify as opium, the drug which even now suffused my being and kept me from immediately lighting up my cigarette while devouring one of Larry's cigars whole, cellophane and all.

"So, anyway," said Larry, "I keep doing this: I take jobs to make movies out of scripts that read like some retard wrote them. A retard who's spent his life doing nothing but watching movies written by other retards. Oh," he interjected, recalling who he was talking to, "I — uh —"

"That's okay, Larry. I don't think I'm technically-speaking a retard."

"No, I guess not. What was it, anyway, your problem?"

Like everyone else, he had heard about it.

"Well, basically I cracked up entirely, and I had to be committed for a while."

"Uh-huh. How ya feeling these days?"

"Much better, except —"

Should I go into it? Well, it seemed only fair if he was considering working with me. Not to mention paying me.

"Yes?"

He took off his glasses and looked me in the eyes. He seemed simply curious.

"I have visits from Jesus. And occasionally I levitate, or seem to levitate. I've also floated up into the air, separate from my body. Oh, and yesterday I traveled through a painting in Mrs. Biddle's house and wound up in 1890s France, where I met the writer Marcel Proust."

Larry took a drag of his cigar, and let the smoke gently trail up from the side of his mouth.

"Sounds like you lead an interesting life, Arnold."

I thought about this.

"It is, actually," I said. "At least now it is."

"Since your crack-up?"

"Yes," I said. "It was pretty mundane really before."

"Working for the railroad?"

"Yeah, that, and everything else."

"Maybe that's why you cracked up," he said.

"Could be," I said.

"I could never understand it," said Larry. "Working some job where you do the same thing every day. I realize that's what most people have to do, but to me it's death. That's why I went into show biz, movies. So, you wanta hear about this script?"

"You don't mind working with someone who's not quite right in the head?"

"Well, you're not going to completely flip out on me, are you?"

"I hope not."

"Because if this is as crazy as you're going to get, believe me, I've worked with lots crazier out in Hollywood."

"Oh, okay," I said.

"Let me tell you about this stupid script."

"Okay."

So a young soldier is on leave in Paris. He meets a girl. They have a wild night on the town. They go to her apartment. Her ex-boyfriend, who has been following them, breaks in. A fight ensues. The soldier gets knocked out. When he wakes up the girl is lying on the floor dead. Someone knocks on the door. He runs out to the balcony, drops down to the pavement...Communist agents. The Corsican Mafia. A band of Gypsy thieves. An attractive Gypsy dancing girl...

"What do ya think?"

"Um, about the story?"

"Yeah."

"It's okay I guess. I read paperback novels like this all the time."

"But it's stupid."

"Oh."

"I want to make it non-stupid, Arnold."

"Well, does the story matter?"

He paused.

"I think you're on to something. What's a story? Just one damn thing leading to another."

"That's true," I said, just to be agreeable I suppose.

"Who cares what happens?"

"Not me," I said.

"You're brilliant. What really matters is what's happening *while* the stuff is happening."

"Or not," I ventured.

"Right. Sometimes nothing's happening while stuff is happening. And sometimes nothing's happening in the first place."

"I find that's quite often the case in my own life."

"But, Arnold, we gotta have something happening. Don't we?"

"I think so. Otherwise —"

"It's boring."

"Right," I said.

"Like real life."

"Yeah."

"We don't want that," said Larry.

"No," I said.

"So, uh, what do we do?"

"Okay," I said. I felt as if my brain were bubbling over slightly, but it was not an unpleasant feeling. "We keep the soldier meeting the girl, and the fight, and him waking up and finding the girl dead."

"That stuff is good."

"Sure. I don't know about the Communist agents though."

"Lose the Commies. What about the Mafia? And the Gypsies?"

"Well, I don't know, Larry. As long as he meets the other girl, the dancer girl."

"Right. We gotta have the other dame. That's essential."

"Sure. You always need a dame," I said.

"Brilliant. Okay."

He grabbed a blank sheet of paper and rolled it into the typewriter.

Chapter 79

"Fade in," said Larry, typing away. "Exterior. Paris. Day. Oh, wait. The title. What're we calling this?"

"What was it called before?"

"*Sidewalks of Blood*," he said.

"*Sidewalks of Blood*?"

"*Sidewalks of Blood*."

"I like that, Larry," I said.

"Yeah, me too, actually. I like the French version even better, *Les trottoirs du sang*."

He backed up the paper and typed in the title.

"All right," he said. "Back to the first shot..."

I'll spare the reader (i.e. myself) my usual second-by-tortuous-second blow-by-mind-numbing-blow account of the next couple of hours. Let it only be said that as we sat there on that hot forenoon composing the opening scenes of our story I effected that escape from the prison of myself which normally I accomplish most profoundly — not in sleep, nor in drunkenness — but oddly enough only when I am all by myself alone in a room composing this chronicle of my body-entrapped life or making my little bad poems. But now I was achieving this not alone but with someone else, traveling with another person into that freedom I've only ever found in the deeper regions of my own self.

At last Larry said, "Damn! This is good, brother! We got almost the whole first act worked out here!"

I didn't even know the movie had a first act, but I kept my ignorance to myself.

"So what about lunch, Arnie? Then you can finally smoke that cancer stick you got in your ear."

Amazingly I hadn't even thought about that cigarette since we had started our work.

I took it out from behind my ear and looked at it. The day had gotten increasingly hot as we were sitting there, and now the cigarette was completely sodden with sweat. I crumpled it up in Larry's ashtray, and we headed into the house, going around it and coming in from the front porch.

Mrs. Biddle and Tommy were playing cards at a small table covered with some sort of Oriental-looking cloth.

They were both smoking cigarettes and they had a pitcher of what looked like Tommy's special iced tea on the table, with accompanying glasses.

"Ah, the scribblers," said Mrs. Biddle.

She was dressed like a lady in a 1930s movie about people on a safari. Come to think of it, Tommy in his cream-colored suit was like someone in the same movie, but the guy who stayed at the plantation and couldn't be bothered to go on a safari.

"Or should I say the typists," she added.

"We deal in the magic of sound and vision, Mrs. Biddle," said Larry. "In dreams. We deal in mystical journeys through space and time. In other words we give the poor yokels what they want: two hours of escape from their miserable little lives."

"I'll drink to that," said Tommy.

"Yeah, speaking of which —" said Larry.

"Some of Tommy's special iced tea?" said Mrs. Biddle.

"Thanks, Mrs. Biddle," said Larry, "but I was thinking of something in a more alcoholic vein."

"Help yourselves," said Mrs. Biddle, gesturing towards a drinks cabinet. "Ice and beer in the kitchen."

"Oh, allow me," said Tommy, rising.

"Sit the hell, down, Tommy," said Mrs. Biddle. "These are two grown men and they are more than capable of getting their own drinks."

"Yeah, take it easy, Tommy," said Larry, heading over to the liquor cabinet. "What are you drinking, Arnie?"

"Whatever you're having," I said.

"Old Crow and soda it is then."

Larry made us a couple of tall strong drinks, using one of those old-fashioned soda siphons. He didn't bother going into the kitchen for ice.

We chatted a bit with Tommy and Mrs. Biddle. Tommy wanted to know what our movie was about, and Larry told him what we had so far.

"I'm enthralled," said Tommy. "Then what happens?"

"We have no idea," said Larry. "But we'll think of something."

"Write me in a part," said Tommy. "I could be an undertaker or something."

"We'll think about it," said Larry.

"You're not going to forget our tea date, are you, Mr. Schnabel?" said Mrs. Biddle.

"Absolutely not," I said.

"We're gonna grab some chow," said Larry.

"Help yourselves. You know your way around that kitchen."

Larry and I went in to the kitchen, and Larry made us a couple of ham and cheese sandwiches, and we each had a beer, sitting there at the kitchen table.

Larry said we should break for the day and pick it up again tomorrow. That was fine with me.

Somehow it had been gotten across to me that we were indeed going to write this screenplay together. Larry hadn't mentioned money again, but frankly I didn't care. When you've written nonsense for nothing but your own idle amusement your whole life you get used to it. And what else would I be doing with my time, anyway? Staring into space? Watching re-runs of *M Squad* and *Johnny Staccato*? Watching the hairs on my arm grow?

Daphne came into the kitchen.

"Oh my God," she said. "I am so hungover."

She sat at the table with us. Hungover or not she was stunningly beautiful. She wore a dress with little red and blue flowers all over it, on a white background. I think the flowers were zinnia.

"Have a beer," said Larry.

"Oh, shut up," she said. "I never want to drink again!"

"I told you not to try to keep up with Frank and those guys."

"Never again! They're not human! They never even went to bed. They just drove off this morning for Atlantic City, something about a dice game, and then they're all performing at the 500 Club tonight. Do you want to go?"

"I don't know," said Larry. "It seems like a lot of work, driving all the way up to A.C. just to see those guys. I mean I heard them all sing all last night, and I didn't even have to move."

"You have a point. Do you think Tommy has any of that special iced tea he makes?"

"Yeah, I believe he and Mrs. Biddle are having some now in the living room."

"Oh, good, let me get a glass."

She jumped up, got a glass out of a cupboard, put some ice in it from the freezer, and left the kitchen.

"Nice kid," said Larry. "But don't mess with her, Arnie. Dick Ridpath's in love with her."

"Oh, I wouldn't —" I started.

"I saw the way she looked at you. It's just if she gets you alone you might justifiably be tempted."

"Larry, really —"

"Women dig madmen, Arnie. Don't ask me why. But nobody gets more action than a maniac. Not even movie stars. Although it occurs to me that those two métiers are not mutually exclusive. But really, it would kill Dick if he found out. 'Cause he really likes you, too."

"You don't have to worry, Larry."

"Come to think of it though, it's the same deal for women. It's always the nutty dames that drive guys nuts. I know this has always been the case with me. Normal chicks, you know, nice everyday gals, I don't know, they just leave me cold. I like them as human beings and all, don't get me wrong, but I just don't want to, um, you know — hey, that girl of yours — Clytemnestra?"

"Elektra."

"Boy, that chick, Arnie, I'll tell ya —"

"What chick?" said Daphne, coming back into the kitchen with her glass full of dark special iced tea now.

"You, baby," said Larry.

Chapter 80

Daphne sat down and took a good long gulp of the iced tea. She put the glass on the table, still holding it, staring pensively off at nothing in particular and probably gauging the tea's effect. Her lips opened, she sighed.

"Well, that's an improvement, " she said. And then, commandingly, "*Larry.*"

"At your service, miss."

"Will you be a darling and go get me some cigarettes. There should be a box on the big coffee table in the living room. I should have grabbed one myself but I forgot."

"Of course."

Larry got up and left and she watched him go.

She leaned across the table towards me. She smelled like a garden.

"Quickly now. Did Dick speak to you about me?"

"Uh –"

"What did he say, and if you lie I'll be able to tell and I'll be very angry."

"He asked me if he should marry you."

"What did you tell him?"

"Well, I, uh, um, I sort of told him that, uh –"

"Stop hemming and hawing. It's not attractive."

"Sorry."

"Do you think we should get married? And I'll tell you right now that if you hem or haw I shall scream."

"I think you should wait a few years," I said, not so much because I thought it was a good idea, but because I didn't want to hear her scream.

"'A few years,'" she repeated. "So you think that's best?"

"What's the rush?" I said.

"Good question. I'm only nineteen after all." She rattled the ice in her glass and took another but smaller drink. "What's the deal with you and this Calliope person?"

"Elektra," I said.

"Elektra," she said. "Well?"

"Um, she, uh — she and I —"

"She *is* very pretty, isn't she?"

"Uh, yes."

"Intelligent, too."

"Yes. More intelligent than I am."

"Poof."

"Poof?"

"You're sleeping with her, right?"

"Well —" I realized that I was breaking out in a sweat again, for about the twelfth time that day — "we haven't exactly *slept* together –"

"You know what I mean."

"Yes," I said, my sweat immediately turning cold.

"Does she like it?" she asked. Then, "Wow, you're blushing."

Her mouth blossomed into a great smile, her eyes flashed, the hot sweat streamed like a river down my back.

(And where was Larry? How long did it take to go to the living room and back?)

"Okay," she said. "You don't have to answer that. But I was watching how she looked at you. I think she likes it. I think she likes it very much. So, are you two going to get married?"

"I don't — think so," I said.

"Why not?"

"Wouldn't a better question be 'Why'?"

"Fair enough." She rattled her ice cubes in the glass again. "Do you like to swim?"

"Very much," I said. "I go for a long swim every day."

"Come for a swim with me. I warn you I swim like an absolute fish."

I wasn't sure about this.

"I just had lunch," I said.

"So go home and change into your bathing suit and we'll take a little stroll or sit on the beach while you digest your lunch, and then we'll take a nice long swim."

My problem — or I should say one of my problems — is I don't know how to say no to people.

"Okay," I said.

"Good. Oh, here's Larry."

Larry came in with a carved wooden box; he opened it and held it out to Daphne, who picked out a cigarette and waited for Larry to put the box on the table and then take out his matches and give her a light.

"Thanks," she said. "Arnold and I are going for a swim, Larry."

"Oh, really?"

"Yes. Want to come?"

"No. I think I'll take a nap."

She picked up her glass, rattled her ice one last time and then polished off the rest of her iced tea.

"Okay," she said. "I'm just going up to get into my suit. I'll be right down."

And she flew gracefully out of the room, leaving behind only the trail of her cigarette smoke and the flowery scent of herself.

I had stood up as she left the table, and Larry had never sat down again. He looked at me.

"Woo boy," he said. "What did I tell you about women and maniacs?"

I looked at the box of cigarettes on the table. On the one hand I wanted to smoke two or three of them simultaneously while stuffing the rest of them in my various pockets. On the other hand I figured I had gone this long, why not keep moving and see if I could hold out till after my swim?

"All right, Arnie," said Larry, and he grabbed my shoulder. "I'm gonna hit the hay. Good luck."

"We're only going for a swim."

"Sure. Good luck anyway." He pinched up the sodden material of my shirt from my shoulder. "You're drenched with sweat."

It was one of those statements to which no reply seemed necessary, or wise.

"Same time tomorrow?" said Larry. "We'll dive into that second act."

"Sure," I said.

"Do what I do and try not to think about it till then."

"Okay," I said.

That would be easy for me. I barely think about my writing even when I'm doing it, let alone when I'm not doing it.

He patted my shoulder one last time.

"Enjoy your, uh, swim, Arnie," he said.

"It's just a swim, Larry," I said.

"Sure, pal. See you tomorrow."

He straightened out my shirt collar for me and then walked out of the kitchen. I sat down again and stared at the open cigarette box.

I reached over and closed the lid.

Chapter 81

After a while it occurred to me to wash up our lunch plates and glasses, and I did so. Then I sat down again and stared at that cigarette box. There it was, just sitting there. There was an ashtray on the table too, with some of the ash from Daphne's cigarette in it. I picked up the ashtray, took it over to the sink, washed and dried it, put it back on the table, sat down again.

I stared at the box.

My head began to throb, and my throat went dry. Here we go again. I grabbed the box and opened it. There they were, serried in all their lung-destroying wonderfulness. Filterless, just the way I liked them. I picked one up. Chesterfield Kings. Not my brand, but a good brand, an admirable brand. I looked around for a light. A box of wooden kitchen matches sat invitingly on a shelf by the stove, not six feet away. Six feet to euphoria. Six feet to glory. Did I want to live forever? What was so bad about cancer after all? And was it worth it, another five or ten or twenty years of life if I couldn't even enjoy a cigarette now and then? But then I recalled that awful coughing fit this morning.

I gnawed my dry lower lip and stared at the cigarette.

Where was Jesus now?

Nowhere. It was just me, me and this Chesterfield King.

What the heck, one wouldn't kill me.

But then I heard a sound like an approaching small cantering pony. I dropped the cigarette back into the box and closed the lid just as Daphne burst into the kitchen, wearing a one-piece shiny green bathing suit, an unbuttoned flowered shirt, sandals and a sort of sombrero, and carrying a large straw bag with shoulder straps.

"Okay, I'm ready, let's go," she said.

I got up and followed her out of the kitchen.

I don't think I've described Daphne yet, except to say that she is beautiful. She is tall, and slim, with dark hair, not very long dark hair, with bangs. Unlike most women's hair these days her hair seems not to have been shaped into a simulacrum of a spaceman's helmet with sprays and glues; it's soft, like a child's, and she keeps it out of her face with barrettes or clips. She also seems to eschew make-up except for a rather deep and red lipstick.

She exudes an aura of physical strength, and her walk reminds me strikingly of the stride of the boxer Sugar Ray Robinson.

"We're going swimming, Grandmom," she said to Mrs. Biddle when we reached the living room.

"Oh are you? So you're a swimmer, too, Mr. Schnabel?"

"He loves to swim," said Daphne, coming around to look at Mrs. Biddle's hand of cards.

"I used to swim," said Tommy, "for miles. In the Philippines. One time I was attacked by a shark."

"Did he bite you?" asked Daphne.

"No. I punched him in the nose and he swam away. After that I stopped swimming though."

Daphne came around and peeked at Tommy's cards.

"Who's winning?" she asked.

There was a notepad on the table and a pencil. Tommy glanced at the pad.

"Mrs. Biddle is up by forty-seven cents."

"Okay, 'bye," said Daphne.

"Mr. Schnabel," said Mrs. Biddle.

"Yes?"

"I'll see you at four."

"Four o'clock, right."

We went out, and as we were going down the steps into the bright heat of the day Daphne said, "My grandmother likes you. And like Dick she doesn't like a lot of people."

"Older women always like me," I said.

"Yes, you're very polite. Old ladies like that."

She strode along beside me, and I fought the urge to stare at her sideways. I didn't entirely succeed, and as we made the turn left onto North Street I almost fell off the curb, but Daphne didn't seem to notice.

"I dislike nearly everyone also," she said. "My mother and father however like all sorts of people, so perhaps misanthropy skips a generation. How do you like Tommy?"

"He seems nice," I said.

"He's very nice. Completely addicted to his laudanum, but he wears it well. When he gets too addicted to get out of bed my grandmother sends him to a drying-out place. Then he starts right up again a week or two after he gets out."

"I hope your grandmother isn't —"

"Oh no. She'll have a glass of his special iced tea in the morning, especially if she's hungover, but she has an iron will. Like me. I'm very iron-willed."

In no time at all we were at my aunts' house. My young cousin Kevin was sitting on the porch, reading or re-reading his Tom Swift book.

"Oh, boy," he said, when he saw Daphne.

"And what is your name?" said Daphne when we came up the steps.

"Kevin Armstrong," he said, his mouth agape and all but drooling. Don't ask me how this kid will handle it when he reaches the age of puberty. He'll probably have to be kept on a leash.

"Okay, I'll be right down," I said.

I went in through the screen door, and it could have been worse, this time it was only my mother and my Aunt Edith who were in the living room, standing and staring out the window at Daphne.

"Did you have lunch, Arnold?" asked my mom.

"Yep, I had lunch at Mrs. Biddle's."

"That lady on Windsor Avenue?"

"Yeah."

"What were you doing there again?"

"I'm working on a screenplay with a fellow I met."

"What's a screenplay?"

"It's a movie."

"You're writing a movie?"

"I guess I am."

"Who's the chickadee?" asked Aunt Edith, loud enough for Daphne to hear her out on the porch.

"She's Mrs. Biddle's granddaughter. We're going swimming."

"How many girlfriends do you have, Arnold?" asked Aunt Edith.

"She's not my girlfriend."

"She's a little young for you, isn't she?"

"Okay, I'm gonna go up and get into my bathing suit."

"Aren't you going to invite her in?" asked my mother.

"Oh. Okay."

I went back to the screen door.

Daphne was reading Kevin's book over his shoulder, with her hand on his shoulder. He looked as if he were melting.

"Excuse me, Daphne? Would you like to meet my mother and aunt?"

"Oh, I'd love to."

I opened the screen and she came in, with Kevin right on her heels.

I introduced her, and then headed out of there and upstairs.

On the third floor I knew I had to be very careful. It seemed to be impossible these days, or these nights as well, to go by Miss Evans's door and not have her pop out, so I went by on tiptoes.

I made it without incident up to my little attic room. I changed into my swimming trunks, stuck my wallet in the pocket of the trunks, put on a clean t-shirt, slipped on my flip-flops and grabbed a towel.

I opened the drawer under my night table. Sure enough, there was a pack and a half of Pall Malls in there. I picked up the opened pack. Then I put it back and shut the drawer.

I went down the steps and once again tiptoed down the hall toward the stairs.

This time I didn't make it.

She opened her door just as I came abreast of it.

"I thought I heard your step, Arnold. You have the lightest footstep of any man I've ever known. Like a dancer. Oh, you're going swimming. So also was I going to go."

True enough, she was wearing a bathing suit. A two-piece this time. Red and black polka dots on a white background.

"But I suppose you're not going alone, are you?" she asked.

"Uh, no," I said.

"No, of course not. But wait. I'll walk to the beach with you. Come in." What could I do?

I came in, leaving the door open behind me.

She busied herself gathering towels, suntan oil, a book, a notebook, pens, God knows what else, all the time chattering about how nice the party was last night. She seemed to be bending over quite a bit while doing this, and I tried to look away and think about baseball.

"Oh!" she said suddenly. "I took your advice and went to that nice Father Reilly. Look what he gave me when I told him I wasn't Catholic."

She picked up a paperback copy of the *Baltimore Catechism* and showed it to me.

"And this too."

Next up was a paperback of *The Lives of The Saints.*

"And this."

She held up a nice set of shiny black rosary beads.

"He gave you all that?"

"Yes, he was so nice."

"He had all that stuff in the confessional?"

"No, silly. He invited me to chat with him, and we met for lunch at the Cape Coffee Shoppe."

"Oh, great," I said.

Possibly great for me, anyway, although I wasn't so sure how great it was for Father Reilly.

Chapter 82

At last Miss Evans seemed to have all her stuff collected and she walked up to me and said, "Do you think I'm frivolous?"

Even I know that if someone asks you if you think they're anything less than perfect that the absolute last thing they want to hear is the truth.

So I said, "Oh, no, not at all."

"You're so kind," she said, taking a step closer.

I backed up and hit the edge of the open door.

"Shall we go then?" she asked.

"Um, I think I'd better use the bathroom first," I said.

It's true to say that I had just then realized that I needed to urinate, but, more pressingly, I felt the need to escape from this woman, even if it was only for a couple of minutes.

I staggered backwards out the door, turned and quick-marched to the bathroom down the hall.

Inside I turned the bolt and stood for a moment with my back to the door. I was sweating again, and now I needed a cigarette more than I had all day, or all my life. I felt like I was about to be led to a firing squad. Didn't they give the condemned man a cigarette with his blindfold?

I went to the bowl and proceeded to do what I had supposedly come in here for. This was the first time I had emptied my bladder since leaving the house that morning, and what with all the iced tea I'd drunk, special and otherwise, plus that one strong highball and one beer, it took a while, and as I stood there I had the strongest feeling that Miss Evans was standing right outside the bathroom door, waiting, listening. It was most disconcerting. I swear, if it weren't for Elektra I would have decided just to let Miss Evans have her way with me and be done with it. After all, she was very attractive, physically anyway, and at least then I wouldn't have to deal with the continual anxiety of running into her in the hallway. And here she was, waiting out there, listening to me peeing; waiting, for me.

What would she say, or do, when she saw that it was Daphne downstairs with whom I was going to the beach? What if she pulled a switchblade from that big beach bag and attacked Daphne, or me?

I finished my business, flushed the toilet, and, as it performed its usual symphony of a truckload of pots and pans being dumped down the side of a rocky slope, I washed and dried my hands.

I went to the door, but then I stopped. Was Miss Evans out there? I leaned the side of my head forward, listening, but I couldn't hear anything.

I turned the bolt on the lock, as quietly as I could, then put my hand on the doorknob, but then I paused and put my ear even closer to the door.

Not a sound.

But that didn't mean she wasn't standing right out there, holding her breath.

I took my hand off the doorknob and went to the bathroom window. It was a casement window, open, with an adjustable screen in it. I took out the screen and stood it on the floor against the wall. I stuck my head out the window.

Running down the side of the house, just to the right of the window, was a drain pipe, fastened to the house by rounded brackets every four feet or so, both pipe and brackets painted many times over through the hundred and four years of this house's history. Directly below the window on the ground down there was a purplish-pink cloud of rhododendrons in full bloom.

I have experienced much insanity over the past seven months or so, but I must say that usually the insanity felt like something that was happening to me, that had descended upon me, rather than something I myself willingly chose to embrace. What happened next I'm afraid fell in the latter category.

I threw my towel through the window, and, without letting myself think about it too much, I climbed out after it. Halfway through it occurred to me that it might have been better to force myself out feet-first, but I didn't feel like hesitating, so I continued to wriggle through the little window, while simultaneously reaching to my right with my left hand to grab ahold of the pipe.

With one last heave my legs came out and seemed to drop past me while I swung my right hand over to join the left on the pipe. Unfortunately the weight of my body and the force of gravity and the fact that I was neither Batman nor Spider-Man resulted in my hands bursting away from the pipe and my body falling backwards away from the house, and I saw the blue sky spinning above me and I caught what I presumed was my last glimpse of life, the upside-down fleeting image of the yellow-shingled, green-shuttered house across the way as I plummeted head-first, when suddenly I stopped just above the first floor windows.

Floating right before me, right-side up, meaning upside-down to my way of looking, was Jesus, in his khakis and old t-shirt, with his usual lit cigarette in his hand.

"Oh Arnold," he said.

"I know," I said.

"Is this any way to die? Jumping out of a third-storey window just to avoid walking to the beach with some goofy woman?"

"It seemed like a good idea at the time," I said.

He shook his head, I guess in bewilderment, put his cigarette in his mouth, reached out, grabbed me, and twirled me around so that I was now right-side up.

"All right," he said. "Try to bend your knees and roll when you hit those rhododendrons."

"I will," I said, sheepishly, and I dropped without further ceremony into the shrubs and tumbled out onto the stone pathway.

I lay there on my back for a few moments. Above me I saw only that pristine blue sky.

I seemed to be okay. I pushed myself to a sitting position. I had a bruise on my right knee, and my swimming trunks were stained from the flowers I had just crushed.

I reached over, grabbed my towel, and got to my feet.

I tried to fluff up the rhododendrons, and I kicked some of the destroyed flowers under the bush.

Then I hobbled around to the front of the house, and went up the steps. I tapped on one of the cross-slats of the screen door.

"Daphne," I said.

She was sitting in there, chatting with my mother and aunt, and Kevin was sitting next to her on the couch.

"Arnold," she called, "how did you get out there?"

"I, uh, went out the side way," I said.

"Oh."

Neither Daphne nor my kin questioned why I would come out the side way and all the way around to the front porch instead of just coming through the house from the stairway like a normal person. But then of course no one there thought me a normal person, and quite justifiably so.

I held the screen door open, Daphne got up, said goodbye to my mother and aunt and Kevin, and came out through the door past me.

"See ya," I said to my family members, and I let the door close.

We went down the steps.

"You're limping," said Daphne.

"Yeah, I fell."

"Are you okay to go swimming?"

"Sure, let's go."

I started to limp even faster. I was afraid that Miss Evans would come running out the door after us.

Daphne took my arm and we headed up Perry Street in that thick August sunlight.

I wondered how long Miss Evans would wait outside that bathroom door. But I couldn't worry about that now.

Chapter 83

When we got to Washington Street I said, "Do you mind turning down here?"

"No," she said, and as we strolled along the pavement past the shops, I noticed people looking at us. Then I realized they were looking first at Daphne, and then at me. She was still holding my arm. So this is what it was like to walk with a beautiful woman. And I retroactively realized that the same thing had happened on the few occasions when I had walked somewhere with Elektra.

I don't remember people looking at me much back when I walked everywhere alone (or with my mother). What was there to look at? But walk with a beautiful woman and you leave the anonymous horde and join the aristocracy of the race.

When we got to Jackson we turned right, and when we reached Elektra's shop I asked Daphne to wait while I went inside.

Elektra was behind the counter, with Rocket Man, and they were both talking to prospective customers.

Elektra was wearing a loose dress I hadn't seen before, pale blue, with a cloth belt, her arms and throat bare. She had most of her hair tied back somehow and she was showing some rings to two ladies. She smiled at me and gave me a nod, and I waited, looking at the jewelry in the display cases.

After a minute she left the ladies to discuss the rings between themselves and she came over to where I stood.

"Hello, lover. What brings you in here?" she said softly.

"You," I said.

"Let me come around, big boy."

She came out from around the counter, took my arm and led me over to the corner of the shop, by some cases that held necklaces and bracelets made with Cape May diamonds.

"What's up, Arnold baby?"

"I just wanted you to know that I'm going swimming with Daphne. From the party last night. The badminton girl."

"You are?"

"Yeah, she's right outside."

Elektra looked out the window, and there was Daphne, smoking a cigarette, and blatantly looking at us. Daphne waved, and Elektra gave her a little wave back.

"Lucky you," said Elektra.

"I didn't want you to think I was doing something behind your back," I said. "But she asked me to go swimming with her."

"Oh, Arnold. It's okay. You are going to try not to have sex with her though, right?"

"Yes," I said.

"I was joking."

"Oh, sorry."

"Although I wouldn't blame you. She's a doll."

"Don't worry," I said.

"How's your chin?" She put her hand on the spot where the coast-guardsman had socked me.

"It's okay," I said.

"Did you hurt your leg last night? I notice you seem to be limping a bit."

"I —" I had decided to try to be totally honest with Elektra, but in this case I just couldn't do it. So I gave her the short version. "I took a slight fall," I said. "But I'm okay."

"Okay, good. Look I gotta get back to my ladies over there. Do you want to do something tonight?"

"Yes," I said.

"Good, drop by around eight, we'll go get a beer. Now, go swim with Daphne."

She gave me a pat on the arm and went back around the counter to deal with the ladies again. I went back out to Daphne.

We walked on up Jackson to the beach, and the nice thing about her, she didn't ask me any nosy questions about Elektra, just as she hadn't questioned me about why I wanted to turn onto Washington Street instead of heading straight up Perry to the beach.

She did ask me if I was reading anything interesting, and I mentioned *The Waste Land*, and Miss Evans's novel.

"But I'm really more interested in this book *This Sweet Sickness*," I said.

She asked me what it was about, and I told her.

"That does sound good," she said. "I'm reading this new Salinger book, *Raise High the Roof Beam, Carpenters*?"

"Never heard of it," I said.

"Have you read any Salinger?"

"I don't think so. But he sounds familiar. Does he write detective novels?"

"No, I don't think so. This book's made up of two long stories. The first one's about this guy during World War II who gets a pass from the army to go to his brother's wedding, except the brother doesn't show up. At the wedding."

"Mm-hm. Why?"

"Beats me. Cold feet I guess. But I'm only about halfway through it, so who the hell knows?"

"He wasn't murdered?"

"No, I don't think so. And then there's another story in the same book, called 'Seymour: An Introduction'. Seymour is the missing brother, I believe."

"Ah. Maybe that one explains why he didn't show up at the wedding."

"Maybe. But I'm afraid even less will happen in that one than in the first one. I kind of wish I were reading your book. Call me old-fashioned, but I like books where people get murdered."

"Me too," I said.

So much for literary dialogue.

She asked me if I had a beach I liked to go to, and I told her about my near-deserted beach in that long cove sweeping down toward the Point. She said that sounded swell.

By the time we got down there I had well digested my lunch, and although I was still limping from my fall I felt ready for a good swim. The sky had grown overcast, and the air was hot and heavy. We stuck our towels and stuff behind some scrub, and then we splashed out onto the pebbly sand into the surf, and after we'd strode in to waist-deep we both dove in simultaneously, just as if someone had fired off a starter's pistol.

She wasn't kidding about swimming like a fish. I've gotten pretty good, but she kept up with me all the way as I headed straight out for a couple of hundred yards or so. I stopped and turned, and she was bobbing right there beside me, barely out of breath, the water streaming down her face, her dark hair shining like the coat of a seal.

She spat a stream of water in my face.

"Which way now, Aquaman?"

"I like to swim down toward the Point."

Without a word she flipped around and swam away, with great smooth strokes, her shiny green suit coursing through the darker green water. I took off after her.

We swam all the way without a stop to past the old beach-defense bunker, and as we came parallel to the convent with its long white walls and its burnt-umber roof, Daphne at last turned on her back and gasped, "Oh, my God, you're relentless! Look, I have to rest, let's go in here."

And before I could say anything she was shooting like a torpedo in to the nuns' beach.

I followed her in.

She staggered up out of the surf, shaking her hair, went up past the pebbly shingle and onto the sandy part of the beach, fell to her knees and then dropped onto her back just above the reach of the tide. I walked up and sat beside her.

"Look at me," she said.

I did.

"Look at my chest absolutely heaving."

I did, and then tried to make myself look past her, at the dark green water, at the steely sky.

Her hand reached up and picked a bit of seaweed off my knee. She sighed deeply. I looked at her again, and she turned towards me on her hip, the side of her face in her hand and her elbow in the sand.

"What would you do if I made a pass at you?" she said.

"I would run back into the ocean," I said.

"Good. Because I'm not going to. Because you're Dick's friend. And because you have a perfectly nice girlfriend with Elektra."

"Right," I said.

The air seemed suddenly still, and even heavier than before, almost palpable.

"I'm going to close my eyes for just a bit," she said. "But don't let me sleep for more than five minutes."

"Okay."

She lay back with her arm over her eyes.

I sat and looked out at the dark green water, here where the great bay met the ocean. A heavy mass of purplish cloud was coming up from the right, from the continent. I lay back in the sand, with my hands behind my head, and closed my eyes.

I felt something on my chest, and opened my eyes again. Daphne, sound asleep, had thrown her right arm over me, and her head, partially covered by her left arm, had snuggled next to chest.

Oh well. I closed my eyes. And fell asleep.

I dreamt I was being rained on, lying in our tiny back yard back home in Olney, but the raindrops were black from the smoke of the nearby Heintz factory. I woke up and realized I was being rained on in real life.

I threw Daphne's arm off me, and shook her shoulder, woke her up.

"Oh, my God, it's pouring," she said.

"Yes," I said.

"Come on, let's go up to that big house and sit under the porch."

"Can't we just go back into the ocean?"

"What, and be struck by lightning? Come on."

"But that's a convent."

"So what?"

And she was up and off, padding quickly up the beach through the rain to the rear porch of the convent. I got up and followed her.

A great crack of thunder shook the earth, and so I broke into a trot, when suddenly all the world lit up all around me with bright white light and the earth flew away from my feet and the world went black.

I opened my eyes and Jesus was standing there. He had that eternal cigarette in his fingers. The rain had stopped, although the sky was still overcast.

"You okay, buddy?"

"Yes, I think so," I said.

He was still in his casual seashore attire, except now he had an old denim jacket on over his faded blue t-shirt.

"Here, grab a hand," he said.

I took his hand and he yanked me to my feet.

I looked around.

We weren't on the beach any more.

We were at the foot of a green hill, with lots of shrubs and trees, scattered rosebushes here and there, some geraniums and rhododendrons seemingly planted at random, blotches of pink and red and pale blue against the green.

The rich dark grass was slightly overgrown.

We stood by a wrought-iron gate, beyond which a cobblestone path wound up to a very large Victorian house, dark yellow and green and brown, with a broad columned porch, and spires, gables, chimney pots, balconies, a slated roof the color of dull garnet.

I was still wearing my bathing trunks, but they were dry, and I was dry.

"Where are we?" I asked.

"That's my father's house," he said.

"Am I dead?"

"That is a very good question, Arnold."

"You don't know?"

"If I knew for sure I'd tell you. Between you and me it doesn't look too good, but, look, we'd better go talk to Peter and my old man. You want a cigarette?"

"I might as well have one," I said.

He patted the pockets of his wrinkled trousers and his jacket.

"Damn. I'm out." He held out the cigarette he was smoking. "Do you want to finish this one?"

"No thanks," I said.

"There should be smokes up at the house."

He opened the iron gate.

"Come on," he said. "Sooner we go up there, sooner we know what's up."

I went through, he shut the gate behind me. We started walking up the winding path to the house.

"By the way, Arnold, I am so sorry about that lightning bolt. Believe me, I had nothing to do with that."

"That's okay. I guess we all gotta go sometime."

I didn't want him to feel bad.

"Believe me, I wouldn't have saved you from falling out that window if I knew that an hour later —"

"Really, it's okay," I said.

"Well, okay then. I must say I'm a little surprised you're taking this so well."

"Well, it could be worse," I said.

"How could it be worse, Arnold? You're probably dead."

"True, but the thing is, it did happen pretty soon after I went to confession. So, I guess I'm still in a state of grace, because — well —"

"Because you didn't have time to have sex with Elektra again."

"Yeah," I said.

"Okay," he said. "Good. So you've got that going for you."

We came to the porch steps. A grey-bearded older guy wearing a plaid hunter's cap and a worn yellow canvas jacket or short coat was apparently napping in a wooden armchair by the front door. There was a small table in front of him, with what looked like a big thick leather-bound ledger of some sort, a jar of ink, a black fountain pen.

"That's Peter," said Jesus.

We went up the steps.

"Peter!" he called. "Wake up. Company."

The old guy opened his eyes, blinking.

Chapter 84

"I brought a friend," said Jesus. "Arnold, this is Peter. Peter, Arnold Schnabel."

I went over and said, "Please, sir, don't get up," and extended my hand. He looked at it with a slightly befuddled-looking expression, and I wondered if I had committed a *faux pas*. Should I have saluted instead? Or bowed?

But he took my hand and gave it a quick shake.

"Pleased to meet you, Mister — what was it?"

"Schnabel, sir."

"Schnabel, Schnabel —"

He took out a pair of wire-rimmed glasses from somewhere within his coat, put them on his nose, and picked up the big ledger.

"Arnold, right?"

"Yes, sir," I said.

"How do you spell this surname — S-H-N-?"

I spelled my last name for him, and he nodded and turned through the heavy pages.

An old Meerschaum pipe lay on its side on the table, a leather tobacco pouch, a box of Ohio Blue Tip kitchen matches, a chipped heavy glass ashtray, all of which made me think of cigarettes, and the fact that I didn't have one

"Okay, here we are," he said. "Schnabel, Arnold. What are you, Jewish?"

"Well, uh, Catholic actually –"

"Not that it matters," he said.

"I mean I was, you know, raised Catholic, and, uh –"

"I just said it doesn't matter."

"Oh, sorry," I said.

"The time for being sorry is over, pal."

"Oh," I said. "I'm –"

I was just about to say I was sorry again, but I checked myself.

"You're what?" he said.

"Nothing?" I said.

"Okay," he said. "Fine. Now, just let me just check this over." He ran his finger back and forth down the page, the way I had seen speed-readers do on TV. "Okay. Good. Good. Oh, sad. Mm-hmm. Okay. Good, good. Uh-huh, good, good — uh-oh, wait, not so good — this prostitute in Germany."

"Well, that was just the once, sir. My buddies got me drunk. I think they suspected I was a virgin. Which I was. Anyway, they got me drunk, and —"

"All right, okay. I see here you confessed it, like, the very next day."

"Yes, sir."

"That's good. Okay, let me just skim through this. Good, good, very good, very good. All good. Good, good, good. Not bad. Hmmm. Not — *too* bad. Hmm."

He continued to talk and to mumble to himself, reading the story of my life. Personally, I was getting bored just thinking about it all, but I suppose this was his job, and he was used to it.

I felt very awkward, standing there in my bathing trunks, without even my flip-flops on my feet. Also it was just a little cool out there on the porch. Oh well, I had spent much of my life standing around being bored and uncomfortable, why should my afterlife be any different?

"*Whoa!*" said Peter abruptly. "Mental breakdown this past year I see."

"Yes, sir. Sorry."

"What did I just tell you about 'sorry'."

"Oh," I said. "Right. Uh —"

"Anyway, it's not necessarily your fault, Arnold. Lots of people have mental breakdowns."

"Right. I'm sorry. I mean —"

"So now you're sorry for being sorry?"

"Yeah," I said. "Sorry."

"Are you fucking with me?"

"Not intentionally, sir."

I heard Jesus chuckling.

"I fail to see the humor," said the old guy.

"Sorry, Peter," said Jesus.

"Don't *you* start," said Peter.

He went back to the book.

"Okay. Okay. Hmm. Sad, but okay. All right. Okay. Okay. Oh. Wait. Not okay. No, not very okay at all."

He looked up at me over the lenses of his glasses.

"All right, what's up with this Elektra girl, Arnold?"

"Oh. Um — uh —"

"Peter —" said Jesus. He was leaning against the porch rail, nursing the end of his cigarette.

"What?" said Peter.

"I told him it was okay."

"You told him it was okay."

"Yeah. The poor guy hadn't had sex in — what? How long, Arnold? Twenty years?"

"Well, not quite twenty," I said. "It was like — uh, eighteen years?"

"Eighteen years," said Jesus.

"I don't care if it was fifty years," said Peter. "It's still a mortal sin."

"Oh. Like you were some saint, Peter."

"I *am* a saint," he said.

"*Now* you're a saint," said Jesus. "I knew you when you weren't so saintly. So give the guy a break. Anyway, two things. One, he went to confession this morning and received absolution, from a Father, what, Hogan —"

"Reilly," I said.

"Reilly," said Jesus. "Check it in your little book there."

Peter looked at the book again, running his finger along the words, his lips pursed, reading, and then he nodded.

"Okay, good," he said. He looked at Jesus. "But you said two things."

"Yeah, the other thing is, we're not quite so sure Arnold's dead yet."

"What?"

"Go ahead and check, skip ahead a little there —"

Peter turned to the book again, running his finger down the page, and then he nodded his head.

"Okay," he said. "Right."

"So I think we need to talk to my old man," said Jesus.

"Uh-huh," said Peter, but he was still looking at the book. Then he looked up at me again. "Okay, backing up a little bit – this meeting with 'Elektra' at the jewelry shop earlier today —"

"Yeah," I said, "well, you see, I just wanted to let her know I was going swimming with, uh —"

"This — Daphne person."

"Right. I didn't want Elektra to think I was doing something behind her back."

"Noble, Arnold. Really noble. But what is *not* so noble is what you were *thinking* about while you were being so honest and forthcoming with her."

"What I was thinking about?"

"Yes. What you were thinking about. Ahem. *The soft curve of her caramel-colored neck. The swelling of her breasts under the thin material of her blue dress. The way she smells like —* like 'butterscotch', isn't it?"

"Well, sometimes," I said. "Other times it's like, like this smell you get when you walk by certain bakeries really early in the morning, or —"

"Stop. You're breaking my heart. I know what you were thinking about, Arnold, and it had nothing to do with eating some butter cake fresh from the oven.'

"Oh, come on, Peter!" said Jesus, pushing away from the rail and coming over to us. "For Christ's sake, the guy is only human —"

"The thought is as culpable as the deed."

"Give me a break."

"Look, I'm not saying this is necessarily a *mortal* sin. I *am* saying it's a sin."

Jesus reached across me to stub out his cigarette butt in Peter's ashtray.

"All right, fine. Look, you know what? We're going in."

The old guy was back to reading the book, running his finger along the page.

"Oh," he said, "and this, here, when you're lying next to this Daphne on the beach here —"

"But I —"

"Yeah. 'But'. There's always a 'but'."

"But —"

"Let's go, Arnold," said Jesus, and he grabbed my arm.

"But —"

"What?"

"Should I go in just like this? I mean, in my bathing suit?"

"Don't worry about it, you're fine." He pulled me over to the door, and opened it. "Come on."

I glanced at Peter.

He shrugged, closed the book. "Go on," he said. "Whatever." He took off his glasses, put them away inside his canvas coat, and picked up his pipe and tobacco.

"Let's go, Arnold," said Jesus.

"Okay," I said.

He held the door open and I went in, but not without some misgivings.

Chapter 85

Jesus closed the door, then turned to me, shaking his head.

"That guy is too much," he said. "Sometimes I think he's *looking* for reasons to keep people out of here. I don't know, almost two thousand years on the job. Just between you and me, I think he's just a *little* burnt out."

He shrugged, and gave me a little tap on the shoulder.

"Come on. Let's go find my father."

We were in a hallway or large foyer, with faded floral wallpaper, a few small tables, a couple of umbrella stands, a few hat racks and coat stands. But no umbrellas, no hats, no coats.

We came out into a large Victorian living room, with a dull parquet floor and worn Persian rugs (or Persian-style, what did I know?), lots of brocaded armchairs and sofas dressed with antimacassars and multicolored pillows, tasseled table lamps, a large chandelier overhead, and a grandfather clock, stopped.

None of the lights were on, but a rippled soft light came through tall stained-glass windows.

"Oh, wait," he said, "you wanted a cigarette."

He went over to a low coffee table by the largest sofa, and picked up an ormolu cigarette box and opened it.

"I don't believe it," he said. He showed the black inside of the box. "Empty."

"That's okay," I said.

"This box is supposed to be kept filled at all times."

"No, really, it's all right," I said.

"Okay. My old man will have some smokes in his office."

"Really, it's okay," I said, for what felt like the eleventh time.

"All right," he said. And then, "Boy, there's like no one around. But *he*'ll be in. He's always in. Come on."

He led me across the room to a another hallway, a long and wide hallway, down which we went. Dozens of paintings hung on the walls. I know next to nothing about art, but most of the paintings seemed old, meaning about a hundred years old to extremely old, meaning very primitive-looking rough wooden icons that must have dated from the middle ages, perhaps even the dark ages. Unsurprisingly, most of the paintings seemed to have religious themes.

"Maybe someday your picture will be on this wall," said Jesus.

"I doubt that," I said.

"That's what Saint Augustine of Hippo said," he said, nodding toward a portrait presumably of that doctor of the church. "Oh, hey."

He stopped at a small table that had a carved ivory cigarette box sitting on it. He opened the box.

"Damn," he said. "Empty again. Oh well."

We walked down the long hall for several minutes, then came to another large room, even larger than the first room, but more sparsely furnished and considerably darker.

"Okay, across here," he said.

We walked across the enormous room. My leg was bothering me, especially what with walking barefoot on these hard parquet floors.

Jesus glanced over at me.

"I'm sorry, this place is just too big."

On the other side of the room was a wide, winding, carpeted staircase, and up we went. On the second floor we went down another hall, this one with no paintings but lots of statues, of saints and the holy family and the various members of the holy trinity.

Which reminded me.

"Hey, can I ask a question?"

"Sure, Arnold."

"Is the Holy Ghost here?"

He stopped for a moment and looked at me.

"I have no idea," he said. "Why?"

"Oh, no reason. I was just, you know – curious –"

"Okay, well, don't worry about him. Come on."

We turned into yet another hallway, this one with only an occasional painting, along with a few small tables with vases on them, but no flowers, and at last we came to a large and sturdy-looking door.

"Okay," he said, "you ready?"

"Not really," I said.

"Oh. Well, just be yourself, Arnold."

"Do I have a choice?"

"About going in?"

"No, about being myself."

He looked at me, nodding his head very slightly.

"Okay. Look, let me just go in and let him know you're here first. Do you mind waiting just a minute?"

I wondered if I had a choice about this either, but I said, "No, not at all."

"All right. I'll be right out."

He turned the doorknob, and, without knocking, he opened the door and went in. I didn't want to seem nosy, and so I looked away as he did so. I heard the door close behind him, and I stood there, waiting.

My leg was hurting. There was a chair way down the hall, but it seemed prohibitively far. And after all, he had said he'd only be a minute.

Five minutes passed. And nothing.

I put my ear against the door, it was a big old carved wooden door. I couldn't hear a thing.

I waited a few more minutes, and now I had to go to the bathroom.

A couple more minutes. I really had to go now.

I went off down the hall. I came to a door, and I tried the knob. It was unlocked. I opened it.

It was a large office and a man sat behind a desk. He looked up from some papers.

"Yes?"

"Sorry," I said.

"Can I help you?"

"I was just looking for the, uh, for a — um —"

"A bathroom?"

"Yes."

"Down the hall, then left, make the first right, you'll see one two doors down. On the right. Okay?"

"Okay."

I quickly started to back myself out. Despite whatever Jesus had said, I felt very self-conscious standing there in my swimming trunks, barefoot.

"Down the hall, left, then right, two doors down."

"Thanks, got it," I said.

I went out.

Down the hall.

But which way down the hall?

I kind of hated to do it, but I decided to go left, farther away from where I had come.

Chapter 86

I won't bore my dear ideal reader (i.e., myself), with a detailed chronicling of the next twenty minutes or so, if that's how long it was. Maybe it was an hour. It sure felt like an hour, or more. But I did go down the hall and make a right and then a left (or maybe the opposite), and I did try the second door I came to, but it was locked. I tried to backtrack, but I'm pretty sure I took a left when I should have taken a right (or vice versa).

Five minutes later, an hour later, who knows, I tried my twenty-fifth or thirtieth door, and this one opened. And it was that guy behind the desk again. He was still going over some papers, but he didn't seem upset at this, my second interruption of his work.

"Hello. You found the restroom okay?"

I couldn't bring myself to tell him the truth, that I had been wandering quite lost all over this enormous house for the past hour or two.

"Yes, I did," I lied. "I — just wanted to thank you."

"You're quite welcome. Do you know how to get to where you want to go now?"

"Oh, sure."

"Well, okay, then."

"Okay," I said. "'Bye."

He waved his pen at me and looked down again at his papers.

I closed the door, and set off again down the hall in what I believed to be the opposite direction from that I had taken the last time I left the man's office.

I went down innumerable corridors, up and down stairways, through several more great rooms. I found many locked doors and a few doors which opened onto other halls and rooms, but no bathrooms. No kitchens, either. And needless to say I didn't see anyone else.

I really wanted just to go outside and pee behind a bush, but I couldn't find an outside door.

I would have climbed through a window, but all the windowsills appeared to be at least ten feet off the floor. I considered climbing up onto a table and trying to jump up, but my leg was killing me at this point. I think I must have aggravated the sprain when I tried to run up that beach during the rainstorm.

Then I saw this big oriental (or oriental-style) vase. It was about three feet high, just the right height, and it appeared to be empty.

I just couldn't hold it in any longer, so I lifted my alleged instrument of manhood out of my swimming trunks and held it over the mouth of the vase, when suddenly I heard footsteps, the distant sound of a man's sandals on hard parquet floor.

I turned away from the sound, quickly stowing away the damned thing, and, looking over my shoulder I saw Jesus rounding the corner into the hallway in which I stood. We were about fifty feet apart.

"Arnold!" he called, almost sliding to a stop on the floor. "I've been looking all over for you! What are you doing?"

"Oh, just, um, admiring this vase."

I patted the gilded edge of its mouth.

"Yeah," he said, walking toward me down this long corridor. He must have found cigarettes in his father's office, or somewhere. Anyway, he was smoking. "It's a nice piece," he said. "Ming Dynasty, I believe. But why didn't you wait?"

"Um, I had to go to the bathroom."

"Oh! I'm sorry, I really didn't think it was going to take so long. So you found the bathroom okay?"

"Oh, sure."

"But what are you doing way over here in the north-east wing?"

"I got a little lost," I said.

"Oh, I *am* sorry."

"It's okay," I said. "So, do I go to see, uh, him now?"

"That's the thing," said Jesus. He had finally reached me. He gave me a pat on the arm.

"We talked it over. I know, we talked a little too long. But he's decided it's okay for you to go back."

"You mean I'm not dead."

"Nope."

"So — I don't talk to him?"

"Not necessary."

"Oh. Uh —"

"What?" he said, I guess he could tell I was holding something back, he was the son of God after all. "Spill it."

"Well," I said, "I guess I was just a little curious to — see what he's like."

"You'll find that out someday, Arnold, when you really die. But look, you're going to live! Be happy!"

"Right," I said, and, anyway, what I wanted most at that moment was just to pee.

And then I was lying on the beach in the pouring rain and that nice young nun I had met the other night was leaning over me and kissing me. She drew her lips away. What was her name?

"Ah, he's breathing," she said.

Kneeling on the other side of me was Daphne, looking down at me, holding her wet hair back away from her face.

"Hello, Arnold," she said.

"Hello," I said, the rain splattering down into my face like drops of life.

"You were struck by lightning," said Daphne.

"Actually I don't think the lightning struck him directly," said the nun.

"Near enough!" said Daphne.

"Yes, quite near enough," said Sister Mary Elizabeth, that was her name. She looked down at me. She had one of her hands under my head. "You don't appear to be burnt at all," she said. "Do you think you can get up?"

"Yes, I do," I said.

Daphne and the sister helped me to my feet, and I became aware that a half-dozen or so other nuns were standing around us in the rain, the whole lot of us getting sopping wet.

I found that I was able to walk, or limp, even without assistance, although my leg did hurt, but Daphne and Sister Mary insisted on each taking an arm.

Soon everyone was up on the back porch of the convent, and I was sitting in a plain white-painted rocking chair.

"You just rest," said Sister Mary. "We'll get you some water. Would you like something, miss?" she said to Daphne.

"Oh, I suppose a glass of water wouldn't hurt," said Daphne, pressing the water out of her hair with one hand.

Meanwhile, I still had to pee.

Chapter 87

Pretty soon the nuns brought us iced water, along with towels to dry ourselves with. (I want to go on record as saying that these towels were the coarsest I have ever encountered since I got out of the army. I wondered if indeed they were army towels.)

Daphne was less shy than I, and she asked the nuns if she could use their bathroom. One of the sisters took her inside, which left me alone in my wet bathing suit, sitting in a rocker and sipping my water, the rain still coming down, with five or six nuns standing there looking at me.

"It's Arnold, isn't it?" said Sister Mary Elizabeth.

"Yes. And you're Sister Mary," I said with I think more urbanity than I normally pull off.

"Sister Mary Elizabeth," she said.

"Yes, right," I agreed.

"In our order if you just call someone Sister Mary you'll get nowhere. I think we have a couple of dozen versions of Sister Mary Something-or-Other staying here right now. Did you keep your promise?"

"Pardon me?"

"The other night I asked you to promise not to swim alone at night any more."

"Ah." I had indeed broken my word to her, and on that very night, by swimming the whole length of the cove beach on my way back from the Point. But, on the other hand, yesterday I had also promised Elektra I wouldn't swim at night, and, so far at least, I had kept that promise. So I chose the Jesuitical route: "Don't worry, I'm not swimming at night any more."

"Good. Is that your girlfriend? That girl."

"Oh, no," I said.

"She's very young."

"She's not my girlfriend."

"Just a friend," she posited.

"Yes."

"Friend of the family?"

"Well, no —"

"Not that it's any of my business," she said, although she didn't seem convinced of that.

The five or six other nuns hung silently on every word of this inquisition, their hands buried in their black habits, their faces bent forward.

"Are you married, Arnold?" asked Sister Mary Elizabeth.

"Um, no," I said.

"That's good. I don't think your wife would be too happy about you taking long swims with that pretty young thing."

"Well, I'm not married."

"Why not? Good-looking Catholic man like you?"

"I don't know," I said (although I could have come up with at least hundred possible reasons right off the top of my head).

"Stop grilling the man, Sister Mary E.," said one of the other nuns, an older, stout nun.

"I'm only having a conversation, Sister Mary M.," said Sister Mary E. "Would you like some more water, Arnold."

"No thanks," I said. "We should go, really. You've all been very nice."

"But it's raining."

"We don't mind. We were wet anyway."

"You'll get struck by lightning again."

What were the odds of that happening twice? Whatever they were I was willing to risk them.

"I think the lightning's stopped," I said.

"You should rest here. You've just had a dreadful shock. Quite literally."

"I feel fine," I said, but in fact I still felt slightly dazed. On the other hand I quite often feel slightly dazed even without being struck by lightning, so what was the big deal?

"You can't go swimming in that rain," said Sister Mary Elizabeth.

"We'll walk," I said. "Just down the beach. To get our things."

"Let us drive you."

"You have a car?"

"A station wagon. It's the order's."

"Ah."

"I'll drive you."

"Well —"

"I insist."

"Okay." I knew it was hopeless to argue. "If you insist."

Daphne finally came out of the house, accompanied by her guard.

"Your friend Arnold wants to abandon our hospitality," said Sister Mary E.

"Well, I'm ready if he is," said Daphne.

We went around to the side of the house to where, sure enough, an old yellow station wagon was parked. I think it was a Crosley, from around 1948.

A couple of nuns held umbrellas over my and Daphne's heads as we went down to the car.

We got into the front seat with Sister Mary E., with me somehow sitting next to her.

The key was already in the ignition. The sister started up the car, put it in gear, and turned us expertly out onto the road.

"Okay, where to?" she asked.

"Just head down Sunset and we can get off when we get near Cape May."

"Where'd you leave your things? Your — towels and such."

"Our towels?"

"Yes. Where'd you leave them?"

"On the beach, near the end of the promenade."

"Good, I'll leave you off there."

"Okay," I said. I could tell she was going to do just what she wanted to do anyway.

She took her eyes solidly off the road to look smilingly at Daphne.

"What's your name, dear?"

Daphne gave her correct name, but before Sister Mary E. could give her the Spanish Inquisition treatment Daphne struck first and asked her how long she had been a nun.

"I went in right after high school," said Sister Mary E.

"Wow," said Daphne. I glanced at her. She had turned slightly against me, looking down and picking at the damp green elastic cloth of the seat of her bathing suit. I looked away.

"Do you think I should have waited?" asked Sister Mary Elizabeth.

"Frankly?" asked Daphne.

"Oh. You do think so."

Daphne let the seam of the bottom of her bathing suit snap back against her flesh with an almost but not quite inaudible thwapping sound.

"Yes, frankly," she said. "I mean, *I've* decided to wait to get married."

"Why? Do you have a boy you'd like to marry?"

"He's no boy, sister."

"Oh my. And it's not Arnold here?"

"Oh, Arnold only wishes."

"I'm sure he does."

I wanted to put my foot over the good sister's on the gas pedal and press down hard to hasten our trip along, but I resisted the urge.

"Are you allowed to visit people, sister?" Daphne asked.

"What do you mean?" asked Sister Mary E.

"I mean, can you come out from the convent and visit a friend. Like a friend in town?"

"I don't have any friends in town."

"You know me," said Daphne. "And Arnold."

"Oh dear. I don't think we're supposed to do things like that."

"Priests do. Priests visit people all the time. Especially around dinner time. Or the cocktail hour."

"Oh, you're very naughty, Daphne."

"Well, it's true! Priests are always visiting my grandmother."

"Really?"

"I swear."

"So you're Catholic?"

"Well, I was brought up one."

"Oh. So, you, uh, don't —"

"Oh, please don't be offended, sister, but, no. Not really. I don't believe any of it."

"But — don't you believe in God?"

"Oh, I doubt very much that there's a God."

"Really?"

Sister Mary E. took her eyes off the road again to look across me at Daphne, who said:

"Of course I could be wrong."

Sister Mary E. continued staring at Daphne, and it was all I could do not to grab the wheel.

"Sister?" I said.

"Yes?"

"The road."

I pointed at it, and, at last, she looked at it.

"Oh," she said, turning the wheel just before we would have leapt off the asphalt and gone bumping over the dunes and down to the beach.

"How old are you, sister?" asked Daphne.

"Me? I'm twenty-four."

"Twenty-four."

"Why?" said Sister Mary Elizabeth.

"You're still in your prime," said Daphne.

"My prime?"

"Yes. And you're quite pretty. Such nice skin and beautiful eyes. You could have any man."

"I've given myself to Jesus."

"True," said Daphne. And she gazed out at the passing scenery. We were approaching Cape May now, thank God, and Sister Mary E. was turning in toward the beach. The rain was stopping.

"Come visit me at my grandmother's," said Daphne. "If you can get away. Do you know where Windsor Avenue meets North Street?"

"I suppose so."

"It's the really big house on the corner on the side away from the beach. 200 Windsor."

"I don't think I could."

"No one has to know. Come by any time."

"Well —"

"Okay, this is good," I said. "We can get out here."

"Do you want me to wait," asked the sister, "and drive you home?"

"Oh, no, don't bother," I said, pushing against Daphne with my elbow. "The rain's stopped.'

"Not entirely," said Sister Mary E.

I elbowed Daphne again, and she elbowed me back.

"It's just a light drizzle," I said. "It's stopping, I think."

"Well, if you say so," said the sister. "Goodbye. Nice meeting you, Daphne."

"You too," said Daphne.

Finally she opened her door and started to get out of the car.

"Thanks, again, sister," I said.

"You're most very welcome. What's your last name, by the way?"

"Schnabel. Arnold Schnabel."

"Arnold Schnabel. I hope to see you again, Mr. Schnabel."

"Sure. 'Bye."

I got out of the car behind Daphne. I closed the door and went up the steps to the promenade, but Daphne went back around and leaned over by the driver's side and spoke to Sister Mary Elizabeth some more. Standing by the rail and looking over the roof of the car, all I could see of Daphne was the top of her sleek dark head and the perfect sweep of her back. Then I felt guilty about looking at her, and I turned toward the beach, which was now grey and empty in the diminishing drizzle.

I heard the Crosley pull out and drive away. Daphne came up the wooden steps.

"I think she likes you," she said.

"Come on, let's get our stuff," I said.

We walked over to the end of the boardwalk, and down to the cove beach. I was still limping, but the pain was bearable.

Our stuff was still there in the sand, in a wet pile. My towel was soaked, but my old wallet wrapped deep inside it was only a little damp.

Daphne reached into her sopping straw bag and pulled out a gold-plated cigarette case, and then a Zippo lighter.

"Care for a cigarette?" she asked.

"No, thanks," I said.

"You look nervous."

"I really have to go to the bathroom."

"Just go in the ocean," she said. "I do it all the time. Don't you?"

"Well, I guess so."

"Go," she said. "Go."

She waved a dismissing hand at me.

So I turned around and hobbled back into the surf.

I waited until I was in up to my waist.

Chapter 88

Facing away from the beach I pulled down the front of my bathing trunks, and soon part of what had once been me, if only for a brief time — this distillation of my morning Chock Full o' Nuts, and of opiated iced tea, of Schmidt's beer and Old Crow whiskey — oh so pleasurably became part of the great ocean, forever, more or less, or at least until the death of the planet.

I waded back in, and Daphne and I gathered up our sodden things and walked, or rather I limped and she walked, back through the misty drizzle into town.

"What was it like, by the way," she asked, "being struck by lightning?"

"Well, I wasn't really aware of it except I saw this bright light, and then it was like I was falling, and I was, uh, passed out."

"What was it like when you were passed out?"

Here it occurred to me that women ask a lot of questions. But now I wonder: is that true? I shall force myself to ponder this question for approximately one minute...

The minute is up and I think the answer is yes, women do ask a lot of questions, especially if they find their interlocutor interesting, or possibly interesting. Men on the other hand seem happy to go through life not asking questions. I know I myself rarely ask a question. In fact it's more than I can do even to bring myself to ask myself why I don't ask questions. Just the thought of it makes me sleepy.

"Well?" she asked.

"Oh, yes," I stalled, because she was forcing me to ask myself (yet again) what to tell someone who has asked me, knowingly or unknowingly, about one of my psychotic episodes. I decided to tell her about what transpired during my black-out, but to tell it as a dream, which after all it most likely had been. I proceeded thus to give her a digest account of my heavenly escapade, leaving out none of the salient plot turnings, no matter how embarrassing. Because, after all, we can't be blamed for our dreams, can we?

However, the first thing Daphne said after I finished, just as we approached the gate to her grandmother's house, was:

"How do you know it was all a dream?"

Of course I didn't know.

"But who ever heard of such a heaven?" was the idiotic response I came up with.

"Who ever heard of any sort of heaven? I mean, who really knows?" she asked. "What did you expect? Billowy clouds and angels with wings, wearing white robes and playing golden harps?"

"I guess so," I said.

She was standing so close to me in her shiny green bathing suit that she almost bumped me off the curb.

"I'd like to know who started up all this wings and harps business," she said. "I doubt very much that it was anyone who'd ever actually been anywhere remotely near heaven."

"You told Sister Mary Elizabeth you don't believe in any of it," I said, with one foot in the gutter.

"I don't."

"Then it couldn't be true that I was in heaven, could it?"

"Why not? What do I know?" she asked. "Why are you standing in the street?"

"I don't know," I said.

"Come up on the sidewalk, you weirdo."

I did.

"Oh," she said, "don't forget your tea date with my grandmother."

"I won't," I said.

The rain had stopped completely by now, the sky was grey, the air thick and rich with the wet colors and the scents of the geraniums and box-elder hedges running along the front of Mrs. Biddle's property, and Daphne looked more beautiful in this shadowless light than I had ever seen her before in our acquaintance, which although brief in countable minutes already felt long. And I remember thinking — well, never mind what I was thinking, but I was glad I wasn't dead.

Daphne had put her hand on the white-painted gate.

"See you, then," she said.

"See you," I said.

But she suddenly came closer and kissed me, on the lips but briefly. She paused for a moment, looking at me, then turned, opened the gate, and tripped up the slate path to the house.

I limped home.

I went around to the back of the house, near which my aunts have a little wooden shower shack, its boards covered with a rippled sun-bleached green paint that almost seems and feels and smells like something living, like moss or the skin of some strange fruit.

I put my damp wallet on a ledge and showered myself off, keeping my swimming trunks on, and I rinsed off my sandy flip-flops under the shower head.

I got my wallet and walked dripping wet to a clothesline and hung up my sodden and sandy towel. My aunts or mother would perform their magic, and sometime tomorrow this towel, or one much like it, would appear, neatly folded, in my drawer.

Across the yard old Mrs. Rathbone opened the door of her cottage and started weaving my way, this time without her cane, but moving quickly like a slightly damaged but determined little ship of war. It was too late to escape, so I waited; then, realizing it was rude just to stand there and let this old woman limp to me, I limped toward her, and we met near the middle of the yard.

"Hello, Mrs. Rath-"

"Gone swimming?" she asked.

"Yes," I said.

"In the rain?"

"Um," I said.

"What do you think of this Steve?"

"Oh, Steve, he, uh, seems nice."

"I thought he was your friend?"

"He is," I said, "but I only recently met him."

What had he done now?

"He wants to marry Charlotte," she said.

"Oh," I said.

"If I tell you something will you promise not to blab it all over town?"

"Sure."

"Charlotte spent the night with him last night. At his hotel."

"Oh."

"I'm no prude, Arnold. And Charlotte's a grown woman. But the thing is that this is the first time she has ever done anything like this."

"I see."

"At least that I know about. She was in the WACs during the war after all. I have no idea what shenanigans she was getting up to in those WACs, especially overseas. Come to think of it she has always spoken fondly of her time in the service. Perhaps that's why. The shenanigans. Would you care for some wine?"

"No thank you. I need a nap."

"A nap? What are you? A child? An old man?"

"I combine the most boring qualities of both," I said.

"She's with him now. Having lunch allegedly. At the Merion Inn. I hope he's not after her money."

"Steve has a good job, I think."

"Yes. So he says," she said. Of course for all I knew he was an international confidence man or a jewel thief. "One more question," she went on. "He invited me to go to lunch with them. Don't you find that odd?"

"He wants to win your favor," I said.

"He doesn't need my favor."

"He's being a gentleman."

"He's being very strange. I know I practically threw them together, but it all seems to be happening so quickly. And answer me this. Don't you find him shall we say a bit light in the slippers?"

"Um —"

"A little as if sprinkled with fairy dust?"

"Oh, I don't know," I dissembled.

"Well, what does it matter, really? Let me tell you something. You wouldn't know, you're a confirmed bachelor, but believe me, physical relations are by far the least important element in a successful marriage. By far. Which is okay. Get a kid or two out of the way and be done with it, I say. Believe me, after my husband and I had been married five years the last thing either of us wanted to do was — at least with each other — oh, but perhaps I speak too much."

"Oh. No."

"You're dying to take your nap. I think I'll visit with your aunts and mother. Take my arm."

I did as I was told, and together we walked, or I should say limped, around to the side of the house.

Chapter 89

As we turned around the corner to the porch I remembered my escapade with Miss Evans earlier that afternoon. What had I been thinking? And perhaps more to the point, what had I not been thinking? She had undoubtedly turned the whole house upside down when I had not replied to her inevitable knockings on the bathroom door, nor to her salutations and queries and quite possibly screams when she finally opened the unlocked door and found no one there, least of all me.

But as so often in life, as so often period because it's probably the same in death, there is nothing to be done but to face the music, or, as the case may be, the cacophony.

Kevin was sitting quietly enough on the porch in his usual rocking chair, reading a Sgt. Rock comic, but he folded it over his finger as we came to the porch steps.

"Hello, Kevin," said Mrs. Rathbone, holding my arm as we hobbled together up the steps.

"Hi," said Kevin. "You're in trouble, Cousin Arnold."

"What did Arnold do?" asked Mrs. Rathbone.

"He disappeared from the bathroom."

"He what?"

Once again I'll do a kindness for that ideal reader who is no other than myself and I shall not recount word by word the next couple of minutes of conversation, to which I listened but did not take a vocal part in, with Mrs. Rathbone all the while hanging as tightly to my forearm as if we stood on the deck of a small ship in a raging sea.

But I suppose I got bored just standing there, so I went over to my usual rocker and sat down. Kevin's usual pile of comic books lay on the little table to my right, and I was just about to look through them to see if there were any I hadn't read yet when I couldn't help but notice that my own corporeal host was still standing there next to Mrs. Rathbone, with an only slightly resigned look on my face.

I wondered what would happen if I got up from the rocker, walked around myself and Mrs. Rathbone, went down the steps and started wandering around town and the universe. But the thing was I really wanted a nap, so I heaved myself up from the chair, walked back to my body and slipped back into it just as Mrs. Rathbone was saying:

"And where is Miss Evans now?"

"I think she's still laying down."

"Lying down," said Mrs. Rathbone.

"Yeah," said Kevin. "That's what I just said."

"She's *lying* down, Kevin, not *laying* down."

Kevin gave her one of those looks he so often gives me, the "you really are insane" look.

I could see through the screen door the ghostly figures of my mother and all three of my aunts, standing listening and watching.

"Shall we go inside, Mrs. Rathbone?" I said, as suavely as if she and Kevin had been discussing the weather and not my latest madman's caper.

She stared up at me.

"Arnold, how did you get out of that bathroom?"

"I climbed out the window and down the drainpipe." I spoke clearly and distinctly so that my mother and aunts could hear and I wouldn't have to repeat myself.

"Wow," said Kevin. "Did you, Cousin Arnold?"

"Yes," I said.

"But why?" asked Mrs. Rathbone.

"I was trying to escape from Miss Evans."

"So you climbed out a third-floor window?"

My gentle mother now came out onto the porch.

"Arnold," she said, "you didn't really, did you?"

In a flash it occurred to me that this sort of admission might well lead to another and perhaps even longer and more tedious stay at Byberry, so I backtracked, and let the Jesuitisms flow:

"That depends on how you looked at it, Mom."

After all, if one hadn't been looking at that side of the house one couldn't know for sure that I had climbed out of the window.

"Then how did you get out of that bathroom?"

"I — just left."

This in its literal sense was not a lie.

"But Miss Evans said she never saw you leave."

I shrugged. This also is not a lie, merely to shrug.

"Oh, Mom," I said, "look, Mrs. Rathbone has come for a visit."

I lifted Mrs. Rathbone's hand from my arm.

"Hello, Mrs. Rathbone," said my mother.

"Hello, Mrs. Schnabel," said Mrs. Rathbone.

One trick with women I've learned in my humble experience is to get them to talk among themselves, and then in the ensuing confusion you can make your getaway.

"Mrs. Rathbone was telling me that my friend Steve wants to marry Miss Rathbone."

"Is Steve that man who was talking to Miss Rathbone in the back yard all yesterday afternoon?"

Now my Aunt Edith came out through the screen door.

"The one who took her out last night," said Edith.

"That's the one," said Mrs. Rathbone.

"He really upset that DeVore couple, I'll tell you that much," said my Aunt Greta, holding open the screen door.

"Mrs. Rathbone," said my mother, "wouldn't you like to come in and have some refreshment?"

"I wouldn't say no to a glass of wine," said Mrs. Rathbone.

"We still have leftover wine," called out my Aunt Elizabetta, from just inside the doorway.

"From Arnold's girl," said Edith.

Soon enough our little assemblage was moving itself into the living room amidst a whirlpool of feminine verbiage, everyone except for Kevin that is, who stayed on the porch with Sgt. Rock, and who could blame him?

"Good day, Mrs. Rathbone," I interpolated, and headed for the hall.

"Where are you going, Arnold?" asked my mother.

"Taking a nap," I said.

"Oh —"

Her little "oh" tumbled beneath the waves of the other ladies' chatter, and I turned up the stairs.

So far so good. Now I only had to make it past Miss Evans's room and I was home free.

At the third floor stairhead I could hear opera music coming from her room.

I was glad that I was wearing flip-flops. If I had been wearing shoes I'm sure I would have removed them before tiptoeing past her door.

I made it safely to the doorway and the short flight of steps leading to my attic room, and soon I was lying in my little bed, naked to the soft warm breeze wafting in from the window.

I fell asleep and at once I was back in God's house.

I came to the door that opened into that office with the man who had given me directions to the bathroom.

"Ah. You again," he said, looking up from some papers.

"Yes," I said. "Arnold. Arnold Schnabel."

He looked at me impassively, his finger holding his place on the paper he'd been reading.

"May I ask, sir," I said, "what is your name?"

He said something but it made no sense to me, it was a combination of sounds that wouldn't stay in my brain. I didn't want to be a pest though, so I didn't ask him to say it again.

"May I help you in some way?" he asked.

"I want to go home," I said.

"Don't we all," he said. He sighed, and shuffled through a stack of papers off to one side of his desk. With a fountain pen he scrawled something on a few of them and then said, "Here, take these."

He held up a sheath of about ten or twelve official-looking documents.

I came over and took them from him, and it was then that I realized that I was as naked as I had been lying in bed.

"Oh," I said.

"Don't worry about it," he said, capping his fountain pen. He seemed pre-occupied, and maybe a little bored. He picked up a pipe from a holder on his desk, and began to fill it with tobacco from a zippered leather pouch.

I glanced at the papers. It was all some sort of incomprehensible legal mumbo jumbo.

"Take those to the front, show them to Peter, you should be fine."

"Um," I said.

"Yes?" He tamped down the tobacco with his index finger

"Well — can I get some clothes?"

He didn't answer right away, because he was lighting his pipe with a wooden match. I waited, while he drew and puffed, getting it going. At last he said, "What was that?"

"Can I get some clothes?"

He sighed, more deeply this time. He opened a couple of drawers, fingered through whatever was in them, then brought out another document. He uncapped his fountain pen again, filled in a couple of blanks on the form, and then scrawled what I presumed was his signature.

He handed me the paper with an air of finality.

"Down the hall, to the right this time. Then turn to the left, go three doors down and on the right hand side knock and give the lady this form. She'll give you some clothes."

"Okay."

"Good."

Puffing on his pipe, he picked up another batch of papers. He wrote something on one of them.

I stood there.

He looked up. Did I mention he was wearing glasses, horn-rim glasses? He sort of peered over the tops of the glasses.

"Anything else?" he said.

"Oh, no," I said.

"Good day, then."

"Good day," I said. "Thank you."

He was already back to reading his papers, but he gave a little wave with his pipe.

I left the office, closing the door quietly behind me.

I stood in the hall. Let's see, go right? I went right. Then left? I went left. Three doors down? One, two, three. The door on the right. So far so good, but I wondered if I was going to have to go through all this rigamarole of wandering around God's house every time I fell asleep or passed out, for the rest of my life. One thing for sure, if this was heaven then it was overrated.

I knocked on the door.

"Arnold?" said a woman's voice.

"Yes," I said, wearily. I was not looking forward to facing some strange woman while I was stark naked, but unless I wanted to spend eternity walking these halls in my birthday suit I supposed I had to go through with a little embarrassment. "I'm here for my, to get my, to get some, uh —"

"Arnold," she said again, louder and closer to the door, and I woke up to see Miss Evans's face leaning over mine.

From downstairs I could hear the opera music.

Miss Evans put her hand on my face.

Chapter 90

"Arnold," she said, "you were talking in your sleep. I could hear you all the way down in the hall as I was coming out of the bathroom."

She was sitting on the side of my narrow bed.

For a moment I wondered if this was really happening. But her fingers, which were now stroking the hair on my head, felt all too real, as did the quiverings of a nascent and quite involuntary erection.

"Your door was ajar," she said.

How foolish of me not to have shut the door and bolted it. I would try not to make that mistake again.

Let's just be clear on the fact that, yes, I was completely naked, and because of the afternoon heat I had lain down without even a sheet over me. I now tried to reach past Miss Evans's hip to grab the jumbled-up sheet and cover myself, but she was sitting on it.

"I was worried about you," she said, seemingly oblivious to my tuggings on the sheet.

"Why?" I managed to say.

"I thought perhaps you were talking to God."

"No," I said. "Not God. Miss Evans, do you mind getting off my bed?"

"Call me Gertrude, Arnold."

She was still stroking my head.

"Okay, Gertrude," I said.

She didn't get up. I tugged at the sheet again.

"Oh," she said. "You want to cover yourself."

"Yes."

In an attempt at modesty I drew my right leg up, and put my left hand over my mindlessly stirring organ of putative virility.

"You needn't be ashamed of your nakedness." She cast her eye along my body. "Don't be ashamed. You have a beautiful body. A strong, honest, workman's body."

"I'd like to cover myself, please."

"Would it make you feel more comfortable if I removed my dress?"

She was wearing one of these sundress things I suppose they're called. Some light material with coiling green ivy printed over a pale yellow background. The way she was leaning over me I could see a good deal of her breasts anyway, but now with the hand that wasn't stroking my head she started to lift off one of its straps while shrugging that shoulder.

"No," I said. "Please don't."

"No one has to know."

"God will know," I said, in my desperation.

Fortunately this stopped her before she got the strap off, although she left it dangling halfway down her arm.

"Yes," she said. "That's true. I suppose he knows all."

"Yes," I said. "Everything."

With a sigh she got up, and she took the tangled sheet, gave it a little flap, and covered me, at last. Then she quickly sat down again on the side of the bed, effectively trapping me there. She did however lift the strap of her dress up over her shoulder.

I could still hear the opera music from downstairs. Some woman singing in Italian in a very high voice, God knows about what.

"Arnold," said Miss Evans, "I know."

"Know what?"

"That you are a saint."

"What?"

"Where are your cigarettes?"

"In the little table there, the drawer," I said.

"May I have one?"

"Miss Evans —"

"Gertrude."

She opened the drawer, took out my open pack of Pall Malls. She shook one up and drew it out with her lips, like a bird drawing a worm out of a hole in the ground. She lit it with my lighter, which she'd also found in my drawer.

"Oh. Would you like one, Arnold?"

She offered me the pack.

In fact I wanted a cigarette then more than I've ever wanted one in my life, but even more I wanted her out of there, or me out of there, whichever came first, and sitting together smoking cigarettes probably wasn't going to hasten either of those eventualities, so I said no thanks.

"I knew there was something special about you," she said, exhaling smoke toward my little window.

"Miss Evans, I mean Gertrude, I'd like to get up now."

"Don't let me stop you, Arnold. Do you have some place to go?"

I looked at my little alarm clock. It was 3:48. I had napped for over an hour.

"Yes," I said.

"Where? To meet your sultry dark bohemian girl?"

"No. I have to meet Mrs. Biddle."

"Mrs. Biddle? Why?"

"To have tea with her."

"Tea."

"Yes. Please, let me get dressed."

"Okay. If you insist."

She stood up. Unlike me she was short enough to stand up straight under the inverted V of my attic ceiling.

"Could you turn around, please?" I said.

"I've seen naked men before, Arnold. In fact I've seen you naked just now."

"Please."

"Oh, all right," she said, turning, but not moving more than a foot from my bed.

"Gertrude," I said, "could you please move farther away. I have to get my clothes from the dresser."

"Oh, let me," she said. "I love looking through men's dressers."

She stubbed out the cigarette in the ashtray on my night table and went over to the little-boy's dresser which is the only sort of dresser that could fit into this small room, and she began to open and rifle through its drawers.

I sat up, keeping my now somewhat quiescent middle parts covered with the sheet.

"Boxer shorts," she said. "I'm so glad, I detest those other kind. And ironed! Does your mother iron them for you?"

"Yes. Please toss them over."

She did, side-armed, turning only slightly, and almost reaching the bed with them. I reached down and got them off the floor.

"Polo shirt?" she asked. "Or is this a formal tea? Suit and tie?"

I hadn't even thought about it, but I wanted to get this over with quick so I said that a polo shirt and Bermudas would be fine.

"No," she said. "Better wear a suit for such a formidable *grande dame* as Mrs. Biddle. You do have a suit?"

At this she glanced over her shoulder at me but by this time I at least had my Fruit-of-the-Looms on.

I told her I did have a suit, and that it was hanging on a peg on the wall over there.

"Good," she said. She took both of my maternally-folded dress shirts out of the drawer, shook them out and held them up to me. "Which one?"

One is short-sleeved, the other is not. Other than that they're pretty much identical as far as I can tell.

"The short sleeve," I said.

"No," she said, "I think the long." She looked at the label. "Robert Hall." She tossed it to me, and this time I managed to reach out and catch it before it hit the floor. "You should let me buy you a couple of good shirts," she said.

"No thanks," I said.

"You deserve better than Robert Hall."

"Robert Hall's fine for me," I said, putting the shirt on.

She had now gone over to my suit, my dark grey summer Sunday suit, one of the two suits I own, the other one being an even darker grey winter suit now in my closet back in Philadelphia. She looked at the label inside the jacket.

"Who or what is Krass Brothers, Arnold?"

"It's just a men's store," I said. "In Philadelphia."

She tossed me the trousers.

"Brooks Brothers, Arnold. Not Krass Brothers."

"Krass Brothers are fine with me," I said, pulling the trousers on.

"No," she said, coming over to the bed, holding the jacket, feeling its material and frowning. "Let me take you to Today's Squire at least. They seem to have some nice things."

Today's Squire is the fancy men's shop on Washington Street, which I've never actually been in.

"No thanks," I said. I stood up, too quickly, and hit my head on the raked ceiling. "Ow," I said.

"Sit down before you kill yourself. You need socks."

I sat down. She handed me the jacket and she went back to my ransacked dresser. I shrugged myself into the jacket.

"All your socks are either black or white," she said.

I did not deny this.

She tossed a rolled-up pair of the black ones in my general direction, and I nabbed them one-handed, my arm outstretched like Willie Mays catching a hard line drive.

"Someday your mother will be gone, Arnold. What will you do?"

"I'll learn to roll my own socks," I said, pulling them on.

"I've never known a man who needs a woman more than you do."

Who was I to deny this?

"What is this?" she said, holding up my one and only necktie, with its little embroidered badge.

"It's my Knights of Columbus tie," I said.

"So you're a knight?"

"Only of Columbus."

"Yes but still. A knight."

"Give it to me, will you?"

She brought it over, handed it to me.

"A sainted knight" she said. "Or should I say a knighted saint?"

I didn't answer. I quickly wrapped the tie around my neck and tied it. I stood up, or at least I stood up as much as I was able to.

"Wait," she said, coming close to me. She straightened my tie, or at least made motions as of straightening my tie. "There," she said. "I owe you so much."

I suppose I stared at her bug-eyed, if not agog.

"For what?" she asked. "For showing me a miracle. Don't make that face. You were in that bathroom. I know you were. And I waited. And when you didn't come out after my repeated knockings and halloos I was afraid perhaps you had had a heart attack, and I turned the knob and the door wasn't locked, and I opened it and you were not in there, Arnold."

"No."

"You had transported yourself."

"Um —"

"You had transported yourself through space."

"Well —"

"A miracle."

"Um —"

"But why? To teach me? To show me? I'm ready, Arnold. I'm ready to be taught. To be shown. Teach me. Show me."

"I have to go to Mrs. Biddle's now."

"I didn't mean *right* now."

"Okay."

My wallet was lying on my little bedside table, where I had left it; I picked it up and put it in my pocket. I turned and started to go.

"Arnold."

"Yes."

"You're not wearing shoes."

"Ah."

I went over to the corner where my Sunday shoes were, by the wall next to the little chair by my little writing table with my little Remington portable where I type up my little poems. I sat at the chair and began to put on my shoes.

"Listen, Gertrude," I said. "I'm really not a saint. I didn't transport myself by a miracle. I climbed out the window."

"Very funny, Arnold."

She picked up her book, *Ye Cannot Quench*, from the night table, looked to see where my book-marker was.

"You haven't gotten very far in my novel, Arnold."

"I'm savoring it."

"So you're enjoying it?"

"Very much."

"What do you like about it?"

"Everything."

All these lies would have to be confessed to Father Reilly next Saturday.

"My next one will be better," she said.

She closed the book, and put it back onto the night table.

I stood up.

She came over to me again.

She licked her finger and touched up my hair with it.

"Oh, I should comb it," I said.

"No," she said. "The tousled look is good for you. The poet, the knight, the saint."

The Italian lady was still singing downstairs.

Chapter 91

"Well," I said, "I'd better go now."

"Yes, let's go then," she said, although she continued to fool with my hair, as if she were intently adjusting a display of flowers in a vase. "Quickly, Arnold."

I turned, leaving her hand in mid-air, and went down the steps and to the door, with Miss Evans hard on my heels.

It was all I could do not to hunch my shoulders up to my ears, bracing myself against the possibility that she might leap upon my back like a maddened she-baboon.

I made it safely down to the hall, but here the faithful reader will not be surprised to learn that I suddenly felt an intense need to go to the bathroom. I considered skipping it and holding it in till I got to Mrs. Biddle's house, but that would mean having to excuse myself and ask to use her bathroom immediately upon my arrival, causing her to wonder why I hadn't relieved myself at my aunts' house less than two blocks away, like a normal person. And besides, hadn't I had enough high adventure the previous evening trying to find the bathroom at that good lady's house? But opposed to all the above was the prospect of going to the bathroom here, like a normal person, but having Miss Evans waiting outside in the hall, listening to my every urinary and ablutionary sound.

Quite the quandary, and I suppose I stood there trying to come to a decision for a moment or two, or three, like a sweating wax statue, just a scant few feet from the bathroom.

"What's the matter, Arnold?" said Miss Evans, coming around to face me, and putting her hand on my arm.

"Nothing," I said.

She looked into my eyes, I suppose searchingly.

"It's never nothing with you, Arnold. It's always something. And I mean that in a good way. Something. Never nothing."

I hated to burst her bubble, but anyway I said, "Well, really I was just trying to decide if I should use the bathroom."

"Why shouldn't you? I mean if you have to go. Do you have to go?"

"Yes."

"Then go."

"Okay."

I stood there. She was still holding onto my arm.

"Go, Arnold," she said again.

"All right," I said. "But I want to ask you —"

"Anything," she said. "Anything at all. Cross the Sahara on camel's back? Paddle up the Amazon in a dug-out canoe? Cross the Arctic in a dogsled?"

"No."

"Climb Mount Everest?"

"No. I just wanted to ask you not to wait outside the bathroom."

"Oh! Of course! I mean of course not! I wouldn't dream! Wait!"

"What?"

"That scritching." In fact I did hear a scritching noise. "It's the phonograph needle," she said. "The album side has come to its end."

"Well, better flip it over," I said.

"No," she said, "I don't think I want to listen to *Tosca* any more today. I want to go out, out to where there is life, and people, cocktails and merriment. And besides, I'm meeting that nice Father Reilly." She paused, as if to give me space to say something. "Yes," she replied to my non-existent question, "after your miracle today I felt I needed to talk to someone, so I borrowed your aunts' telephone and dialed directory assistance, got the number of the rectory and called him. He agreed to meet me. At the Pilot House. Tell me, Arnold, would it be appropriate of me to order a highball?"

"Sure," I said. Oh, by the way, she was still gripping onto my arm, my biceps, but the blood hadn't gotten completely cut off yet.

"Good," she said, "Do you suppose Father Reilly drinks?"

"I wouldn't know," I said, although I had never met a priest who didn't drink, forget about the Irish ones.

"Well," she said, "I'll cross that bridge when I come to it. Now go, go use the bathroom! Why are you dawdling here? You'll be late for your tea date with Mrs. Biddle."

"Okay," I riposted.

I tried to sidle past her to get to the bathroom, and she turned with me, as if we were performing some painfully awkward square-dance, her hand sliding along my arm but not quite letting go.

"See ya," I said.

"Yes," she said. "I'll see you later. And this time, Arnold, will you please leave the bathroom by conventional means?"

"Yes," I promised.

"No teleportation."

"No," I said, and gently but firmly lifting her hand from my wrist, I disengaged myself and went into the bathroom and closed the door. I stood there quietly, thick seas of sweat oozing from my pores into my clothes. After perhaps half a minute I finally heard her footsteps go away down the hall, and, putting my ear to the door, I could even hear her close her own door.

As swiftly as possible, I urinated, washed my hands, tossed some cold water on my face, gave my teeth a quick brush, opened the door, peeked out toward Miss Evans's room just to make sure the coast was clear, then tripped down the hall and bounded down the steps like an antelope before the madwoman could burst out of her apartment and trap me again.

My mother and aunts and Mrs. Rathbone were all still in the living room, and for good measure Miss Rathbone and Steve were there, too. Steve wore a pale yellow suit and Miss Rathbone wore a nice dress which seemed to be made of pink tissue paper, but they both looked somewhat rumpled, as if they too had recently risen from a nap, but with all their clothes on.

"And where are you off to all dressed up in your Easter outfit?" cried Steve.

"Oh, shut up, Steve," said Miss Rathbone, and I realized they had not been napping but drinking.

"I'm having tea with Mrs. Biddle," I said.

"Oh, how Oscar Wilde," said Steve.

"Mrs. Biddle is a beautiful woman," said Miss Rathbone, and I noticed that she had one of her pink cigarettes in each of her hands. "I would love to do her portrait."

"Portrait of a grand old broad," said Steve. He tried to tap a cigarette of his own into an ashtray and missed.

My three aunts were all looking as intently at Steve and Miss Rathbone as if they were a TV show, Burns and Allen, or Ralph and Alice Kramden.

"Will you be home for dinner, Arnold?" asked my sainted mother.

I told her maybe not, but not to worry about it.

"But we made sauerbraten."

"I *love* sauerbraten," said Steve.

"Okay, see you all later," I said, heading for the door.

"High society," said Steve. "No time for us common folk."

He went on to say something else but I was already out the door.

As a railroad man and a church usher I have always prided myself on my punctuality, and here I was already ten or fifteen minutes late for my tea with Mrs. Biddle. Good for me she only lives less than two blocks away, and so not two minutes after ejecting myself from my aunts' house I was knocking on the stout wooden frame of Mrs. Biddle's screen door.

Chapter 92

No one answered my knocking.

I stood there sweating in my Krass Brothers suit. The heavy wooden door behind the screen door was wide open, and I could see clearly enough past the foyer into that big living room which looked as if Fred Astaire and Ginger Rogers were about to enter it singing a love song.

I called hello.

My leg was hurting again, or rather it had never stopped hurting; I simply now became aware of it again.

I realized there was a door buzzer on the jamb, and I pressed it, but it must have been broken, I heard nothing.

I waited, then knocked a few more times. I called hello again once or twice.

I wondered if perhaps I was somehow mistaken. Had I merely dreamt or imagined that Mrs. Biddle had invited me to tea this afternoon? Or perhaps she had invited me but I had somehow missed a day. Perhaps today was really tomorrow. Perhaps I was dreaming now. Perhaps...

"Hello," I called again, my voice breaking, and I was just turning to slink off when I heard a voice say:

"Oh! Sorry! One moment!"

Forty-seven seconds later Tommy appeared on the other side of the screen:

"Mr. Schnabel! What a pleasant surprise! Please come in!"

He opened the door and I came through.

Tommy seemed to be wearing the same cream-colored suit he'd been wearing earlier, now slightly rumpled, and with his blue and red paisley tie loosened and the top button of his shirt undone.

"Forgive me," he said. "I fell asleep in the chair. Dreaming. Of the old days." He extended his hand and I took it. It was very slender and dry, slightly cool, but his clasp felt surprisingly strong.

I followed him through the foyer and into the living room. He waved a hand at the larger of the two couches in there and said, "To what do we owe the honor?"

"Mrs. Biddle invited me to tea," I said, tentatively, and sitting where I had been beckoned to sit.

"Oh! Of course! I should rouse her!"

"Oh, is she sleeping?"

"I'm not sure. Wait here."

"Okay."

"Fix yourself a drink if you like. If she is sleeping this may take a while."

"Oh. Don't wake her."

I half-rose, half-heartedly.

"Are you kidding?" he said, already on his way out of the room. "She would murder me! Make yourself a drink, or go in the kitchen and fetch yourself a cold beer."

He was gone.

I sat there, the sweat on my back cooling and drying. The room was not air-conditioned, but the ceiling was very high, as were the open windows, and a few well-placed electric fans stirred the temperate air gently.

An engraved wooden cigarette box sat on the coffee table before me, it looked like the same one that Daphne had asked Larry to bring into the kitchen a dozen years ago or possibly just earlier that afternoon.

I opened the box, and there they were, all those glorious Chesterfield Kings, twenty or thirty pristine white cartridges of pleasure. There was also a table-lighter in the shape of a fat smiling Oriental man, the Buddha I think, I suppose he had relaxed and put on weight after achieving enlightenment; this lighter was big and stout, suitable for burning down whole villages or bashing in the skulls of unwary burglars.

I sighed, and closed the box without taking a cigarette, only the Buddha knows why.

A couple of New Yorker magazines lay on the table also, and I picked one up. To tell the truth I've never been a fan of this publication, although I've liked some of the cartoons.

I started to read what I pretty soon realized must be a short story.

A man named Brad comes home from the commuter train and his wife Gillian takes his briefcase and asks him if he would like a cocktail. He says yes, a scotch on the rocks would be nice. A little girl with golden hair comes running into the the room, crying, "Daddy! Daddy!"

I closed the magazine and put it down. Suddenly a scotch on the rocks or even without rocks sounded like a good idea.

I was getting up to go over to the liquor cabinet when someone knocked on the screen door frame.

No one else was there to answer the knock, so I went over to the door. A young woman stood on the other side of the screen.

"Hello," she said.

"Hello," I said.

"Arnold," she said.

"Hello?"

I had no idea who she was.

"May I come in?" she said.

I opened the door and let her in.

She had very short light brown hair, and she wore a simple, almost girlish dress with a pattern of sunflowers on a white background. She carried a rather larger canvas bag, like something a woman would carry to the beach or to a picnic. She wore leather sandals and no socks.

"It's me," she said.

This happens to me a lot. I suppose I really am wrapped up in my own little universe, because my whole life people have been coming up to me and knowing who I am and everything that there is to know about me when I haven't the slightest idea who they are. But I was not to remain ignorant for long.

"Don't you recognize me?" she asked.

"Well —" I stalled.

I did sense something familiar about her. Had I met her at the party the night before?

"Sister Mary Elizabeth," she said.

"Oh," I said. And then, the veil falling at last, I said again: "Oh."

"Do I look that different?"

"Yes," I said.

"What are you doing here?" she asked. "Are you staying here too?"

"No," I said. "I'm just here for tea."

"For tea."

"Yes, with Mrs. Biddle." She cocked her head slightly, furrowing her brow. "Daphne's grandmother," I added.

"Oh. Is Daphne here?"

"I really don't know."

"Is anyone here?"

"Well, I know for sure that this man Tommy is here. He's a friend of Mrs. Biddle's."

"And where is he?"

"Going to find Mrs. Biddle."

"Ah. What a beautiful house. Do you think it would be okay if I sat?"

"I think so," I said.

She went and sat down in a plush arm-chair near the sofa I had been sitting on, putting her big bag on the floor beside her, and I sat back down on the sofa.

"You look quite nice in your suit," she said. "I've only ever seen you in your bathing suit. But still I recognized you. You're probably wondering what I'm doing here."

I thought it politic to hold my peace.

"Daphne invited me to visit her," she said. "When she and I were talking by the car while you waited on the promenade. So I decided to sneak away while the other sisters were saying their private devotions in their rooms. I went out the window, changed my clothes in the old Crosley, and walked into town. My habit is in here," she said, indicating her canvas bag. "What do you think of that?"

Fortunately for me Tommy came into the room just then.

"Oh," he said. "Another visitor."

"Hello," said Sister Mary Elizabeth.

He came over to her and offered his hand.

"I'm Tommy," he said.

She looked at his hand momentarily, then gave him her own hand. I thought he maybe was going to kiss it, nothing would surprise me at this point, but instead he only gave her hand a gentle shake.

"I'm Sister Mary Elizabeth," she said.

"Charmed," he said.

I'll hand this to old Tommy, he didn't bat an eyelash.

Chapter 93

"I'm here for Daphne," she said to Tommy.

"Ah," he said. "I'll go get her. I think she's napping in her room. Everyone's napping." He turned to me. "Oh, I did find Mrs. Biddle, Mr. Schnabel. Sound asleep."

"Oh, I hope you didn't —"

"No, of course I woke her up. Tell you what, just go up to her room."

"Her room?"

"I'll bring you tea up there. You can have it on her veranda."

"I — I — uh —" I said with my usual wit.

"What's the matter? I assure you she's dressed by now. At any rate she won't let you in if she isn't. Or at least I think she wouldn't."

"Oh! No! I — uh —"

I glanced at Sister Mary Elizabeth and she stared back at me blankly.

"Well," said Tommy, "if you feel uncomfortable I could go up with you —"

This seemed like a great idea. It wasn't so much that I was afraid of being alone in her room or on her veranda with Mrs. Biddle, it was just that I was afraid of somehow getting lost on the way there — or of something else perhaps even more disturbing happening.

"Well," I said, "if you have to go up anyway, to get Daphne —"

"Oh, Miss Daphne's room is on the first floor, in the rear, but —"

"Oh."

"But really, it's no problem for me to go up with you."

"Mr. Schnabel," said Sister Mary Elizabeth, "don't make this gentleman have to go up the stairs with you —"

"Oh, I assure you, sister," said Tommy, "I don't mind at all, and Lord knows I could use the exercise —"

"But really," she said.

"It's okay, Tommy," I said. "I can go up alone. Just give me directions."

"Can't miss it, go up the stairs in the hall, first room on the right on the second floor."

"First room —"

"On the right."

"Do you want him to write down the directions?" asked Sister Mary Elizabeth.

Daphne walked into the room. She was wearing white shorts and a yellow polo shirt. Her hair was pinned back away from her ears with red barrettes, and she was barefoot.

"Oh, hi, everybody," she said. "What's up?"

"Arnold's afraid to go to your grandmother's room," said Sister Mary Elizabeth.

"As well he should be," said Daphne. She came over and plumped down next to me on the couch. She had the look of someone just up from a nap. She leaned over, popped open the cigarette box and took out a Chesterfield.

Ever the gentleman, I hefted the heavy fat Buddha lighter and lit her cigarette. She sat, back, exhaling, and Tommy and the sister and I all watched her as if she were an endlessly fascinating movie come to life. Then she yawned and looked at me.

"What on earth are you and my grandmother going to talk about?"

"I haven't really thought about it," I said, which was true, but now I felt a shimmering of disquietude from a fresh new source.

Daphne said nothing, but stretched her arms, and her left arm, the one with the hand holding the lit Chesterfield, stretched behind my head and even touched it slightly; she smiled at Sister Mary Elizabeth: "You sneaked away!" she said.

"Yes," said the sister.

Daphne reeled her long arm back in from over my head, and a fleck of ash from her cigarette tumbled down my nose.

"Won't you get in all sorts of trouble?" she asked.

"What's the worse they could do to me?" asked Sister Mary Elizabeth

"I don't know!" said Daphne. "Send you to Africa?"

"I wish they would," said Sister Mary Elizabeth.

"I'll leave you two young ladies," said Tommy.

"Wait!" said Daphne. "If you're making tea, would you bring us a cup?"

"Of course I'll bring you a tray."

"Ah, thank you, Tommy," said Daphne.

And Tommy was off again.

"Arnold," said Daphne, "don't you have to go up to my grandmother's room?"

"Oh, right," I said.

I got up.

"You know which room is hers, right?"

"Yes," I said. "I think so."

"See you later," she said.

"See ya," I said.

"See you later, Mr. Schnabel," said Sister Mary Elizabeth.

"Call him Arnold," said Daphne.

"See you, Arnold," said the sister.

I nodded to to her, and off I went, outfitted by Krass Brothers, Robert Hall, and Thom McAn, but naked as ever to the universe.

In the hall I went up the stairs and I came to the landing with the painting of the French people by the seaside. I hesitated before the painting. Then I put my hand into it, and into the living and breathing air of this sedate seaside scene. I drew it out again. Perhaps some other time.

I went up the next flight to the second floor and knocked on the first door to the right.

"Yes?"

"Mrs. Biddle?" I called, although I don't know who else I thought it might be.

"Darling, you're here, do please come in."

I opened the door and came in.

"Shut the door behind you, will you?" said Mrs. Biddle, and I did.

It may have been one thing for me consciously to choose not to go back in time again through that painting on the landing; however, as so often in this life, we cannot always choose what we will do, and thus I stepped into Mrs. Biddle's boudoir not in 1963, but from the looks of things, 1933.

The young Mrs. Biddle sat at a dressing table, applying powder to her face with a large puff.

"Sorry, old boy, just finishing my face."

Everything was in black and white, and shades of grey, shades of black and silver.

She threw down the puff and rose from the chair. She wore a silky sort of shimmering gown like the color of moonlight. She came to me and put her hands on my arms and looked up at me.

"Kiss me," she said.

I did, but briefly.

She drew back a bit, still holding onto my arms and looking up at me from under her lowered eyebrows, which were plucked pen-line thin.

"You're not cross with me for over-napping, are you?"

"No," I said. "I was napping myself."

"Good. Shall we go out onto the veranda?"

"Okay," I said.

She took my arm and we went across the room to the open French doors. A little breakfast table and a few matching chairs were out there, but she said, "No, darling, over here, side by side." And she pulled my arm and led me to a small wicker sofa strewn with pillows, cushions, and scarves.

She gently sat down, drawing her legs up under her, and, turning to look up at me, she patted the place next to her.

I sat down.

I looked out through the screening of the veranda, down at the grounds and buildings of the plantation, out at the jungle-covered hills and up at the enormous burnished-steel sky. A hushing and very warm breeze came down over the tops of the trees, and somewhere a parrot squawked thinly, like a human baby with the colic. The air smelled of coconuts and sugarcane, of pineapple and raw tobacco. And of Mrs. Biddle's perfume. My skin was moist under my suit.

"Cigarette, darling?"

She reached over and flicked open the top of a silver cigarette box on the long low glass-topped table in front of the sofa.

"No thanks," I said. "I'm trying to quit. Or at least I think I am."

"Will wonders never cease?" she said. She took out a cigarette, closed the box and tapped the cigarette on its engraved lid.

There was no table-lighter on this coffee-table, so I reached into the pocket of my suit, which was now a very lightweight white linen, and I found a lighter. I lit her cigarette.

"Please relax, dear," she said. "Jimmy's safely down in Manila."

At a wild guess, I supposed Jimmy to be her husband. Mr. Biddle.

"And Tommy as you might or might not know," she said, "is the absolute soul of discretion."

I could definitely see her resemblance to Daphne now that she was so much closer to Daphne's age. She was shorter than Daphne, and her hair was lighter — well, I think it was dyed, to tell the truth — but her eyes, her nose and mouth, her slim but strong figure —

"Why don't you take a picture?" she asked.

"Oh, sorry," I said.

"Oh, please, don't apologize, I love it, an old married lady like me?"

"You're not so old," I said.

"I shall never see thirty again, darling, and for a woman that is simply doddering. But enough of this stupid banter. I'm so glad you came. I've been thinking about you nonstop. Simply nonstop."

"God knows what you think about," I said.

"What do you mean?"

"When you think about me," I said. "I'm myself twenty-four hours a day, and, believe me, it's not that fascinating."

"That's just one of the things I love about you, you dear man, your almost complete lack of narcissism."

"Perhaps if I were someone else I would be more narcissistic."

"I've given the servants the afternoon off by the way," she said. "It's only you and me and Tommy in the house. My daughter is visiting with one of her little friends. So we shouldn't have any interruptions."

She put her hand on mine.

"So," I said, "what did you want to talk about?"

"Are you decent?" called a voice from within her room.

"Oh, do just come in, Tommy," called Mrs. Biddle.

Tommy came out onto the veranda carrying a very large and ornate tray with a tea service on it. He looked very young and dapper, dressed, like me, in a white suit.

He laid the tray on the table: a teapot, two cups and saucers, a sugar bowl and a honey bowl, a little silver pitcher of milk or cream. Tiny little engraved spoons, shiny as drops of rain. There was a pile of small crustless sandwiches on a silver platter, and a couple of small china plates.

"Shall I pour?" asked Tommy.

"No, Tommy, thank you so much; Mr. Schnabel and I are just going to have a little chat for an hour or so."

"Of course. I'll be in the drawing room. Listening to the radio. E.M. Forster is coming on with one of his little book-chats."

"Splendid. Keep an eye on the door, darling, and if anyone comes by, send them away. Say I have a headache."

He smiled and withdrew.

"Now," she said, picking up the teapot. "First things first. Tea." She lifted the lid of the pot and smelled the brew. "Ah, strong and piping hot." She replaced the lid. "I don't think that Tommy's spiked it. But we shall see."

Chapter 94

She paused, holding the pot.

"Darling, I just realized I don't even know how you take your tea."

"Don't feel bad, I barely know how I take my tea myself."

"Milk?"

"Sure."

"One lump or two?" she asked. "Or honey?"

"What the heck, let's go with honey. One teaspoonful."

"That's exactly how I take it," she said.

She fixed our tea. I lifted my cup and tasted it: pretty good, actually.

"You like it?" she asked. "Tommy blends it himself. Assam and something else. And sometimes, yes, laudanum. But this —" she licked her lips appraisingly, "seems to be un-spiked. Or, if it is, it's only just a teeny bit spiked."

She put down her cup and saucer, took one puff from her cigarette and then stubbed it out in a large cut-glass ashtray.

"Here it comes again," she said.

She was referring to the rain, which started just then with a smattering of fat drops exploding against the screening of the veranda, and which a moment later turned into an utter downpour, turning the outside world a dark streaming and clattering grey. The only illumination was from a handful of windows glowing like dying suns from the other buildings on the plantation, small blotches of dull swimming light in this submerged world.

"This damned rain," she said. "Do you ever miss home? Philadelphia?"

"No," I said, "not really."

It was good to sit here drinking sweetened strong tea, out of the downpour, sitting with this beautiful lady. I took a bite of a sandwich. Chicken salad. And very good.

"This racket," she said. "This rain. It sounds like all the heavens are crashing down."

"Don't worry," I said. "They're not."

"No, of course they're not." She put her hand, the one with a wedding ring on it, onto my knee. "You're so strong, Arnold. So unflappable."

"Not particularly," I said. "These people who work on your plantation. They're strong."

"Yes, I suppose they are." She lifted her hand, flexed and unflexed it. "And I suppose you think I'm horribly spoiled."

"No," I said.

"I *do* work you know. I'm up at seven every morning attending to affairs. Tommy oversees the fields and I deal with the house and the ordering and transport and everything else. While Jimmy drinks. Drinks and gambles. Drinks and whores and gambles." She looked away, out at the downpour beyond the veranda's screening. It was like being behind a waterfall. "Perhaps I've said too much," she said.

"Oh, no," I said.

I tried another sandwich. Pork I believe, also excellent.

"I'm horribly unhappy, Arnold. I no longer love Jimmy; and he has never loved me. He married me for my money, I know that now. But if I divorce him my mother will have a cow, an absolute cow. Catholic you know. And my father will be none too happy either, believe me, as Jimmy took all my money and sank it into this hellhole and it's all in his name and if I divorce him I know he won't give me a red cent. What should I do?"

I thought about this a moment, chewing my sandwich.

"Could you wait till Jimmy gets really drunk one day and then have him sign the property over to you?"

She held still for a moment, then took a sip of her tea.

She laid the cup and saucer down.

"That's actually not a bad idea. I could arrange for our lawyer Dr. Rodriguez to be there, all ready with his contracts and stamps and pens. I'm sure he'd be happy to do it. Dr. Rodriguez is slightly in love with me you see."

There was a small plate of cookies on the tray also, I hadn't even noticed them before. I started to reach for one but her hand intercepted mine and pulled it to her breast.

"Feel this," she said. "Can you feel my heart beating."

I could, actually.

"Yes," I said.

I started to pull my hand away, but, not only would she not let go of it, she pulled it under her décolletage and placed it on her right breast, all the while staring into my eyes.

"Um," I said.

"Don't you want me, Arnold?"

"Well, it's just that —"

"Your little — friend?"

"Yes," I said.

She continued to hold my hand on her breast.

"Persephone is it?"

"Elektra," I said.

"Are you going to marry her?"

"I doubt it," I said.

"Why not?"

"I wouldn't want to inflict myself on her," I said, in all modesty.

"Oh, yes," she said. "This alleged breakdown of yours."

"It's not merely alleged," I said. Her breast was warm, and moist, but I suppose no more warm nor moist than my hand was.

"I don't give a damn about your breakdown," she said. "Pardon my language."

"Of course."

Despite myself I felt those ancient stirrings down below.

"Wait, did you hear something?" she asked.

All I could hear was the clattering rain.

She pulled my hand away from her breast and laid it, my hand, on the table.

I reached over for one of the cookies, it looked like a butter cookie.

"Oh, dear," she said, looking over my head.

Putting the cookie between my lips and biting into it — it was indeed a butter cookie, crispy and delicious — I turned and saw a large blond-haired fellow in a disheveled and wet white suit come out onto the veranda.

"Hello, Jimmy," said Mrs. Biddle. "You're back early. How nice. Do you know Mr. Schnabel?"

Chapter 95

Jimmy said nothing at first. He stood there in his wet linen suit, a faint steam rising up from his great round shoulders. He looked like a man who had played fullback in college but who hadn't exercised in the fifteen years since his graduation. He swayed just slightly, staring alternately at Mrs. Biddle and myself. His eyes were small but with large black pupils.

Swallowing my bite of butter cookie I stood up, wiped my hand on my trousers and then extended it, my hand, to him.

"How are you?" I said. "I don't think we've met."

Of course I couldn't be absolutely sure of this, as I had no recollection of being in 1933 before, if that was the year we were in, or in the Philippines, if that was where we were.

He stared at my hand.

"Whatcha doin' here," he said.

I could now smell the alcohol fumes wafting gently from his big body, admixtured with those of cigars and sweat and what I now recognized as female sexual exudation.

"Mr. Schnabel simply stopped by for a visit," said Mrs. Biddle behind me.

I brought my unshaken hand down to my side.

"You're that nut," said Jimmy, to me.

"Jimmy," said Mrs. Biddle.

"I heard about you. Railroad man. Went nuts. Are you nuts?"

"Jimmy," repeated Mrs. Biddle. "Stop it."

"What are you doin'," he said to her, "having tea with this lunatic?"

"He's recovered. Or recovering. Be polite. Mr. Schnabel is our guest."

"I didn't invite him. I go away for a few drinks at the club and you invite some nut case in for tea."

"Stop this nonsense, Jimmy."

"You," said Jimmy, pointing a large bloated finger at me, "Beat it. Hop it. 'Fore I throw you out."

"Okay," I said.

"Arnold," said Mrs. Biddle. "You don't have to go. Jimmy, you're drunk. Go to your room and lie down."

"Shut up," said Jimmy. He was still pointing at me and now he stepped forward and poked me in the chest with that big finger. "Scram," he said.

"Sure," I said. I turned to Mrs. Biddle. "Thanks for the tea and sandwiches, Mrs. Biddle. And the cookie."

"Don't go, Arnold. Don't leave me with this beast."

Suddenly something — I suppose Jimmy's ham-like paw — shoved mightily against my shoulder and I tripped over the tea table, sending it and the tea service clattering and shattering onto the floor. I staggered several steps but managed not to fall down. Mrs. Biddle screamed, I turned, and Jimmy was rushing toward me making a sound like a man whose arm was being twisted behind his back, but in fact both his arms were raised and his hands were clenched into fists, but fortunately for me he slipped on something, I think it was the silver tea tray, and I stepped to one side as he stumbled past me and crashed through the screening and into that almost solid wall of rain, from which erupted a shrieking bellow like a dog being run over by a truck, cut off abruptly by a muffled but loud wet thump.

I stood there looking at the big jagged hole the man had left in the screening. The only sound now was that of the rain, this wet cacophony as if some ocean in the sky had decided all at once to come crashing down to drown the earth forever.

"Oh my God," said Mrs. Biddle. "Are you all right, Arnold."

"Yes, I think so," I said.

I looked at her, she was still sitting on the wicker sofa, but sitting up very straight, with her fists clenched close to her breast.

"Go look, see if he's okay. He's such a bull. I'm sure he's okay."

I went over to the edge of the veranda and looked down through the torn space in the screening. Down through the torrents of rain I saw Jimmy's pale form lying absolutely still face down in the mud of the yard.

"Is he okay?" asked Mrs. Biddle.

"He's not moving," I said.

"Oh," she said.

I moved back a bit from the verge of the veranda. I had been getting wet.

"I'll go down and check on him," I said.

"Wait. Let me look."

She got up, stepped over the tea things on the floor, and came over next to me. She put her hand on my arm and leaned forward, looking down.

"He's not moving," she said.

"No," I said.

"He's not moving at all."

Continuing to hold tightly onto my arm she leaned farther over, holding her other hand over her forehead to keep the rain out of her eyes.

"I think his neck is broken," she said. "Look, Arnold."

I didn't want to, but I did, shielding my eyes from the rain with my hand. It was true, his head was twisted at an unnatural angle. He looked like some enormous puppet dropped in the mud.

Then we saw a man in a white suit come out of the house, carrying a black umbrella. He came down the steps, went over to Jimmy and knelt down next to him on one knee. All we could see was this large black umbrella, and the bottom half of Jimmy's unmoving body.

Then the man stood up and tilting the umbrella towards his back, he looked up at us. It was Tommy.

"How is he?" called down Mrs. Biddle.

Tommy called up something but the downpour drowned out his words.

"What?" called Mrs. Biddle. "How is he, Tommy?"

Tommy called louder this time, cupping his hand to the side of his mouth:

"I'm afraid he's dead, Mrs. Biddle."

She paused, then straightened up and looked at me.

"It was an accident, Arnold. There was nothing either of us could do."

She had continued to hold onto my arm, but now she let go of it.

Chapter 96

We went downstairs. Her living room looked much the same, that is as if William Powell or Carole Lombard might walk in at any second, except now everything was bright and new and polished. Again though, everything was in black or white or shades of grey. It was still only late afternoon, but the windows were almost dark with that thick crashing rain outside.

Tommy came in from the porch just as we reached the middle of the living room. He closed his glistening umbrella and stuck it in an ivy-patterned vase in the foyer.

"If it's any consolation, death must have been instantaneous," he said.

"The poor man," said Mrs. Biddle.

"May I get you a drink, Mrs. Biddle?" said Tommy.

"Oh, Tommy, look at you, your trousers are ruined."

"Don't worry about my trousers now."

"And your shoes. Your lovely white shoes."

"I'm going to make you a drink," he said. "Why don't you sit down. You've had a shock."

"I don't think I can sit."

"Mr. Schnabel —" said Tommy. He was heading toward the drinks cabinet.

"Yes?"

He made a movement with his head, but I wasn't quite sure what he meant by it, if anything.

He stopped, and pointed to the larger of the two sofas. Then he pointed to Mrs. Biddle, and then back to the sofa.

"Oh," I said. "Oh. Mrs. Biddle, come on, sit down."

"Will you sit with me?"

"Sure."

I sort of guided her over to the sofa, although God knows she knew where it was, and she sat down. I sat next to her, to her left. She put her hand on mine.

"Will you have a cocktail, Mr. Schnabel?" asked Tommy.

"Okay," I said.

To tell the truth I really felt like I could use one at this point.

"Whiskey and soda?"

"Sure."

"Ice? I can go get some from the ice box."

"I'll just have it the way Mrs. Biddle is having it."

"No ice then."

Tommy went to work preparing three drinks, using a quart of Old Forester and a large glass soda syphon. Outside the rain drummed down, like a million tiny bongo drums played by a million tiny madmen.

"Should we get the boys to bring him in?" said Mrs. Biddle, her voice breaking slightly.

"Not until the police get here," said Tommy over his shoulder.

"The police?" she said. "Will that be necessary?"

"It would probably be for the best in the long run."

"I suppose you're right," said Mrs. Biddle. "I hate to think of him lying out there in that mud."

"Can't be helped," said Tommy. "Oh. Does anyone want a little something extra?" he asked.

He turned and held up a small brown bottle, taking the cork from it as he did so.

"Yes, Tommy," said Mrs. Biddle. "For my nerves, thank you."

"Mr. Schnabel? A touch of laudanum?"

"Well, just a little," I said.

I wasn't quite sure if any of this was really happening, so I saw no harm.

"Will you ring the police, Tommy?" asked Mrs. Biddle. "I don't think I could bear it."

"Certainly. But may I make a suggestion?" he said, bringing three tall drinks over to us on a silver tray.

"Of course," said Mrs. Biddle.

"Let me telephone Dr. Rodriguez. I'll tell him the situation, and we'll let him handle it."

"Do you think that's best?" she asked.

Tommy laid the tray on the coffee table in front of us.

"Yes, I think so," he said. "Bottoms up now."

We all took a glass. Tommy didn't sit, but stood with his drink on the other side of the table.

"To Jimmy," he said.

We all drank.

"Well, I must say I needed that," said Tommy. "I'll telephone Rodriguez now."

He took his drink over to a side table on which a white telephone sat.

"Light me a cigarette, Arnold," said Mrs. Biddle. "One of those in that box there."

The box was the engraved wooden one I had seen here before. The table lighter in the shape of the fat Buddha was there also. I opened the box and offered it to her, she took out a cigarette, and I gave her a light with the smiling philosopher.

"Won't you have one, Arnold?" she said, in a soft voice.

I think I actually sighed, because I really did want one. But I had gotten this far today without one, I had gone through so much, somehow I felt like holding out, whether any of this was real or not, so I told her no thanks. I have to say I think the laudanum-spiked highball was a factor in my being able to abstain.

"Hello," said Tommy, speaking in a loud voice into the telephone receiver. "*Hola*. May I speak to Dr. Rodriguez, please. Tell him it's Tommy, from the Biddle plantation." He put his hand over the phone, and looked to us. "He'll be right on."

"Tell him to hurry, Tommy," said Mrs. Biddle.

"I will," said Tommy. "Oh. Dr. Rodriguez, Tommy here. Yes, how are you? Listen, there's been an accident, and Mrs. Biddle asks that you come right over. Yes. It's Mr. Biddle. Jimmy, yes, he fell, and, well, he broke his neck I'm afraid. Yes, he's dead I'm sorry to say." He listened for a few moments and then put his hand over the mouthpiece again and looked toward Mrs. Biddle. "He wants to know how it happened."

"He stumbled and fell off the second floor veranda," said Mrs. Biddle.

Tommy repeated this down the telephone line.

There was a pause, and then he said, "Yes, he had been drinking I fear. Yes. Yes. Very sad. Yes. Listen, Dr. Rodriguez, do you think you could, um, deal with the police concerning this. Yes. Yes. Thank you. *Muchas gracias*, doctor, *adiós*."

He hung up the phone.

"Well, that's done," said Tommy. "He said he'll drive right over, and after he has, uh, assessed the situation, he'll call the appropriate person in the police."

"Oh good," said Mrs. Biddle.

Tommy started to walk over towards us with his drink.

"Oh wait," said Mrs. Biddle.

Tommy stopped.

"April," said Mrs. Biddle.

"Oh, right," said Tommy.

She turned to me.

"My daughter," she said.

"Oh," I said.

"Tommy —" she said.

"I'll take care of it," said Tommy. "I'll call. Shall I — shall I tell her?"

"Yes," said Mrs. Biddle. "Or, no. I'll tell her. But dial the number for me, will you please, Tommy?"

Tommy went back to the telephone.

"May I make another suggestion, though?" he said. He held his drink in his left hand, and with his right hand he draped the telephone cord over his left wrist.

"Of course," said Mrs. Biddle.

With his right hand Tommy picked up the telephone and brought it over to us.

"Let her stay at her little friend's house for a few hours. At least until they take the — until they take Jimmy away."

"Of course," she said. "I wouldn't have thought of that. Thank you, Tommy. You're such a brick."

"It's nothing."

He laid his drink down on the table, and, still standing, he dialed a number on the white telephone.

"You're a brick, too, Arnold," said Mrs. Biddle, patting my hand. "I want to thank you so much."

"For what?" I said.

Tommy, cradling the receiver to his ear, reached down with his left hand to take a cigarette from the box.

"Just for everything," Mrs. Biddle said.

Tommy, waiting for someone to answer on the other end, picked up the fat smiling Buddha and gave himself a light.

Chapter 97

After a moment Tommy said a few words to someone on the telephone, and then he said to Mrs. Biddle:

"They're getting April now. Are you sure you want to tell her? I could break it to her gently."

Mrs. Biddle hesitated, chewing one side of her lower lip, then said, simply, "Give me the phone."

I felt awkward. It seemed that Mrs. Biddle should have some privacy while telling her daughter that Jimmy had suddenly died.

But then it occurred to me that perhaps my presence, baleful as it often seemed to me – condemned as I was for life to put up with it – even so might make this difficult moment somehow easier for her. Besides, I learned a long time ago that I wasn't put on this earth for the purpose of not feeling awkward. Far from it, I have felt awkward for approximately 95% of my waking life, and for a not insignificant percentage of my sleeping life. But still I thought perhaps the thing to do would be at least to get up from the couch, perhaps to go and stand at a window, gazing out at that crashing rain relentlessly attacking the outside world like an army of angry monkeys wielding stout bamboo sticks. And indeed I started to get up, but Mrs. Biddle — who had taken the phone from Jimmy and was sitting very upright, holding the receiver to her ear with her right hand while holding a cigarette in the other — whispered:

"Don't get up. Stay."

So I stayed. A few long moments passed into the present and then into the past.

"Hello," she said, finally, into the phone. "April — what? No, you don't have to come home yet. What? Well, yes of course you can stay over there tonight if you like. Of course. Yes. Oh, you won at canasta? That's marvelous, darling. Eight dollars, golly. Yes, dear, of course you can buy anything you want with it. Yes. Nancy Drew books? Yes, lovely. But listen, April, the reason I'm calling —"

She paused, and then put her hand over the mouthpiece.

"How do I tell her?" she asked, looking from Tommy (who was still standing there) to me.

Tommy didn't say anything.

She said to me again, "How do I tell her, Arnold?"

I could hear a young girl's voice coming from the phone, saying, "Mother, are you there?"

"Just tell her," I said. "There's no easy way."

Suddenly she handed the receiver to me, and then put her hand over her mouth.

I put the phone to my ear.

"Hello?" I said.

"Who's this?" said the girl's voice.

"I'm a friend of your mother's. Arnold Schnabel."

"Arnold what?"

"Just call me Arnold."

"Okay. I'm April."

"I know. Listen, April, I have some bad news. Your mother wants me to tell you because she's —"

"Upset," whispered Mrs. Biddle through her fingers.

"She's upset," I said.

"What is it?"

"I'm afraid your father has had an accident."

"An accident? Is he dead?"

"Yes, I'm afraid so."

"Did he crash his car?"

"No, no, he, uh — he fell off the veranda on the second floor."

"Was he drunk? He must have been drunk."

"I think he'd been drinking, yes," I said.

"You're sure he's dead."

"Well —"

"Did you take his pulse?"

"No, no, I didn't, but — Tommy —"

"Tommy said he was dead?"

"Yes," I said.

"Well, he must be dead then."

"Yes," I said.

There was a pause here, but it didn't feel awkward.

I realized that both Tommy and Mrs. Biddle were staring intently at me. Then April spoke again:

"Can I talk to my mother now? Do you think she's able to talk?"

"Let me ask," I said.

"That's a good idea," said the little girl.

I put my hand over the mouthpiece of the phone and turned to Mrs. Biddle.

"April wants to know if you're able to talk now."

Mrs. Biddle still had her slender fingers over her mouth, but after a moment she lowered them.

"How is she taking it?" she asked.

"Not too badly," I said.

She hesitated again, chewing her lip, then took the receiver out of my hand.

"Hello, darling," she said.

This time I did get up, taking my drink.

I shrugged at Tommy, he shrugged at me.

I walked over to one of the large front windows and looked out through the torrent. I could see the white blob of Jimmy's body out there, being pummeled by thousands of gallons of rain, lying in the mud as if it were floating in a dirty lake.

Mrs. Biddle's voice spoke softly behind me, murmuring to her daughter.

I turned away from the window. Mrs. Biddle still sat very upright on the couch, her head inclined to the telephone receiver, one long bare arm reaching out to tap her cigarette into the big glass ashtray.

Tommy had sat down in a leather easy chair, and, with a cigarette between his thin lips, he was cutting the pages of a book with a knife.

I wondered if I would ever make it back to 1963. After all, I did have a date with Elektra that night.

Chapter 98

What if I had to stay in this world, for the rest of my life?

I supposed there could be worse fates. Apparently I belonged at least somewhat in this present universe. After all, young Mrs. Biddle and Tommy seemed to know me and accept me. Perhaps this indeed was my real world, and I merely suffered from a delusion that I lived in 1963. But, if that were the case, then I was apparently suffering from a severe case of amnesia regarding this present world of circa 1933, which as far as my memory served, had only begun for me perhaps an hour before.

On second thought, perhaps my real life was in that world of the 1890s that I had visited yesterday with Dick, and both this 1930s universe and my previous 1960s world were merely bizarrely realistic psychotic fugues. Psychiatrists and literary historians of whichever future this document finds itself, I forward this question over to you.

Oh well, as Tommy had said regarding leaving Jimmy in the mud and the rain, whatever my situation was, it couldn't be helped.

Or could it?

I went over to where Tommy sat. He was now reading the book whose pages he had been cutting. I saw that the title was *The King in Yellow*.

"Excuse me, Tommy?"

He looked up, smiling.

"Yes, Mr. Schnabel?"

Mrs. Biddle was still talking with her daughter on the phone.

"I have to use the bathroom," I said, in a low voice.

"Oh, go right up," he said. "There's one in the back of the house but the one on the second floor is much nicer. Do you know where it is?"

"I think so," I said.

So far this house had seemed almost identical to Mrs. Biddle's house in 1963.

He smiled again and went back to his book. I started to head for the hall but suddenly Mrs. Biddle called.

"Arnold, where are you going?"

I hesitated, and fortunately Tommy came to my rescue. He cleared his throat and pointed to the ceiling, in the direction presumably of the bathroom.

"Oh, go right ahead, Arnold, darling."

Waving her hand at me, she went back at once to her telephone conversation.

I went out of the room and down the hall, then up those all-too-familiar stairs.

I stopped at the landing. Now that I really looked at the paintings I saw that only one of them was from 1963, the one with the French vacationers by the seaside. The other two paintings seemed to be different. Unfortunately neither one seemed to depict a house in Cape May, circa 1963.

I put out my hand to the French painting again, and, after pausing only a second I thrust it into the painting, into that fresh crisp seaside air.

After a moment or two I pulled my hand back out. Sure, I could climb on through, and perhaps I would meet that nice Monsieur Proust again, but the last thing I needed or wanted now was to go even further back in time.

I went on up to the second floor, but instead of going to the bathroom (even though I did in fact have to go), I went back to Mrs. Biddle's door. I had closed it behind us when we left her room earlier.

I had an idea, and I had nothing to lose from trying it, even though by doing so I would be committing the rudeness of entering a woman's bedroom on my own and uninvited.

I took the traditional deep breath and put my hand on the doorknob.

I closed my eyes and took another breath.

Then I said to myself, or to whomever, *Dear Jesus, please let me come home; I promise to be a good man if you do.*

"And if I don't, then what? You're going to be a bad man?"

I opened my eyes, and there he was, standing to my right, smoking one of his Pall Malls as usual.

He now wore a rumpled, stained, apparently once-white tropical suit (of the same sort I wore, and as did Tommy, and as had the late Jimmy). He wore a formerly-white, sweat-stained fedora, and a grey-and-black striped tie, loose at the unbuttoned collar. He had a two-or-three day's growth of beard, and his hair, although not its traditional shoulder-length, was at least a month overdue for a cut. Nevertheless he looked somehow dashing, like a professional gambler, or gun-smuggler.

"Are you surprised to see me?" he asked.

"To be honest, no," I thought but did not say. I didn't want to talk aloud, for fear of possibly alarming Tommy or Mrs. Biddle, even if they were all the way downstairs.

"You haven't answered my initial question, Arnold," he said.

I had already forgotten what that was.

"Will you be a bad man if I don't arrange to return you to, you know —"
I sighed. I know it's impolite to sigh, but I couldn't help it.

"No," I said, silently. "I'll at least attempt to be good, either way, I suppose. As good as I can manage. Which may not be saying much."

He smiled and put his hand on my shoulder.

"Arnold, may I make a suggestion?"

"Sure," I didn't say.

"Stop asking me for favors. Despite the common superstition, I – and I think I speak for my father and for the Holy Ghost as well – I, we, are decidedly not in the business of answering prayers. Okay?"

"Okay," I said.

"Good. Now go back to doing whatever it is you were going to do."

"All right," I said, this time aloud, despite myself.

I closed my eyes again. My hand was still on the doorknob.

I held my breath, opened the door and stepped through.

I opened my eyes and the room, the world, was in color. I let out my breath, and without looking back I closed the door behind me. I could hear talking out on the porch.

I walked slowly and carefully out to the French doors that opened onto the porch, and there, sitting side by side on a wicker sofa, having tea, were myself and the older Mrs. Biddle. She was telling a story, smiling, and I was listening, holding a teacup.

Beyond us I could see through the screening at the other end of the porch the sun going down over the houses and the trees, amidst pale wispy clouds, beginning its journey across the continent and over the Pacific, on to the Philippines and points beyond.

The air smelled of magnolia, of honeysuckle, of the Atlantic Ocean.

I walked over to myself and Mrs. Biddle, and then I stepped into myself.

I looked at Mrs. Biddle from my eyes.

She had changed into what I believe is called a summer frock, with little red rose petals on an orange background.

"I never saw him again after that night," she said. "Soon afterwards he went back to work for the railroad, and they transferred him to Mindanao. He was killed in the war. Am I boring you?"

"No, not at all," I said.

"People always think their own lives are so fascinating."

"I'm not bored," I said.

"Is it terrible that I was happy that my husband died?"

"No," I said.

"I did feel guilty. I went to confession about it, and the priest absolved me."

"Well, there you go," I said.

"The only thing is, I didn't really believe in the church or God or any of that, and I still don't. I only went to confession to ease my conscience."

"That's why a lot of people go to confession," I said.

"Yes but still."

I gazed out through the screening at the breathing world all green and white, blue and orange and every other color.

"Excuse me, Mrs. Biddle," I said, "what was that man's name again? The guy — the man – who —"

"Who didn't kill my husband?"

"Yes," I said.

"Arthur," she said. She looked away. The reflections of the failing sun lit up her face and she looked young again, or anyway younger. "Arthur Schaefer," she said.

"Arthur Schaefer," I repeated.

As Miss Evans would say, *mon semblable, mon frère.*

Chapter 99

She sighed, looking away toward that sinking sun spilling streaks of liquid red and orange and yellow across the sky, its watery light filtered by the porch screening turning the skin of her face into the color and seeming texture of a ripened peach.

For some reason — perhaps for many reasons, or perhaps for the single reason that I am not quite right in the head — I touched her face, if only briefly, running my finger down her cheek.

Needless to say she turned and looked at me, her eyebrows raised quizzically. But far from getting angry and slapping me, she said only:

"Have another cookie."

I took one. They were the same butter cookies she had given me back in 1933.

"I love to see a man eat," she said.

I chewed and swallowed.

I became aware that this was the same porch I had been sitting on last night, but a different part of the porch, and that the room I had just walked through, Mrs. Biddle's room, was the one in which I had only barely escaped the advances of Miss Evans. All of that seemed so long ago, certainly much further distant in time than my more recent visit here, in 1933.

"Did you ever re-marry?" I asked.

"No. Once bitten," she said. "Why have you never married?"

I've been asked this question so many times in my life, and I've always responded with something stupid, or inadequate, or both.

This time I told the truth:

"I don't know, really."

"You remind me of him," said Mrs. Biddle.

She didn't say his name, but I knew who she meant: my double.

"He was a regional manager for the railroad," she said. "One day they found him naked, walking along the rails, headed into the mountains."

This sounded like something I would do.

"They hospitalized him in Manila for a month. He was convalescing with some neighbors of mine when I met him one day. He —"

Mrs. Biddle looked up, over my shoulder. I turned. A woman of about my age had come out onto the porch.

"Hello, mother," this lady said. "Introduce me to your friend."

I stood, swallowing the last of my cookie and wiping my hands on my trousers.

"This is Mr. Schnabel, April," said Mrs. Biddle. "Arnold, this is my daughter, April."

April held out her hand and I took it.

She wore pleated tan slacks, sandals, a white blouse like a man's sport shirt, tucked in under a wide black belt. She had dark blond hair brushed back from her forehead and fastened somehow behind her ears.

She wore a single strand of white pearls, and a diamond glittered on each of her ears.

"My daughter has told me all about you, Mr. Schnabel," she said, holding onto my hand. "I hope you don't intend to relieve her of her virtue."

"Absolutely not," I said.

She still held onto my hand.

"You seem oddly familiar," she said.

I could have set these ladies' minds at rest, and told them it had been me with Mrs. Biddle that rainy day thirty years before, that it had been I who had broken the sad news to young April on the telephone. But, not particularly wanting to be hustled onto the next ambulance back to Byberry, I said nothing.

April relinquished my hand.

"So you're writing a screenplay with Larry?" she asked.

I had almost forgotten about that.

"Yes," I said.

"I love Larry's movies. They're so lurid. I hope there's a murder."

"Oh, yes," I said.

"Good."

She was a beautiful woman, taller than Mrs. Biddle although not so tall as Daphne. When I had spoken to her on the phone I had had a mental image of a childish version of Daphne, with blond ringlets, and now the womanly April stood before me, an older version of Daphne, a younger version of her mother.

"You don't say much, do you?" she said.

"I think it's best I don't," I said.

"Are you staying long, April?" asked her mother.

"No. I have a flight for Africa the day after tomorrow."

"Always traveling," said Mrs. Biddle.

"Never a dull moment," said April, reaching past me to take one of those butter cookies. She smelled like fresh butter.

"You and Mac," said her mother.

"Busy as bees," said April. She bit into the cookie.

"April's a journalist, Arnold," said Mrs. Biddle.

"Oh," I said, as usual not challenging Oscar Wilde as one of history's great wits.

"He's not impressed," said April, chewing her cookie. "Sit down, Arnold, please."

I resumed my seat.

"Just wanted to say hi," said April. She put the remainder of the cookie back onto the plate. "I'll leave you two. Oh."

Daphne had just come out onto the porch, with a red-headed girl in a light-blue dress covered with little metallic black cross-hatchings.

"Hi, mother," said Daphne to April. She kissed her mother's cheek. "This is my friend Mary Elizabeth."

"Hello, Mary Elizabeth."

"Very pleased to meet you," said the girl, young woman rather.

"And that's my grandmother there," said Daphne. "Everyone calls her Mrs. Biddle."

"Hello, Mrs. Biddle," said Daphne's friend.

"Hello, dear," said Mrs. Biddle.

Being an inveterate gentleman, I had risen from my seat again, and there I stood.

"Arnold, how do you like Mary Elizabeth's make-over?"

I had no idea what she was talking about; so of course I do what I usually do when this sort of thing happens, I faked it.

"Excellent," I said.

"I dyed her hair 'fiery auburn'. It's the new her."

"Do I look stupid?" asked the girl, addressing me, and it wasn't till then that I realized that this was Sister Mary Elizabeth.

"No," I said.

In my defense I'll say that she was also wearing red lipstick, and eye make-up.

"A man of few words," said April.

"Few spoken words," said Mrs. Biddle.

True to my description, I said nothing, instead of what was on my mind, namely that I felt as if I were floating in this shimmering filtered red and gold light in a great pool of time, the past and the present flowing through me like light through a stained glass window, into a future which would soon enough be the past, if it wasn't already.

Somewhere a blackbird cackled, and the trees in the yard shook their leaves in a gust of wind from the ocean.

I became aware that a few seconds had gone by. As so often in my life, by keeping quiet I had disquieted my fellow human beings. I scrambled through my brain, if not for a witticism, at least for an acceptable banality.

I came up with nothing.

"Q.E.D.," said April.

Chapter 100

"Do you want to go out with us, Arnold?" said Daphne.

"Go out?" I said. Again threatening neither Oscar Wilde nor Levant in the rapier wit department.

"Yeah, to get a beer or something."

"Well —"

"Go ahead, Arnold," said Mrs. Biddle, lighting a cigarette with a paper match, "keep an eye on her. Try to keep her out of jail if you can."

"Um, uh," I replied.

"Go on, Arnold," said April. "Live a little."

"What do you say, Arnold?" said Daphne.

"Well, I — uh —"

Daphne had changed her clothes also. She wore a yellow dress, with straps, and flashes of orange light danced along the fabric each time she moved. She too wore lipstick, of a brownish red, and also eye make-up, although not as much as Sister Mary Elizabeth did.

"Do you have plans?" Daphne asked me.

Suddenly I recalled that — a circumstance which would have been incredible a couple of weeks ago — I actually did have plans.

"Well, yes," I said.

"A date with Elektra?"

At last someone who got her name right.

"Yes," I said.

"When?"

"Eight o'clock."

"Good, we have plenty of time for drinks, and then you can go to Elektra. Or even have her join us if you like. You should see her, Mary Elizabeth. Stunning."

"Really?"

"Simply stunning."

"You're not turning lesbian on me, are you?" said her mother.

"What if I am?"

Sister Mary Elizabeth put her hand over her mouth.

"All right, enough of this madness," said Mrs. Biddle. "Help me up, Arnold."

I took her proffered arm and did what I could. In her free hand she had taken up a pack of Lucky Strikes from the table, and a paper book of matches.

"Hand me that walking stick."

Her cane was leaning against the wall near the end of the sofa. I handed it to her.

"How's the bum leg?" April asked her.

"I'll never dance the Watusi again," said Mrs. Biddle.

"My mother broke her leg dancing the Watusi," said April to me.

"I can think of no better way to have broken my leg," said Mrs. Biddle.

Somehow our small army made it down to that living room, no longer in black-and-white, but now looking somewhat like a living room from a 1950s movie, but a movie taking place in the 1930s, if that isn't too complicated, and somehow I think it is.

Tommy suddenly loomed up from somewhere as we were all milling about in this Technicolor world suffused with all the colors of the rainbow and some others I had never noticed before.

"Going out for drinks?" he said, to me in particular. "I'm frantically jealous."

"Come with us," said Daphne.

"Go out? With the young people?"

"Why not?"

"Oh I don't know."

This went on for a while, and a lot more seemed to go on while I stood there and smiled like an idiot whenever some sort of reaction seemed to be called for regarding what seemed like the twenty-seven conversational paths which were being trampled on more or less simultaneously but which were probably only ten or twelve in number; and all I know is that finally the four of us, Daphne, Sister Mary Elizabeth, myself, and yes, Tommy, were walking (well, I was limping, my leg was still hurting) along North Street together, the two girls in front, Tommy and I walking side by side.

"Drinks with the young people!" said Tommy again, as he had several times before.

"Oh wait!" said Sister Mary Elizabeth, and she stopped, turning sideways to Daphne and putting her hand on her arm.

I noticed they were both carrying purses. Daphne's was red plastic, Sister Mary Elizabeth's was black leather, although I suppose they both belonged to Daphne.

"I don't have any money," said Sister Mary Elizabeth. She removed her hand from Daphne's arm and put it on the purse she held in her other hand. She stared at the purse and then back at Daphne.

"Oh," said Daphne. "Not a cent?"

"Not a red cent. I've taken a vow of poverty."

"Right. Come to think of it I only have a few dollars."

Both the women looked at us. Their dresses, a glowing blue on Sister Mary Elizabeth, a flashing yellow on Daphne, and their skin – Daphne's tanned like polished oak, the sister's white like a statue in church – pulsed in the bright failing light falling through the trees.

"I suppose I've got twenty or so on me," said Tommy.

"That'll get us started," said Daphne. She turned to Sister Mary Elizabeth. "But what you need to understand, Mary Elizabeth, is we're women. We don't really *buy* drinks."

"We don't?"

"I certainly don't."

"That seems hardly fair."

"Life is completely unfair," said Daphne and she turned and started walking again.

The extremely attentive reader will be aware that I had still not managed to go to the bathroom since leaving my aunts' house about a century ago. As we approached my aunts' house I said, "Excuse me, can I just stop here briefly?"

Daphne turned.

"Why?"

"I want to change."

Of course I couldn't say I had to use the bathroom. Not in front of a nun. Even if she were dressed in civilian clothes, and wearing make-up.

"Changing out of your conservative dark grey suit?" said Daphne.

"Yes," I said.

"Good," she said. "We're not going to a funeral, you know."

Chapter 101

"If you like," I said, "you can go ahead, and I'll meet you."

"Oh no," said Daphne. "We'll wait. Can we dawdle on your porch?"

"Uh, sure," I said.

So I led the way, unlatching the wobbly bloated wooden gate (perhaps someday I will fix it, if I can find some time in my hectic schedule) and stepping onto that mossy bluestone path to the porch just as Mr. and Mrs. DeVore — the young couple who had proven to me the night before that although there may be human limits to pain or to pleasure there are apparently no limits to banality — came wheeling around the side of the house and immediately assumed expressions which would have been suitable if President Kennedy and all his clan had suddenly arrived to play a brisk game of touch football.

"Mr. Schnabel!" said Mrs. DeVore. "We heard all about your evening out!"

"Oh, yes," I said, not stopping.

"Sinatra!" shouted Mr. DeVore. "Ol' blue eyes!"

"Uh, yeah," I said, making it to the porch steps.

"And who are your nice friends here?" demanded Mrs. DeVore.

I was trapped, so, turning at the top of the porch steps I quickly declaimed:

"Mr. and Mrs. DeVore, this is Tommy, and Daphne, and Sister Mary Elizabeth."

"Sister Mary Elizabeth?" said Mrs. DeVore.

"Just Mary Elizabeth," said Sister Mary Elizabeth.

"Oh," said Mrs. DeVore.

"Arnold was joking," said Daphne.

"Heh heh," said Mr. DeVore.

"Heh," said Mrs. DeVore.

"I have to change now. Excuse me," I said.

"Where are you all going?" said Mrs. DeVore as I turned away, and I heard Daphne say "Nowhere" as I opened the screen door and almost toppled over my cousin Kevin who had been standing inside the doorway unbeknownst to me.

"Who are those people, Cousin Arnold?"

"My friends," I said.

"Lady!" he suddenly yelled, catching sight of Daphne.

"Hello, cutie!" she yelled back, and the little scamp shoved past me as if the house was on fire.

But now I faced a phalanx of wide-eyed familial old-womanhood right inside the doorway, my mother, my Aunt Elizabetta, Aunt Greta and good old Aunt Edith.

"It's that girl," said Edith. "His new girlfriend."

"Arnold," said my mother, "did you eat?"

"Who are all those people?" asked Elizabetta.

"Which one's his girlfriend?" asked Greta.

"She's not my girlfriend, I had something to eat, thank you, Mom, those are my friends, and they're just going to wait while I change," I said, and I went around their flank, through the living room room and dining room and kitchen, down the hall and up the stairs, taking two or three steps at a stride, sore leg or not.

On the third floor I slowed down, and walked carefully, quietly, as if through a mine field, holding my breath, past the always treacherous doorway to Miss Evans's room.

I got past it safely and made it to the bathroom. I bolted the door behind me, then tested it, just to make sure. Then I went to the toilet, unzipped, freed my organ of micturition and of at least potential procreation, and allowed my bladder to empty itself of urine.

And as it all streamed so gloriously out of me, I thought of that fateful rainy afternoon so long ago. Had I been in some measure responsible for Jimmy's unfortunate demise? Had I — with that lowest and even unconscious degree of will which can nevertheless produce terrible and even fatal actions — stuck out my foot and tripped Jimmy, causing his great drunken bulk to hurtle forward and off through the screening of that second-floor veranda? Who knows? I had to admit that the world was undoubtedly better off without his presence, but still, it was not my prerogative to hasten his departure. I would have to remember to confess these thoughts to Father Reilly next Saturday. I wasn't sure however if it would be a good thing to mention to him that this incident occurred thirty years ago.

Of course most likely it had all been a waking dream. But are we responsible for sins committed in our dreams? I would perhaps bring this up with Father Reilly as well, unless I sensed that I had already tried his patience enough for one day.

I zipped up, washed my hands, looked into the mirror. I can't even say how gratifying it was to see myself, not in tropical linen, but in my slightly iridescent Krass Brothers suit which looked sometimes the color of wet cigarette ash, occasionally almost black like the asphalt of a city street at night, and other times, like now, the color of a storm cloud about to burst.

I decided to go whole hog, and brushed my teeth.

Feeling pretty good about myself I put my ear to the door, just to make sure that Miss Evans wasn't coming or going (I felt I could recognize her step by now, as quiet and ghost-like as it often seemed to be), then opened the door and went out to the hall.

Luckily for me it seemed to be exactly the same hallway I had left a few minutes before, and I went on up to my attic room.

Once again my mother had worked her magic. My narrow bed was made, the room was swept and dusted. A clean white polo shirt and a fresh pair of madras Bermuda shorts lay folded on top of my dresser, and I changed into them. I exchanged my Thom McAn brogues for my Keds, worn raffishly with no socks, and I ran a comb through my hair, bending down into the small round mirror on its swivel.

I opened the night table drawer which held my cigarettes, my trusty Pall Malls. I picked up the open pack in there, and my old Zippo lighter. Then I thought, no, and I put them back and closed the drawer. You see, I wanted to live.

I hurried downstairs, come hell or high water and everything between.

I felt that the world — this world, or any other world I might wander into — I felt that all this world was my oyster, or as much mine as anyone's.

THE END
of the first volume of the memoirs of Arnold Schnabel

APPENDIX
SELECTED POEMS OF ARNOLD SCHNABEL

This sonnet was written in the first week of Arnold Schnabel's commitment to the Philadelphia State Hospital at Byberry, during that very dark January of 1963. Originally published, as were all of Arnold's poems during his lifetime, in the *Olney Times*.

"One Night"

One night the ceiling opened and I rose up slowly;
above my house I twisted round, looked down and back
on Nedro Avenue, B Street, and the Heintz factory;
black smoke billowed from a gaping maw-like stack,
smoke enveloped me and all was dark;
like a dead cinder upward I floated and spinned:
I called to God for light, a tiny spark:
He did not answer. The reason? I had sinned.
For fifteen years I stared at the night within my head
and then at last I slept for another fifteen,
till I awoke firmly bound to a clean white bed.
It's been several days and now the bed is not so clean,
and neither am I; each night I watch the ceiling yawn,
but I am well-strapped in: I await the dawn.

This poem was submitted to the *Olney Times* by Arnold Schnabel in early March of 1963, just a couple of weeks before his release from the Philadelphia State Mental Hospital at Byberry.

"A Guy Named Jesus"

A guy named Jesus came to see me last night;
He opened my door and for a moment just stood there;
"Hello," he said, then, shutting the door tight,
He came to my bed and pulled up a chair.

"My name is Jesus," said He, and extended His hand;
I took it and shook it, His grip was warm and firm.
"So," He said, "You've had some trouble, I'm led to understand."
"Yes, it's true," I said, "For I am a lowly misbegotten worm."

"Poppycock!" said He; "and by the way, may I smoke?"
"Dear Lord," said I, "smoking's not allowed in patients' rooms."
"But you forget," said He, "'Tis I who make the rules! (Ha! a joke!)
But fear not, for there's nothing like a butt to dissipate the glooms."

And taking from His pouch a lighter and a pack of Pall Mall,
He lit us both up and said, "I have come, you see, to set you free,
from your absurd travails, and your own self-made Hell."
"I deserve only Hell," I cried, "and free I deserve not to be!"

"I'll be the judge of that," He said with a winning grin,
"that is, of course: the Holy Ghost, My Father, and Me.
So stop this nonsense, for I want you to begin
That long journey home to Avenue Nedro and B."

A guy named Jesus came to see me last night,
a simple Jewish carpenter smelling faintly of wood;
we talked until the first faint glimmerings of light,
and when He left I slept the sleep of the good.

This sonnet first saw light in the May 18, 1963 number of the *Olney Times*. By this point one wonders if Silas Willingham III – the editor of that august and generally upbeat paper – was even bothering to read Arnold's increasingly disturbing poems before running them. But we can only be thankful that print them he did.

"The Day of the Worm"

When I was a lad, so many years before my fall,
I feared strange moist days like today,
days of spring, after rain, a sky of steel grey,
when it seemed that no one was outside at all,
or if they were, they were always several blocks away;
and on such days whilst walking aimlessly around,
I would notice a plethora of worms arising from the ground
and wriggling across the wet concrete pathway,
millions of them, rising up, implacable and blind;
what did they want, and why were they here?
I wanted only to be home, and to leave behind
their vileness, their inexorable legions, and my fear.
and, now, from the damp loam of my soul what new creatures
arise, silent, smiling, and with my own features?

Another ingenious sonnet, bravely or obliviously published in the May 25th 1963 issue of the *Olney Times*.

(A note for the young people: The *Schaefer Award Theatre* came on at 11:30 on Saturday nights and showed movies with only one commercial interruption. This show introduced a generation to such classics as *On the Waterfront*, and, yes, some perhaps not so great ones like *Desirée*.)

"The Schaefer Award Theatre"

The Schaefer Award Theatre, and this is my reward:
Brando on the screen, and in my hand a beer;
Mother upstairs, asleep, and nothing untoward
shall disrupt this quiet night with madness or fear.
I have gradually stopped taking the little capsules;
they were a wall between me and life and, yes, this:
the keening and swooping of these razor-winged rascals
who zoom past my sofa with a chilling hiss;
I do not mind them much; somehow they always miss,
and so I drink my beer and watch the movie *Desirée*;
Jean Simmons is so very lovely as Mademoiselle Clary;
when the devils flock in front of her I bat them away
with this poker; I refuse to let them scare me.
But I mustn't relax my guard. Victory goes to the wary.

Originally published in the special "Summer Fun" supplement to the June 1, 1963 issue of the *Olney Times*; it's nice to see that Arnold Schnabel (now on an open-ended leave of absence from the railroad) has gotten away with his mother for a vacation in Cape May, NJ. They stayed at the guest house of his three maiden aunts, the Misses Greta, Edith and Elizabetta Schneider.

"Frank's Playland"

In old Cape May I walk with my mom
through air thick with honeysuckle and suntan oil;
the sun explodes like an atom bomb,
and human beings lie beneath it to broil;
we walk along the shimmering promenade,
by the lunatic ocean and screaming sand,
and, somehow, although it might seem odd,
I long to enter the darkness of Frank's Playland;
I loved this place back when I wasn't a fogey:
nickelodeon and skee-ball and photograph machine;
and, overseeing it all, old Frank with his stogie,
his belt-hung coin-changer, and his jokes so obscene;
now I, the boy, am quite as old as back then was he;
I peer within: Frank's ancient face stares out at me.

This sonnet struck the pages of the *Olney Times* like a bolt from the heavens on June 22, 1963. Arnold Schnabel at the time was recuperating from his mental illness at his aunts' place in Cape May and apparently deep in a course of intense close reading of his young cousin Kevin Armstrong's comic books.

"The Hawkman and I"

Or would perhaps I were the Hawkman, fitted out
with a special belt made of Nth metal
and a pair of wings allowing me to fly about
in mask accipitrine and an arsenal
of ancient weapons and of course my wife
and partner the Hawkgirl, who shares my life
as Carter Hall, archaeologist and curator,
but secretly Katar Hol, a cop from Thanagar,
from which planet I brought the Absorbicon,
and with which I could instantly absorb
every single thing known by every last human
who ever lived on this spinning green orb,
all their fears and loves, all their final words;
I should also be able to converse with birds.

Arnold Schnabel published this sonnet without fanfare in the July 6 1963 issue of the *Olney Times*, where it went completely unnoticed by the critical and academic establishment, only to rise up again in 1978 when Sid Vicious declared it his favorite poem. Frequently anthologized, Harold Bloom has called the poem a "companion piece to 'Abandoned'" and I would agree; but it works perhaps even more powerfully considered by itself, preferably at 4 AM, in that hour when consciousness teeters precariously on that rusty razor's edge between despair and madness.

"Inspiration"

People often ask me, "Where do you get
your inspiration from, a brand new poem
every week, fifty-two weeks a year yet?"
It's really not so hard, or so I tell them,
not so hard at all once the poet learns
that no one really cares how well he writes,
that it doesn't matter if his spirit burns
or hides like a dog through Byzantine nights;
this poet is incapable of writing well
anyway, but even if he were, it still
wouldn't matter; very few of us can tell
the difference between ambrosia and swill.
And that's okay; now he is ready to sing.
Nothing stands in his way; not a thing.

Another life-affirming sonnet. First published in the *Olney Times* of July 20, 1963.

"Swimming"

Off to my right a girl's dollhouse convent
and a little boy's toy lighthouse model;
the yawning sun begins its grand descent
and the gulls and jackdaws cheer and yodel
as the bay catches fire one last time;
my arms and legs in animal motion,
my breath the meter, my muscles the rhyme,
I feel I could swim across this ocean;
I take one great lungful of breath and dive
down deep to where all is green and quiet
down through a world where the dead are alive,
and, strange to say, so also am I, yet
up I burst to the light, and head towards
the shore, and home, to write these words.

A truly sublime sonnet from Arnold Schnabel, first published in the July 27, 1963 issue of the *Olney Times*, and harkening back bravely to his famous poem "One Night" (which latter was composed immediately following his breakdown and commitment to Byberry).

"The Hammock"

After a modest lunch of liverwurst
on pumpernickel, washed down with iced tea,
it is decidedly far from the worst
thing in life just to rise and go nicely
lie myself down in the hammock out back
(hooked from an oak and the rear of house
and fashioned from an old potato sack),
content as a dog, a cat, or a mouse,
or even as this tree, or the great sky
flickering through the living boughs;
I do not fear rising into that eye
of fire, nor do I ask the whys and hows;
if the sky should want me, let it take me;
I'm as ready now as I'll ever be.

This unassuming little sonnet appeared first in the *Olney Times* of August 3, 1963. It is notable however for being the first of Schnabel's poems to make a possible reference to the smoking of cannabis.

"Escaping the Heat"

It's too hot to think, to write or to create,
and so to escape the oppressive heat
I go to see some friends who operate
an air-conditioned shop on Jackson Street.
My friends make trinkets from pebbles they go get
Off the beach, and from shells and other stuff on it,
from nothing much at all, just as a certain poet
of my acquaintance will jury-rig a sonnet
from the flotsam and the jetsam of a life
he's somehow always forgotten or declined to live.
My friends seem happy nonetheless to see me,
and we go back to the workroom (the air rife
with solder) where they're so very good as to give
me a smoke, as we sit and talk of the Bodhi Tree.

Arnold Schnabel made an unusually direct foray into the mystery of his sexuality in this sonnet ("Not merely perfection, but perfection squared," as Arnold's friend the author and poet Horace P. Sternwall put it), first published in the August 10, 1963 edition of the *Olney Times*.

"Committed Bachelor"

My life's been a series of more or less
humiliating moments, and so much
more often more than less; I've made a mess
of all my fitful bold attempts to touch
another human being (except for
my mom) and in that rather rare case
of someone else presuming the rapture
of my company I will always race
for the nearest exit, out of the fear,
bordering on certainty, that there must
be something deeply wrong with a person
so desperate; and also they are just
so homely usually, and worse than
that, dull; and thus is curiosity
trumped by the demon dubiosity.

The following brilliant sonnet — which sheds a bemusing light on Arnold Schnabel's newly unleashed sexuality — was submitted by Arnold to the *Olney Times* for the August 10th, 1963, issue. Not surprisingly — considering its bold treatment of a subject matter which Arnold had always previously dealt with in the most thickly-veiled terms if at all — the poem was rejected by the paper's editor, Silas Willingham III. What is slightly surprising is that after almost twenty-five years of publishing Arnold's poems on a weekly basis (Arnold had continued to submit poems by V-mail even when serving with the army engineers in the European Theatre in WWII), Willingham had only rejected one other poem, "Committed Bachelor" (q.v.) which Arnold had submitted apparently just a few weeks previously. Upon finding "Dialogue in the Confessional" unsuitable for the family audience of the *Olney Times*, but not wanting to leave Arnold's fans bereft, Willingham had second thoughts about "Committed Bachelor" and ran that in the August 10th issue instead.

"Dialogue in the Confessional"

I went to confession and told the priest
about what I had done and that Jesus
had said it was okay; I heard the least
intake of breath; "Sex is not to please us,"
he said after a long pause, "but to bring
children into the world, within the state
of holy matrimony." "But the thing
is," I said, "no man and wife procreate
each time they perform the act; is it wrong
then, when they do it and fail conception?"
"No, no, of course not," he said, "just so long
as they're wed, their love is no exception
to the rule." "Right," I said, "But what if, say —"
"Three Hail Marys," he said. "Now go away."

This sonnet first appeared in the *Olney Times* of August 17, 1963. The *Olney Times*'s venerable editor Silas Willingham III would appear to have resigned himself to Arnold's new frankness; either that or he simply published the poem unread beforehand.

Biographical evidence tells us that Arnold was at this time reading T.S. Eliot's *The Waste Land* for the first time, but, as usual, he seems to be blithely resistant to literary influence.

"My Invisible Friend"

I know it's not strange for a child to
have an invisible friend, but what of
a man of forty-two? It seems wild to
be seen talking not of love but of
matters carnal, over a cigarette
and a beer, to a man no one can see,
even if, as he won't let you forget,
He is the son of the Divinity.
It's true that He came to me when my night
boded well never to end, and He led
me back to a day that was filled with light,
but now it would be nice if He, instead
Of showing up quite in person, would just
Say hello in a mote of sun-drenched dust.

The *Olney Times* had been printing a poem a week by Arnold Schnabel for twenty-five years by the time this stunning sonnet appeared in the issue for August 31, 1963, and in all that time Arnold had never before published a poem that could conceivably be called a love poem.

Better late than never.

This poem can safely be assumed to address his new (and apparently first) inamorata, the Bohemian jeweler Elektra.

"You Asked For It"

You asked me to write you a poem; oh
well, luckily for me you didn't say
that it had to be a good one, and so
I'll mention your eyes, not as bright as day
nor dark as the night, nor deep as the sea,
but deep and dark and bright enough for me
to swim in, to dream in, and to live in;
and then your skin, and what it has given
to someone who once wished to leave his own;
and your laughter that awakened the clown
inside a scarecrow made of flesh and bone,
so that he sits now putting these words down
on paper: a trite, embarrassing mess,
but perhaps not entirely meaningless.

Made in the USA
Middletown, DE
29 July 2019